DAWN OF THE RAZIEL

Volume One of the
Causality Saga

By Ian Chan

To my family….

The galaxy is a vast and complex place but whether viewing it in the tiniest detail or at its grandest scale, there is an ever-present property, a building block of its geometry. In mathematical terms it is called Phi and has a value of 1.61803.... Many think of it as the Golden Ratio, others the Divine Proportion, but whatever name you identify it with; Phi seems to be part of our make-up, hard-wired into our mind as an archetype of beauty. Present in every facet of life and occurring throughout the entirety of nature it is said to be the sign of God.

Prologue

The life force permeating the universe ebbed and flowed in an ambient sea, it drifted endlessly with the sub-space currents, felt the draw of gravimetric tides, broke in waves along event horizons and bubbled in a froth of quantum foam, but for the first time in an age something urged it towards harmony and purpose. Such will impressed upon the cosmos had only happened once before in the vast memory of existence and that event had transpired to shape the very fabric of the universe itself.

At the galactic core, in the storm of a hundred synchronous hypernova, Mazzaroth was the first of the celestial bodies to take its place in a divine configuration, a cosmic arrangement that would not occur again for another 4.6 Billion years. The corona of the white star weaved and danced as if moving to the tune of the universe's long forgotten song, now remembered. Mazzaroth remained what it always was, nature's fusion factory, a star, but like looking into the brightness of a person's eye you could perceive a sentience in its sparkle.

With Mazzaroth's new vigour, the desire upon the infused energy intensified, the first cog in a grand galactic combination lock, slowly opening to glimpse the magnificence hidden on the other side.

Kesil in the nebula of lanterns, a triple blue jewel burst into glorious brilliance as it reached its zenith along the Golden Spiral. The lighthouse of creation momentarily had a beacon of blazing sapphire that outshone all for light years around.

The flow surged, transforming into a rolling torrent crashing into the tapestry of space time, barely held back like a failing dam creaking under the pounding tumult of an astrological tsunami.

Finally, Eden the oldest planet in the galaxy slowly arced across space, the foundations of the planetary focal point rumbled and warped as it crept into the turbulent stream of energy. The sheer power of the encompassing forces threatened to tear apart its core, but Eden's heart was ancient and strong. In a dimensional eclipse it reached its apex, the whole planet began to vibrate, space hummed in anticipation and then it happened; a rift into the realm of God was torn asunder.

In the night sky of Eden, lightning crackled and thunder resonated through the air as microscopic rips began to pull apart the very fabric of space and time. Branches of light leaked out into the darkness, growing in intensity until the manifestation of the rift opened in a roar of radiance and music. A shining tree hung in the night sky and from under its illumination the power of the universe's creator poured through, breathing life into the firstborns..........

1 - The Dawn

It's cold......

Michael stirred.

The bright white light was blinding, his pupils were fully dilated and the instant ocular overload had ignited a fierce headache that stabbed at his brain. His subconsciousness instinctively screamed for his eyes to close and his body to turn away from the tormenting exposure, yet his commands echoed around his head unanswered.

It was as if he was staring directly into the flaming Sun barely risen in an inky midnight sky, but where he should have been radiated in the warm rays of photons, only chilling beams rained down through his icy breath.

He could feel his naked skin laid out upon a freezing slab, his nervous system openly accepting sensory input but strangely unreactive to the uncomfortable stimulus.

Michael's consciousness carried out those internal reality checks to determine a dream state versus the vividness of wake, but it repeatedly reported confusing results. Yes – I can see; yes – I can hear; yes – I can smell; yes – I can taste; yes – I can feel, but all aspects of his body were paralysed, rejecting his every will.

Am I in a lucid dream? I can't be, I remember the dream I had last night, I talked to my gran, but I know she passed away years ago! he confirmed to himself as he smelled and felt the disturbance of heavily disinfected air.

Yes - I am conscious.

Yes, I am awake!

Michael could hear movement all around him and fleeting shadows moved on the edge of his peripheral vision. Blurry shapes loomed over him, he found it hard to distinguish form or feature under the uncomfortable bright glare.

"Hello!" he called out. How loud it sounded in his mind but no noise passed his lips.

Each dark shape then became solidified as they made brief contact with his bare skin. He tried to shout out as the blunt sensation of pressure was applied to numerous points around his head, "What are you doing?" he roared silently. The effort was somehow draining.

The figures seemed to pause at his unsaid anguish, but it made no difference. His unknown antagonists never relented, intrusively examining his body for what seemed like an eternity, with each callous touch more painful than the last.

"Stop .... Please!" he forcefully tried to plead.

The distress of helplessness surged through him, panic called out to his lungs to gag for oxygen but his nervous system continued to defy his commands.

A high-pitched sound began to whine over him like a drill, overloading his auditory senses with its severity. Suddenly a device creaked over his face, blocking some of the light painfully bombarding his retinas, yet it remained fuzzy in its close proximity. The mechanical device began to move and pixel by pixel an extending appendage came into focus. Michael's brain exploded with dread and he struggled violently against his invisible shackles.

A vivid voice wandered to the forefront of his perception, drowning out the harsh senses overwhelming him. The harmonious voice strangely bereft of any emotion reverberated around his head as the advancing metallic needle pushed slowly against his pupil, "Do you know the potential contained within you?"

The words lingered like a stubborn mental imprint, the surface tension broke and the sharp point punctured into his eyeball.

No, no ……. Horror finally engulfed him.

"Noooo!! Stoopppp!!!" A lamp flew untouched across the room smashing into a hundred pieces as had many before it. Sweat poured from his drenched body, his eyes shot backwards and forwards in a panic, the rapid gasping breaths almost bringing him to the point of hyperventilation. His muscles continued to spasm and his clenched fists cramped as he gripped on the cotton sheet in paralysed dread.

Michael had just woken from a nightmare, that same nightmare that has plagued his mind for the last year and a half. It lurked there in the concealment of the subconscious, ready to strike when he passed into sleep, a foreboding place where imagination had been slain, a decaying corpse fed upon by a parasite. Nothing existed there now but for that nightmare. Yet in the reality of wake such terrors of the mind would fade, washed away by the flood of consciousness. Not for Michael, his mind had been permanently wounded, each perfect little detail etched deeply into his psyche, festering there, oozing every bit of fear and pain he experienced. In an endgame of spitefulness, eyes open it played on endless repeat, antagonising the inside of his skull. Eyes closed he relived it, relived it like it was the first time.

His conscious mind gradually kicked in and the realisation of where he was began to clear his mind in a breeze of bitter relief. To him waking up was but a temporary amnesty into a slightly lesser nightmare that was his life. He lay there wide-eyed feeling the contractions of his heart slowly weaken as his pulse returned to normal. The pain shooting around his muscles subsided yet the perpetual ache in his temples continued to throb as if his head was clamped in an ever-tightening vice. He blinked hard; the horrible sensation continued to burn behind his watering left eye, a sympathetic bodily response to a ghostly trauma it had been tricked into suffering.

Michael let out a despaired sigh*, another day gone and another rung climbed on the ladder to nowhere.* And Wednesday's sucked the most, it was psyche evaluation day with the shrink.

With an exhausted effort Michael heaved himself off the flea ridden mattress laid upon the floor and carefully trod over the broken porcelain towards his semi-derelict bathroom. His kidneys ached as he relieved himself. Michael grimaced with the pain as he tried to force himself upright, spraying the toilet seat with a splatter of blood-stained urine. He reached for his toothbrush from a discoloured plastic cup, "Shit!.... No toothpaste."

Michael's eyes searched around until he saw it perched on the side of the mouldy tiled window seal. His apartment was three floors up yet the stench of garbage still wafted through the air vent that was inserted in the bubbled glass. He grabbed the almost empty bottle of brown liquid and shakily unscrewed the metal cap. He threw the last dregs of the leftover whiskey into his mouth and after a few swirls and a gargle, swallowed hard. Michael threw the empty bottle into his tarnished bath that was acting as a temporary bottle bank. The alcohol began to do its familiar magic extinguishing the fire in his optic nerve, slowly flowing through his blood vessels, drowning the sensory receptors in a wave of dulling relief. But the reprieve was all too short lived. A deep seeded Nausea suddenly sprouted, sweeping through his body in a disorienting blow. He stumbled to the bathroom door, steadying himself with an outstretched hand and stared towards his apartment entrance in expectancy. A loud set of knocks rattled on his apartment door. Then a second set of impatient bangs followed, dislodging plaster from the cracked ceiling in a shower of white powder.

"Michael, I know you're in there!" shouted a women's voice, high pitched but breaking at the end as a result of too many strong cigarettes.

He tried to stay silent but the impulse to retch was too strong. His stomach contents surged up his throat and erupted into his mouth. He doubled up under the violent convulsion, squeezing his hand over his mouth like a man trying to suffocate himself.

"I want my rent, it was due yesterday and you haven't paid for last months!" she fumed as a dog started growling and sniffing at the base of the door.

Vomit squirted between his fingers, smearing his puffed-out cheeks and rolling down the corners of his mouth. With a struggle Michael managed to swallow down the mixture of whiskey and the digested remains of last night's microwave meal.

"Perhaps if you spent less cash on booze, you could pay me what you owe. Don't think I won't catch up with you. You'll have to come out sometime. Eventually you'll need that alcohol fix. And I'll be waiting." the dog gave another angry snarl, "We'll be waiting!"

The nausea always preceded this strange sixth sense, it wasn't knowledge of the future but only what he could describe as a brief confusing perception of what was about to come. It was like another consciousness whispering to him 'Someone's at the door!'.

Michael wiped the chunks of regurgitated food across his sleeve and staggered to the bathroom sink. He twisted the faucet nozzle, the water flowed brown from the corroded pipes but he didn't wait for it to run clear. Michael clutched a handful of dirty water and splashed it over his face. As he did so he caught a glimpse of himself in the cracked mirror.

There was a time not so long ago, more a dying dream than the past, when his reflection was not the ragged shell of a man he saw now.

"How did it get to this?" he asked the gnarled reflection.

But he didn't need the answer; he knew exactly the moments that had led him down the spiraling path to the life staring back at him from the other side of the mirror.

2 - Crossroads

1.5 Years Ago

Michael breathed in deeply, the smell of antiquity filled his nostrils. His fingers brushed over the dusty surfaces of wood and stone, moulded not by modern machines, but by the sweat and guile of craftsmen from a bygone age. His senses took it all in, a potent concoction evoking feelings of mystery and wonder. To him there was something alluring about stepping back into the days of old, into the foot prints of Earth's forgotten cultures, attempting to see through their eyes the wonders of their achievements, imagining how the world changed, gave birth to new civilisations and in turn watched them decay under the relentless passing of time.

Once again, he slowly surveyed the contents of storeroom 3c of the British museum before finally picking up the dossier outlining the origin of the collection, and any accompanying information relating to the generous donation of these items.

"Well this is going to take some time." Michael muttered to himself as he scrolled down the list of objects he would have to examine and catalog.

Yet the workload brought a smile to his face. Being a historian of ancient civilisations wasn't a job to him but a passion that brought him enjoyment and a daily satisfaction that most people wished for.

"Mmh, an Anonymous donor." Michael began reading the intriguing fore note.

"Wow, originally brought to England by an antiquities dealer with a distant connection to Flinders Petrie."

Michael wasn't a get your hands dirty archaeologist type, digging in foreign deserts or excavating damp caves. He was more passionate about piecing together the mysteries of the past from others archaeological finds and historical accounts. And in his mind, there was no other person that contributed more to his line of work than Flinders Petrie, the pioneer of modern-day archaeology and most famously known for his extended trips into Palestine and Egypt.

Now gripped, he read on with eagerness. "This nameless antiquities dealer was linked to a far right-wing group but shared the professor's interest in relics, and in particular, those in Palestine. He was said to be fanatical about continuing the life's work of Flinders Petrie and on one such foray into Palestine, he mysteriously vanished; not heard from again he was finally declared officially deceased."

Far-Right links. Well I understand the anonymity now. He thought to himself.

The fact that none of these objects were properly evaluated or source verified, only amplified his enthusiasm to start hunting through the artefact filled shelves and unopened crates. He quickly lost himself in the task and all thoughts outside it slowly dissolved away.

*

Signaled by his rumbling stomach Michael became aware that he had been searching amongst the collection right through the morning and past lunch. *Just one more box, then eat.* He hadn't found anything yet that really jumped out and tugged on the strings of curiosity, just an excellently preserved ammonite fossil that he knew his daughter would be fascinated with. She had told him on multiple occasions that the pattern of a similar snail's shell was the most beautiful thing she had ever seen. Nonetheless there was still a plethora of sealed storage boxes to investigate. He decided upon a medium sized leather trunk because of its ornate but delicate gold leaf art of Egyptian serpent imagery. In addition, it still had its rusted padlock closed and intact. Usually the purpose of locking meant one thing, to protect something of value inside. Michael grabbed a crowbar from his toolbox, the only instrument not designed to be non-invasive and delicate, and broke open the lock. Inside it was an interior lined with purple velvet and something wrapped in an elongated sheet of stained linen. Putting on a pair of protective white gloves, he carefully unraveled the protective fabric to reveal a partially crumbled scroll.

Should I bring this to the museum experts.... No, I'll be gentle and very careful.

He took the leather parchment to the storerooms examining table and cautiously unrolled the scroll to reveal the black ink of ancient Hebrew text.

"This is interesting, written in carbon soot on vellum, goat or calf I believe. Wow, this is old. No way.... could it be a new Dead Sea scroll?" Michael whispered to himself, as the animal hide parchment brought back memories of the famous Dead Sea scrolls, a collection of ancient manuscripts that were discovered between 1947 and 1956 in 11 caves near Khirbet Qumran, Israel.

"The letter forms are so old, I need to study this in my office." he said enthusiastically, the artefact embodying what everyone in his field dreamt of, the adrenalin and excitement that came with the possibility of a new discovery.

Back at his office, he placed the linen wrapped scroll on top of his cluttered desk and began searching for his paleography and ancient Hebrew reference books. Michael was well versed in the Hebrew language, but some of the text was in an older Paleo-Hebrew dialect and studying the size, variability and style of the text would help him better date it.

He spent the following hours studying every little detail of the scroll, disregarding the waning hunger pangs but not the third vibrating call of his phone in quick succession.

"Hi?"

"Michael, where are you? We expected you back for dinner by now." said his slightly annoyed wife.

"I'm so sorry. I never realised the time. I should've called." Michael replied apologetically.

Claire sighed, "What is it this time? Bella has been asking for her daddy all evening. The poor thing fell asleep on the sofa waiting for you."

"I'll make it up to her tomorrow. We'll go for ice-cream after her therapy." he promised with guilt. "Claire, I think I might have discovered something new, it could be important but I need to make sure I've recorded and verified all the details." he continued, trying to justify himself even though he knew his wife had never understood his fascination with old things of the past.

"Ok Mike, just don't be too late. I'll put your dinner in the fridge."

"Thanks Claire. I'll see you later."

"Bye."

Putting the phone down, he looked outside at the low Sun with a sense of remorse, imagining his daughter sitting waiting for her father with a child's anticipation. He inhaled a focusing deep breath, switched on his deskside lamp and reached for another dusty hardback from his bookshelf.

*

The Sun had long disappeared over the horizon of the London skyline by the time he had finally translated the text and confidently dated the scroll. In his estimation, the antique was over two thousand years old, yet unlike the archeological treasures of its Dead sea counterparts, it didn't contain anything of great religious or historical significance but the fading Hebrew words did talk of something that ignited Michael's imagination. They were the ancient account of an object named as the Lisan key. He lifted his notepad up to the lamp light and read out the English translation:

'Where the finger of the peninsula meets the tongue of the sea, towards the northern edge of Lisan, he threw his vehicle into the bay of Mazra. Born from this iron ark in a fiery furnace, the obelisk took shape, a monument in the original language of man. At its mouth was spoken the truth, the code key, both the beginning and the end, its words of creation can save, for it opens the door to the greatest kingdom of all. Here upon the cape at the bottom of the world, still today you will find the relic that is the Lisan key.'

"Lisan, Lisan…..Lisan. Why do you sound so familiar?" he asked himself as he routed through his desk draws. "Ah ha. Yes. Here we are." Michael had pulled out a tattered programme from a conference that had been held a few years ago inside the BP Lecture theatre of the museum.

He threw his mind back amongst the jumbled memories of that day. The conference had been an open forum for those who had wanted to present their ideas that were slightly outside the realm of the mainstream views of ancient history. Hypothesis such as the Orion correlation, signifying the differing construction date of the Egyptian pyramids, and how those civilisations of Egypt, South America and Asia shared similar architectural techniques and designs long before communication was said to have existed between them. He couldn't remember the context in which it was mentioned, but an elderly Rabbi who was then a well-respected mathematician had taken the stage to propose his interpretation of the real meaning behind the symbolic writings of ancient religious manuscripts. Michael hadn't listened long due to the call of his daily duties but he had attended long enough to hear reference to Lisan and the possible biblical importance of the area, and the mocking response of his peers that ensued.

Right what was that Rabbi's name? I'm sure he can provide some insight on the importance of Lisan. Potentially the meaning or origin of the mysterious words on the scroll also, he thought to himself as he scoured the conference booklet for the agenda of topics and the inset details of the related speakers.

Michael needed to quickly send the Rabbi an image of the scroll and head straight for the tube station. In all the anticipation of the unexpected find, he had again lost all track of time, and if he didn't leave soon, he was going to miss the last train home. He had already missed tucking his daughter into bed and if he ended up spending the night at the office, then he was certainly going to feel the full wrath of his wife. So he took a few photos with his phone and gently wrapped up the vellum parchment in the protective linen with disappointment. Further investigation would have to wait until Monday morning.

*

With the time rapidly approaching 1am, Michael was grateful to disembark the Friday night vomit comet, the drunk and nauscous revelers making it an uncomfortable journey as they boisterously enjoyed a few more drinks or tried to survive the spinning carriages of the last train home. He walked along the dimly lit platform of Little Chalfont station and into the deserted carpark to begin the last leg of his commute home.

Taking a shortcut through the darkness of the winding country roads his mind began to wander, thinking how fantastic it would be if the ancient document spoke of a yet undiscovered artefact, perhaps some sort of important language Rosetta stone, an unheard-of knowledge repository or even as stated a key to a previously unknown lost kingdom. Maybe he would learn more next week when he completed the cataloguing of the collection, or if the Rabbi replied to his email, but for now he had to concentrate on driving. The exertion of the day had finally caught up on him.

"C'mon focus!" he commanded himself as he shook his head and squinted into the light beams penetrating the night.

Michael was beginning to feel sleep calling and the fact that he was on a quiet road in the Buckinghamshire countryside with not a car in site wasn't helping matters. As he approached a distant deer crossing sign illuminated in his headlights he struggled to focus on his surroundings, now wishing that despite today's excitement he had paid more attention to his watch and left the office at a more reasonable hour. With each moment that passed it became more difficult to combat his heavy eyes and it would have been so easy for him to give into his weariness and drift to sleep. Fighting a losing battle, Michael's eyelids finally began to slip over his eyes, his head tilted forward and his car started to veer across the side of the road just when a blinding bright light and an intense chill pulled him from his slumber.

"Oh shit!!" he blurted as he swerved in sudden realisation and found himself scrapping the nearby hedges at the opposite side of the road.

Slamming on the breaks he brought the car to a screeching standstill. Panting he swung his head around to see the vehicle he had almost hit, but was mystified to see a road devoid of cars or lights as far as he could see.

It couldn't have been going that fast. He thought to himself as he exhaled in relief and rubbed his aching eyes. *It doesn't matter. You're ok. Let's just get home in one piece.*

Anyway, he was wide-awake now thanks to the infusion of adrenalin being pumped around his body, he rolled down the window a touch to allow in a cool breeze that should help keep him alert enough to complete the distance home without further incident. He glanced at the dashboard clock, touched the accelerator to move off but immediately took a second take.

"That can't be right!" he muttered to himself.

Michael checked his watch, the big hand was on 3 and the little hand pointed to 4, yes they both agreed, it was 4.15am. Had he fallen asleep, had both time pieces suddenly gone mad. He looked around in bemusement, his surroundings were a shade lighter and he was obviously in the same stretch of road by the deer-crossing warning sign. Whatever was going on, about three and a half hours had somehow disappeared.

Confused and just wanting to get home, he continued onwards. As the adrenalin left his body, he pulled up to his semi-detached house in the small village of Ashley Green.

*

"Daddy is that you?" whispered a child's investigative voice.

"Yes sweetheart, why aren't you sleeping?" responded Michael. He had tried his best to traverse the stairs and hallway with minimal noise but the floorboards would creak annoyingly under the smallest weight. Something that had been on his DIY to-do-list since they moved in years ago.

"I was just looking out the window." explained Isabella as her father crept quietly into her room and over to her bedside.

"What are you looking at?"

"Just the stars daddy…Do you know there are fifty-six stars in the sky right now?" she said staring at the square of space visible from the window.

Normally this sort of statement from a three year-old would surprise a parent, but Michael was unfazed, "Have you been counting them all night?"

"No, I was just looking now." as she clarified one of the street lamps fluttered and flickered off. "There are eighty-three now."

"I don't need to count, is that normal?" But before he could answer she continued, "Sometimes I say what I see and people laugh at me…Today we were saying the days of the week…I said Tuesday is yellow with green spots, sounds like drums and tastes like broccoli…That's why I don't like Tuesday, broccoli tastes disgusting…But I am not joking, it's what Tuesday is…I don't know why it's not the same for everyone else… Should I lie or agree that others are right even though it's not true?"

"Darling, you should always tell the truth." Michael confirmed.

"I want to tell the truth even if other people don't like it…Lying makes me feel bad… My skin feels all wrong… The colours and noises… It's like walking in an ugly picture… I can't explain it… It's just stinky and gross."

Michael couldn't hold in a loving smile although Bella was quite serious about the topic.

"They just don't understand you, or think the way you can." he paused contemplating how he could explain it, "Take all those stars for instance. Do you know that everybody used to think that all the stars and Sun moved around the Earth, that we were the centre of the universe." Michael enacted the movement with his hands, "Those that said this wasn't true were laughed at also."

Bella smiled, "That's silly. It's easy-peasy to see how everything moves together when you look at the sky." As a gesture of the obvious, she put out an open hand towards her poster of the Milky Way, complete with a pin tagged 'We live here!'

"Not for everybody, like it wasn't then. But now these people who were laughed at, they are now thought of as great people with beautiful minds. Just like I think of you." he stroked her hair and caught a quick glimpse of his watch.

"Daddy's what's wrong?"

"Nothing darling, why do you ask?" he replied trying to maintain a guise of innocence.

"Remember the time when you, me and mummy went to see the doctor?"

"Not exactly."

"It was on the twenty-eighth April last year…It was a Friday."

"Ok." Again, Michael was not surprised by his daughter's calendar calculating, but seeing such a young child do this still astounded him.

"You'd both just spoken to the doctor… mummy was crying…And you looked at me…. Your face was like this…Every line on your face was in the same position."

"I think maybe I am just tired." He tried to change the subject, "Speaking of being tired. Why don't you try and go back to sleep darling?"

"I already tried; I couldn't sleep…I was thinking about the day."

"How was your day?"

"Ok, I guess. A…" Isabella's pause was drawn-out, "Am I weird?"

"No of course not. Why would you say that?" Michael took his daughter's hand to give reassurance.

"Tommy at nursery…He asked me why I don't talk to the other boys and girls…Why I always walk away from them when they come close to me." she recollected with a tinge of sadness.

"What did you tell him?"

"I didn't reply…Then he said why didn't I look at him when he was talking to me?... So I looked at him…Then he said that I was starring…He told me I was weird…So daddy, am I weird?" she asked again with a cute naivety.

"Being different does not make you weird. It means your unique and more precious than anything ever created on Earth and all its history. The others will eventually see that."

"Just like Cinderella in your princess books." Michael gestured towards Bella's extensive bedside book case. She was a vigorous reader for one so young. Although she could only manage simple children's books, Bella was 3 years ahead of the average child's reading age.

"I see you've moved all your books around." queried Michael who had not seen this behavior in his daughter before.

"Yes. I wanted to put them in their right place.", she began pointing to each pile of books she had stacked together, "These are ones about princesses…These are stories about animals…Those are the ones about letters, numbers and colours…and that one is about monsters…. I don't like those ones; they are scary to read by myself."

Michael picked up the book at the top of the scary pile. It was 'Where the wild things are' with its humanoid horned beast on the cover. "Did you know the meaning of this book is about a child's growth, how to overcome feelings you don't quite understand, and accept the realities of their lives with help from their parents' love."

"I know I'm different…I want to be like the others though…Playing together and having fun…But daddy, I don't know how." Bella illustrated with hands and face expressing the deepest of bafflement, "Do you know why I am like this? I can understand many things the other girls and boys don't, but I just don't understand this."

"No darling we don't. But knowledge and answers are not always given to us so freely. We must earn knowledge through experience and discovery. If we had all the answers and solutions and knew everything, what meaning would our life have? I for one, wouldn't have a job." Michael tried to explain with a smile.

"You would be bored daddy." she conceded.

He gave her a jovial wink, "Exactly! That's what makes life fun. And the most beautiful and powerful knowledge is always the hardest to discover."

"Then will I ever know how?"

"I am sure of it, but one step at a time." Michael moved Isabella's hair off her face and behind her ears, "I'll tell you what, the first thing is to just smile. You have the most beautiful smile, its infectious and it makes others happy and want to smile too." Just talking about it made him smile unknowingly.

"Should I then give Tommy a hug?... Tommy smiled at Lucy once and she gave him a hug…And he shouted that it was yuckie."

"Then Tommy doesn't know what he's missing." he laughed softly. "And do you know who needs a hug right now?"

Bella jumped onto Michael's lap and squeezed her arms around his neck. "I always feel better after talking to you daddy."

"Me too." he mouthed.

"Oooo, that's such a good cuddle!" Michael gave her a playful squeeze back making Bella giggle out loudly.

He kissed his daughter on the forehead, "Right young lady. Time for you to go back to sleep before we wake up mummy."

"Do I have therapy class tomorrow?"

"Yes sweetheart, but if you go to sleep right now, we will get ice cream afterwards! How does that sound?"

Bella grinned cheekily and quickly slid under her duvet, rolled until tightly wrapped in the covers, and pulled in her mannequin doll close to her nose for comfort. "Good night…Love you daddy."

"Love you too." responded Michael as he tiptoed out of her room and pushed across the door. "Sweet dreams."

Now physically and mentally exhausted the one thing he wanted more than anything else at that moment was his bed. Little did he know that this would be the last time that he would look forward to sleep.

3 - Perception of the Mind

"Michael….. Michael….." his name echoed elusively on the wind, lost amongst the tempest of thoughts swirling around his stormy mind.

"Michael!" The psychiatrist repeated in a more assertive tone, "Are you listening to me?"

"Yes, sorry." He turned his eyes from the painting on the bare bricks of the office wall. The room was spacious and airy, warm rays of Sun flowed from the skylight above and down onto the natural parquet floor beneath his feet. "With all the plants and bright white surfaces here, I expect you chose that painting because it complements the perception of positivity you are trying to achieve."

"Your daughter, you are avoiding the topic Michael." suggested the psychiatrist as she placed her notepad on her lap and sat more upright in her designer leather chair.

"Did you know that is a painting of the Hanging gardens of Babylon? One of the seven ancient wonders of the world. Many people had come to accept it as just a historical mirage. But persistence in one person's belief has uncovered new evidence, findings that have suggested it could actually be real, and was constructed in Nineveh, the capital of the ancient Assyrian

Empire."

"I don't think my art selections are relevant to the topic right now." she replied trying to deflect further immaterial chat.

"To me it is. Did you know that an image like this, scientific revelations like this would excite me like a child on Christmas morning. I would get butterflies in my stomach and my imagination and intrigue would run wild." He paused and looked at the painting once again, "Now I feel nothing. Not a thing."

"This is clearly a consequence of what happened, but to understand it, we need to first resolve why did it happen...Michael, every time I ask this question you avoid the answer."

The psychiatrist eased her posture in the high-backed chair. "Perhaps if you close your eyes and layback in the sofa. It will help you relax and focus your thoughts."

"Closing my eyes has never brought me peace, it just allows the horrors to be seen more clearly." he responded with despondence.

"Ok then. Just try and think back to what happened in your own words. Take your time, and remember anything you say here is just between us."

The psychiatrist took a look at her watch, 5 minutes passed in silence. "You haven't said anything in five minutes, just tell me what is on your mind right at this moment?"

Michael sighed. "How is it possible to prove that I have adhered to accepted morality and the laws of a government, if my body is not governed by the known physical laws of the universe?"

The psychiatrist was slightly surprised and taken aback by the comment. "Please carry on." she insisted as she scribbled down notes.

"Should I demonstrate this internal influence, this deviation against what we know as reality? The very nature of showing, just proof that it's uncontrollable and a far greater threat to Bella than they already believe. Not just a danger to her but to everyone around me."

"Ok good, you have mentioned your daughter's name for the first time. That is progress."

"What progress?" he looked at the psychiatrist despairingly, "I can't control it, but all I can be sure of, is that others would want to. Especially those responsible for this change in me."

"Those responsible? Michael, we spoke about this before. The court was very convinced with the course of events. You cannot continue to assign blame to others without substance."

The familiar thoughts ran through Michael's head. *Others…How do I speak of that missing time without adding to their disbelief in my sanity. Even now, I still don't have a clue who did this to me.*

"So what choices do I really have?" he continued, "With proof, all I see is a cage without a key and a queue of doctors with their tests. So, do I continue to hide this torment, somehow find the evidence that someone did this to me? Those that create a disease usually create the cure. Could this all be reversed and prove I am no threat to my daughter, that what happened was just an involuntary reaction."

"This is what we are trying to do right now. Heal you, understand and eliminate the affliction that made you do this to your daughter."

"This is exactly what I mean. You think I snapped, a mental defect to be repaired or a genetic disposition in my brain that you need to rewire around. Just another crazy drunk that exacted abominable harm on those they supposedly loved."

"It's not about what I think or my opinion. It's about discovering the psychological origin of this illness and giving you the help you need."

"Sitting on this uncomfortable sofa, talking about the mess my life has become an hour every week is certainly not going to solve this. Nor is it going give me a relationship with my daughter again."

"Let's be brutally honest here. These sessions are one of the prerequisites for why you are not sitting in a prison cell right now. You need to take responsibility for your actions and accept the ongoing consequences of those actions…You did this to her; can you at least accept that?"

"Yes, it was my action…But I will never accept responsibility for those actions."

"Acknowledgement is the first step to moving forwards. An initial step to maybe seeing your daughter again." returned the psychiatrist.

"You know…A wise person once told me, that truth is a beautiful picture to walk in, but to tell a lie is stinky and gross." as he recalled it, for a brief moment a beam of happiness broke through the façade of gloom.

But all too quickly it faded behind the cloud of reality as the office began to hum and the two glasses of water began to vibrate on the glass table separating them. Michael rubbed his head as the familiar ache bludgeoned his temples.

"Sorry, those planes fly lower and lower to city airport these days." the Psychiatrist commented with a fake grin.

He gulped down the glass of water and focused on the painting once more, "Acknowledgement is to accept a historical mirage. But I promise you this, I will be taking responsibility and accept the consequences of my actions going forward. To not pursue my belief in the truth would be to lose the only wonder this world has to offer me."

*

Michael left the Nightingale hospital, on Lisson Grove, London. As a specialist mental health institute, he felt the glares and pre-formed judgement of those that witnessed him exit. His sullen and fatigued look made it easier for them to form those opinions, drug addict would have been his first choice if the shoe was on the other foot. And he would not have seen them as a victim of circumstance seeking help, but no different than a thief or a petty criminal.

But am I any better? he questioned himself as his fingers clasped the object in his jacket pocket. Something he had acquired on his last day of work and at the time justified as a deserved severance pay. Compensation was not readily afforded to those laid-off in such a shower of shame, even though he had dedicated almost twenty good and honest years to the museum.

He ignored the wordless glances of passers-by and began to take thirsty mouthfuls of liquid from a dark fizzy-drinks bottle he had pulled from his carrier bag. As he did so he exhaled in a look of alleviation. But no bubbly sugar solution filled the merchandised plastic, rather his ever-present friend who could help him more than any psychiatrists' words, malt whiskey. As the alcohol began to drown out the headache and he started to feel a more solid connection between his feet and the paving slabs, Michael began to walk with purpose towards Marylebone station. By the time he had arrived at the correct tube platform, performed a short sprint to jump between the closing doors and bustled for a seat, he was exhausted.

"Noooo!! Stoopppp!!!" There was a loud thud as the carriage experienced a solid shunt. The familiar sounds of the tube train bellowed in his head, the screech of wheels against tracks, the whoop of changing air pressure in the tunnel. He had unknowingly nodded off and that nightmare had seized its opportunity to take hold once more, yet the most disturbing thing about the experience this time was the faces of the people staring at him. Embarrassment welled up inside him, as couples muttered then smirked, others ushered their children to a safer distance from the weirdo, and worst of all, the eye contacts of pity.

It doesn't matter what these people think. They have no idea what you are going through. They have no bearing on your life. The voice of Michael's negative self-talk sprang to his defence as it had done on an increasingly more regular basis. And with that mental clarification he unscrewed his masked booze bottle and took a hefty swig.

The tube train then began to brake sharply as it approached the next station. Luckily for him, it was his stop and curtailed any prolonged uncomfortable atmosphere. Michael quickly left the carriage and made his way onto the streets of Soho. He took a quick look around to get his bearings then strode off in the direction of a quiet and innocuous looking side alley. Amongst the trash dumpsters and steaming vents stood a metal bar covered shopfront. The nameless outlet had a few display cabinets containing secondhand silver and gold trinkets in the window but very little else to convince you it was a reputable business. He knew about this place due to his superficial involvement in recovering some stolen artifacts that appeared for sale at the property. Ignoring the criminal connection Michael believed that it was the perfect location to get the object in his coat pocket engraved. With a conviction hanging over him he couldn't risk a legitimate shop recognizing it for what it was.

A small bell tinkled as he walked inside and from a shady desk in the corner a plump weathered face lifted up.

"Yes, what can I do for you?" the man questioned as he dragged on a cigarette and locked away the small pile of money he was counting.

"I need some jewelry engraved."

"You can do that at most jewelry shops on the high street, what brings you here?" the shopkeeper asked suspiciously.

Michael pulled the object from his jacket and discreetly placed it on the counter. With some nervousness he pulled his hand away to reveal a silver bracelet capped on each end by the heads of two golden rams facing each other, a beautiful object he acquired on his last day of work. He was sure it would take years before the museum realised it was missing, if at all. His last day wasn't your usual time of farewells and reminiscence, rather two cardboard boxes and 30 minutes to collect his stuff. Before being hushly escorted out a side exit. It didn't leave him much time to sift through the 20 years of accretion. So he took his notes, some personal objects, his favourite reference books and of course the bracelet. One thing he regrettably had to leave behind was the scroll without ever discovering what the Lisan key was. Yet that was the other side of the fence to the life he stood in now.

"That looks to me like you have yourself a very old and rare trinket there. How did you get it?" the shop owner probed.

"I came here to avoid those questions." Michael wondered if he really knew what was in front of him. It was a piece of ancient Greek jewelry brought back from a dig near Greece's Parthenon temple on the acropolis that overlooks Athens; a wonderful example of the craftsmanship of that time.

"Of course. And that discretion comes at an uplifted price…Of course."

"How much?"

"Forty-five pounds."

"What. Forty-five pounds!"

"Well this isn't going to be your modern-day machine engraving. Such a delicate item will require manual methods, skill of the hand, and of course discretion."

"Ok." Michael conceded.

"I'll tell you what geezer. Why don't you sell it to me? Seems a pity to damage such a nice little piece like that. I'd give you a good price…Seventy-five." he suggested.

"No, it's not for sale."

"I'll give you a ton. Best offer you'd get around here." Negotiated the shifty dealer.

"Please, just engrave these words on it…." He was unable to say the them aloud so he placed a piece of paper on the counter, one with a very simple message.

'Daddy Loves You'

4 - Curiosity

Cruising at 22,500mph the exploratory spacecraft had passed within the orbit of the irregular moon and was now nearing the end of its approach phase after traversing the cold void of space on a prospecting mission to look for the signs of an ancient habitable environment. The robotic space probe represented the pinnacle of its builder's technological expertise and ingenuity, and for the duration of its lonely voyage their state-of-the-art scientific cargo had remained in its dormant state.

On-cue the predestined wake-up call executed the probes complex lines of computer code; initiating the pre-programmed approach sequence that had taken the brightest minds of the era great labors to devise. The curving horizon of the planet was now in full view; there were no blues and greens that signified the beauty of thriving life, yet the eon old scars stood as a beacon to a past shaped by the undeniable surge of nature. This was not an expedition out of requirement, but an undertaking to quench the insatiable thirst for knowing the unknown, answering the questions that drew their gaze to the heavens.

Out of all the worlds that they had observed, this one was in tangible reach, one that captivated its watchers and left mystery in its path as it crossed the expanse of the sky. After 250 Solar days and 350 million miles of navigating the harsh black vacuum, negotiating radiation showers and asteroid fields, it had finally arrived; yet it would be the next seven minutes that would ultimately decide the fate of their quest for knowledge.

The probe had penetrated the alien air, smashing into the atmospheric particles at 13,000mph. If eyes were present, they would have beheld a dazzling fireball as hot as a star itself blazing across their skies. But with the searing heat and mega forces subsiding, the cutting-edge technology had pushed its construction to its very limits and survived the journeys ultimate test; to be rewarded on the other side by the wondrous sight of a soaring three mile high mountain rising out of its primordial crater.

Throughout its trek across the extreme setting of space, the precious cargo hibernated safely in the protective embrace of the aero-shell, and now just two miles above its target area the exploratory machine was exposed for the first time to a strange new world. And in tribute to meticulous planning and inventiveness, it gently touched down on the extraterrestrial surface in a perfect landing that barely disturbed the red soil beneath its wheels.

Back in NASA's Mission control at the Jet Propulsion Laboratory, California, the tension was building. All attired in their blue insignia shirts and lanyard security passes, the NASA scientists sat at their stations listening in anticipation to the data being relayed over the headsets. An oversized American flag on the rear wall provided the backdrop for a series of pedestals and two extensive rows of black consoles further forward. Every compact station was staffed by an enthusiastic scientist following the direction of the mission leaders posted at two separate desks at the front of the elongated command room. The three other walls were inset with large glass windows that allowed observation from the surrounding areas which were home to the multitude of media and other support staff. Mounted on the partition walls were a number of big flat-screen TV's that displayed imagery and reports on the spacecraft's progress, some of it coming directly from the intermingled cameramen who were documenting every aspect and detail of the iconic NASA mission. This particular mission was part of NASA's Mars program, a long-term effort of robotic exploration of Martian geological and geochemical history; specifically, the red planets past capability of supporting small life such as microbes or extremophiles. To achieve these goals, the Mars Science Laboratory rover carried the most advanced and sophisticated suite of instruments designed for scientific study ever sent to Mars.

Mission control had now received confirmation that the probe had successfully detached from the cruise stage through its deep space network of antennas. The nerves and excitement were visible on the faces of all those that had spent many years of their life preparing for this moment. Their chance to input significantly into mankind's knowledge of a world outside our own and the possibility of making first contact with extra-terrestrial life, living or dead.

Silence fell across the room as the mission controller relayed that the Mars Reconnaissance orbiter had begun to track the probe.

"One minute to entry."

The scientists looked at their displays hoping for positive data on the spacecraft's progress; but they all knew that the radio signals from the Mars probe had taken fourteen minutes to reach the Earth. In reality the rover had already failed in its mission or was successfully landing in a momentous achievement of human engineering.

"We are now beginning to feel the atmosphere." announced one of the NASA mission control. As he did so, one scientist in the back row re-checked her completed message on the terminal screen. Activating the encryption cipher, she waited for the cryptographic characters to be assigned before pressing transmit and piggybacking the secure communication on the torrent of information already being streamed out to the world.

COM-12, touchdown expected
14-minute signal window
Quad 51: Aeolis Mons 4.36°S 137.26°E
Cydonia Mesa: 40.45°N 9.28°W
2 hours to relaying range of Odyssey orbiter
Wind sensor advised

A few anxious minutes passed while all incoming technical data was scrutinised when the mission controller declared, "Seven minutes of terror are underway."

The media circles covering the mission immediately began outlining what this meant on their news channels and social media feeds. 7 minutes of terror was the term they had given for the vital phase where the automated computer would take full control of all the Entry, Descent and Landing stages and the overall fate of the mission. Every detail had to work perfectly and seamlessly; any miniscule deviation from this would otherwise result in likely mission failure or destruction.

Each tick of the clock seemed to pass in slow motion, building the pressure until it could be momentarily released two minutes later when the next confirmation came in, "Parachute successfully deployed."

The Mars Odyssey orbiter had now entered observation range and began transmitting data back to Earth as it tracked the probe from its position two and a half miles above the red planet's surface.

"The retro-rockets are firing, velocity fifty metres per second. Stand by for sky crane."

A pin drop could be heard as they all held their breaths in anticipation. It was the first time that the pioneering sky crane or soft-landing technique had been implemented by NASA. Their suspense would be ended very shortly in anguish or joy, but the sixty second wait felt like the longest of their lives. The pause continued; then those two wonderful words came.

"Touchdown confirmed!"

Mission control erupted into scenes of jubilation as waves of relief and ecstasy filled the air. Everyone involved grabbed their nearest colleague and hugged them in congratulations and hi-fived all those in celebratory reach. A feeling of liberated anxiety was clear on every expression, the euphoria that the many years of hard work had not been in vain was infectious. They had done their job but the question still remained, would the Mars Science Laboratory do its?

The rover, equivalent to a one-tonne robot sat there within its twelve by four mile landing ellipse on an alien world that no one had ever stepped on before. It was situated in one of the four landing candidates that had been nominated as potential sites that could have provided the right geological environment to have supported Microbial life. The 3.5 billion-year-old formation had been named Gale Crater and it was a specific area at the base of the colossal mountain, known as an alluvial fan, which provided the intrigue for their studies. The natural characteristic was likely formed by water carrying sediments and its corroded channels in both the giant mound and crater walls suggested the enticing evidence of flowing liquid. At the foot of the mountain designated Aeolis Mons these vast deposits were the strata that unveiled the tale of the planet, each layer a historical page of the distant past waiting to be turned. A planet's life story that would be uncovered by the mobile laboratory as it painstakingly worked its way upward, using its state-of-the-art sampling and analysis instruments to scrutinise the material composition layer by layer. Through its endeavors hopefully ploughing the way to answering that big question, are we, or have we always been, alone in the universe?

As the Mars Science Laboratory initiated its automated systems tests in readiness to survey the Martian landscape; swirls of dust rose as a sharp angular shadow was cast across the rover's weather station.

In NASA mission control, the commotion had only begun to die down when one of the scientists loudly exclaimed, "It's a wheel!"

The first low-res image from Mars had arrived, a black and white picture taken by the front hazcam to confirm the rovers orientation. Everyone in the command room looked to their nearest display as the scientist projected the image onto the numerous big screens.

"It looks like we've also captured the rover's shadow in the crater."

Another larger image started loading up soon after; the pixels popping up row by row in a teasing reveal to show the crater walls on the alien horizon and dust particles obscuring the hazard camera. With wide grins the NASA scientists initiated their review of the landing site on the other world.

"No big rocks in site, it's a relatively flat spot. The terrain looks nice and level but it appears we have blown up a dust cloud with our descent engines."

The various news agencies reporting on the mission began

sharing the first images from the Mars Science Laboratory with the global population. They would not be expecting more detailed high-resolution images from the Martian environment for at least a couple of hours due to the transmission window of NASA's signal relaying Odyssey orbiter.

One of the first jobs of the exploration program was to find areas where life may have survived had it ever evolved on Mars. If that primary goal was achieved and these places discovered; then they would know exactly where to conduct future missions to search for the direct signs of life. Now that their robotic research rover was safely on the planet, everyone at NASA was eager to get the Mars Science Laboratory started on its purpose without delay.

As the NASA technicians scorned over the data they were receiving from the rover's high gain antenna, the on-board computer confirmed that it had completed the series of automated test sequences to make sure all its systems were operating as expected. This was when one of the technicians noticed a blip during the rovers checks on the immediate environmental conditions, a sudden failure in one of the weather station instruments.

"I think we must have sustained damage from the dust and stones thrown up by the descent thrusters? One of the wind sensors in the robotic arm is malfunctioning."

5 - The Bilderberg Group

Michael swigged from his antique hip flask and slapped it down on his cluttered desk. The beams of the morning sunrise penetrated his moth-eaten curtains illuminating his chaotic workspace and highlighting the dust particles floating in Brownian motion. He never used to be a big drinker, but not so long ago after that night, he discovered that alcohol was the only thing that seemed to give him any release from his torments. A lesser of two evils he would tell himself, but that was before both had conspired to drive him to something far worse. Now he had to live with it, embedded so deep it was much a part of him as breathing. There was no dangerous downward spiral of abuse, no glimmer of hope at the end of the tunnel. He was already at the bottom of the pit of despair slowly drowning in the filth of anger and guilt.

He was sitting at his computer reading the ramblings of another whack job on a conspiracy theory web forum, a crazy old fool ranting about how he was horribly violated and his head implanted with a device by little grey aliens. Clicking the embedded video, a leather skinned man in denim dungarees appeared on his media player, 'So you take them there loops of copper wire.' The hillbilly was in a wooden shack full of tools and an obvious moonshine still. 'Connect this here truck battery and there y'all go. Usin done made ya a mind shield.'

"This is ridiculous." concluded Michael as he closed down the internet browser in frustration. He drew the line at making D.I.Y alien proof headgear.

He was getting nowhere, there were no answers, that tiny drop of salvation of someone else to blame seemed so far out of reach. He could feel the dull pain hammering on the sides of his temples, scratching across his brain like wildfire claws, the presence of a shrieking monster trying to dig its way out, intensifying as it spread along every neuron and cumulating in an eruption of agony behind his eyes. On occasions these attacks were heralded by gradual indications, but usually as it was now, they came without warning.

"Argghh!" he let out a growl of annoyance at the piercing ache while his keyboard and mouse began to rattle violently as if a localised earthquake had struck with him at the epicentre.

The clatter began to echo loudly in his head, his heart raced and the cruel world around him blurred. He snatched for his antique decanter. Gulping down the brown spirits, that precious liquid that kept things bearable. The liquor oozed down his throat, adding to the alcohol already being pumped through his arteries. A numbing warmness flowed around his body, beat after beat dispelling the disquiet conflict in his mind and the debilitating pain, for now.

Can this day get any worse? he asked to any higher power listening.

Every day was already an existence of hardship but this morning had brought new meaning to the word rock bottom, it was Isabella's 5th birthday and over a year since he had last seen her. Michael looked to the postbox for that letter which could have elevated his mood, but alas nothing, life spat on him as always. He had written to her every week without fail but no response or acknowledgement that his daughter was even receiving his letters had ever come.

How could I expect anything different after what I did? No one understands what I'm going through, yet still, it's nothing to the suffering and pain I brought upon my daughter.

Michael scalded himself in his head. No apology will heal the life she had before her now, but stupidly or not, he always thought he could do or say something to make that wound a little less agonizing.

In his hands he held up that special something he had for her this year, and inspected the message he had engraved on the silver jewelry with the two golden ram heads. An extra touch that had cost him the vast majority of his weekly dole money. The so called 'Full English Breakfast' microwave meal and supermarket value alcohol in front of him served as a stark reminder of the daily diet he was forced to survive upon as a consequence. It was such an object of beauty and rarity; in mythology a symbol of energy, power and strength. Everything that his daughter represented to him, and for her birthday, it was worth the lesson in manipulating the most meagre of budgets.

He slumped in his armchair, the ripped tartan pattern exposing the foam and bent springs inside. It was a piece of furniture he had found dumped outside a large town house in one of the more upmarket streets in his area. Michael slowly turned the bracelet through his fingers. He washed down the remains of his cheap processed meal with a skinful of whiskey from his walnut veneered flask, placed the trinket in his breast pocket and allowed his eyelids to turn the lights out on everything else but the gloom of his self-pity.

"Nooo!! Stoopppp!!!" An old geographic globe that was balanced on a leather-bound stack of 'lost civilisations' volumes was now tumbling across his floor.

"God damn you!" Michael cursed loudly, questioning if there would ever be a moment of peace for him.

The phantom paralysis and the dance of his cramping toes took a few seconds to subside. The clammy heat aggravated his skin and that familiar smell of stale air began to fill his nostrils.

"I really need to get out of this dump." he told himself looking around at his depressing studio flat in west London.

It was one particularly bizarre character on the Internet forum that, on cue, gave him that perfect reason. 'Ping!' …. Ping! … Ping!' His computer was making sharp pinging sounds signifying the appearance of the message chat box on his screen. It was a member of one of the many conspiracy web forums he frequented these days probing for any clues that could give him the answers to what happened to him that night. It was a sorry state of affairs that these strangers were the only ones that seemed to take him seriously. Most of them were clearly insane but if you wallowed in crap long enough, something useful would always float to the top. And when he started hearing about similar stories of bright lights and lost time he dived right in, head first. Normally he didn't take seriously what many of the conspirators said but this guy was different to the other crazies, he seemed to have a solid group of well-informed connections and his information was always backed up by the most respected posters.

Fox: Hey Truth Seeker, you there dude? I think I have something you might want to hear!

Michael cleared the sleep from his eyes and took to his keyboard.

Truth Seeker: Hi Fox, what is it?

Fox: Was speaking with Gandalf and get this, he said that one of his contacts had been given info from a security officer of that place Dulce. Say's it totally trustworthy!

"Dulce, been hearing a lot about you lately." he muttered to himself.

It was only a day or two back that he was reading a local newspaper story written by a hack in Albuquerque, New Mexico regarding the recent spate of missing person reports of native Indians within the Jicarilla Apache reserve. The home site of the Jicarilla Apache nation was situated in the rugged mesas of northern New Mexico right next to the nearby town of Dulce.

Truth Seeker: Dulce….. Ok, I've heard about it. What does it have to do with me?

Fox: Well he said some secret government agency has been abducting civilians and messing with their heads and stuff!

Truth Seeker: What agency?

Fox: Not sure, but mentioned something about a uniform insignia with a triangle and three stripes

Truth Seeker: Means nothing to me. What are they doing to these people?

Fox: Supposed to be part of some crazy-shit mass experiment they are doing

Truth Seeker: Any details? Are these people missing time, experiencing changes to their bodies?

Fox: Didn't say, but has something to do with brainwashing for sure. That's got to cause some headaches…right?

Truth Seeker: Can you get more information?

Fox: That's the thing. Since he made contact no one has seen or heard a thing from him. Disappeared from the face of the Earth man….

Truth Seeker: Damn it! Was there anything else that could help?

Fox: Only that they are also mutilating cattle

Truth Seeker: Well nothing like that is happening here. I need something I can go on. What about the UK?

Fox: Are you kidding dude! Your end of the pond is the talk of the forums today!

Truth Seeker: Why???

Fox: It's the Bilderberg man!

Truth Seeker: Shit yes…. It's today, worth a try

Fox: Could be dangerous but you know those cockroaches will know what's going down

Truth Seeker: You're right. If someone knows what happened to me then it's there.

Fox: Good luck but gotta go, can't stay on too long, don't want to be tracked. Will let you know if I get more, be careful. They have eyes everywhere

Truth Seeker: Thanks, keep me posted

Fox: Will do. Live long and prosper dude

He had almost forgotten that the infamous meeting was taking place in central London that very day. It was said to be a gathering of the Bilderberg group. Michael had learnt of them; they were at the heart of many a conspiracy theory. It was the unofficial name given to a conference held annually and attended by people with huge influence in business, media and politics. A place where whoever was involved in destroying his life would surely attend.

Michael clicked on the Wikipedia page for the group and once again read over the summary of its origin, 'The original Bilderberg conference was held at the Hotel de Bilderberg, near Arnhem, from May 29 to May 31, 1954. Polish expatriate and political adviser, Joseph Retinger, concerned about the growth of anti-Americanism in western Europe, along with a number of others, proposed an international conference at which leaders from European countries and the United States would be brought together with the aim of promoting understanding between the cultures of the United States of America and western Europe.'

He accepted that this may actually be an accurate account of how it all started but the online consensus of his like-minded community certainly had different beliefs now. Presently with it being an invitation only gathering attended by not only prime ministers, presidents and royalty, but by media and oil barons, political figures, central bankers, international financiers, leading business persons and defence experts. They were convinced that as a meeting shrouded in secrecy and extravagance, this behind closed doors collection of powerful figures secretly fixed the fate of the world.

Michael grabbed a pair of ragged jeans and the only t-shirt that didn't stink of week-old body odour and alcohol. He motioned to the door where his trench coat was draped over a replica Easter Island Moai statuette when he heard footsteps and the grunting of an eager dog. The land lady was outside in the hallway. The nausea reared once more and burning stomach juices swelled in his gullet. It was that intuition again; he could feel the agitation emanating from her. Michael would randomly feel that connection, literally a gut feeling from a person, there essence momentarily piercing him like the blade of a turning knife. She was frustrated that she had to leave for a few days; Michael's rent money would have to wait. Crouching down with his weight against the door; he spat sour bile into a dying Yucca plant as he listened to the echo of the high heels and scratching paws disappear down the stairwell.

*

One hour later Michael exited Green Park underground station. The weather forecast had said it would be clear blue skies all day but unnatural looking layers of white cloud had rolled in overheard casting a shadow over the area. He momentarily watched the hustle and bustle of commuters and tourists, *how simple life used to be* he thought to himself as he brushed shoulders with the world he was once a part of. Feeling like he was moving against the direction of everyone else he started walking down Piccadilly towards the Ritz hotel, the prestigious location of this year's Bilderberg conference.

Security was out in full force, scores of private body guards were escorting their assigned V.I.P.'s through the famous entrance and local police were scrutinising every person, methodically searching any one that wanted to get close. There was no way he was just going to walk through the front door today, especially without the required security passes or tied to the party of an influential dignitary. Michael took another swig of whiskey, swallowed with a grimace and decided to make his way round the back of the 133-room luxury hotel.

Behind the Ritz was the grassy expanse of Green Park with its ample cover of trees. Michael kept his head down and wandered onto the pathway amongst the runners and dog walkers. As he left the commotion of the main street and circled to the rear of the building, the show of security quickly tailed off. Although there were still plenty of guards patrolling the area, this presented him with the best chance to get inside the hotel without being spotted. Michael took a seat upon one of the many benches, the smell of half eaten kebab and chilli-sauce made his stomach rumble. His hand reached for the nearby bin but he wasn't that desperate just yet; he snatched a sauce stained newspaper from the top and unfolded it out in front of him. Scanning the inside pages, he kept one eye out for the right moment to approach the brushwood that backed onto the Ritz. He was distracted by an article on the annual tally of missing children in Brazil, a staggering number, when a lull in passer byes finally came and grabbed back his attention. He dumped the tabloid back into the wire bin and walked purposely towards the tree line. Once under the cover of some foliage, he quickly examined the skirting fence and found a big enough break in one of the fence panels to fit through. Squatting in a patch of undergrowth; Michael sipped from his hip flask waiting to make a run for a service door he had spied in the distance. Fifteen minutes he had waited before his opportunity came; the meeting must have started as patrolling guards had momentarily disappeared. Michael squeezed and forced himself through the muddy gap in the fence, tearing his terracotta army t-shirt in the process. A souvenir he had purchased on his second visit to see the prized artefacts when they had come to an exhibition in London. He unraveled the hooked brown strands of cotton and sprinted across a short patio for the service door. He tugged at the handle but it did not budge. As he tried to catch his breath, Michael cursed himself for being so stupid; *of course they wouldn't have left the god damn door open!* He kicked the heavy metal door in an involuntary rage, this entity of anger fully directed towards the unmoving handle. He was about to yell out at the pain shooting through his foot when there was a blunt crack from the lock. Michael tentatively tried the handle once more. It rattled loosely in his hand; the sturdy internal mechanism broken in pieces. The door pulled open. This was the only occasion he could remember when one of these strange phenomena actually caused him any benefit. Michael didn't waste a second of his lucky break and stuck his head in the doorway. It was silent and clear. He quickly slipped into what looked like the exterior side entrance to a laundry room. But as he went to pull the door closed and slide across the lower bolt lock, his hip flask slipped from his jacket pocket and clattered across the outside paving slabs. The metal and polished wood clanged against the stone, and as it rattled to a stop, he could hear the two-way radios of the guards' crackle into life and the sudden sound of running footfalls approach from around the corner as they reacted to the distant noise.

"Shit!", he didn't have much time, he needed to hide fast.

He scrambled to the floor burning holes into his jeans and grazing his knees, finally scooping up his silver and brown flask after a number of fumbled attempts. The guards' footsteps were getting close now. Michael dove into the laundry room and hauled the door shut, sliding the thick bolt across the base of the exit just as two burly guards came into sight. He didn't think he had been seen but he needed to move fast just in case. Rubbing his bleeding knees in irritation, Michael pulled himself up and hastily left the laundry room. He entered a set of deserted corridors; he couldn't stay out in the open for too long and there was no way he could enter the lobby area of the Ritz without causing suspicion. His muddied hands and trashed clothes would immediately attract unwanted attention. First things first he found an empty bathroom and began to wipe the dirt from his skin and jeans trying to clean some respectability back into his appearance. As he attempted to turn his long brown trench coat inside out, his head began to ring painfully. He stared at himself in the mirror trying to focus the blurry reflection of weeklong stubble and cavernous black eyes, flipped the leather lid of his scratched flagon and took a big gulp of whiskey to try and dull the sharp aching in his brain. Michael shuddered while he swallowed the burning brown liquid. As the alcohol flowed down his throat it seemed to have the desired effect of dulling his senses. While the buzzing in is mind was momentarily masked, it was replaced with the echo of a muffled voice. It was coming from the air vent. *The conference* he thought to himself, Michael gazed at the thin grill, *I can fit in that.* With his head still thumping he mounted the wash basin and gave the vent cover a strong yank; his first attempt loosened two of the screws and with another couple of wrenches the grill popped off. He took a deep breath and heaved himself into the tight opening, leaving the grill resting at its entrance.

Michael followed the sound of voices through the claustrophobic vents until he finally reached its source. A wonderfully extravagant venue full of candelabra covered tables beneath gold and crystal adorned chandeliers. Michael was looking over the Music room of William Kent house which adjoins the Ritz hotel. The room was full, he estimated over a few hundred high profile people were sat in groups being indulged with the most expensive champagnes, finest entrees and all listening intently to the current speaker. Michael thought he recognised the rotund and bearded man as the Time magazines person of the year, a big hitter in the world of business and certainly someone with great influence. He lay silently still in the vent listening to each speaker in turn; an hour passed of people discussing global warming, announcements of business mergers, U.N peacekeeping requirements, new laws needing to be passed to combat terrorism and the troubles of the Middle East, but nothing seemed to be related to him or any of the popular conspiracy theories that were smeared across countless web pages.

I thick haze of cigarette smoke had begun to drift towards the ceiling of the room. No one seemed to bat-an-eye at the fact that they were breaking a countrywide rule of non-smoking in public buildings, a rule they all thought they were clearly above. Michael was now beginning to get the shakes, not because of the cold air blowing through the vents but due more to the fact that all that was left in his hip flask was the strong fumes of fermented alcohol.

Without the dulling effects of the whiskey, Michael's head started to feel like it was being crushed in a vice again. Everything seemed to be closing in around him, his heart rate increased and breathing became difficult. As panic began to set in, he glimpsed two gentlemen seated close to the nearby door quietly take their leave and exit the room. Michael couldn't explain it but he was getting a nauseating feeling in his gut that he should follow these strangers. He didn't know if it was this strange intuition or the intensifying claustrophobia that was urging his being to search for larger confines, but he squeezed himself around and back into the network of vents.

Regularly checking the direction of the two men through the numerous grills, he followed the sound of their voices down a couple of abandoned corridors into a second dining room. This one did not contain an air outlet like the other rooms but fortunately housed a maintenance hatch leading to a crawl space above the rooms ceiling. Michael began to breathe a little easier now he was in a less confined area and dragged himself over the wooden beams and insulation to a tiny spy hole left by the repositioning of the grandiose chandelier. Through his limited view he could make out a long highly polished table with at least fourteen people seated around it, and wafting through it, the strong-smelling aroma of chamomile. A thick set man, looking in his late fifties and seemingly a high-ranking military officer, stood and faced the two gentlemen who had just joined.

"Report!" he asked in a deep gruff voice.

One of the new arrivals addressed the table, a dark-skinned man of pacific looking descent with a large set of claw-like scars across one side of his face. "The turnout was much as we expected; all the world's most influential and powerful people in monetary, political, intellectual and ecclesiastical circles, but there were some interesting developments."

"More worrying I'd say Mr. Pierron." added the second new arrival, a tall slender man with black rimmed glasses and a neat side parting.

"Please explain Dr. Kuzminski." asked the old military man.

"Well General Allen, one of the suspect multinational corporations funded by a consortium of international bankers and oil barons has bought out one of the leading suppliers of power to the United States; and now combined control over sixty per cent of the populations' electricity demands, cornering a market resource that should not be monopolised as such. What concerns me more though, is the plans to bring out a number of new laws in the face of the current threat of terrorism. In brief, motions towards circumventing data protection acts and methods of identification and tracking that will basically undermine the western world's basic human rights. More so to bestow the UN with further powers to legally interfere with nations and states who do not adhere to the best interests of the people in that room."

"This stinks of the FEMA situation and the Patriot Act all over again." commented a large balding man.

"Doesn't it quite Judge Kidd. What I believe we are looking at in that room could be the first steps of a single world authority or group of powerful elite, in a situation where they can influence and dictate every facet of economy, law, religion and even war for their own ends." summarised Mr. Pierron, "A particularly scary thought."

Shit! This is nothing more than another damn collection of conspiracy theorists with a bit of money and too much time. Michael started to think to himself, believing it was an extreme stretch of the imagination to have come to such conclusions from what he had heard in that music room.

A middle-aged woman also in military uniform stood and leaned over the table. She had an odd look and feel about her, like her skin didn't really fit her body.

"Listen, you must not let your focus wander, there is more at stake than human rights and the greed of Earth's wealthy minority. What of the resources I need to complete my work! The sands of time are heaped heavily against you!"

"Against us!" The general repeated before propositioning for everyone to sit, "Ok, these are indeed disturbing reports but Corporate is right, we have more pressing matters to attend too. The day of judgement is fast approaching and we must be prepared. Dr. Kuzminski, how did things go with BHP Billiton?"

"They were very curious as to why we would be interested in what they believe are empty coal mining facilities. But as soon as Mr.

Pierron gave them our offer, suffice to say they were more than happy for us to purchase all of them, no questions asked."

More business talk, this is a waste of time. I need to start thinking how the hell I'm going to get out of here. Michael's shakes were getting worse; now pouring with sweat he was beginning to feel great agitation and discomfort.

The general continued, "Excellent, I can report this to the Egregor. He will be returning tomorrow for debriefing at Alton Towers HQ. The Egregor will be pleased with the acquirement of further resources, but his interests will lie more in operation Darwin. Dr. Heaney this is your department." sending his gaze to a moustached fellow taking a deep gulp of his chamomile tea.

"As you are aware, our role in operation Darwin is observation and cover up. I fail to see, even if successful which I don't believe is viable in the time scale presented, how it is going to help in the current situation. Although as asked, my team has been monitoring case MC One-Nine-Eight-Zero. As of yet we have not seen any significant developments. His employment has been terminated; he remains a recluse inside his own home and only surfaces to take a trip to the local off-license. He is no more than an alcoholic with an obvious violent tendency. In my opinion we are wasting our time and resources best directed elsewhere."

"My father and the Egregor founded this organisation, so I know from the beginning that this has been of great importance to him. Therefore, I would like a full report ready for his arrival tomorrow. Please tell me, where is Michael now?"

On the mention of his name, Michael's heart skipped a beat and his pulse began to race, the sound of which was almost drowning out the voices below.

Dr. Heaney's left eye wandered as he looked towards the general. "Well Sir it's rather strange, there appears to be strong atmospheric interference over central London from an unknown source. It is messing with our tracking equipment and we lost him as he entered the affected area."

"Find him, bring him in if you need too!" ordered General Allen.

Anger ignited inside Michael, the bastards had ruined his life and there was no way they were going to get their filthy hands on him again. Breaking through the mental shackles, this secondary state of consciousness erupted like a volcano.

As all his emotions burst to the surface, the wooden beam taking his weight cracked beneath him. The splintering support collapsed and the chandelier dropped from the ceiling, shattering across the solid table followed by Michael and a deluge of plaster. He crashed violently upon the table and off onto the floor, while the members of the meeting fell out of their seats in shock and surprise. Michael jumped to his feet and made for the closest exit, a large curtained window. The strange looking woman known as Corporate, with unexpected speed moved to intercept him. In an unconscious act, one of the loose chairs shot across the room smashing into the oncoming woman's chest, slamming her against the wall and down to the carpet. Michael stopped for a split second in concern, but as he stared at the crumpled body, he thought he saw her face flicker, if only for an instant, yet just enough to reveal reptilian like features.

The site of two men lunging for him dragged him out of his shock. He darted forward and flung himself through the window, sending shattered glass onto the soft grass below. Michael scrambled up to his feet and sprinted for the park. Just as the others made to pursue him a team of security burst into the Wimborne room.

"What's going on, is everyone alright?" queried the lead guard with his finger ready on the Taser trigger.

The stern face of the general looked to the window and case MC 1980 running off into the distance, then back to his people. "Everything is fine. Just an accident with the chandelier."

As the confused security left the room, the general picked up the chair that seemingly flew unaided across the room. "Dr. Heaney, a waste of time you say!"

6 - The Path not Chosen

It was an unusually hot day for the wet Autumn the north of England was experiencing. A doting mother placed her daughter onto a swing in the middle of a lush grassy park. Children ran around them shouting and laughing, enjoying the weekend with their families, but the girl on the swing didn't make a sound. Instead she waved her arms and created varying shapes with her hands, signs which her mother understood perfectly.

"Ok darling, I will push you higher but make sure you hold on tight" replied her mother while signing back to her daughter.

"Right, one more go and we need to go get lunch before dad comes." Again signing and mouthing the words expressively.

She glanced over to her daughters' grandparents sat on a nearby bench watching with fondness. Her husband had been on a business trip and she had taken the opportunity to visit her parents to get some appreciated time with their grandchild.

Her mobile began to ring. She held up her finger then made the phone sign before her daughter ushered over Nana and Gramps.

"Hi love, it's me. I'm still more than an hour away on the train." updated her husband, "It's was a pain getting from the hotel to the station. You know how London traffic is."

"Why didn't you just get the tube?" she asked.

"I wasn't in the mood. I'm getting pressured to agree to some law changes but I'm not having it. Just boring work stuff honey."

"Well try to forget about it if you can. Your daughter is looking forward to a weekend with a happy dad. Just give me a call when you arrive."

She walked back to her family as them and everyone else was oblivious to the events unfolding at the top of a multi-story car park in the centre of town.

Asam was a surgeon at Walkergate hospital in Newcastle and it was his turn for the weekend shift but today he never turned up for work. There was nothing wrong with him, feeling as healthy as he had ever felt and with nothing more important to do. However, Asam had an incredible urge to drive into the centre of town, a compulsion he could not explain. His hand involuntarily flipped the indicator and he pulled his car to the side of the road. A new Porsche he had rewarded himself to celebrate his promotion to chief of surgery.

He stepped out of his car and began to walk through the busy streets. There was a feeling of detachment from reality, like a connection had been severed between his consciousness and his brain's command centre. His mind aimlessly searched down various synaptic pathways continually hitting unnatural roadblocks to its cognitive freedom. He was well aware of himself and his decisions, but it was another part of him that was the pilot at the controls.

Twisting and turning down side streets, Asam had no idea where he was going but his body seemed to know the way. After entering an unknown building and climbing some flights of stairs, Asam found himself at the top of a small multi-story car park in the most crowded area of the city. Somewhere locked away at the back of his mind his real-self shouted out that this situation wasn't right, but he carried on regardless towards a large white van parked at the edge of the structure. Asam didn't know why but when he pulled the handle of the vehicle, he wasn't surprised to find it swing open. He proceeded to step into the driver's seat and fumbled for the keys in the ignition, they were there as he inexplicably knew.

Asam looked at his gold watch, a gift from the colleagues that he should have been sitting down with now, drinking a coffee and discussing the latest sports cars. It read 12.59pm. The surgeon's arm rose, it was shaking, maybe the piece of him that knew this was wrong was fighting the urge. It was futile, as his watch hit 13:00 Asam turned the key and for a split second afterwards a whisper of "No!" hung in the cabin, as the wave of reality returned.

There was a flash of blinding light and a deafening rumble in the air, children and their parents looked to the skyline in terror.

The child on the swing did not stir; she looked at her mother wondering why her face looked so scared. "What's wrong mummy?" she asked in her sign language, but her mother did not reply, all she could do was wrap her arms around her daughter as a wind of searing flame engulfed them.

*

Elsewhere across the globe Chi Hon's old and run-down fishing trawler pumped out thick black smoke as it chugged into the shanty town harbour. Every day without fail Chi Hon would sail out at sunset to bring home a catch that would hopefully raise enough money to feed his family. Today was no exception, he began his exhausting routine as usual but today his patchwork wooden boat arrived with a meagre haul of fish on deck and while the Sun still hid over the horizon. The seafood market workers just assumed it was due to a problem with his boat or a bout of severe sickness as the reason for such an early return from the Yellow Sea. No fisherman would cut short their struggle to make ends meet unless there was a major problem.

With the economic explosion in China many cities around the country had experienced a significant upturn in their prosperity, especially in Qingdao. That greater revenue had even filtered down to the poorer echelons of Chinese society, with more demand for fish, the price per kilo of catch naturally went up. But it meant Chi Hon had to work harder to reap the benefits while he could as like other provinces in China, they were already seeing that growth steadily plateau. That extra money was much needed income he was able to send back to his struggling family back in Xinjiang. His parents, siblings and extended family were fruit farmers, but due to the ugly disputes between Hui and Uyghur ethnic groups and the subsequent crackdown by the Chinese government, theirs and others grape exports were heavily hampered in the region.

The port labourers knew something was different with this unusual site the moment Chi Hon disembarked his boat and motioned for the market, leaving his vital income to lie upon deck under the spoiling humidity. He walked emotionless through the dealers as they prepared troughs of ice and scales for the fleets of fishing boats to return. His regular buyers called out to him with greetings but no response or acknowledgement came. It was not because he did not hear them, their voices were crystal clear in his head; something unexplainable blocked every bit of him that wanted his vocal chords to scream out. He was in a walking dream looking through his own eyes from the end of a constricting tunnel with spots of light blocking the exit. As he ambled out of the shanty market and towards the town centre, his thoughts went back to that of his wife and children waiting for him at home hoping to hear of a successful day at sea.

A combination of the drying salty water and the rough tarmac path began to badly blister his bare feet but any pain was securely locked away as Chi Hon stopped beside a parked rusty van. The one thing he always felt blessed by was that he had the gift of free will and the ability to use that to provide for his loved ones, yet he had reached the moment where he had come to the devastating realisation that even that had been stripped away from him. He was now just an observer to his own determined fate.

The Sun was yet to rise over the busy city of Qingdao but for miles around the sky was lit with the energy released by splitting uranium atoms.

7 - Whispers in the Shadows

Deep underground somewhere within the mountainous border of Afghanistan and Pakistan, a set of men waited nervously, eyes transfixed to a double wooden door elegantly carved with crown adorned serpents. Red drapes embroidered with gold thread hung from the chamber walls and a thick Persian rug cushioned the hard-cold surface beneath. Dozens of topographic maps of the outside lands were laid out upon the central elongated table weighed down with empty artillery shells, their edges fluttered under the warm draught being pumped in through the vent that was hewn out of the stone wall. Apart from the occasional cough due to the dry air, the attendees were silent; the only noise a background hum of a nearby electrical generator. There was nothing to be said or speculated until he arrived. The person they were waiting for was known only as the Pindar, a mysterious man with such global influences that he was someone to be seriously listened too.

The Pindar was standing in a dim room barely lit by flickering candles; although he was one of the most powerful men on Earth, even he still had a master. Out of the shadows a harsh whispery voice filled the air.

"So it has begun Pindar, we come to the last stages of a plan, over ten thousand years in the making. You will make them understand in no uncertain terms that the United Nations has targeted them for the introduction of occupational forces, something they cannot do legally without immediate threat to the security of the member nations. You will force into their minds the belief that without a ruthless stance of co-operation, certain death and defeat would shortly fall upon them."

The figure in the shadows raised his head; the light barely penetrated the darkness surrounding him, but enough to reveal the black slit of a snake-like eye hidden within an outline of turquoise jade.

"Now go do what you were created for." hissed the masked figure.

The Pindar bowed and made his way to the door, he was there for one reason, to communicate the wishes of the Masters to their pawns. He made his way down the lavishly carpeted corridors excavated out of mountain rock to a pair of heavy wooden doors. Composing himself he stepped through. He was immediately met with a wave of questions, "I demand to know what is happening!", "Why have we been summoned here?"

He raised his hand and looked at the attendees with an intent gaze. The Pindar could drive fear into any man with a mere glance. His eyes were penetrating, with a yellow hue about them. His face was pale like it had never seen the Sun and permanently flaking with some kind of skin affliction.

"Gentleman sit." The Pindar commanded with a soft German accent. They done as he asked in silence.

"Thank you all for attending. I wish it was in better circumstances. I will get straight to the point as what I am about to tell you will require swift counter actions.", the Pindar removed his suit jacket, plain black except for a triangle tipped with a golden eye and beams of light stitched into the pocket. "As of twenty minutes ago a number of small nuclear devices detonated in numerous United Nation member states, which include the US, UK, and Russia."

There were some joyous reactions to the news but the majority in front of him wore heavily worried faces.

"I am certain none of you here know who is responsible, as none of you were. This was done not by any country or rogue militant group, but the leaders of the UN themselves!"

The representative of Libya spoke, "Why would they have done such a thing?"

"A reason, a cause, an excuse! A new international law has recently been passed that allows the United Nations to invade and occupy any country that threatens world security with the use of nuclear weapons. It is no coincidence that every member of the permanent Security Council has been attacked, any single member of that group has the power to veto any action decided upon by the council."

"Let the infidels come, their blood will stain our land red!" spat the Iranian leader.

"You clearly do not understand! This new law circumvents all rules of war; this will not be like Iraq or Afghanistan. Bombs will rain indiscriminately from the sky, poisons will infect your water supplies and chemical gases choke the life out of your lands. Only when all that is left of your country are a few impoverished people and your natural resources, will the so-called peace keepers step foot onto your soil. Had not the rhetoric already begun against your nation?"

"But the world would not allow it!" stated a shocked Syrian Minister.

The Pindar smiled, "Do not be so naive, did the world stop the invasion of Afghanistan over one atrocity? Did the world come running to the defence of Iraq when allied nations attacked on the grounds of non-existent weapons of mass destruction? No!! The world watched on their TV screens and did nothing! The UN has strong evidence that you are responsible and in addition, plan further imminent attacks. To the eyes of the world you will have the blood of millions on your hands. Don't you already with the reported chemical attacks on your own people? Their voices will be silent!"

The Syrian Minister suddenly lost his confidence in the ethical stance of the global society.

"The Democratic People's Republic of Korea has broadcast the development of nuclear weapons. Even with our token dismantling of facilities, America's distrust of our government remains strong. They will certainly come for us. We do not have the power to fight an all-out war against the UN or America. What can we do?"

The Pindar took a deep breath ready to respond to the North Korean ruler, "There is only one thing you can do, admit to it."

This caused an avalanche of outbursts, "Foolishness!" "How would this help?" "We would give them exactly what they need to for their evil crusade!"

The Pindar raised his hand again to command silence, "No, the opposite. They do not expect you to admit to this. The reach of the United Nations is not unlimited; they will target at the most two of your nations as prime perpetrators and throw their full military force at them. It will not stop there; they will regroup their forces and each of you will follow like dominos." The jaundice eyes of the Pindar looked at each of the men in turn, "But imagine, the United Nations faced with the combined forces of your countries! Your faith, courage and resolve will strike fear deep into the heart of the UN. You will stand together and tell the world if the oppressors attack your people, you will not bow to their evil, you have justice behind you and will not hesitate to retaliate with your full might. What they have witnessed this day is but a mere breeze compared to the storm that would be unleashed upon them!"

8 - The Incident

July 6th 1947

"Colonel John Allen, Counter Intelligence Corps." he answered as he picked up the phone.

"Colonel Sir. This is Major Marcel, Five Hundred and Ninth Bomb group of the eighth Air force. Apologies for such a late call."

"How can I help you Major?"

"Colonel Blanchard requested I call you for assistance. There has been an aircraft crash in Corona. The wreckage remains unidentified and seems to be spread halfway across the Foster ranch."

"When did this happen?" inquired the colonel.

"The Chaves county sheriff told me that the ranch foreman found the debris four days ago. Supposedly came down the evening before, during that god awful thunderstorm."

"Standby Major." He advised as he covered the mouth piece of the phone.

"Lieutenant." Colonel Allen hollered over to a nearby soldier encamped behind a huge radio system and a desk full of filed flight and radar reports, "What have we had in the air within our vicinity since July second?"

The young lieutenant hastily searched through his documents before replying, "Other than our official planes out on training exercises, and a single rocket launched from White Sands… Ehhh… Just Project Mogul sir."

"Shit." he cursed to himself.

Colonel Allen signaled to his listening subordinate as he advised Major Marcel on the phone, "Major, Captain Cavitt will assist you. I want you both to find the foreman, we will need his help in locating the debris. Then get yourselves out there in the morning."

"Yes Sir." acknowledged the major.

"This ranch foreman, did he take any of the debris from the crash site?" questioned the colonel.

"Yes sir, he brought some to the sheriff's office. I inspected it myself sir. It's unlike anything I've seen." confirmed the major.

"Ok Major. You've done a great job so far. I'll send some MP's to the sheriff's office to collect the wreckage. Captain Cavitt will be with you shortly."

"Thank you, Sir."

Colonel Allen hung up the handset and turned to the men present, "Right, main goal is to locate and retrieve all fragments of this craft and lockdown access to the site. Sheridan, who's your most trusted man?"

The captain removed his tilted uniform cap and scratched his head, before momentarily answering, "Bill's a good man."

"Sergeant Rickett, I want you to drive down now and locate the body of the wreckage. As soon as you have, notify me straight away. Understood."

"Absolutely Sir." responded the young soldier, trying to hide the pride from the faith put in him.

Within hours, Colonel Allen, his most loyal men and a group of MPs were on their way to the Foster ranch in a convoy of military vehicles. They were heading to rendezvous with Sergeant Rickett who had swiftly located the main body of the wreckage. The ranch area was a wilderness of dirt, hardy grass and shrubs. There were no natural or artificial light sources penetrating the gloom, and outside of the light cones produced by the convoy of vehicles, there was endless darkness.

Upon pulling up beside the headlamps of the sergeant's jeep, Colonel Allen jumped from his Dodge truck and made his way to the stationary sergeant.

"Sergeant report." The colonel requested but there was no response.

"Sergeant Rickett... Bill!" he called with more assertiveness.

The young soldier finally turned in response, "Sorry Sir... The main structure of the wreckage is there." He pointed his flashlight at the hull of metal ten feet in front of them embedded in a mound of dirt.

"Sir, there is several bodies. The poor people, they're are all dead... Badly disfigured... Sir I don't..." he reported weakly before his words cut off, clearly shaken by the scene.

The colonel did not immediately respond, seemingly perturbed by the sight. He surveyed this pivotal tragedy illuminated within the range of the flashlight, letting an uncomfortable silence pass before finally speaking.

"Ok son. It's a scary and horrible thing you've just seen but I need you on point right now. You'll have the time to think about it after the job is done." advised the colonel sternly but with empathy.

"Yes Sir. Yes of course." As he said it, you could see him mentally shake his hampering emotions.

"Good lad." The colonel turned to his accompanying group and addressed them in an authoritative voice, "Right men. MPs I want you to set a perimeter around this site, no one gets in or out without my say so. You, you and you, go with Sergeant Rickett and locate the bodies. The rest of you start loading the wreckage on the trucks. Work fast, questions are for later!"

One hour had passed and everyone involved was clearly unsettled, but under the reaffirming guidance of Colonel Allen they had maintained their professionalism. In total fifteen deceased bodies had been discovered by the small contained group of his most trusted men and placed in their accompanying medical vehicle. Nearly all but the main body of the craft had been retrieved and they were just about to assemble together to recover the broken hull when Sergeant Rickett shouted out.

"Colonel Sir! We have one alive!!"

As Colonel Allen motioned towards the location of the sergeant, a humming noise began to fill the air.

"Sir! There is something here vibrating hard, I think it's part of the engine!!" The end of his sentence was barely audible under the amplifying buzz.

Whatever it was, the noise sounded like it was overloading fast and every soldier in the vicinity ran for cover. Sergeant Rickett and Colonel Allen crossed paths as they both sprinted in opposite directions.

Inside the mangle of metal, the colonel grabbed the barely moving hand, arousing a feeble groan from the body. He could see the malfunctioning power source beside him and felt the intense vibration rattle through his bones. As toxic smoke spewed from burning material and melting metal, Colonel Allen heaved the lifeless figure out from under the ensnaring rubble and onto his shoulders. With all his effort he hauled the survivor across the tremoring and rugged ground to the protection afforded behind a military jeep. But no sooner had he dropped behind the dusty rubber of the wheel; a muffled blast ripped through the remains of the wreckage.

The colonel shook his ringing head and looked at the diminutive figure in his arms. Soldiers ran frantically around him and the stifled voice of one MP echoed in his ears; "Colonel Sir, are you ok!... Oh sweet lord, is that a child!"

Colonel Allen never replied but continued to lock his gaze into the dying eyes of the survivor. As they finally closed over, the connection of that moment broke and the colonel's face twisted with despair.

"God no... Medic!!!"

The colonel bewilderedly rose to his feet with the immediate arrival of the MD. He could see that it was dawn and the Sun would soon be rising. He walked over to a soldier carrying a large mobile radio system harnessed to his back and took the handset. He radioed back to his office and connected with the lieutenant than manned the communication and radar system of the Counter Intelligence Corps.

"Lieutenant, this is Colonel Allen. Listen carefully, do we have any project Mogul surveillance balloons in the sky right now?"

"Ehhh... Yes Sir, one." answered the young soldier as he double checked his itineraries.

"Bring it down right now." he ordered.

"Right away Sir. Transmitting signal to begin descent close to your location."

"You misunderstand lieutenant. Release the ballast immediately."

"But Sir… That means it will drop like a stone and crash." the confused lieutenant tried to explain.

"Correct lieutenant."

"Ehh Right… Affirmative… Impact expected in fifteen to seventeen minutes Sir, two clicks due north."

He turned to his trusted men that had now gathered for orders, "Right gentlemen. I need you to collect every fragment of that wreckage double-time, get it and the corpses back to the base infirmary and lock it all down. I'm afraid the Russians are going to know about Project Mogul!"

"Excuse me Colonel, you mean to tell the ruskies about our spying operations?" queried Sergeant Rickett surprised.

"I don't think we have a choice now." the colonel announced, "Sergeant, I have a task for you. Go meet Captain Cavitt, Major Marcel and the ranch foreman. Assist them in locating the mogul balloon crash site and make sure the major gets that wreckage back to Roswell AAF."

"Understood Sir." confirmed Sergeant Rickett.

"Tell Captain Cavitt to find anyone else who saw the wreckage and gather any fragments they may have took. I want to speak with them personally."

9 - The Voice

Countdown: Minus 17 hours before multiple nuclear strikes

"They're looking for me... Tracking me... How?" Michael was trying to process the situation as he paced up and down a damp and dimly lit side street between two concealing buildings.

Once he had made his escape from the meeting room window of the Ritz, he had run as long as his unfit body would allow him. Scampering between alleys, rushing through department stores and hopping on and off public transport when his burning lungs screamed for a break. He was no super spy, but he had hoped that his chaotic movements would cause enough confusion to give him respite to formulate his next steps.

"Someone following me?... No, they mentioned atmospheric interference over central London... Got to be electronic... Surveillance cameras?... Would have seen me coming out of tube in that case... Satellite?... But they said interference from an unknown source, so not weather."

A mind full of conspiracy theories bounced around his head, hundreds of hours of research adding fuel to the fire of each possibility. From microchips in the head to foreign objects implanted just under the skin, and run-of-the-mill tracking devices attached to his clothes to even entertaining the idea of astral projection and anal probes.

"It's got to be a chip of some kind!" he deduced as a garbage truck pulled-up to empty the dumpsters lining his momentary hiding place.

He needed another place to provide some privacy and something to fix that recognisable feeling welling up inside of him. And by sheer fluke, at the other end of the side street, the bleak and rotting sign of a run-down pub shone like it was being pointed out by an angel.

With a triple shot of spirits Michael made his way down the sticky carpet stairs and into the rank toilets. Laying down his tumbler on the metal cistern he locked the cubicle and started to remove his sweat soaked clothes. As he removed each piece of clothing, he thoroughly checked them for anything out of the ordinary such as odd buttons or hardened knots, until finally he was down to his underwear. With the help of the stainless-steel partitions he began scouring his body for a scar, lump or strange mark that could possibly be the result of an implanted tracking device, when in the smudged reflection he noticed the old dog bite. The wound he had received from a nasty tempered Alsatian when he was a young kid. He still remembered the pain of its fangs piercing his skin.

That night, the morning after! A light bulb in his mind flashed on. The mark left by the beast's teeth had brought another memory to the front of his mind.

He located the culprit tooth as he remembered the throbbing toothache he had had the morning after that night of missing time. A molar on the left side of his jaw just after his bottom wisdom tooth. Not wanting to diminish his courage with hesitation, he downed the triple shot, took his bottle opener key ring and immediately began to wrench at the molar. He whimpered with pain after each crank of metal against enamel. It was five attempts and an area of butchered gums before it started to loosen. Almost on the point of passing out, he took one more fervent attempt. Finally with a muffled yell of agony and a splatter of blood, the tooth broke away, its roots still firmly embedded in his jaw bone. Holding his face in agony, he spat the white and red chunks into his hand. Wiping the tooth down with bathroom tissue, he could immediately see it was unusually hollow and inserted inside was a small metallic chip.

"Find me now you bastards!" he uttered to himself as he crushed the device under his shoe and flushed the broken fragments down the toilet.

*

Michael gazed out of the coach window, swilling whiskey around his mouth to numb the pain of the bleeding hole in his jaw. It was a three hour trip up the M1 to Alton Towers and as far as he knew there was only one place of that name. The United Kingdom's most famous theme park was built north of the village of Alton in Staffordshire. It opened in 1980, was currently owned by Merlin Entertainments and apart from a few well reported incidents in the news, it was about as much as he knew of the place. He had visited Alton Towers only once before long ago when he was a teenager, he noticed nothing out of the ordinary then and it certainly hadn't cropped up in any of the conventional conspiracy theories he had ever read about. At first he thought he must have misheard the name, a theme park housing some type of government base was a crazy idea, but after thinking about it further, it wasn't really that farfetched, in fact it made perfect sense. Who would expect it, a secret facility within a legitimate business visited by over two million people each and every year. From what he had heard back at the Ritz, this person they called the Egregor was going to be there tomorrow, the man that was responsible for destroying his life, a man that had the answers. That was if he was a man, Michael couldn't get the reptilian glimpse out of his mind. Had he imagined it, he had drunk a lot that morning and his head was thumping in the melee, but that split second was so vivid.

The coach shuddered and the engine rumbled into life. Sitting alone on the backseat, a torrent of mixed thoughts surged through his head.

What the hell is going on?... Who are these people?... Why am I not disappearing, going off the grid as the forums called it, instead of turning up on their doorstep?... Will they make me disappear forever? The wave of uncertainty triggered a subconscious flight reaction as his muscles tensed and he sprang up off his seat ready to sprint for the exit. Only subdued by the jolting of the coach as it accelerated away from its bay.

His mind used the pause to reinforce his next steps. *Hiding will not give me the answers I need... I've looked at every alternative, these people are the only ones that can give me a solution that could give me back my old life... The worst case, I exchange one nightmare life for another, or permanently be freed from the torment of living altogether.*

This made his thoughts stray back to the gathering at the Ritz and the words that were used to sum him up, 'He is no more than an alcoholic with an obvious violent tendency.' The lonely journey up the motorway allowed nothing but the time to contemplate.

What really had they expected to see from me?... Have they watched me as closely as they alleged?... If so, then did they not see me slowly lose myself in paranoia as strange involuntary sensations infected my body and objects began to move around me?... Were they observing me when I tried to explain away these weird manifestations as breezes through an open window, passing heavy goods vehicles or even mock me when I employed an exorcist?... Did they feel the disorientating nausea and debilitating headaches that await me around every corner and strong emotion?... Had they played some part in so so many medical examinations I underwent searching for a physical cause that could be treated, then look from afar every time I visited the deer crossing sign hoping for some answer to it all?... Answers are the least I deserve after what they've put me through!

Still all the rationalization and internal talk to justify what he was doing did not drive him onwards to make that step-after-step towards the waiting unknown. The courage and focus to drag himself onto that coach came from a single source inside his wallet. Michael reached for it from his trouser pocket and delicately removed the only picture he had of his Bella. The trimmed wallet sized photo had been taken after the incident. Most people would have a plethora of photos outlining important moments and random instances of daily life readily available on their phones. But Michael no longer owned one and for many and numerous reasons the data of his past had long been erased. So when this most rarest of objects appeared before him he took it. In a desperate act he had broken into the hospital ward to see her, and while the on-duty nurse had run off to fetch security he stole it from the medical file that recorded his daughter's progress.

His head weighed down by the heavy chain of guilt looked upon the image. She was still trying to smile, that same innocent smile that lit up his heart each time it beamed at him. But now her twisted and melted lips would eternally cage in that beauty. No one would ever see his little princess again; never penetrate past the mask of blistered and disfigured skin that covered the majority of her body. He ran his finger over the outline of her bandaged face, flicking through his fading memories of Isabella like a smoldering picture book.

"I'm so sorry." he mouthed to the image as a tear trickled down one cheek.

Before he did this to her, there was already something that distinguished his daughter from the other children her age. It wasn't something physical or easily noticeable but she had been diagnosed with an autistic brain disorder. A rare condition that required much attention, and considerable time and effort from Michael and his wife to make sure that they done all they could to help her develop the social and self-care skills she would need in the future. Although destined to face problems with social interaction and communication as she grew older, Isabella displayed an astounding memory and creative thinking for one so young. Her remarkable brilliance or talent in certain psychological areas provided a stark contrast to her overall limitations, a trait said to be common among those who suffered from the exceedingly rare phenomenon known as Savant Syndrome. Her life would have been a hard-enough road to travel as it was, but he would have been there standing supportively by her side each difficult step of the way. Now he had made it a million times tougher, thrown in her path obstacles of pain, suffering, loneliness and the cruelty of human prejudice. And at this moment in time there was not a single thing he could do about it. This was his reminder if he ever needed one of the wrongs he had to right, to do what was necessary to try and repair the unfixable no matter the sacrifices he would have to make.

Resolve once again strengthened his being, today he was taking the first rung on the ladder to answers and the first question that needed to be answered was; 'What did they do to him?'

The coach pulled up as the Sun was setting over the tree lined horizon. The passengers disembarked to check into their onsite hotels for the evening and Michael followed them onto the gravel car park to avoid looking suspicious. This was about as far as he had planned, all the money he had to his name barely covered the coach ticket and the mandatory bottle of whiskey. Beyond getting here, all he knew was that he had to locate a way into the theme park grounds.

With the distraction of over excited kids and the scramble for their baggage, Michael slipped behind a second empty coach and used the cover of the failing light to sneak his way into the trees and up to the fence that bordered the park. As darkness moved in, he followed the rough wooden barrier until he came upon a small gate that was probably used to bring in equipment. He scaled it easily enough and jumped inside the borders of the park with minimal commotion. Security was non-existent, but then who would want to sneak into a theme park at night when all the rides were off. Michael found himself crouching in the midst of eerie woodland. He trod carefully over the heavily leaved ground barely able to see the tangling vines that threatened to drag him down into the sinister shrubbery. Wandering through the moss laden trunks, the uneven foliage under foot finally got the better of him and he stumbled to his knees, his outstretched arm grabbing a branch wrapped around the cold touch of metal. Michael pulled himself up to face the bizarre scene of a white minivan gripped in the embrace of vengeful crushing roots. He quickly moved on and approached what looked like the ruins of an old manor house reaching out of the encroaching forest; following the odd stonework he felt his way around a corner and reeled; momentarily startled as he found himself confronted with the unmoving stare of a ghostly figure. It took him a few seconds to realise that the hooded bust was merely a wraithlike statue and slightly longer for his body to stop shaking from the jolt of adrenalin. Out in front of him towered a giant structure, a rollercoaster of some type by the look of its silhouette. Under the pale moonlight he could just make out the large wrought iron sign overheard; he was standing in an area known as the dark forest. One of the many themed locations designed to depict a supernatural wood disturbed by the recent excavation of an ancient burial ground.

Taking a sip from the liquor bottle to calm his nerves, he made his way to a diminutive hut named tormented treats that was fashioned to resemble a haunted crypt. The lock on the door was easily broken with one of the many stones lying on the side of the cracking walkway. Finally some good luck, it was a fast food outlet, a welcome change from the tasteless ready meals of the past week. Michael gouged himself on tinned hot dogs and chocolate, knocking back the whiskey until he passed out with the bottle clutched close to his chest to protect it from any wayward spirits that also wished to silence their tormented souls.

*

As the first drops of the Sun crept through the tree tops to wash away the menacing atmosphere of the dark forest, Michael woke with a shout; "Noooo!! Stoopppp!!!"

His body took longer than usual to let go of the nightmare and accept the confines of the cramped cabin as utensils slammed against the walls. Approaching chatter undulated in his head from loud to quiet making it difficult to judge the distance. Michael forced back control of his limbs from the attack of spasms. Gargling some whiskey to wash the morning taste out of his mouth, he quickly chucked the utensils back into their guessed places and ran for the cover of undergrowth towards the rear of the food hut. Looking out from behind the foliage he could see the first of the park's workers coming into sight around the ivy-covered columns. It wouldn't be long until a small army was out in force preparing the area for the flood of fun seeking visitors.

Ok, get it together. What do I do now? Michael thought to himself, as all around him became a hive of activity.

He unraveled the resort map that he had stolen from his makeshift bed and breakfast and scoured the rides, gardens and buildings. One jumped out above all others as a potential base of operations, the parks namesake; the semi-derelict gothic style country mansion. He knew that it had to be the oldest building here and most structures of its type had lower levels. Not only that, back in World War 2 the war office requisitioned Alton Towers as an officer training unit along with all the secrecy that such facilities entailed.

Michael continued to hide in the bushes until the first visitors began to enter the dark forest and enthusiastically queue for the first run of the day on the Th13teen roller coaster. Casually stepping out among the excited throngs, he proceeded to walk head down towards the once splendid stately home situated at the centre of the vast grounds. Once inside he set off searching every part of the renovated building that he could gain access to and after half an hour he had already come up against a number of heavy locked doors and supervised areas. After exhausting all the accessible sections of the structure, he realised just how hopeless this exercise was.

How did I ever expect to find a secret base; or an office or wherever this Egregor was. Yeah, of course I was just going to walk around a huge, busy place like this and stumble on a door with his name on! he cursed his naivety.

He slumped on a crumbling wall, filled up his walnut veneered flask and polished off the remainder of the bottle. The futileness of it all incited the pounding in his head when he heard the crackle of a walkie-talkie.

"Sshhhhh... Code blue.... Sshhhhh... X-Sector .... Black hole site..."

Michael looked curiously up; the radio talk was coming from a maintenance man that was passing by. He couldn't help but stare at him; a feeling in the pit of his abdomen like someone tearing at his stomach with their bare hands was somehow ringing internal alarm bells. The brutal signal was telling him something wasn't quite right with this guy. Trying to remain inconspicuous he followed the man a short distance towards the location of one of Alton towers original rides, the indoor rollercoaster known as the black hole. There was already a lengthy queue for the ride but the maintenance guy bypassed them all and walked straight into the main entrance.

"Excuse me there. I've lost my child and have just been informed that she has been found and is waiting for me inside. Do mind if I quickly skip in here and get her?" asked Michael somewhat nervously.

After a short pause, likely due to the fact that he probably reeked of alcohol, the family standing at the front of the queue let him past. He stepped onto the platform just in time to see the waiting visitors being held back as the man climbed into an empty carriage. As it moved away into the artificial void, another pulled up behind it to take its place.   There was a space left at the back of the waiting carriage which Michael didn't hesitate in jumping into. Sitting down in the one-man car, he made sure not to bring down too tightly the metal bar that was designed to hold him against the uncomfortable seat. With a little jerk the red and black metal frame slowly rolled forward into the gloomy tunnel. Michael wasn't here for the ride and knew that there was only a short period until the rollercoaster would charge down a steep drop. So at the moment he was enveloped by the pitch black he began to squeeze himself out from the under the restraining bar and pulled himself up by the protective side pads. As soon as he was free, he reached into the darkness, feeling his enclosed surroundings for a way off the carriage. The coaster paused, maximising the anticipation before the plunge, he scrambled for something solid. His hand gripped a piece of scaffolding above his head just as the carriage cascaded down the tracks with a chorus of screams. Michael could hear the shrieks of delight trail off into the depths as he was left hanging in the blackness. He'd better do what he was going to do and quick, behind him he could hear the excitement of passengers as they jumped into the next carriage. Michael swung his legs back and forth and found a foothold on some further scaffolding. With a few quick maneuvers he began to scale down the exterior framework as the sound of wheels against tracks rattled over his head. Around him glowing beach ball planets and replica LED stars barely lit his footholds, extravagant decor designed to give the thrill seeker the feeling of actually falling through a black hole in the depths of space.

After a few minutes of descent, he came to another set of tracks, ones that didn't appear to be part of the main ride. Running parallel to the rails was a thin metallic shelf which Michael dropped onto and shuffled along. This ledge shortly opened up into a wider platform then abruptly stopped at a solid black wall. Parked beside him was an empty roller coaster carriage and recessed into one of the walls was a single innocuous wooden door. Screwed into the brown oak was a small brass sign engraved with maintenance cupboard. Michael tentatively opened the door onto a cramped room dimly lit by a single red light. Stepping inside he began to rummage through the contents stacked upon riveted metal shelving. There were a few tools, cans of oil, containers of nuts and bolts, basically your typical store room. Michael swiped at a box of bulbs in anger when the door swung shut behind him. There was a sharp jolt and the sensation of movement. He went for the door but there was no interior handle or any way of opening it. He tried to force it open and hammered on the surface with a heavy wrench but the door returned more resistance than expected from mere wood. There was another shudder and everything seemed to stop. The door lock clicked, Michael slowly pushed it open. Peering out, he found himself starring down the barrel of a gun, there was a muffled pop and everything around began to blur out of focus, then blackness took him.

*

Michael stirred; it felt unusual to wake without the sense of panic and smashing objects. The calm was so unnatural that his immediate thoughts were that of something being seriously wrong. This was the first time in what seemed like an eternity that he had woken and not had that nightmare. His eyes sticky and still feeling groggy, he went to rub his face but his hands wouldn't move. He tried once again with increased effort, but his arms did not respond. This felt different to the bodily paralysis that he often experienced. Michael gave a hard yank and as he did, he could feel the restraints rub tight against his wrists.

Noooo! Michael opened his eyes. He was strapped to a bed dressed in a hospital gown with numerous wires attached to his body. He looked around frantically with terror flowing through him; he was in what resembled some type of lab. It wasn't his nightmare again, things were different, the room was dim but there was no white light or the fleeting glimpses of an unidentified presence. This lab was deserted. The machinery hooked up to him began bleeping furiously. Michael struggled, wildly trying to break free from the restraints. Each violent effort digging the leather deeper into his wrists and ankles, his flayed skin was raw from the friction and blood seeped onto the bed sheets. The door to the lab slid across and a blurred figure appeared in a flood of light from whatever was outside. One of his hands got lodged in the tubular framework of the bed and his heart rate accelerated as a man dressed like a doctor came rushing in.

"What the hell are you doing to me!!!" screamed Michael.

"You shouldn't have woken yet. Please calm down!" requested the Doctor as he hastily pulled out a syringe and selected a small clear vial from a glass cabinet.

"Nooooo!!!!" Michael roared. There was a loud crack as a couple of finger bones snapped in his attempt at escape. The unyielding bonds broke apart and with a swinging blow from his fist, the Doctor dropped the syringe. In one motion Michael leapt from the bed trailing wires and drip feeds, grabbed a scalpel from the bedside tray and aggressively slammed the Doctor against the wall, the glistening steel blade held a hair's breadth away from his jugular.

"Now I will only ask you one more time, what are you doing to me?" he asked with a desperate menace, pushing the razor edge of the blade against his neck, a trickle of blood seeping from its touch.

The Doctor began to sob, "Please don't hurt me.... Please.... I've done nothing to you. I was just going to sedate you so you don't hurt yourself."

"You bastard! Do not lie to me!!" Michael knocked him against the wall once again, his swelling fingers struggling to grasp his shirt. "I found the tracking device in my tooth. You've changed me inside, you made me hurt my daughter! Now tell me before I cut your god damn throat!!"

Speaking of Bella with such vitriol in his actions, rocked him with deja vu. What would she think of him? He remembered a time when his daughter had pushed a girl to the wall and threatened her with a waving pair of plastic scissors for making fun of her.

He had asked her to promise to never do anything naughty like that again.

'I promise daddy. Being bad is dark, a cold night with screaming.' Bella gave an expressive shudder as she explained, 'Being good is bright, a warm yellow light.'

'I want to always stay in the light, and I always want you to stay there too.' she took his hand in concern, 'Promise me you'll stay out of the darkness.'

She had kept her promise where he couldn't.

A voice echoed over the labs communication system breaking his flashback, "Michael this is not a course of action you wish to take. Please put the surgical instrument down."

There was something familiar about that voice.

"You've pushed me to this point. I have no other choice. If you don't give me answers right now, I will kill him. Do you understand!!" he shouted into the air at the unseen antagonist.

"I do not believe taking a life is in you. I will give you the answers you seek but first you must release the doctor. As he has stated, he has done nothing to you."

Although still disorientated, with those words he now realised why he knew that harmonious tone.

"You!! Your voice plagues my nightmares; I hear it every time I close my eyes. Who the hell are you?"

"I am the Egregor." the pitch of his voice had never changed once.

"The Egregor. Operation Darwin, you are responsible for everything!" The primal urges for revenge ran strong but Michael felt compelled to listen to the voice. This is what he had come here to do, to get answers. He knew he could not murder someone. What if he did manage to escape, he would be back to square one and these people would always be there hunting him wherever he went. He threw the shaking Doctor to the floor and watched him scurry out of the door that he had entered through. He looked at the scalpel in his hand and let it slide slowly from his grip to clatter against the tiles soaked by the leaking bag of saline solution.

"Michael, it is time we talked." Behind him a mirrored wall creaked and the stone grinded in its tracks as it began to slowly slide across.

10 - MUFON

Countdown: Minus 2 ¼ hours before multiple nuclear strikes

The smell of chamomile wafted into the small conference facility as a mustached man with a wandering eye took his place among the two dozen or so people already seated. Dr. Heaney sipped from his freshly made infusion as he surveyed the people entering the room. After the meeting at the Ritz hotel he had decided to travel to northern Kentucky for this year's MUFON international Symposium, a place where he could determine how well the goals of COM-12 had been met and follow up on an interesting lead that had recently come to his attention. The Mutual UFO Network was an American non-profit organisation created for the systematic collection and analysis of UFO data with the ultimate goal of learning the origin and nature of the UFO phenomenon.

If COM-12 had been effective in their objectives then the topics, new data and incidents discussed here at the symposium would not be attributed to the work they were involved in. He had spent most of the day following the mainstream MUFON schedule of guest speakers, listening to the accounts of their own personal experiences, the debates over new evidence and the continuing defence and national security questions raised over their existence.

As usually was the situation, once all new data and cases had been reviewed there was little information that related back to COM-12; a positive outcome meaning that their important work still continued to remain covert. The negative and the more worrying consequence of these findings was the question over where this plethora of new data and incidents originated each and every year. So many encounters of the third kind, sightings and strange accounts could not all be explained away by mistaken identity, wild imaginations or pure falsehoods. This was something COM-12 needed to take seriously and investigate. That was why he had chosen to attend this side speaker who was due to discuss the connection between the US government and the UFO phenomenon, and more interestingly for Dr. Heaney, the possible implantation of foreign devices into the brains of the population. For him, if these cases were not real then this seemed like one way of introducing these experiences into people.

The speaker coughed loudly to get his audiences' attention. A blurry image of a one-dollar bill filled the screen. As the gathering people quietened and made themselves comfortable, the speaker adjusted the projector and the intricate green print came into focus.

"Hi everyone and thank you all for attending. Today I would like to discuss matters that for me are more than just mere information for you to be aware of. What I tell you today, I believe is an extremely important warning, one I hope you will think about, digest and ultimately act upon. This is something that affects us all, our security, our freedom, not just that as individuals but possibly that of the whole human race.

Most of us are here today to discuss the evidence of the UFO phenomenon, of the existence of extra-terrestrials, debate the merits of that evidence and what it truly means for us. That is a topic for the others outside this room. I am not here to prove or convince anyone of the existence of little green men on Mars; my aim is to show you that the UFO phenomenon is in fact the doing of our own government or at the very least, plays a significant part in it."

The speaker paused to wet his throat with a glass of lemon flavoured water. Among his listeners there was no mumbling of disbelief or discontent. The majority of people had come to the

MUFON symposium and this room because they were believers, conspiracy theorists or those looking for answers that conventional explanations could not give. And Dr. Heaney was one of the latter.

"Ok, let us ask why the government is responsible for the UFO phenomenon and the facets that are widely associated with it. Imagine for yourselves that if you wished to carry out heinous acts against your own people, things that break every human rights law, goes against what every man, women and child on this planet sees as wrong but wanted to avoid any accountability for it. What better way than to blame it on aliens! What I mean by this is you suggest a culprit that answers to no human law or policed by any force on Earth, a guilty party that cannot be proven or disproved, one treated in such a jovial light that it is accepted as a matter for a psychologist to cure rather than a soldier to fight back in your defence. I believe as do many of my like-minded peers that this is a scheme initiated by our own government, specifically those in it who wield the power and make the decisions, those that we know as the Illuminati."

Again the speaker paused to allow his audience to absorb what he had just said. Dr. Heaney took the moment to view the response of the people surrounding him. There were some that nodded in agreement; others muttered its conceivability, a handful that seemed disappointed there was not more focus on extra-terrestrial life being involved. It was as much as he had expected to see, apart from two figures sitting towards the back of the room that he hadn't noticed earlier. The man and women dressed in plain black suits bared no interest in what the speaker had said but instead were intently scanning the reactions of the audience members. He turned his gaze away as not to draw their attention and slowly drank from his waxed paper cup in contemplation. There was a tap of wood from the podium out in front and a hush slowly filled the room.

"So what reason would our government have for doing such a thing?? The simple answer is control, money and ultimately power! There are signs and evidence everywhere, and they are not shy of rubbing their existence and omnipotence in our faces; in their arrogance they know we are looked upon as crazy conspiracy theorists unable to stand up against their hidden rule. Yes, individually we are mere nuisances that they can discredit and extinguish at any time, but as a united people we can force out the truth, shout loud enough as to make the world question what is right before their eyes. That is why I am here today. I don't expect you to blindly take my words as gospel, but I hope to open your eyes with material evidence to what is really happening out there. Let me begin with the tangible symbol of what has brought these Illuminati to their apex of power; that is money, specifically the one-dollar bill. Take a closer look at it on the screen, also if you have one in your pocket then feel free to take it out and inspect it yourself."

Dr. Heaney looked around the audience with the noise of many people reaching for their wallets and handbags, slipping out the notes. Most of the people in the room smiled or turned the money in their hands with curiosity, except for the couple seated towards the back whose expression remained impassive and serious. The woman dressed in a practical suit and white shirt buttoned to the top was more interested in the content of her mobile phone than participating with the suggestions of the speaker.

The speaker picked up his pointing stick and poked it towards the projector screen. "Now look here, what do we have? The great seal inset with a thirteen tiered pyramid, an emblem of their ancient past and representation of the Thirteen ruling families of their hierarchical system. In fact, the number thirteen is prevalent in many places on this bill. Count the stars on the right-hand side. Thirteen illuminated stars for the thirteen colonies, the thirteen original ruling family lines. On the bird's breast there is a heraldic shield covered with thirteen stripes resembling those of the thirteen original states on the first American flag, those original states being the territories of the Thirteen ruling families who founded the United States. Grasped in talons of the bird, thirteen leaves and olives and thirteen arrows, for me symbolising that they will achieve what they believe as peace, the olive branch, through means of war, the arrows. Finally, the string of thirteen pearls leading off either side of the edge of the bill. The white pearl the symbol of unblemished perfection, of purity, the untainted blood line of the ruling families running all the way back to the beginning and then all the way into the future. A fascist and unmistakable belief that they are better than all others and how this must always remain the case! Again, let's look at the motto under the stars, 'E Pluribus Unum', thirteen letters and Latin for 'Out of many, one', out of all the nations there will be one, controlled by the mouth, the head of the bird. That one nation on Earth will have rule over all others and be led by none other than the Illuminati. No wonder they say thirteen is bad luck, an unlucky number. In many countries, cultures and religions there is a stigma against the number with no agreed upon theory as to this association. Let me put to you my belief that the original Thirteen ruling families have brought pain and destruction upon the world throughout all history and against all peoples that has burned the notion of this number with evil so deeply that it has persisted throughout the ages. The saying goes 'Thirteen, unlucky for some, not for others.' I say unlucky for all that aren't one of the Thirteen ruling families."

It was plain to see among the listeners, that the speaker was fueling the fire of those with minds already full of conspiracies with his own interpretation of the symbolism present on the dollar bill. Those who were more sceptic seemed to be slowly accepting the possibilities as he produced his evidence that was beginning to seem too numerous for mere coincidence. Overall everyone appeared to be very interested in hearing more including Dr. Heaney.

Taking his pointing stick once more he moved it up to highlight the great seal and one of the letters in the lower banner. "Right, let us continue. The great seal and its deeper messages. It is embedded with an anagram, and if we draw a six-pointed star, the Star of David, or Solomon's seal, its points touch various letters in the mottoes."

He pointed out the lines of the star and the letters they traced. "It spells Mason, for many just another name for the Illuminati. And before you say this star pattern is a coincidence, then take a look how the thirteen stars are arranged on the other side of the bill, yes, in the formation of the Solomon's Seal also. Now I want you to put your attention to the top of the pyramid, we have the All-Seeing Eye, the eye of providence; it represents divine providence watching over humankind and symbology of the

Illuminati at its most blatant. This more than anything shows you the view of superiority they have of themselves over us all. I said before, I am not here to prove or disprove the involvement of aliens but look closely at the eye, the skin surrounding it, would you say that is human like? The detail is quite clear; it is scaly in nature. And being at the pinnacle of the pyramid where the eye of God should be, what does this tell us about who is really in control? Is this the true face of the Illuminati?"

Dr. Heaney then pulled out one of his own dollar bills, spilling some of his chamomile over his jacket. He removed his handkerchief from the front of his pocket and it was then that he thought he caught the gaze of one of the suspicious characters looking at him. She quickly turned her head and went back to whatever was holding most of her attention on her mobile phone. He sipped his drink and inspected the bill more closely. He could see how the skin around the eye could be interpreted in such a way but wasn't wholly convinced it wasn't just a characteristic of how it was sketched for the printing press.

"So what do they want? What is their goal for the world? Well, funnily enough they have no qualms about advertising this to everyone on the one-dollar bill. Let me elaborate on this. In one phrase everything is summarised; 'Novus Ordo Seclorum', for those of you that don't speak Latin, it translates to 'Secular World Order'. Yes we are talking about a New World Order. A new order for us all fashioned and ruled by the Illuminati. And moving to the base of the pyramid MDCCLXXVI or seventeen seventy-six, the date the Illuminati were formed or possibly the date this New World Order was conceived, coinciding with the signing of the Declaration of Independence. Look above that, the further Latin words, 'Annuit Coeptis', 'He approves of the undertaking', who approves? The person whose eye that is? This also can be interpreted as 'announcing conception'. So, are they really announcing to us the conception and their approval of a New World Order?.. I strongly believe so! Finally, that bird of prey on the seal; clearly a bald eagle, an avian unique to North America, supporting on its breast the shield of the American flag. It seems the founders of the United States were fond of the prominent eagle imagery of the Roman Republic. For what reason, I am not sure, maybe its ideals and goals bore comparison to their own, or maybe there lies a deeper historical link. A link possibly shared in the eagle adoption of the German Confederation and Nazi Germany. Like the Aquila, the standard of the Roman legion, and the national insignia of the Third Reich, it has its wings outstretched, displayed in a heraldic manner. Outside of here take the time to count the differing number of feathers on the left, right wing and tail, then lookup the degrees of rites within the Freemason's society. I will let you make your own connections with that. But the main point I want to show with this, is that the great seal was not originally sporting a bald eagle. Please look at these images."

On the projector screen three images appeared of the great seal. One was a black and white engraving, another a photo of a printing press die. While the last was a large framed oil painting. "Here we have three examples of what the original great seal looked like. An engraving by one of the original designers, James Trenchard, a photo of the first original seventeen eighty-two die of the great seal, used until eighteen forty-one and today displayed in the national archives in Washington D.C; and lastly a colour painting by an unknown artist in the St. Paul's Chapel, New York City. Now tell me, is that bird a bald eagle? Obviously not, there is little similarity to the national bird of the United States of America; it clearly resembles one well known mythical bird of fire!... So, is that eagle a herald in flight? For me that is a phoenix of a New World Order rising out of the ashes of an ignorant world."

He took a dollar bill from his own wallet and a lighter from his shirt pocket and began to set it alight. Well I for one will not let a New World Order rise from these ashes. A few people in the crowd copied his act of defiance and began to ignite their own dollar bills to sporadic clapping from the audience.

The two suited in black had barely changed expression, but upon this show of defiance they looked wholly unimpressed.

"So you are probably wondering; this is just imagery on a piece of paper, what does it have to do with the UFO phenomenon? Well we know throughout history how difficult it is to rule humankind, our urge and choice of freedom always pushes us to reject Draconian authority, a level of control required for any New

World Order. How do you stop the voice of people like me, people like you? How do you muzzle the will power of one's mind? You must first gain control of that mind. This leads me to the topic in which I have a personal association to, the cranial implantation of devices among the US population."

This subject was what most interested Dr. Heaney and seemingly the same could be said for the two odd characters at the back of the room. This was judging by the fact that the women immediately put away her mobile device and the man's demeanor drastically changed as the speaker spoke his last words. On the screen the depictions of the great seal flicked away to show several slides of alleged implants supposedly discovered in the brains of US citizens. On the last image there was a tiny bloodied object beside a surgical ruler. It was a circular metallic ball laid out upon some hospital gauze. Dr. Heaney had used implants as tracking devices before but they were simple micro-chips similar to that used in a lot of hi-tech military grade gadgetry and certainly not inserted into the brain of a subject.

"This inauspicious little thing is a souvenir of my own abduction. I barely remember it, but one day I found myself wandering the streets of Manhattan with no memory of the last couple of days. Following this I tried to continue my life but then I began to suffer from regular and severe nose bleeds. During a subsequent CT scan to determine the cause, this mysterious article showed up lodged in my brain. The medical specialists were luckily able to remove it through my right nostril with a not too invasive surgical procedure. Unable to explain what the object was, these so-called experts of medicine and science dismissed it as an unknown foreign body that could have found its way there unnoticed in many different ways, and that they had seen much more bizarre things turning up in the human body. The most important thing and the only matter I agreed with them upon, was that the object was removed without any physical harm to me. But that just wasn't good enough, I wanted, I needed answers."

He was not the only one looking for explanations to that riddle, Dr. Heaney wanted them also. He wondered what it was about how we were wired that made us crave meaning, and answers for everything that we do not know or understand. Where would the human race be without that ingrained drive for knowledge? He wouldn't be sitting here right now; the speaker wouldn't be standing before him and Michael would still be drinking himself to death in some flea ridden room. Dr. Heaney had always had trouble maintaining focus, not just with his wandering eye but also with a wandering mind. His thought patterns would compete, racing off in various strands becoming a tangled web of disorganisation. It was a type of attention-deficit hyperactivity disorder, but chamomile always calmed his nerves and soothed the impulsiveness of his mind. Drinking the last of his lukewarm herbal tea he returned his concentration to the matter at hand.

"There has been research and evidence for this going all the way back to the nineteen sixties. It was not until the nineteen eighties that I got involved after I discovered my own. By then many implants had been removed and studied from various locations on the body, but my interest was in the implants of the brain due to my initial personal circumstances. I managed to persuade the physicians to let me keep the implant they found in me and since then I have over time collected similar objects found in people who have had comparable experiences, or had them drop from their nostrils in intense nose bleeds. Many of these shared a traumatic abduction experience, some involving extra-terrestrials and some like myself without the memories of alien participation. What was strange about the medical results was that if the object was truly an innocent foreign object, it didn't create any internal infections that you would expect from a foreign object in the body. So using my own funding, I was able to get mine, and a few other devices analysed. The objects were covered by a hard, dense, dark grey membrane wrapping itself around it like some type of cocoon. The thin membranes were composed of proteinaceous coagulum, hemosiderin and keratin, all typically found in the surface of your skin, hair or nails, seemingly making the device avoid every possible rejection crisis. I say device but none of the objects had any discernable electronics inside, although they did have some magnetic properties and glowed with a yellow green colour under certain fluorescence lighting. Now this is the interesting part, there seems to be some connection between the implants and the pineal gland in the brain. The small endocrine gland is located near the centre of the brain, in a little cave behind and above the pituitary gland, which lies behind the root of the nose and governs the circadian cycle through the optical nerve. I suspect that most of you do not have a medical doctorate like myself, so let me explain. It is located directly behind the eyes and activated by light. Initially travelling from the retina, the nerve impulses journey via the pineal nerve to the pineal gland. The pineal gland is therefore a photosensitive organ and an important aspect in the body's timekeeping. As well as that, it appears to play a major role in sexual development, sleep patterns, metabolism, hibernation and seasonal breeding in animals such as cattle. From such a nerve, serotonin sends the pineal gland information to produce melatonin, thus regulating the circadian rhythm which is a roughly a twenty-four hour cycle of biochemical, physiological and behavioral processes in living entities. Where am I going with all this you may ask? Well I mentioned the device has some magnetic properties and an electromagnetic field can change the production of melatonin. This surplus can produce some surprising effects in the human body; such as analgesic effects, hallucination and light spots in vision, shorter pregnancies or pronounced healing. So in conclusion, these devices could be used for some kind of mental or behavioral conditioning, altering serotonin levels to cause confused perceptions, most likely enacted during an abduction incident. It is not surprising to me that a lot of these abductees would involve little grey aliens with monstrous black eyes. Although I believe that these are evidence enough, it appears that I am part of a tiny minority that agrees. The mainstream scientists give it very little attention because the lack of verifiable evidence. I have even offered myself and the implants in my possession for scientific research, but strangely no academic authority seems to be interested in the truth."

He continued to explain how he believed the government would use this cranial persuasion and control to make the desired population more malleable to their will. What his theories were on how they could be monitoring devices gathering experimental data or possibly for planting information into the subject. On how this might be done by individual or group activation through some type of long-range radio transmissions by a super powerful transmitter apparatus within North America.

The scientific facts about the claimed implants were what Dr. Heaney wanted to know, the rest of the speaker's opinions were of less importance to him, however he decided to attend until its conclusion. If what he had presented was true then it could explain a great many things that had continually concerned him, and as a consequence this required more thorough research and resources, something that COM-12 could provide in abundance. This would take a carefully worded proposition to the speaker when the opportunity presented itself, and that chance came as the speaker wrapped up his ending speech of spreading the word, following their intuition and too question everything. Then on a final note inviting anyone with queries or information that might help him in his investigations.

As the energised and thoughtful audience began to leave the conference room, some passed on their gratitude, others second-hand leads to further information and contacts, the rest left with a head full of radical notions to digest that spat in the face of the conventional perception of the world around them. Dr. Heaney remained in his seat to wait for his turn in a more discrete setting, an idea shared by the curious couple in the plain black suits. The last of the attendees passed out into the main hall of the northern Kentucky convention centre to mingle with the vendors and discuss with the mass of like-minded contemporaries, the topics that they could not do in your usual day-to-day gatherings. Placing his waxed paper cup under his seat, he straightened his tweed jacket and approached the speaker as he carefully packed up his slides in a slender wooden box.

"Excuse me there. May I extend my congratulations on a very thought-provoking discussion." Dr. Heaney offered his hand in greeting.

"Thank you." The speaker shook the doctor's hand with a somewhat suspicious gaze. "How can I help you?"

"On the contrary I would like to offer you my assistance. I work for an organisation that I believe would find your research intriguing, and could provide the advance resources required to investigate and ascertain the possible workings of these implants. We would of course recompense you for the loan of the relevant objects for the duration of the studies. You would also have complete access to the collated data to do with as you see fit."

"Sure, and my evidence would quickly disappear in a mysterious fire at your facility or in some unforeseeable accident." The speaker was clearly distrustful of any organisation interested in his work and maybe there was good reason for this.

"Ok, to ease your apprehension, I could promise you and a small team of observers admittance to our facilities to oversee the testing, and the authoring of full legal documentation to maintain transparency of our collaboration." This would increase the cost of this endeavor tenfold now. COM-12 would have to mock up a new facility and transport the necessary hi-tech equipment to the site as they could not clearly allow access to any non-security cleared civilians into the current COM-12 facilities. But the extra expenditure was worth the answers they could yield if the speakers so called evidence was genuine.

"Then in that case I will definitely consider your offer but first I need to know who you work for. The government? A privately funded company?"

"Privately funded." Dr. Heaney was expecting this line of enquiry as he clearly had a mistrusting nature. So as they spoke his mind wandered off racing along tangents providing various answers and counter questions until it found one with less chance of providing a dead end.

"And your interest in this?"

"Entertainment, more specifically gaming. Video games are a multi-billion dollar business and the competition is cut-throat when it comes to producing the next level of customer experience. Currently the push is for three-D and augmented reality, but my company want to think beyond the next generation and force the boundaries further, make the experience more immersive not just in the sensory manner, but emotionally too. To be successful in the entertainment world you have to think outside the circle, when everyone else is thinking outside the box."

"It might not come as a surprise, but I would be against such emotional manipulation. I see it as a fast road down to subliminal advertising and targeted merchandise addiction. This is to a degree toying with the free will of the population, but still a long way off what the government is planning on doing. Perhaps its imagined use in the world of video games would raise the awareness of the technical possibilities in the media. Maybe others would then take my work seriously." The speaker paused, "Do you have a contact number or a card? I will get in touch with my decision."

Dr. Heaney flicked through his pouch of numerous contact cards and handed him one printed with the company logo for Merlin entertainment watermarked behind a single mobile number and email address. He knew telling the speaker the truth was obviously impossible, a story of pure scientific intrigue would have sent warning signs in a suspicious mind; in this day and age when something is too good to be true then it usually wasn't. The best way was to offer a motive of monetary gain and a lesser evil when compared to an intention of mass domination of free will.

"Thank you, I look forward to it." He turned to leave and spotted the two suspect characters surveying him. As he sent them a glance, they both turned their attention to the speaker and motioned from their seating. Perhaps now that he had finished, they had an equivalent offer to present to the speaker. But as he entered the now deserted corridor leading to the main reception area, he looked back for one last inquisitive peek to see them instead follow in his footsteps and heading towards the door. Dr. Heaney's own paranoia started directing his thoughts this time and he slipped through a close by fire exit. He could have joined the many others enjoying their breaks between the next lecture or forum, but who was to say they weren't working with others in the symposium. Taking two flights of stairs he exited the building into a small alley way at the back of the conference centre. There was no hint of anyone following him and confident he had lost his potential pursuers, he bent over and tried to get his breath back.

"Getting as paranoid as that speaker in your old age." he muttered to himself just when another side door further down the alley opened, and the man in the black suit stepped out. Dr. Heaney twisted around to walk in the opposite direction but stood there blocking his passage was his female partner. Now sporting dark black glasses, they both slowly approached him.

"I think all of us needing the fresh air of this fine smelling alleyway would be too much of a coincidence. Why are you following me?"

"We will be the ones asking the questions." stated the woman with a quirky smile.

Dr. Heaney ignored her. "Why would you be interested in the speaker yet pay such little attention to what he actually had to say?"

The woman gave a fake chuckle, "That is my line of questioning for you. Why were you so interested in his work? We saw you have a nice little chat with him at the end."

"You spent a fair amount of time engrossed with your phone. Perhaps playing a short game of Angry Birds or Tetris? I am in the video game industry. A device that could illicit emotional responses could be valuable for new gaming experiences. Imagine integrating a pleasurable stimulation upon the completion of a level or destroying a bad guy."

"Enough of this bullshit. Imagine a shock of pain each time you answer a question incorrectly." threatened the man as he pulled out a miniaturised cattle prod. "My colleague ran you through our systems. We know you have attended MUFON a number of times now, but there seems to be no other information in our intelligence records and that pisses me off. Now who do you work for?"

"Surely the lack of government records ought to tell you that you shouldn't be bothering me. I'm not prepared to give you any further information." countered Dr. Heaney.

"Is that supposed to worry me?" The man raised his charged weapon. "You come to MUFON offering assistance to a nuisance already nullified. Which means I can be sure of one thing; you are not one of us. Now again who do you work for?"

"What concerns you? That he is right about the government?" reproached Dr. Heaney.

"We set up MUFON so that we could bring together all the trouble makers and traitors spouting their conspiracies and propaganda. Here we can keep tabs on them and deal with them as and when we need too. But what bugs me more than them, are the ones who sit there silently listening to the filth leaving their mouths, seeking to undo our work with their hidden agendas. Now we can't have that."

As he raised the pronged tip of the weapon to his face, a beeping and buzzing emanated from the women.

She took her mobile device from the inside of her suit jacket. "This is going to take a bit longer than we have. It's happening. We need to go."

Dr. Heaney turned to her. "What's hap..."

There was a loud crackle and Dr. Heaney dropped limply to the floor from the intense electrical shock to the back of his neck.

"Then it looks like he'll have to come with us."

11 - The Hidden Power

The rubber tyres of a Learjet 36A smoked as they touched down on the runway tarmac after its journey from the Middle East. Taxiing to a nearby hanger the plane slowed to a halt and released its cabin steps. The Pindar disembarked his private jet with a twisted grin across his face. He was to return to his Bavarian state mansion in Germany to convey some important information to his brethren. Waiting at the bottom of the steps was his personal stretched limousine with its tinted bullet proof windows and all the amenities anyone could wish for. From within a pair of knee-high stiletto boots swung elegantly out.

"Welcome back Pindar." She spoke in a seductive tone that would put most men into a trance. An attribute that would have been surpassed by flawless beauty if it were not for a leather patch covering her left eye.

"Thank you, Frau Wulf." The red-haired woman was dressed in a snug fitting suit, black leather boots and swathed in a polar bear skin with its taxidermy head draped across her shoulders like a trophy. She was his second in command and born into his family somewhat enigmatically. The Pindar remembered well the uproar over her birth. Frau Wulf's mother was an estranged cousin of his, and her father still to this day remained a mystery. That was the problem. It was a rule among his kin and ancestors that no child could be born or marriage sanctioned outside that of the noble families. This was to ensure that their bloodline remained pure back to their most important of roots. Knowing this his cousin carried the child in secret, but nothing could stay hidden from them for long. Finally, they caught up with her during the labour. Although she died during child birth, she did confess to the father not being one of the noble families, a suspicion confirmed when the baby's body showed no sign of the skin affliction that affected all members of their bloodline to some degree. By law the child would have been terminated, but what was concealed behind that eye patch saved her that day. "What brings you back here?"

"I have some delightful updates for you regarding our test work in Alaska." Frau Wulf spoke with an upper-class English tone but still carried the hint of a German accent that originated from her childhood.

"Reports can be given over video link."

"And there is only so much snow one person can take."

"But is it not baby seal clubbing season?" he commented with complete sincerity.

"The delectable fun obtained by smashing in the skulls of their cute chubby faces loses its appeal somewhat once you watch the life wisp away from those puppy dog eyes for the hundredth time! Besides sealing season is closing early due to population decline and I anticipate you will personally be enchanted with the news I bare." she gave him a wicked smile as she disappeared back into the stretched car.

"Is that so? Then I look forward to hearing it." replied the Pindar joining her inside. He had chosen Frau Wulf to oversee the Alaskan project for the same reason he had made her his lieutenant. She was deeply loyal and no matter the consequences would without fail get the job done. Whatever it took, to a point where the others believed she harboured something truly evil inside. Therefore, she was perfect to manage the delicate situation in Alaska, considering its moral repercussions and the detrimental implications to the people of the world.

"As you are quite aware our testing has proven frightfully successful in arousing randomised effects. We have all witnessed the wonderful widespread results that we were looking for with bated breath. The evidence of their overall effect is agreed by all to be quite irrefutable, no? Yet to my dismay the ability to target a location specifically has remained dastardly out of reach." she let out a breathless sigh of disappointment. "Well new data suggests this may no longer be the case." She handed the Pindar some satellite imagery from over the Asian continent. "You see the delicious patterns across these areas."

"Most interesting indeed. Then the question is how has this benefited me?"

"The rice crop yields in these areas have been, well the devastation is just blissful. Hence leaving a certain someone's companies as the front runners in rice production, and of course there remains a huge demand for the cheap staple diet of the world."

"Well not so cheap now. This is our chance to tighten our grip on many countries, especially in the current economic crisis we have engineered. Sometimes a simple grain can be just as valuable a currency." The Pindar spoke with a nefarious smile. "Not to mention how much richer this will make us."

"Has made us! The shares have doubled and I have already authorised a significant increase in export charges from South America, India and China on your behalf. The new figures are truly a delight."

"Then this is most welcome news. So, Frau Wulf when can we expect its other functions to be operational? I am sure that MAJI would be pleased with its swift completion."

"The scientists seem to think it may be some time before any remote capabilities are accomplished. Of course, I have told the buggers that they think wrong. It will be ready when we need it. I can be quite persuasive! The little darlings are rather scared that they might find themselves hanging around my neck like this scrumptious fur." She gave the freshly skinned polar bear hide an amorous stroke.

"And where possibly would they get such an idea."

She let out an evil cackle, "Quite! Someone's been digging into my past indiscretions I suspect. It was only a bit of fun, all work and no play leaves a lady a little frustrated." Frau Wulf's past was an enigma to most of those who had the misfortune of crossing paths with her. Few knew her name but those who had heard of her reputation or had experienced first-hand her sadistic disposition during her early days in Germany called her Frau Wulf, or in English Ms. Wolf. She herself happily adopted the title finding it quite delightful. She turned to the Pindar with a devilish eye, "Anyway a modicum of healthy fear never did anyone any harm! They'll literally kill themselves to get it completed."

"Of that I have no doubt. Now, since you have travelled so far with such pleasant news, I think it is only right that I show my hospitality and lay on a little hunt for you. The grounds have quite the selection of big game." The Pindar and Frau Wulf chuckled together as they travelled towards the Bavarian countryside with the snow-capped Alps climbing out of the distance.

*

The log fire in his lavish study was blazing; he sat down in his antique leather chair and lit up a 1937 La Corona. The Pindar picked up the only piece of modern equipment in the whole room, a remote control, and pointed it at a large oil painting above the fire place. It was no ordinary piece of art but the original 15th century 'Gardens of Earthly delight' by Hieronymus Bosch, not the copy that was given to the Prado Museum in Madrid. As the impasto images of Heaven, Earth and Hell slid away from the wall, a collection of maple framed TV's were revealed. A total of thirteen stacked in a pyramidal type arrangement. From the top down, one by one they flickered on in turn. On each of the screens were displayed between one and five figures, both male and female, all in their own luxurious backgrounds and attired in fine garments bearing the symbol of a triangle pinnacled by a golden eye with beams of light emanating outwards. Most oddly of all, many exhibited the same pallid and desiccated face as the Pindar.

"Welcome my brothers and sisters."

Everyone raised their right hand and using their little and fore finger gave a short two fingered salute.

"As head of the Thirteen ruling families it is my duty to notify you, the family representatives, that our plan is preceding perfectly, the group of Nations that we have worked so hard to manipulate and demonise to the world have agreed to stand together in the face of the UN threat."

There were smiles of satisfaction coming from each monitor.

"I have communed with the Masters; our New World Order is approaching. Now all that is left is to use our power and influence to nudge the other side into taking the course of action that we desire. Can I trust that this will not be a problem?"

A chubby bearded gentleman from a TV situated on the second row down spoke up in a deep southern American voice.

"There was some discontent with our mass surveillance motions at the Bilderberg gathering. I expect our main adversary capable of blocking these in the International Court of Justice, will have a sudden change of heart with the recent turn of events."

"Yes quite." agreed the Pindar, "Any other consequences of note we should expect from the fallout of our preliminary collateral targets?"

From the bottom row another man spoke up in a South African accent, "Qingdao mineral mining operations price took a nosedive for some unforeseen reason." The grey-haired balding man gave an arrogant smile as he relayed the news, "Given the current circumstances, I am sure our reduced takeover offer will now look too good to be true. The same could be said with our real estate interest on the coastline. While rich in sea resources, who would want to invest in ruined lands and poisoned water now?"

"So, I can report to the Masters that the timeline will remain on schedule?" asked the Pindar as he watched affirming nods from each TV.

"This will not present any problem. This is what we have always done; for over a millennium the Thirteen families have manipulated the world. Our voice falls on important ears and our persuasion strong. We laid the foundations of its conception; the UN will do as we command." An elderly, white-haired, American woman from a screen on the second row gave the final confirmation.

The Pindar picked up the remote control, gave the family salute and switched off the pyramidal display.

She is right, many times have we used our vast wealth and connections to play two sides against each other for our own agenda.

The imagery surrounding him was proof of that, this very room epitomised the power running through his bloodline. He gazed around his study absorbing the supremacy that could be traced back through the eminent eras of the past, each one herding humanity towards their end goal now within his touching distance.

12 - First Contact

Countdown: Minus 2 hours before multiple nuclear strikes

Anger still coursed through his veins as Michael peeled off the wires taped to various recording points across his torso. The sliding wall had gradually revealed numerous pieces of computer hardware, a plethora of monitors and video displays showing the bed he had just escaped from. He extracted the drip needle in his arm which had dug awkwardly into his muscle during the scuffle with the doctor. His broken fingers had begun to throb uncomfortably but the breaks seemed to be clean and his digits straight enough.

The moving partition eventually disappeared into the side wall and he found himself standing before a concealed room that housed a broad monitoring station of some type.

"Please enter." the hidden voice came from a high-backed chair at the centre of the curving station.

Now he stood there in that strange situation, an unknown place where all barriers had fallen between him and this Egregor. It was as if he had finally unlocked the door that had imprisoned him for an eternity. All his suffering, the pain and constant torment, so long without reason or hope. The emotional fallout of it erupted inside of him in explosions of fury and burning hatred but confusedly tempered by the deluge of curiosity and fear.

As his surroundings began to shake with the intensity of his emotions, Michael strode purposely towards the chair facing the control desk. "Now tell me what the hell is going on!!" he yelled as he yanked the seat around.

Immediately he stumbled back from the invisible blow of shock.

"Please control your anger and things shall be made clearer."

Michael was speechless, his mind overloaded with a hundred different thoughts and contradicting bodily commands.

"How are you feeling? We have repaired your orthodontic damage and removed the poison from your body; you will have no dependency on it now."

Michael felt the inside of his jaw with his tongue, the unpleasant gaping hole seemed to have healed. The Egregor was right, he also no longer had the craving for alcohol and the shakes that came along without it, but all thoughts of himself had left his mind.

"What are you?" Michael finally let out, the only words he could manage. The person sitting before him was either severely deformed or not human at all. He was staring at a bulbous grey head with oversized and almond shaped black eyes.

"I am Egregor Krill." was the reply from the short slit of a mouth. "But I suspect you are referring to my appearance."

Michael did not answer. His heart was pounding and his legs had lost all of their sturdiness.

"I am Egregor of the Ashtar Co-operative, an extra-terrestrial race from a system a vast distance from Earth and ..."

"An alien!" he stuttered. Michael had read the rantings of many conspiracy theorists; the personal accounts of abduction and catalogue of so-called alien images but nothing had prepared him for the reality.

"Yes if you will, I am alien to this world but believe it or not I am here to help you."

"Ok, this is really happening... Get answers... Bella." His mind was still in shock at what was before him but the rage inside quickly dislodged the disorientation of the situation. "Then tell me! Why have you done this to me?"

"This was not done to you by anyone. I have been told you have developed certain abilities and of course you search for an explanation for these. I can tell you they originated within yourself. They have always been a part of you. Finding you was pure luck, a chance meeting that may turn out to be one of great importance."

"Then what happened to me that night? It's haunted me ever since. You don't know what it has done to me, my life... my daughter!" Although he was finally getting some of the answers he had longed for, Michael was fighting to contain the resentment and the need to unleash his blame.

"Throughout many of your Earth years, in accordance with the Grenada treaty, we have been taking humans from across the world. Acquiring them so that we may run our necessary tests."

"Against their will!!" Michael's voice rose up another level but the diminutive figure showed no sign of intimidation.

"We had no other choice. What would you have us do? Ask them to assist out of their own free will and allow us to perform the required examination. Imagine the world's reaction to what we were doing, imagine their reaction to us. Our need and yours was too great. It had to remain secret, it was the only way." As Egregor Krill talked, his blank eyes, flat diamond shaped nose and gaunt cheeks showed no emotional cues; in fact, his whole body never once portrayed any hint of expression.

"But at what expense? Destroying my life, maybe others also, leaving them psychologically damaged and mentally scarred!"

"Yes, a moral dilemma. Most know nothing of their ordeal. It is only the rare few, those strong of mind, that have been known to recall varying degrees of the procedure."

"The rare few! You can read about thousands of these cases in books and on the internet. Your image is everywhere, not just on conspiracy and science fiction websites. I can get you on a god damn key ring!!"

"Yes, this concerns us greatly considering the predominant number of these cases are unrelated to us. We have been given the title of 'The Greys' in common literature, and it remains a puzzle as to how we have been shed in such tainted light, but what is important is that the majority of the population do not believe in us. We have worked hard to keep our operation a secret; however, this will not matter soon."

"Why have you abducted me and the others?" Michael's initial responses had been reactionary with emotion, but now he forced his logical mind to takeover and proceed like this was a routine archeological puzzle.

"The crucial question, why? Long ago we discovered the children of Earth were somehow special, as a race, humans have great potential. And you Michael are extraordinary among them, this you have already witnessed first-hand. So why have we done this, it was because we were searching for people like you."

"What are people like me? What's happening to me?"

"This is something we are not entirely certain of. The genome of the human race has rapidly evolved for ones so young. In theory, a biological structure as complex as DNA should not have evolved in the short period between the formation of your planet and the first appearance of complex life on Earth. Even with the expansive scientific knowledge of the Ashtar, vast regions of coding held within your DNA continues to remain a mystery. It is an instruction manual for humanity, one we can interpret, yet still fail to comprehend the ultimate purpose of its design." Egregor Krill began to explain.

"So tell me, are you saying this affliction is genetic?" Michael asked inquisitively, as a genetic defect was not beyond human science to repair, let alone an advanced intergalactic civilisation.

"That is our belief. Contained within your strands of DNA are the genetic blueprints that define the characteristics of every individual human, each with unique combinations of genes. We do not have a consensus on the function of every gene even though the Ashtar share many similar genetic traits. The truth is that in the average homo sapiens, in fact every other life form that shares a similar molecular structure, most of it does not have a function; that is any function that can be utilised. You are different; much of your genome no longer lies dormant but is lighting up, actively tapping into a connection between your body and the fundamental attributes of nature. An evolutionary potential that we have no explanation for."

"Then turn them off!" he requested with insistence.

"No we cannot. Do you know the potential contained within you?" Egregor Krill repeated the exact same words that had concluded every nightmare.

"I don't care." Michael retorted before Krill could speak further, "You said there are others like me? Experiencing the same thing?"

"Yes there are others, increasingly more so, as time moves forward and human populace grows. The Ashtar have discovered further, that individuals within a specific genetic lineage share similar DNA markers, and some of those have latent genes that are active; and as a consequence, imbuing them with unique traits, perhaps even abilities considered a peculiarity. But please be clear on one fact, there is an immeasurable contrast between you and all these others. There is no one like you."

"Then turn all these genes on in the others." He felt guilt the second he suggested it. Effectively attempting to substitute a stranger's suffering for that of his own.

"That is not how it works. The Ashtar would have accepted the immorality of such an action given the alternatives." Krill conceded, yet displayed no modicum of feeling either way.

"But you mention lineage, genetic ancestry? We've never been close but I'm sure none of my family has gone through what I have, my daughter is remarkable but nothing like what's happening to me." Once more he felt himself searching for that finger of blame for that one discriminative thing that picked him out above all else.

"Correct, again we do not know why. For that very reason we are required to perform an invasive test to determine subjects of special interest."

"You mean sticking a needle through my bloody eye!" The sheer memory of it making his eye water and sting.

"Yes. Unfortunately the only method of diagnosis available to us. It is a probe inserted into the anatomical centre of the brain within the pineal gland. At the quantum scale there is a detectable energy signal, reminiscent of a consolidated brain wave. The Ashtar have never observed that energy spectra within the defined scope of significance. That was until we found you."

"Then what makes me different?"

"In honesty, the Ashtar do not know why the genetic makeup of the human race has such potential; the origin of these abilities still remains a universal enigma. But your distinction, perhaps it is nothing more than a random mutation in the code of your DNA. An aberration of humanity, but a fortunate one for it."

"I still don't understand. How can my DNA make things move around me?" he asked disbelievingly.

"You have experienced telekinesis, an ability to influence matter. We hypothesise that you are able to manipulate energy at the tiniest of quantum levels where the fundamental forces interact. In basic terms just as your body can create a small electromagnetic field and produce electrical impulses with proton motive force, it can also directly influence other forces such as gravity, but only now on a grander scale."

"But that doesn't explain why I'm affected by these gut feelings, some type of sixth sense which triggers unbearable headaches and nausea." Michael continued to question. He had always lived a consistent life of mediocrity that literally changed overnight. There had to be an external cause to this. Nothing else made sense.

"Most interesting. Our research points to many humans having this ability to some degree. The cases suggest that there may be some tenuous connection between the human mind and the world around us. Maybe the beginnings of a fledgling telepathy or the awakening of an ability to translate quantum probabilities that define real world outcomes. You can call it intuition, yours is just a more developed sense. Again, we do not know how such abilities can manifest themselves. As for your headaches and nausea; unfortunately, they are a by-product of your body engaging genes that it is unaccustomed too and has never utilised before. They will eventually diminish as your physiology learns to cope. Your determination to poison your body did not help."

"You don't know what it was like hurting what's most precious to you!" Michael responded with anger at the Egregor Krill's judgmentally sounding words. "You have given me these probable causes and possible explanations, yet the fundamental fact is that none of this happened until after you abducted me!"

Krill's dark oval eyes stared unblinkingly at Michael, "I must reiterate that this disposition was always contained within you. It could have been pure coincidence but I agree that the Ashtar finding you may have awoken what once lay dormant. Conceivably it was an emotional response to the ordeal, an organic defensive reaction to our examination, or a manifestation to answer the call of our search that opened up Pandora's box so to say. In that respect I admit responsibility for what has happened to you since, but I do not regret any of your hardships. The consequences are far more important."

Michael's blood began to boil at the lack of remorse shown by the Egregor, "More important than maiming my child, condemning her to a sad, lonely life of ridicule and rejection?"

No response came as he seemed to be hit by flashbacks deep in his psyche.

"Do you know every night I used to watch her sleep, gave her a kiss on the forehead and told her how much I loved her… Before I left her side, I would absorb myself in every changing detail of her face. Imprint her image in my mind, so that the mental picture would always be with me, in my dreams or if the worst ever happened… Now I've lost it, that picture of her face has been tainted in my memory, replaced by one that is not the daughter I knew. Even the faded images I have left in my dreams have now been taken from me!" Each sentence Michael spoke increased with strength and vehement. He looked glaringly at the unemotional alien, "You've already clarified that my misery is of little concern!... But tell me what is so god damn important that my daughter's suffering means nothing to you!!!" Sparks flew from one of the consoles behind the diminutive form as a searing pain in Michael's head almost floored him.

Krill's deadpan gaze seemed to grow in intensity, "What is? Let me tell you young one. You and your people know nothing of what is out there. In the vastness of the galaxy there are many species…."

"Then I did see some reptilian creature at that meeting!" interrupted Michael clutching his head.

"Fortunately an advocate to our cause, but there are countless species out there of different forms, advancement and beliefs that are not. Many of which are dangerous, however there is one out there, more powerful and evil than you can possibly imagine and they are coming to Earth. They are known as the Sin."

"Why?" he instinctively responded. His mind confused, in a chaotic state of flux between intense emotion and the rationale of logic.

"To wipe the human race out of existence."

"Again why? What threat are we to them?" Michael rubbed his temple trying to block out the headache.

"Now… None what so ever. They come because of an ancient prophecy telling of a race known as the Raziel, a young species that would eventually be the harbingers of their doom. The Sin believes them to be you. They are single minded in their quest for galactic domination, only fearing one thing, the prophecy, and they will not rest until its cloud of uncertainty has been eradicated."

"Have they not been told that we aren't the Raziel?" There was a moment of silence, "Are we?"

"We do not know. The conception of this prophecy was from a time long before the Ashtar. The Co-operative has their doubts. In the grand diverseness of the galaxy, the human race and its biology is not vastly different to countless other species. But as I have said, it is this hidden potential that makes you unique. Like all prophecies, they are mere words, unfortunately for us all; they are words the Sin strongly believes in. Are you the Raziel, perhaps given time you would become them, however by that distant future the Sin would have long vanquished the galaxy. Raziel or not, in this present, it matters little against the might of the Sin Supremacy."

Michael was once more speechless. He didn't know whether to believe it all, but then again after the things that had happened to him and the truth sat before him. "How long do we have?"

"That is unknown to us; we only know they are coming." Egregor Krill gestured Michael to a nearby chair. "Please rest, the stress on your anatomy is clear, even to one still unfamiliar with human physical nuances." Michael did not argue; the fatigue and pounding in his head had drained the last strength in his body.

"Our endeavour began over seventy years ago; an Ashtar warship was patrolling within this sector of space when a small vessel was detected heading towards your planet. Only a handful of races would have ever lain eyes upon such a craft before and still exist today. One of those was the Ashtar, although not for an age. To our alarm and dread it was a Sin seeker ship. We pursued the craft into your solar system and opened fire. Even though the craft was a modest reconnaissance vessel; compared to our warship it was an even match. After a fierce battle we managed to destroy the Sin craft, but not before it broadcast a message in the vicinity of Earth. The Ashtar ship sustained major damage in the encounter and unable to maneuver the craft they had no option other than to attempt an emergency landing on Earth. They made their best efforts to control their descent towards a deserted area of your United States of America but their speed was too great. They crashed on the outskirts of a small town known to you as Roswell, New Mexico."

Michael's drawn face seemed to liven up upon the mention of that infamous location.

"I deduce you have heard of the incident. Fragments of the Ashtar warship were scattered across a substantial area but the main bridge section containing its occupants terminated in the soil of a local ranch. Military representatives from the nearby Roswell army air field shortly attended the scene and altogether retrieved fifteen deceased Ashtar from the wreckage. Fortuitously a single Ashtar survived the crash that day and that survivor owed their life to the bravery of Colonel John Allen Snr. I believe you have already made an acquaintance with his son.

Just prior to the sole survivor of the crash falling unconscious, he was able to pass on important information to the colonel.

The Ashtar have the ability to use telepathy, able to communicate with each other with only the medium of their thoughts. This ability is incompatible with humans but we have had limited success in passing on data to the human mind using a dangerous telepathic transfer.

With the understanding that he was gravely injured the Ashtar took what was in probability his final chance to warn the human race. Utilising all of his strength and concentration he projected the knowledge of their impending doom at the hands of the Sin and impinged how crucial it was to take the correct course of actions. Although we do not know where or who the message was meant for, we were able to decipher it and with my last words I told Colonel Allen what it said, 'Prepare for judgement, we are coming!'"

"That survivor of the crash was you?" Michael exclaimed.

"Yes fortunately."

"That was over seventy years ago! What makes you think they're still coming?"

"Space is inconceivably big. You do not know the Sin as I do, many more years may pass, but without doubt, the day will come when they fill your skies with their vessels of war."

"Then it could be another hundred or more years before this happens; outside my lifetime. Listen, I don't really care about anyone else on Earth, right now all I care about is my daughter. Everything, every action, every consequence has less meaning without her. So again, I ask you... I will beg if I need to... Please stop what is happening to me, only then I can see her again, try to make up for what I've done... You have that ability, right???" Michael looked to Egregor Krill with a mind full of hope.

"No, I do not. The preference of the Ashtar Co-operative aside. We do not have the scientific knowledge to stop or reverse the transformation happening within you... But there is someone who can help you."

"Who? I want to see them now!" he demanded.

"Michael, I propose a covenant. I will bring you to this person and after you have conversed with him, if it is your wish, we will use our resources here on Earth to allow you to once again see your daughter. Not from afar but real contact."

"And how will you do that? You know what I did to her. She is in the US now with her mother and grandparents. The decision was made by a court of law; I am forbidden to go anywhere near her."

"Michael, you should be well aware of what we are capable of doing. All I require in return is you allow me to show you something first."

"How do I know what you have told me is the truth, how can I be sure you will keep your end of the bargain?" To accept everything this emotionless alien had said and to freely submit himself to them was a giant leap of faith.

"Michael, what does your intuition tell you?"

13 - Task of the Pindar

In the dark, deep within a secret underground facility somewhere in the United States of America.

A figure adorned with a plumed head dress of vibrant feathers entered the shadow of a crude laboratory. The modified cave was dank and water dripped from the rusted pipes routed along the glistening wet walls. Old dated equipment furnished the ominous space like it was assembled from an amalgamation of scrap yard remnants.

"The Ashtar have ceased all activity on the planet. This can only mean two things." he reported with a whisper.

A mosaic masked form motioned awkwardly from behind some type of red chemical bath, which was interconnected by a number of thick plastic tubes snaking across the stone floor and air like a tired spider web. The mask resembled a skull with four bands of turquoise and black jade; the lower jaw in turquoise and finishing with a black polished upper cranium that tailed off into a deer skin hood. All that was visible behind the central jade band was the reflection of two snakelike eyes. "Ah... Quetzalcoatl, the bearer of good news as always!"

Chilling screams echoed in the background. "Tezcatlipoca, it appears you are enjoying your work too much."

"You have come to tell me something, so I suggest you get on with it. As you can hear I have important work to do." He was dressed in pitch black garments broken by copious jewelry and a breast plate of smoky mirrored material.

"Yes those grey skinned meddlers. Firstly they have either found what they were looking for, or secondly the Sin is close!"

Tezcatlipoca was mute for a moment while he contemplated this development. "There presence has not been witnessed in over seventy years, not since their reconnaissance vessel was destroyed sending that message. A single brief transmission over so many years of silence!"

"You know the nature of the Sin as I do; it is not a question of if they will come, but rather when they will come. There is not a force out there that can stop them."

"It displeasures me to say, but I agree with you. The activities of the Ashtar have no bearing on our goals but the Sin….. If they arrive before our work is complete, they will destroy the human race, every last one of them. Our ultimate objective would be an impossible task."

"We must accelerate our work. If the Sin is near, it is vital that we are prepared; hence the reason for my little offerings. If by some fortune their arrival is delayed, well our objectives will be closer to realisation and there will be no one to interfere."

"Quetzalcoatl, our control on this planet is not absolute! In accelerating our work, we risk being discovered."

"Your opinion of the risks is irrelevant to me. This is the quickest method to achieve our goals. You know what is at stake for us!"

Tezcatlipoca hissed loudly showing his extreme disapproval. A black and white monitor in the background slowly refreshed between various video feeds casting a menacing eye over the unknown locations. A static filled image of a suited man entering an elevator blinked up onto the screen, momentarily halting the exchange.

"The Pindar is here", as Tezcatlipoca pointed this out, a further barrage of screams reverberated in the air. The blood curdling sounds seemed to pierce the stone confines from all directions simultaneously.

Behind the dusky orange of a horned beak, a scaled snarl was almost perceptible on Quetzalcoatl's face. Tezcatlipoca knew it was directed at him but choose to ignore it. He limped over to a far console integrated with switches and dials. Under the dark draping fabric his right leg below the knee was substituted with a fused snake statuette made from the same substance as his breast plate; glass that had the appearance of a smoke-filled mirror. With an obviously disappointed groan he flicked a couple of switches. A blue liquid pumped into the chemical bath mixing the fluid to a luminescent purple. With a twist of another dial the new mixture siphoned through a number of drainage tubes away into the shadows. Almost immediately the disturbing shrieks and groans tailed off to leave only the echo of rattling pipes.

The lift doors shuddered open onto an underground level that few people had ever set foot on and were allowed to leave. The Pindar stepped out, adjusted his tie and made his way towards the lab of Tezcatlipoca. The corridors were claustrophobic and gloomy. Cob-webbed lighting flickered randomly with the buzz of surging electrical currents. Each time the illumination levels fluctuated, arachnids and other beastly insects were momentarily highlighted scuttling in the slimy cracks and damp corners. The smell of rotting meat clogged the humid air so you could almost taste it at the back of your throat. An odour that grew more pungent as the Pindar moved deeper into the facility along with the temperature and spectre of danger. His skin started to grow clammy and beads of sweat seeped on his forehead. As he arrived at the entrance, he dabbed the perspiration with his silk handkerchief.

"Enter!" requested Tezcatlipoca.

"Masters you have summoned me."

"I have a task for you. You are to have something delivered to your new collaboration of rogue nations." disclosed his feather embellished Master, passing over a manifest of stained and crumpled paper.

"What is to be delivered to them?" he replied as he looked through the list of countries and GPS coordinates untidily sprawled on the lined sheets.

Tezcatlipoca raised his clawed hand and pointed a long thin finger in the direction of an array of monitors. There were several of varying sizes and design, all mounted to the wall with tubular framework, latches and bolts. Many of them only displayed the fuzz of black and white static but the one of interest was a large colour TV with a polished wood effect chassis. On the screen at least a dozen or more devices were visible, each the size of a fridge carefully stacked together in some kind of concrete storage facility. Each one had an unmistakable warning symbol adhered to its side leaving the Pindar in no uncertain terms what these objects were.

"Nuclear Weapons!!" the Pindar muttered unable to hold in a gasp of surprise. "Master what if they use them? The initial nuclear attacks were of our will. Unimportant targets, carefully chosen collateral damage that served our purposes."

"You question us!" Quetzalcoatl spat in a threatening tone. "You are the tongue of the Serpent. Your place is to communicate our wishes to the others without question."

"I apologise Master. I only think of the agreement we made on your behalf between the Thirteen families and the others." replied the Pindar in a humbled manner.

"We know full well, the agreement that was made. We suggest that you personally make sure that they select their targets wisely!" spelled out Tezcatlipoca. "To make sure of this we have provided specific instructions for one of the devices ourselves."

"And another thing, make sure MAJI use their military connections to provide indisputable evidence to the UN of their imminent danger." added Quetzalcoatl.

"What evidence?"

"Why you and your dangerous gifts of course!"

"If that is your will." answered the Pindar unable to hide his look of anxiety.

"Now leave us. Your New World Order will be born out of the ashes." commanded Tezcatlipoca.

The Pindar left the gloom and stench of the lab. As the creaking elevator doors closed on him, Quetzalcoatl turned from the monitoring video link to his associate. "He questioned you, do they suspect the nature of our real plans. That they are mere pawns, this New World Order just a stepping stone in something far more important."

"No, you give them too much credit. The Cult of the Serpent and MAJI still believes we share the same goals as they do. As for their so-called secret societies and the rest of the world, they know nothing of our existence. He has grown arrogant with the power and wealth he has become accustomed to. Something he forgets we have granted them and can take away just as swiftly. For now he is of use to me, once that is passed I will send a message to the others at his expense."

"I suggest you begin to accelerate your activities. It is the one that lived who has commanded it!"

Tezcatlipoca replied with an irritable hiss as he left the lab, "It will be done!"

14 - Hope beneath the sand

Countdown: Minus 1 ½ hours before multiple nuclear strikes

Egregor Krill dismounted from the high-backed metal chair and rose up on his spindly three toed legs. He stood no taller than 4ft high, his body grey and gangly except for a pair of thick forearms preceding his elongated four fingered hands. He wore garments resembling a tight-fitting wrap of bandages that ran from his ankles, covered his torso and up the length of his protracted neck. Over the graphite shaded cloth some type of ornamental platinum collar hung down across his gaunt rib cage.

"Would you please follow me." Krill asked as he wandered towards a side door.

"How about my clothes!" responded Michael tugging at the light green sheet loosely tied around his body.

"Yes of course, they are located behind you." Krill gestured towards a side recess in the medical bay.

He could see his clothing laid upon a cold steel table with his personal objects. Michael immediately stepped across the threshold between rooms, picked up his antique flask beside the silver bracelet and popped the lid. The calming aroma of liquor filled his nostrils.

"You do not require that substance."

"I will decide what I do and don't need. I've already agreed to come with you." Although he knew he didn't have much choice if he wanted any hope of repairing the two lives that had been destroyed. "When you have come up with a solution to my pain then I'll stop looking to this!" Michael held up the walnut veneered flagon and took a gulp. He closed his eyes and let out a sigh of satisfaction.

Egregor Krill stared on unblinkingly, turned his back and moved towards an automated door. "Then when you are ready, I shall be waiting."

After he had changed back into the dirty and tatty clothing, he put his objects back inside in his jacket pockets, momentarily eyeing his daughter's photo. *I promise you sweetheart, I'll make things better.* He drew in a deep breath, slowly exhaled and made his way out of the medical bay, through the hidden monitoring chamber and through a sliding glass door into a passage with a large extractor fan overhead sucking any stray particles into its filtration system. The second of the opaque glass doors was situated a short distance ahead, the separation forming a small quarantine area. He stood before the sliding glass and exited straight into a colossal library housing wall to wall books, journals, computer terminals and stacks of papers. Michael stared around in reverence at its sheer scale. This place had countless books and manuscripts that must have been hundreds, perhaps thousands of years old and would have put the museum's collection to shame. Unlike the museum there was no hint of dust upon the books or shelves, the air was dry and clean, surgical like.

"This is the central knowledge repository." notified Krill who stood there waiting for him.

"Whose knowledge repository?" questioned Michael.

"COM Twelve."

"And who are they?"

"As I recovered in a hidden facility within Roswell army airfield base, Colonel Allen Snr with the help of a group of trusted colleagues, twelve in total, started to take measures to cover up the crash as nothing more than the remains of a downed weather balloon. This was no easy task in the climate of mistrust running throughout the human race, and created deep suspicions in many facets of the United States. Knowing the importance of secrecy, they initiated the formation of a covert agency that has grown in its influence and power. It has been designated COM Twelve, referring to the committee of twelve that created it. You dropped in upon the current leading twelve at the Ritz. This facility is their headquarters."

Exiting the grand library, they proceeded into an area that resembled a hi-tech office environment with rows of computer stations all facing a huge curving wall that acted as one gigantic media display. Across its area, world maps, live video footage and satellite imagery flashed on and off producing a central command area that NASA would have been proud of. The initial clamour of conversations died away and a hush blew over the room as each person spotted Michael's entry. He passed someone staring at him who he thought he recognised as the tall dark-haired gentlemen with spectacles from the Ritz. He wasn't the only one gawping at him. Nearly everyone in the room was; which Michael found weird considering the company he was walking beside.

Passing through some 'authorised personnel only' double doors, they walked down a short corridor of staff offices to another set of identical doors. Entering into a hub of activity they were met with the sound of grinding metal and a fountain of superhot filings showering the concrete floor. Military types, scientists and people dressed as park staff seemed to be monitoring and testing the base systems; the largest group overseeing the transfer of what looked like the segment of a missile using an overheard system of pulleys and rails. It became clear it was an engineering section as he passed schematics of the theme parks rides and structures, rollercoaster tracks being employed as some type of magnetic catapult and most bizarrely of all, someone welding a section of the McDonald's golden arches sign with a special surprise loaded inside.

"Why have a base of operations here?" queried Michael as he surveyed the dual-purpose objects hidden in plain sight.

"Firstly, there are certain advantages that such cover provides. An entertainment facility of this type allows COM Twelve to bring in vast quantities of material, hi-tech electronics, heavy machinery and to excavate deep into the ground without question or suspicion. Where else could you maintain such a military base underground as well as on the surface and preserve secrecy. This headquarters is more than a concealed location for COM Twelve to carry out their endeavours. I hope you will never need to see the full capabilities of this facility. You will shortly see the second reason why this location fits the needs of COM Twelve."

Apart from the way they entered there were two other exits to the engineering workshop. One a wide opening where the pulley rail system ended and a heavy-duty conveyor belt began; after the haulage platform at its mouth it ascended at a steady gradient presumably to some outlet at ground level. The other was an arched space uncovered by a raised shutter, the cellar like area was plain and empty apart from a single opening at its centre and the protruding pipes lining its ceiling. Krill led Michael to the circular aperture lit from above by a directional spot light. They began to climb down a steep iron staircase bolted to the bored hole, clearly given away by the striation marks of a bulky drill bit. Michael doubted he was being escorted to COM-12's personal wine collection to fill his flagon with some expensive vintage. A notion quickly confirmed as he reached the bottom of the spiral steps to find himself standing at the far end of a short passage facing a vault type door and two heavily armed sentries. Here one of the soldiers indicated to a piece of apparatus akin to a filing cabinet, while the other stood ready hand on pistol. With a few taps of his control tablet an optical device resembling a blacked-out scuba mask rose from inside the portable machine. Both of them were subjected to a retinal scan before an internal electronic lock clicked and the soldiers allowed the pair to pass.

Behind the protected doors was a bending spherical tunnel plated in brushed steel and overlooked every twenty metres or so by a mounted rail gun that followed their every move.

"What's with the armed guards and oversized machine guns?" asked Michael, the presence of the targeting barrels making him slightly uncomfortable.

"Merely a precaution. Where we are going, there remain a few unanswered questions."

They finally reached a cylindrical steel door. Krill placed his hand on a full-length panel like a pane of black glass and allowed it to scan his hand and body. On a rectangular screen adjacent to the panel a real time MRI image scrolled vertically. The lights above the scanner flashed green and a computer voice announced 'Authorisation accepted'. With a loud grind the bulky metal entrance popped inwards and slid round to one side. Behind the door was a cramped circular cavity that had been hewn out of the surrounding rock. Suspended by a thick cable in the centre of the cavity was a platform just large enough for two people. They both stepped out onto the platform as the metal door slotted back into position and locked behind them with a deep thud.

There was a sharp jolt and the platform began to drop steadily as if in a bucket being lowered into a well.

"Ok, so are you going tell me what's down here?" inquired Michael as the pace of the descent picked up.

"The sub-global system, about five hundred metres below us." answered Krill as he removed two silver pieces from a hidden compartment on his collar.

"Ok. So will I be needing them?... What are they for?"

"The Ashtar birthplace is a dark world, although its star shines with a brilliance similar to your Sun, the atmosphere of our planet was dense, filtering the majority of the incoming light. This resulted in the Ashtar species evolving eyes that were proficient at absorbing the maximum quantity of photons. Although we have become accustomed to the intensity of light here on Earth, the illumination down here does not agree with our optical sensitivity." Krill explained as he slipped the silver pieces over his large black eyes like contact lenses.

The platform abruptly came to a standstill at the bottom of another cavity which required a similar body scan to exit. The arcing door slid across and Michael followed Krill out into a space large enough to enclose a two-story house. He was standing in a white crystalline cave that sparkled with a metallic like impurity. Krill was right; the light down here was strange. Michael looked for its source but it seemed to be emanating from the rock itself. There was a pungent smell like overly strong garlic permeating his nasal passages suggesting to him that his surroundings were home to some type of phosphorous compound.

Towards the back of the natural cave, a gulley was eroded away leading to large circular openings at opposite ends of the side walls. No water was present to suggest it was the origin of the smooth deformation, in fact the air was exceedingly dry and after inhaling a few times he could feel the dehydration in his mouth. Inset within the channel was a thin cylindrical structure containing a hollow interior and capped at each end by a rounded cone. The object appeared to consist of the same material as the cavern rock and seemed to undulate up and down as if on an invisible river.

"Please step in." asked Krill directing him to the hovering rock.

"Is that what I think it is?"

"I apologise I am not aware of what you are thinking. As mentioned Ashtar telepathy does not function with human beings although unexpectedly I am able to feel a tangible connection with your psyche. It is a transportation vessel for the sub-global tunnel system."

"I didn't mean lit... Never mind. So down here you have your own underground network?" This didn't surprise Michael much, as amazing feats of underground construction had already taken place in the world he knew, such as the London Underground and Channel Tunnel. What did intrigue him though was how it worked. There were no rails, no electrical or chemical equipment that could act as a power source, nothing but fashioned rock as far as he could tell.

Inside the crystalline vessel there were two protruding formations housing a clear marble roller ball embedded in their tops. They were located at either coned end just under a transparent slab of the same material that acted as a window.

"Are you ready?"

"Wait, where's the seatb..." Before Michael could finish his sentence, Krill edged the ball forward, and the pointy cylinder shot off like a bullet down the nearby tunnel entrance.

Through the window Michael could see the walls of the tunnel flash past him in a blur. The whole transport system seemed to be quarried from the same surrounding rock that contained the white crystalline impurities and radiated its own light. At the velocity they were travelling, it was impossible to tell the layout or scale of the sub-global system. But what he was able to perceive was that more than one section existed, as now and again he would see Krill flick his wrist in a direction and the vessel would hop into an adjacent tunnel without so much of a hint of a course change.

"You've built a transport network deep underground like our tube system, but how does it run?"

"No, the sub-global system already existed. We do not know who created it, only that it was constructed almost ten thousand years ago. The tunnel network is vast spanning the entire globe, but we have only managed to chart a tiny percentage of its totality. It runs along veins of Lodestar; a strong magnetic material you can see glistening in the rock strata surrounding us. It is what powers the system and propels this vessel along its tunnels."

"That's impossible!" Michael blurted out in astonishment, "Mankind was in the Mesolithic period, the end of the last ice age. Most of the population were mere hunter-gatherer communities. They couldn't have completed such a feat of engineering." Michael could not disguise the surprise in his voice. Everything he had learned about archaeology told him that ancient human civilisations had constructed remarkable things but the sub-global system was something entirely different.

"Who built it remains an unanswered question. Hence our security measures at such entrances."

The magnetic train slowed momentarily before Krill with a flick of the wrist slipped it down another adjoining tunnel and accelerated to its travelling speed that was impossible to estimate visually.

"The Lodestar is now mined by COM Twelve owned operations. Its properties are the basis of many advanced technologies that are sold to fund such facilities as the headquarters you have just encountered. We also require it for another purpose which you will discover later."

"The air down here is warm." Michael ran his hand across the phosphorescent rock but it was cool to the touch as you would expect underground.

"We postulate that the sub-global network reaches considerable depths; the system perhaps reaching as far as the planets heated core."

"But why haven't …"

"It requires a certain degree of concentration to circumvent this tunnel network successfully." cut-off Krill, "There will be time for questions when we arrive at our destination."

Michael restrained his curiosity and decided instead to digest everything he had discovered so far. He had learnt much but there was still so much more that was left unanswered.

In the stifling air drowsiness blew over him and his chin slowly dropped to his chest. Again the nightmare did not take him, locked away somewhere in the dark recesses of his mind by the chains of answers. This time Isabella's faint face floated before him, his daughter's grey eyes and pretty features smiled back at him with innocent affection. But where there should have been love and happiness, only anger welled. A blinding headache exploded with the undesired emotion. Her smile distorted to shock as the skin on her face began to blister, peeling away piece by piece. He tried to reach out for his daughter but her flesh began to melt away under the searing heat engulfing them. Isabella let out a soul-destroying cry of pain, 'Daddyyyyy!!!'. Warm tears boiled as they ran down his cheeks, 'I'm sorry princess… I'm so sorry.'

"Sorry for what?" Krill's harmonious voice once again smothered the confines of this new nightmare.

"Eh… Sorry… Sorry I fell asleep." Michael replied as his senses brought him back to his slumped body on the seat of the transportation vessel.

"No apology is required. You slept for a short period only."

"We've stopped. Where are we?"

"Approximately four hundred metres below the Sahara. More precisely the region known as the Tenere desert in northern Niger."

"Africa already! It didn't feel as if we were travelling so fast."

"The inertial effects are minimal. The capsule including yourself are propelled by the generated magnetic field. On average our velocity exceeded several hundred miles per hour."

Michael took a swig of whiskey and disembarked onto the smooth sparkling floor and examined the architecture. They had

119

come to a halt at a similar white rock cavern, except this one was much bigger in size and looked a lot more artificial. With its squared off corners and refined cylindrical columns towering to the ceiling it resembled some eerie opulent tube station. The area of the extended platform was devoid of any equipment or sign of life except for a big hanger type door recessed into the cavern wall at the opposite end to the vessel.

"Tell me, what are we doing here? Is it sand you want to show me?" he commented with cynicism as he followed the rubbery textured body of Krill. In the natural cavern light purple veins could be seen branching out just under his pale skin and pear drop shaped skull.

Once at the huge steel door, Krill again placed his hand on an access pad and submitted to a body scan. There was a repeating beep like you would hear from a lorry reversing and a solitary red light above the panel started to flash. The hanger door began to slide across revealing a lift wide enough to accommodate a couple of average sized cars and another pair of ominous looking rail guns mounted to its ceiling.

"I do not believe all the sand above us would be of any benefit in the coming battle." he answered as the doors closed across and the lift began to slowly ascend.

If there was any sarcasm in the Egregor's response it was beyond Michael's ability to detect. Anyway, this wasn't important to him as the lift stopped and opened into a wide metal plated room without any sign of an exit.

"Please step out of the lift." requested Egregor Krill.

Michael surveyed the walls and ceiling; each square segment had a smooth protruding sphere. The lift doors closed behind them. "What, no giant machine guns this time?"

"No. Something significantly more deadly." replied Krill stoically.

Michael decided he would rather not know the details as he sensed movement below his feet. Momentarily the lift doors behind them slid across once again but this time onto a hub of activity.

"Welcome to the 'Earth Advanced Research Facility.', base of operations for COM Twelve's scientific and technological research." Krill announced.

They were standing behind a Perspex wall looking onto a scene straight out of a James Bond movie. On the other side of the protective screen was a hanger the size of several football fields. This place seemed to be carved straight out of the rock with only a single immense sandstone column holding up the weight of desert ceiling above. It appeared to be home to what must have been hundreds of scientists working on all sorts of magnificent contraptions. Out in the distance he could see a lofty metal pylon with a sphere on top blasting bolts of lightning at a suspended piece of metallic debris. To Michael it looked like some sort of gigantic Van de Graff generator that was popular in many school science classes. As he watched with interest, static jumped excitedly around the spheres surface, arcing out in a deafening crackle and burning a deep hole into the solid hanging target.

"Please could you put on the protective garment and eye wear before we enter the testing area." To the side there was a collection of vacuum-packed lab suits and goggles of all sizes.

Michael put on the white body suit and wrap around glasses. To him the material didn't feel like the run of the mill lab attire, it was more like he had just slipped on a layer of jelly. However, unlike jelly when he gave it a tap, it did not tremble or depress under his touch but instead hardened on impact. He tugged on the fastening Velcro of the protective clothing and to his surprise although still stiff, the pain in his recently broken fingers had all but vanished.

Once correctly attired he took a position beside Krill in front of the transparent wall and waited for the concealed section of tough plastic to retreat into the ground.

Krill walked through into the testing area just at the same moment a hovering piece of electronics exploded, sending a shower of green sparks and metal shards in their direction. Michael was peppered with minute shrapnel and a jagged piece of an electronic component that was now embedded in the chest of his suit.

"Shouldn't you be wearing some protective clothing?" pointed out Michael as he fastened the Velcro zip right up to his chin and pulled out the broken circuit board that was loosely lodged in his garment.

"My body is not as fragile as it appears young one."

Michael followed Krill towards the far corner of the hanger trying not to show his fascination with everything around him. He still harboured blame for everyone involved with his situation and particularly Egregor Krill. He mustn't forget the reason he was here. They passed a group of scientist figures working on a semi-organic object akin to an old gramophone. It was beaming a perfect holographic image of a rust coloured rock face out above the hangar floor. One scientist motioned to the strange device and shut down the projection revealing an antique blue police box that had been veiled behind the life like hologram. Krill seemed particularly interested in the results as the observers shook each other's hands in congratulations, bar one exception whose face remained stony and impassive. Michael thought for a moment that it was the strange faced woman, the one named Corporate from the room at the Ritz, but before he could confirm his suspicions Egregor Krill interrupted him.

"Let us continue."

"What are they all doing here?"

"At the COM Twelve headquarters they concentrate on their business development, which you can see is vital due to the funding needed to run such a facility, secondly to cover up the existence of the Ashtar, our activities here on Earth and to debunk the conspiracy theories related to our research. This is done by their high connections and influence in the business world, Air force and Navy intelligence circles. Although as you have implied not entirely successfully. Through their endeavour, this facility was possible. It is where the greatest minds of this planet have come together to prepare for the invasion of the Sin."

"What can they do?"

"You will see." Krill stopped on the exterior of a 10ft high free-standing cage structure. The metal mesh enclosing an area that all the other researches kept their distance from.

Inside the walls of twisted wire and poles, a single scientist worked. The individual was wearing a glossy black helmet and adjusting a long glove similar in style to motor bike attire.

Krill slid the door latch across and led Michael into the cage, "I would like to introduce you to the head of research for this facility, Dr. Tesla."

The scientist, tapped the side of the helmet then realised the noise was coming from behind. Turning around Dr. Tesla caught sight of them and waved towards Krill.

"Watch out!" shouted Michael between gags before scrambling behind a shelving unit.

There was a split-second pause as the others glanced at him in confusion when a bolt of lightning ejected from the glove and blew apart the head of a mannequin a few feet away.

"Dr. Tesla?" spoke out Krill in an un-phased tone as smoke and the fine plastic remains of the mannequin's head floated around them.

"Wooooh, needs a little adjustment I think." claimed the muffled voice of Dr. Tesla as the scientist attempted to waft away the dust, "Krill! Nice to see you, what can I do for you?"

"I would like you to meet Michael" invited Egregor Krill as Michael stepped out from behind his shield of furniture.

Dr. Tesla approached him glove hand outstretched, "Nice to meet you, how do you like EARF?...... Get it, Earth Advanced Research Facility!" the scientist mumbled with a soft voice imbued with enthusiasm.

Michael took a slight step backwards giving Dr. Tesla an un-amused and apprehensive look.

"Oh, I'm sorry! I guess I should take this off." commented Dr. Tesla removing the glove that had decimated the dummy moments ago, "Just a second." The Doctor took off the helmet to reveal a youthful and geeky looking female whose dark hair was held back from her face by a replica Wonder Woman tiara. "Targeting helmet and shock glove, based on my father's research" she added as she placed the objects on a cluttered table nearby.

"Let's try this again." Once more presenting her hand.

"Hi." Michael wasn't really in the mood for niceties but shook it anyway.

"So you are Michael then." stated Dr. Tesla looking him up and down, "Looks normal to me; although I was expecting someone a bit more presentable, perhaps athletic and a little less odour!" she remarked to Krill.

"What am I doing here?" Michael groaned, "Is this who I've come to see?" He was beginning to get irritated.

"No. Where we need to go, we will require transport. Dr. Tesla, would you please do the honours."

"Really! Oh fantastic!" She glimpsed around the workshop pointing at things and muttering to herself. "Ehhhh ok. Follow me!"

Dr. Tesla left the Faraday cage through a back exit and briskly walked along the rough exterior of the underground hanger temporarily stopping to witness some ceramic veneered suit with wings being submitted to the scorching exhaust of a suspended jet engine. She gave an enthusiastic thumbs-up to the attending scientists, "Looking good! Should be ready for full flight testing soon!" She carried on towards a set of massive blast doors which required Dr. Tesla's personal security card to enter. Down a short and wide corridor of the sandy rock, they came to another pair of equally unyielding blast doors. With a big grin, she swiped her card through the access panel and stepped down into the exposed section.

"This is Seber!" she announced proudly.

They were standing on a viewing platform overlooking an area that resembled an enormous mechanics garage but with something far more interesting than a beat up truck to work on. In the middle of the holding bay stabilised on a set of makeshift locking clamps was what Michael could only describe as a giant amber pebble.

"What the hell is that supposed to be?" muttered Michael to himself.

Dr. Tesla looked at him like he was some type of imbecile.

"What is it? It's Seber, only the most advanced ship in the galaxy, and most likely the last of its kind. That's why we call it Seber, its Hebrew for…"

"Hope." Michael finished.

"You know Hebrew!" she replied impressed and slightly surprised.

"At university I always wanted to learn a language to supplement my historical studies and Hebrew seemed to appeal to me at the time." he responded impassively examining the structure of the vessel.

"Oh, a scholar. You didn't look like the type. What happened to you?" Dr. Tesla inquired.

"Long story. Maybe you can ask your Egregor sometime."

She gave Krill a short glance and started tidying away a few tools.

"She doesn't know what happened to my daughter?" questioned Michael in a hushed tone.

"It is not a common knowledge that I have shared."

"What is not common knowledge?" quizzed Dr. Tesla overhearing Krill's words.

Michael ignored the question and kept his attention on Egregor Krill, "So is this your salvaged ship, the one from Roswell?"

"Oh no! The Ashtar Co-operative have nothing like this! No offence Krill." answered Dr. Tesla on his behalf.

"None taken Doctor."

She commenced to tell the historical background, "This was discovered right here above us, buried in the sand. In nineteen eighty-six a nomad travelling through the Tenere desert stumbled upon a section of Seber protruding from a dune. Believing he had discovered the crash site of a meteorite he contacted the only university in Niger, the Abdou Moumouni Dioffo university in hope of selling its whereabouts to them. Through COM Twelve's academic connections, we learnt of this amber meteorite and sent out a team to investigate. On discovering what he had unearthed we paid the Nomad and the university quite a substantial sum of money to keep quiet on its discovery and location. Just in case anyone's curiosity into our own interest began to raise its head, we supplied the university with what we told them was a segment of the space rock, in reality a piece of asteroid with a section of fused glass mixed in with a sprinkling of the desert sand. After that the university thought nothing of it. Rather than try and relocate the ship and risking news of our discovery being leaked, we built this facility around it. It initially started off with what you see below you but quickly expanded when construction of this room led to the detection of the sub-global tunnel network. After a good clean we found out it was relatively undamaged, although we established Seber to be well over two thousand years old! Really quite fascinating don't you think?"

"Yeah, quite!" replied Michael with a hint of sarcasm although he thought Seber was probably the most amazing archaeological discovery made on Earth. And that was saying something considering he had just learnt of the sub-global network.

"Do you want to have a closer look" asked Dr. Tesla with

excitement.

"Do I have a choice?"

The three of them led by Dr. Tesla made their way down the metal staircase onto the main level of the holding bay. They walked up to the underbelly of Seber but there didn't appear to be any marking on its exterior signifying a possible entry point into the craft. Standing beside the gleaming amber of the unnaturally smooth surface, Michael could now gage the size of Seber. At its widest point it was about 15 metres in diameter and about 7 metres from top to bottom. The back of the alien ship was broader than the front which gave it a side profile like that of a Stone Age spear head and from above the silhouette of an egg.

Michael ran his hand over the surface; it was warm to the touch and felt like solid marble without imperfections. He watched as Dr. Tesla also placed her hand on Seber's hull but with altogether different consequences to his. The once solid walls began to ripple as if they were alive and like a glass blower manipulating molten glass, the crafts surface moulded itself into an archway and entry ramp.

Dr. Tesla sent a smile towards Michael's astounded face. "The outer shell of Seber is a nanobot fluid. It solidifies into a super hard substance on contact with anything other than itself, like the air around us. It is also able to repair itself and cast the fluid into different forms." explained the doctor tapping the newly formed ramp. "A rather remarkable substance actually."

Michael inspected the solidified formation with curiosity, looking for any sign to indicate its once flowing form. He removed the protective lab suit and followed Krill into the interior of Seber. Meanwhile Dr. Tesla whistled happily to herself as she hurried about outside pulling on levers and pressing buttons. Michael was surprised at what he saw in the interior, he was not expecting to walk inside and be able to see the entire holding bay through the structure of the craft. The walls that appeared amber on the outside were in fact crystal clear on the inside just like one-way glass. Michael stroked the clear surface, to the touch its texture and warmth matched that of the rest of the rigid outer surface. He almost had a clear 180-degree view around him, only broken by four glowing stud-like bulbs, equidistantly implanted within each quarter of the shell, and a large rear compartment enclosed by dark amber walls.

"Yes, the nanobot fluid produces a polarised shell allowing asymmetric transmission of electromagnetic radiation. Please join me in the command level." requested Krill.

By the time he had turned around Krill was gone. The section of the ship he was standing in was like living quarters containing seating areas and a whole manner of objects he didn't recognise. Above him was a grey ceiling bound by a circular ring of some cloudy plastic type material. In the centre of the ceiling was a circular opening large enough for a person to fit through.

Must have been where the Egregor disappeared too. Michael thought to himself as he stepped underneath the hole.

There was a piece of stone on the floor below his feet. Michael could feel that the circular plate beneath him was at least a few degrees colder than the surrounding area. The rest of the floor had a rubbery grey look to it like the ceiling and was only broken by sections of what he thought was furniture and four large transparent portholes. Michael looked around him but there didn't seem to be any type of steps, levers or anything of the kind that could help him up.

"How do I get up?" Michael shouted through the hole as he tried in vain to reach its rim.

"Simply jump."

Wait! Did I hear that right? Krill didn't seem to have a sense of humour so Michael gave a sigh and leaped upwards with his arms outstretched.

To his bewilderment, at the apex of the jump his body failed to fall under gravity but floated upwards through the hole quite gracefully and then hovered momentarily until he took a step onto the solid floor of the upper level.

"Low gravity transition plates. Please take a seat." said Krill.

This upper section of Seber was identical to the lower level in size except for the rear compartment it had below. But in contrast this area had a number of console clusters laid out along the periphery of the inner walls. Michael placed himself down onto one of the console seats. Immediately it felt as if the material moulded around the contours of his body. He went to swing the chair around to face Krill but it never budged, instead the entire console swung to correspond with the movement of his body. The terminal screens in the arm rest and in the integrated console appendage were flat and soft to the tips of his fingers; each had a display like a touch screen computer. Surprisingly the hi-tech screens were in English, this told Michael that whoever this previously belonged to spoke our modern language or the people at this facility had succeeded in interfacing with its technology. In each corner of the central appendage display was a digital red button, Michael motioned to select one of them on the screen, *Let's see how this works, can't do any harm.* Just as his finger drifted over the virtual button there was a shout of a woman's voice that was more like singing.

"Don't touch that!! Weapons control!!!" Dr. Tesla had momentarily popped her head through the hole before vanishing again to the lower level.

Michael pulled back his hand disparagingly. "So who built this then?" he inquired struggling to contain his curiosity.

"Seber was constructed by a truly ancient race known as the Elohim. In fact, they are known as the eldest race in the galaxy." enlightened Krill.

"Dr. Tesla said this is probably the only one of its kind, so you must know more about these Elohim. Have they died out? Destroyed by the Sin?"

"Not entirely, just the knowledge of where they all are is lost to us."

The doctor stuck her grease smudged face back through the level transition hole, "We're ready to rock and roll!"

"I do not understand." returned Krill with a blank expression.

"Oh sorry! We can go." translated Dr. Tesla with an apologetic face.

"Hold on! Go where?" challenged Michael with a growing concern.

"That way!" Dr. Tesla pointed directly above them before jumping into her seat.

Michael looked up through the opaque shell of Seber. There was a shaft running vertically for about a hundred metres ending at a hatch that was sliding apart to reveal a clear afternoon sky of untainted blue and a thin veil of falling sand.

The desert floor above was lifeless for miles around, the only thing differentiating this spot from any other in the one hundred and fifty-five thousand square mile expanse of sand, was a single ring of black rocks and the dark hole opening within them.

"Ready?" she asked rhetorically with her finger poised over the controls. Without considering any potential answers Dr. Tesla pressed the pad on the console and let out an excited shout "Woo hooooo!"

Seber darted upwards at an incredible pace. Michael went to gasp in anticipation of the G-force he was expecting to experience, but there was no sensation of his stomach being forced towards his ankles. No hint of acceleration or even noise. The walls of the shaft rushed passed him, only just wide enough to accept the full width of the soaring amber pebble. Seconds later he was watching the sea of yellow and brown that was the Sahara Desert retreat into the background. Further seconds past and the green of Europe and South Africa appeared into view, and then he was in orbit.

"You can fly this thing?" muttered Michael, more to himself than asking the question.

"Huh! Why because I'm a woman? I'll have you know, Seber is my project and there is no one more qualified than me to take her controls!" retorted Dr. Tesla

"What?.. No! We're in a vessel thousands of years old looking down on Earth." Michael responded still staring towards the green and blue sphere in awe.

"Of course! The Elohim built things to last, and obviously with a little bit of my own expertise, Seber is as good as the day it rolled out of the shipyards." she added with pride and less defensively.

"Is this what you wanted me to see?" Michael gestured towards Krill.

"Earth from the surface or Earth from space, it doesn't apportion you the perspective you need. We are going to Mars."

"Mars!" exclaimed Michael, "You've got to be kidding me? It's millions of miles away!"

"Correct. But we are not bound by the scientific limits you are accustomed to."

"Right… How long will it take to get there?"

"Ohhh, hopefully the press of a few buttons." answered Dr. Tesla excitedly.

The clear ring that constituted part of the floor separating the upper and lower levels became aglow. Blocks of light began to flash on, one after the other, completing a loop before terminating and starting the process over again at an accelerated rate. Accompanying the flashing lights was a pulsing sound of something powering up that intensified with the increasing speed of the blocks of light. As the illuminated ring became a solid band of white, the space around Seber began to blur in and out of focus. The Earth behind them and its partner, the moon up ahead, seemed to shimmer like someone flicking a light switch rapidly. The blurring amplified and just before losing all detail, Michael thought he saw intense flashes of light bursting from the different regions of Earth simultaneously. Everything shot back into focus and where the green and blue jewel once was, there was only empty space. Michael span around, the silvery radiance of the moon no longer floated before them, replaced now with the unmistakable rusty colour of Ares the god of war.

"Wooo!! I knew it would work!" yelled Dr. Tesla.

"What! You mean you've never tried it before?" snapped Michael.

"No, this was our test flight. Successful I'd say" remarked Dr. Tesla with a smile.

"Successful! What if it didn't work?!!" countered Michael.

"Dr. Tesla tells me we could have partially materialised here while the rest of our molecules remained in elliptical orbit around Earth, if I comprehend correctly."

"You've understood perfectly Krill. If I was you Michael, I would count all my fingers and toes." she suggested with a snort.

"Yeah great, haven't you people already done enough with my molecules! What just happened?"

"Quantum entanglement drive, Seber is also the fastest ship in the galaxy. The principle is simple really; we basically entangle all ours and Seber's particles to the destination we want. The instant we are fully entangled, an exact copy is created at the designated coordinates, the original ceases to exist and we find ourselves in our new location. It's the only one of its kind, the Elohim seem to be able to manipulate a dimensional plane that no one else can reproduce. Anyway, won't go into the technical details, but we just travelled about a hundred million miles quicker than you could say warp speed!"

Michael's head was spinning; he didn't know what to say but knew exactly what he needed. He reached into his jacket pocket and pulled out his carafe of whiskey.

"You know that stuff's not good for you!" called over Dr. Tesla.

The insinuated criticism of others who didn't know the whole picture riled him once more, "No, being abducted by bug eyed aliens and accompanying crazy scientists on experimental jaunts across the solar system is not good for me!" he replied knocking back a good measure of spirits.

"Ok, I will keep quiet and fly... Inertial compensators down twenty-five per cent." she whispered to herself.

Seber sped towards the fourth planet from the Sun, making a series of spins around its tiny orbiting moon Deimos, that in Dr. Tesla's words were to blow off the cobwebs. As the alien craft looped the huge rock, Michael felt the extreme change in inertia tug on his internal organs, almost causing the alcohol to come straight back up.

"Enough already!" shouted Michael trying to hold in his stomach contents.

Dr. Tesla tapped the console a few times and Seber started to level out and the effects of inertia began to dissipate.

"Hey Michael, look to your right!" she commented innocently.

Michael switched his attention to the starboard of the ship, only a few kilometres away he could see another spacecraft orbiting Mars. A small aluminum cube equipped with a satellite dish and two solar powered wings extending from opposite sides.

"That's Mars Express launched by the European space agency to map atmospheric and geological aspects of the red planet. It's one of three functional space craft in orbit; well sent from Earth anyway."

They left the exploratory craft in the distance and headed for the planet. Seber hit the thin predominantly carbon dioxide atmosphere. Mars red surface rushed towards them. A colour given to the planet by a layer of iron oxide dust created when oxygen from its ancient atmosphere was absorbed into the Martian rock. The ship dove down over a heavily cratered area, a billion years of brutal pounding leaving a hundred thousand eternal scars. Dr. Tesla levelled their angle of descent and adjusted their trajectory to a heading north-west taking them directly into the path of a violent and vast dust storm that raged over a quarter of the planet.

The hematite sand battered Seber's hull, visibility was only a few feet in the sea of red that enveloped them. The ship suddenly plunged through the driving wind, leaving the fierceness of the storm and into a silent darkness.

"Where are ....", before Michael could finish his question the air around him lit up, the light seemed to emanate from the nano-fluid that encased Seber and easily pierced the gloom for some distance. To one side of the ship Michael could see them hurtle past miles of solid rocky wall whose base was lost in the black depths below.

"We are travelling within Valles Marineris, it's a giant canyon that is oh, about, one hundred times longer than the Grand Canyon on Earth and roughly three times deeper." explained Dr. Tesla with an impressed sound to her voice, "Although only half the radius of Earth and one tenth its mass, Mars is home to some extraordinary features that dwarf those that can be found within our oceans and continents."

Once they had sailed the length of Valles Marineris the storm above had lost most of its power and density. Seber skipped out over the red desert leaving its sands swirling in its wake and hit a vast upland region of Mars known as Tharsis. A plain flattened by lava flows and resident to several humungous volcanoes.

"Michael that over there is Olympus Mons" stated Dr. Tesla pointing towards a colossal lump of rock that rose endlessly skywards, "It's the biggest mountain in the Solar System, rising up to fifteen miles above the surrounding plain. Everest is dwarfed in comparison."

"We will shortly arrive at the intended coordinates" notified Krill as Seber broke through the tail of the storm.

They continued to pass across the Martian surface leaving the monster mountain behind them until it was a pimple in the distance. As the line of sight began to clear, more and more of the landscape began to creep into view, Michael looked out towards the horizon and slowly rose from his seat, "Oh my… Is that…"

Dr. Tesla grinned, "It certainly is!"

15 - Aquarius

The American delegate to the United Nations Security Council paced up and down his office high up in the UN headquarters based in Manhattan New York. He gazed out the lofty window to the waiting city, the waiting world below. Pushing open the window designed to stop would be jumpers, he thought to himself that perhaps this would be the easy option. Once extended to its furthest point, it locked into its preventive position. He placed a knee on the window ledge and raised himself to the breezy opening, sucked in the fresh air and loosened his plain blue tie so it hung messily around his neck. Deep black hollows framed his eyes and small bloodied razor marks spotted his face, showing clearly that his focus lay away from the pastures of sleep or the mundane task of shaving. Today had been a most difficult one; tempers were frayed after hours of heated debate concerning the course of action that must be taken in the face of the recent devastating attacks of terrorism. They had just convened for a recess having made little progress and still remaining a million miles away in terms of a consensus decision on a plan.

The United Nations had never before faced a situation of such consequences since it was founded in nineteen forty-five, when fifty countries signed the United Nations charter in hope that this international organisation had the ability to intervene in the conflicts of other nations and ultimately prevent war. Although now it consisted of 192 member states comprising the General Assembly it was the responsibility of the Security Council to make the decision that would shape the future of the world. The Security Council constituted fifteen member states made up of 10 temporary seats and 5 permanent members that were the United Kingdom, United States, Russia, China and France. It was these 5 permanent nations that held the real power to pass a United Nations Security Council resolution that all member governments had to carry out under the United Nations Charter.

Being the most powerful nation on Earth, the United States of America held a significant sway in the council's policies and the US representative was a very influential figure among his delegation. He walked across the American flag rug and adjusted a plaque on the wall with his sweaty hands; it was the charter that outlined the purpose of the United Nations. In his mind he read out the words that he had used more times than he could remember to convince his colleagues to sanction the proposals of the US;

1) To maintain international peace and security, and to that end: to take effective collective measures for the prevention and removal of threats to the peace, and for the suppression of acts of aggression or other breaches of the peace, and to bring about by peaceful means, and in conformity with the principles of justice and international law, adjustment or settlement of international disputes or situations which might lead to a breach of the peace;

2) To develop friendly relations among nations based on respect for the principle of equal rights and self-determination of peoples, and to take other appropriate measures to strengthen universal peace,

3) To achieve international co-operation in solving international problems of an economic, social, cultural, or humanitarian character, and in promoting and encouraging respect for human rights and for fundamental freedoms for all without distinction as to race, sex, language, or religion; and

4) To be a centre for harmonizing the actions of nations in the attainment of these common ends.

The American took his gaze from the charter; the acts of terror were so devastating and momentous that everything outlined on this engraved stone was in severe jeopardy and no matter how he interpreted the words; their countermeasures would go against everything they had sworn to uphold. He saw no other choice; the UN was being backed into a corner and if they didn't act, then the US or a number of the other permanent five would and risk alienating the rest of the world or worse. It wouldn't be another Afghanistan or Iraq; any retaliation was going to make them look like a playground squabble.

His office door swung open distracting him from his thoughts. "Who are you? You can't just walk straight in here!" snapped the US representative.

"You do not need to know that." stated a man with a composed voice. The man dressed in a plain black suit and wearing dark sunglasses shoved his security clearance badge into his face. The US representative had never met someone of such high security clearance and he had been to meetings with some of the highest ranked generals in the American military.

"Then what agency are you from, FBI, CIA? Not many people can just waltz into my office no questions asked."

"Also something you do not need to know." replied the man calmly.

"Then what do I need to know?!" asked the representative in anger.

"Is the correct question.", the man put his hand inside his black jacket, removed a large brown envelope and placed it on the desk.

The US representative sat down in his leather chair and emptied the contents of the thin package in front of him. They were photos, magnified satellite imagery of some military camps and close up shots of equipment being delivered to these foreign bases, equipment he clearly recognised.

"These are from Iran and North Korea. Where did you get these?"

"The source is not important, only what you have in your hands. I trust you know what to do with these and what course of action needs to be taken. We will be monitoring developments very closely."

"Who's we? Who do I say I got these from??" he shouted after the man in black.

The mysterious agent gave the photo waving UN delegate a lengthy deadpan gaze, turned his back and exited the office without another word.

The door to the room closed and the US representative fumbled impatiently through his desk draw. He hurriedly lit a cigarette with a shaking hand, flouting the buildings strict non-smoking policy, and once again examined the images.

The agent only known as Aquarius II passed into the blue painted corridors. As he did so he whispered to himself. "Who I work for? It's better if you don't know."

It was of extreme importance that his organisations involvement in this situation remained unknown and that the how and the why of their incriminating evidence maintained its secrecy. Knowing any of this would sow the seeds of doubt and second thoughts into a person made of weaker stuff than him. Many wouldn't understand the necessity for such measures. Ultimately, the national security of the United States was at stake.

Aquarius II had operated in foreign countries for most of his service, but increasingly now it seemed he was spending significantly more time engaged within the borders of his own. This type of errand was a bit different to his usual duties but the all-important atmosphere of intimidation was still essential. As a veteran agent now, his vast experience meant he was satisfied that the delegate had got the silent message. From looking at an individual's face you could read a lot about a person, their character, emotions and most importantly intent, but having two black voids over what some people called the windows to the Soul made that advantage one way. That's why the dark glasses were standard issue; be it a psychological response to a social barrier or a natural physiological reflex, there was something unsettling about not being able to see a person's eyes.

Aquarius II stepped into an adjoining art decorated hallway and approached a group of Russian delegates in intense discussion outside the Security Council chamber. As he passed them by, they fell into whispers, closed ranks and gave him a sideways stare of mistrust.

"This would never have happened if we were still the Soviet Union" spat one Russian in his mother tongue.

"The price of capitalism." added another believing that their Russian language gave them secrecy enough.

Unbeknownst to them, although his Russian was rusty Aquarius II understood perfectly, *Still brainwashed by a broken dream. One of our greatest achievements destroying that delusion.* He replied to them in his head.

How things have changed. He thought to himself with despise. It was not so long ago that these Russians were the greatest threat to the United States of America and the driving force that had led them to their current position. And now members of their government walked and talked freely in one of his country's most secure buildings. Times had changed and priorities had shifted since the simple days when he first enrolled to serve his country, when things were black and white, good and bad.

Aquarius II continued down through the busy lobby of the UN building. As he walked, he observed and interpreted the faces of the individuals he passed.

Two Chinese representatives. *That stern exterior hides nothing, your isolationist demeanor only adds to the obvious. Your fear of losing control.*

A group of UK delegates. *You walk and talk with importance, but you fear making the decisions required to win. You believe you paint yourself a bigger target to these terrorists. You fear culpability.*

A French ambassador. *An air of arrogance yet you want someone else to lead, you fear your own competence.*

Aquarius II stood amongst these people from every continent and there was one evident commonality among them all, undeniable fear of what the future held. He cared little for them or their irrelevant feelings, there was only one nation of people that concerned him.

He reached the security checkpoint at the lobby exit, turning around he raised his arms for the personal body search and looked at all the foreign dignitaries scuttering around trying to do what was best for the global good. These men and women, their emotions and families were as real to him as any American's but he still struggled to find any shred of empathy for them.

Finally my country will see peace and security for the first time in its long

history. If you knew the lengths we had gone to for that taste of utopia, a future where the people of the US no longer had enemies or lived in the fear of imminent danger. I'm sure you would see our collaboration as deplorable, our actions despicable, but for all the lives saved it would be worth it. Your nations will reap the benefits of your sacrifices, although mere echoes of our great country, the consequences of what we have done will mean that for generations to come, they will have the privilege of being born into a world free from chaos.
He silently told them all.

Aquarius II left the building and those in it to make the decisions he had help lay out. As he walked down the steps into the United Nations plaza a moral conflict raged inside him. Moments ago, he had justified to the world his unethical methods and those of the organisation he represented, yet he still struggled to justify the sacrifices of innocent Americans to himself. He was as patriotic and strong willed as they come, but so many of his people had suffered and died, children too, and they would not be the last. That protection, trust and liberty afforded to them by the constitution coldly ignored under an ever-increasing list of justified compromises. This was not what he originally signed up for, maybe his morality and integrity had slowly diminished and became blurred over time, or perhaps the lengths he was willing to go to had expanded with his life's end game in site.

Once more he shook the weakness of doubt off. *Yes they are the very people I do this for. But the United States is more than any one person or group, it's an ideal and symbol of something much greater. What we are doing will deliver the American dream to all its citizens and bring about a change that will see advancements in all walks of life that we could only have imagined. A future worth sacrificing much for. Too many American's had died already, many more are threatened. Such evils must be done in the face of our greatest threat. And I will carry that burden for all of them!*

16 - Scapegoat

The Year 1996

The officer stared out the window, his gazed fixed on the trees bordering his quarters in Langley. He sat upright in his immaculate ceremonial uniform; hands interlocked upon his empty desk. It had been many months now, this room was no longer a place for a well-earned rest as a guest of the CIA, it was really just a holding cell in camouflage.

He was never one to think too much and reflect on what he was doing, it was always second nature, a calling which he felt compelled to answer. Now contemplative thought was all he could do to try and make sense of the situation of limbo he currently found himself in.

I always knew the government would not associate itself with the operations I was involved in, but… What had I expected?… For the great service I did my country, I expected a Distinguished Intelligence Cross for my fortitude and exemplary courage. I was ready to die, satisfied that if I did, all that would be remembered of my sacrifices for our nation would be a solitary star displayed on the Memorial Wall in these headquarters… Maybe being the disowned patsy is the ultimate sacrifice for me?

Before the officer could rationalise any further there was a loud knock at his door.

"Enter, it's open." he rose to face the door, assuming his ridged

139

formal posture.

"At ease soldier." Spoke a smiling man with a folder as he passed the stationed guard and into the quarters.

"Yes Deputy Director Sir." responded the officer while he saluted and awkwardly tried to relax his body.

The Deputy Director of the CIA was of an unathletic build, had his dark but greying hair neatly combed and was entirely unassuming except for a bright multi-coloured tie of mosaic blues and reds. "Now please take a seat, I wish to discuss some things with you." he asked as the guard closed the door behind them to provide the privacy they required.

"Yes Deputy Director Sir."

"First things… As of the Fifteenth, I am now the acting Director of the CIA." updated his visitor.

"Congratulations Sir."

"Fortunately for the both of us the director abruptly resigned… Let's just say he and the establishment saw things a bit differently."

The officer nodded in acknowledgement and joined his important guest at the small dining table. The acting director placed the thick dossier out in front of him and opened it up, "So officer, this in front of you is officially your whole life." He began to flick through the ensemble of documents, "A Member of the US Navy DEVGRU, SEAL Team 6, drafted into Special Operations Group within the NCS. Exemplary service record I must say."

"Thank you, Sir." he replied while considering his service history. Up to that point those pieces of paper probably did contain his entire life. But it was when he joined the National Clandestine Service that all official lines got blurred. It was a semi-independent service of the CIA and he was drafted into the Special Activities Division specializing in operations that included high threat military or covert activities with which the US government did not wish to be visibly affiliated. It was adeptly, some thought, named SAD for short, but traversing a realm where overt military or diplomatic actions are not viable or politically feasible meant he could autonomously serve his countries' interests.

The director flipped to the back of his file, "But now we have this big shit storm of brown staining this last page.", he lifted his head from his notes and sat back legs crossed, "I know you've repeated the mission report many many times, I've read your statement, so I don't need to know the detail. But I want you to tell me it in your own words, face to face. I don't care about this diplomatic bullshit; nobody is writing anything down here."

"Right, of course Sir.", the officer took a breath and put his mind back, "I was running black ops in Chechnya helping the guerrilla forces plan their movements to gain independence. The tension in the region was on a knife edge, Russia's reach was weakening and the powers that be informed me to do what I could to insight rebellion and further destabilise the Russian rule."

"Absolutely we did." the director admitted.

"That's when I gained intelligence on a significant way I could do that." he made the eye contact that prompted further confirmation.

"And your target was a political figure of very high value to us. He was a hard-line extremist, highly influential within the hierarchy of the Russian government. A dangerous individual with a personal hatred of our great country and the principles it stands for. It was a big risk, but as someone who wanted to bring back the glory days of communism and the Soviet Union, it was the right play."

"I discovered the target would be stopping for a limited time in Budyonnovsk, roughly seventy miles north of the border. I'd never received intelligence on his movements between Russian cities before, it was a one-off opportunity. So, I helped organise an offensive… In a column of military trucks, I accompanied a large group of Chechen separatists into the city and stormed the police station and city hall… Inside the government office I hunted down the target and took him out." the officer recounted with no hint of emotion towards the kill.

"I'm not afraid to say, that was a game changer for us in the area."

"But before the separatist forces and I could retreat, Russian reinforcements arrived. Too caught up in raising their flags on top of the government buildings… Maybe I could have pushed them out of there sooner, but the symbolic nature of those flags is a stronger motivator for rebellion than any words or action I could ever perform."

"Yes, patriotism is a powerful weapon." the director agreed, "So, then we have the incident. It's been labelled as the Budyonnovsk hospital hostage crisis. Estimated one hundred and fifty civilians dead and over four hundred injured."

He looked back apathetic to the casualty report, "We holed-up for hours, but in the end we had to fall back into the residential districts. Seizing the hospital was the only way we could maintain a tactical advantage. We only did what was necessary to secure an agreement for our escape."

"Ok. So let me tell you how the US administration see this in the light of the world. They are appalled by the deaths of innocent men, women and children in an unjustifiable and criminal attack. No such American involvement was authorised." summarised the director.

"I fully understood when I signed-up that they would exercise plausible deniability." conceded the officer. He observed the pitted complexion of the director's skin trying to interpret the hidden facial indicators.

"I am sure... Now let me give you the unofficial feelings." he proposed, "They are still appalled by the deaths of innocent civilians, but to add further. It was a calamity that had gone against their mission objectives. The Chechen rebels had been severely discredited to the world and this crisis has instigated unwanted negotiations and ceasefire... They think there will be a signed peace treaty within the year." He let the officer ponder that for a moment.

"This is the thing; I became deputy a few weeks after this happened and since then they continue to cut our funding and criticise our transparency. You know, the administration still wants their answers from the CIA and now that specifically means me.", the director paused and smiled at the officer, "So you see, I've personally come here to give you one opportunity to tell me exactly what you think of that?"

The officer focused on his micro expressions, those unfakeable tell-tale signs that occurred universally on everyone's' face. Sometimes flashing up in bursts as fast as a quarter of a second it took great skill to read. As he echoed the displeasure from Washington there was an unmistakable but not easily noticeable give away. One side of his mouth raised slightly; it was clearly contempt.

"They... They are..." the officer still struggled to speak freely. It felt like insubordination, the habit of compliance with his superiors and the words of his government were difficult to shake.

"Go ahead, say it like it is. It's off the record, just me and you."

"Sir, they are wrong!" he forced out. The expression of pain on his face seemed to be caused by saying those very words.

"And why?" the director questioned as he smiled more broadly.

Many times had the officer seen malice and falsity behind a smile so he examined the director's face in detail. The lines of his crow's feet were strong near the outside of his eyes. A wrinkle ran down from his outer nose to outer lip and the corners of those lips were drawn back and up. He was definitely happy to hear his response, not in a funny way but a contented way.

"Yes it might lead to a peace treaty, but I have ensured that any chance of a communist resurrection has taken a significant blow, even fatal. None of them were there, risking their life's behind the lines amongst those Chechen fighters. They were tired and demoralised. That crisis and the following ceasefire allowed them a moral victory, time to rest and most critically rearm."

"Yes certainly, the Russians have never gained the initiative since. But what about the civilians that lost their lives? How do you feel about that?"

The officer looked at him directly in the eyes, he saw no hint of deception in them, just genuine interest in the answer to that question. He had always been honest with his statements detailing the incident but was never entirely forthcoming with his personal feelings relating to it. Now his questioner had asked that very thing specifically and his answer would remain truthful.

"Those people that died... Innocents most likely, but I feel no guilt. They are not my people, just foreign collateral damage that had to be sacrificed to achieve what was necessary for the greater good of the United States of America."

"Ok. Then what about this, where you find yourself now? You know they want you to stand trial in a military court for your crimes."

"Instead of being hailed a hero, even if unsung, I find myself an outcast in my own country, by a government I would stand by without exception." The sadness and anger clear in the officer's voice, "But if a scapegoat is what my country needs then I willingly submit myself."

"Yes, we do need a scapegoat… But I believe you are worth more to your country than a scapegoat."

"Yes, Sir I believe I am." he concurred.

"The world is changing, the threats are changing, and we need to evolve to combat this. The trick is to see where the danger might come from in a post cold-war world. Is it the transformation of Russia and China, rogue states like North Korea, Iran, Iraq or other forms of terrorism? To those that make the decisions on funding for the CIA I've appealed to its original mission. Which was to prevent another Pearl Habour."

The director undid his suit button and leaned in, "But we cannot do this by just being narrowly focused in our strategy, remaining ethically consistent with America's values or by working within the framework of international law. As you know very well, the CIA will bend the boundaries of these rules, but in its current iteration it will never be able to ensure the national security of the United States of America."

"Sorry Sir, I am not following." The officer was puzzled as to the direction of the conversation.

"What if I told you there was a truly clandestine organisation of like-minded individuals out there. One that answered to nobody and able to exist and operate outside the shackles of our administration or global scrutiny, one that the CIA was but an instrument to manipulate. Imagine being able to go on the offensive, destroy our threats before they even become a danger and seek them wherever they may hide. They and you understand what needs to be done, some would say actions that were unethical, that our current establishment will never ratify, fund or consciously allow. This is not just a very real chance to secure the defence of our great nation, but to make sure it is never threatened again." as the director explained his hands became even more expressive. He was truly impassioned by this vision.

"You want to recruit me Sir?"

"Correct officer."

"But what about my current predicament?"

The director took the last page of his dossier, screwed it up and threw it in the nearby waste paper bin. "This is a lot to think about and process. This calling will require a lifetime commitment. It is Christmas in six days, I will return in four and then I will take your answer."

17 - Majestic

The Year 1996

Four days later the officer was again sat upright at his desk in his ceremonial gear in contemplation. The snow fell thickly outside his window and as he had expected, there came a knock at his door.

"Enter it's open."

"Officer... I assume that tells me your answer." The director was looking towards a duffle bag on the methodically made bed.

"That is correct Sir, my answer is yes."

The director smiled and walked to the waste paper bin. He held up the officer's dossier, "This is the only record of your existence." He dropped it in the metal container, pulled some lighter fluid and matches from his velvet overcoat and preceded to set fire to it. "Follow me."

As the flames incinerated his years of service, he grabbed his duffle bag of personal items and followed the director out of his quarters. There was no guard this time, only another man in the exact same ceremonial dressage that without a word of acknowledgement crossed their path and into his newly vacated quarters.

"Who's that?" asked the officer as the door closed behind them.

"The ghost of your past and the United States involvement in the Budyonnovsk crisis disappearing."

With little fanfare and absence of officiality, they promptly and quietly exited the building and into a waiting black SUV. The officer had been in one of these before. It was a mobile communication fortress, armoured from bullets and explosives, windows that blocked out any external view and fully sound proofed.

The doors auto closed and the director turned to him, "You ready to go on a journey?"

"Yes Sir."

The vehicle pulled off, crunching the gritted snow and left behind the formally unnamed CIA headquarters in Langley. "I'm sure you're aware of the unofficial CIA motto, 'You shall know the truth and the truth shall make you free'. Well I am going to tell you a story about our secret control group and what we are doing to ensure a future of America that we both hope for. It's a long trip so I will start at the beginning."

The officer was intrigued as to what covert group could possibly exist that the CIA or the NCS were totally unaware of.

"On the twenty-fourth of September nineteen forty-seven, President Truman authorised with an executive order, the creation of an ultra top-secret arm of the US military that only answered to the President of the United States. It was made up of the top military and scientific personnel of the time and created solely to investigate anything UFO related, of advanced technology or even alien in origin. Its task was to determine their origins and dangers, and provide guidance on the necessary courses of action needed to protect the interests and national security of the United States of America."

Interesting, it was formed almost at the same time as the CIA.

The director allowed the officer to absorb that information before continuing, "Now the important thing. It was only known to exist by a select few in the government and with ultra-secrecy, comes ultra-clearance, ultra-authority and ultra-deniability. The resources to be able to access all personnel, facilities and data available to the US, make anything classified to all but themselves, and the free reign to utilise the latest technological R&D. Trusted with the power that no other agency or military organisation wielded, that control group was codenamed MAJI."

MAJI?… I've never heard of them in any intelligence chatter. The officer thought to himself, not making the comment as he never expected he would know of them.

"I'm not going to give you a history lesson here but I want you to understand the moments that led MAJI to where it is today… Back then was a time of high paranoia, we were post World War two, technology had advanced, people had begun to fear the commies and everyone seemed to pay more attention to the skies. Maybe it was a cumulation of all these factors but something had certainly caused a dramatic surge in these unknown events. So, there was a mountain of UFO, alien, generally weird sightings and reports from both the American military and the general population. In fact, right across the world, hell, the term flying saucer was being thrown across the news on a regular basis… So under project Grudge they investigated everything of interest and as you would expect, most of it was crap. You name it, natural phenomenon, mistaken identity, wild imagination, drug induced hallucinations or elaborate hoaxes." The director spoke casually as if talking about last night's episode of x-files.

The officer was not put off by the notion of UFO's. Too him they were just objects that the standard military or regular citizens could not identify, and he knew full well what lengths certain agencies would go to provide false information into the public domain.

The director's facial features took a more serious tonicity, "But as the saying goes, there is no smoke without fire. There were definite lines of investigation that could not be explained under any of those categories. Something unknown was certainly happening out there and MAJI were determined to find out what that was, who or what was responsible and ultimately if it posed a threat to the security of the United States of America."

The officer felt the change in momentum of another left turn. Although he couldn't see out of the SUV, he was still able to maintain a sense of his direction, and by his bearings they were heading somewhere towards Dulles international airport.

"Increasingly as they investigated these very concerning events and reports, more unanswered questions cropped up. As they probed into them, MAJI hit information firewalls, well executed cover-ups or were down right blocked by influential senior officials. A surprise considering the executive powers they were awarded... Anyway, when you knock on enough doors and knock on them long and loud enough you will eventually get someone's attention. And MAJI certainly did."

"There was another agency, Sir?" questioned the officer.

"No... Not an agency operating under the government or any other nation for that matter, no foreign coalition or secret service. Imagine MAJI sitting in your shoes right now, just realising that the scope of power you wielded, that the influence, resources and capabilities of your organisation were, let's say, restricted in comparison to another hidden in plain sight, but like us wished to remain concealed at all costs." His eyebrows raised with the reveal. A physical emphasis employed to promote the feeling of surprise in the listener.

Yet the mention of an entity superior in means to America immediately invoked the image of an enemy, "Who?"

"The Cult of the Serpent."

"A Cult? I've never heard of anything like them, Sir." The very words Cult and Serpent shouted religious fanatics and treachery to him but he reframed from assumptions and continued to listen intently.

"No one had heard of them before. They've existed for a very long time in recorded history. When something has been around for that long, successfully shying away from public view... Well, inevitably they become invisible like a natural socio-political background noise. Perhaps by another name then, we refer to them as the Illuminati?"

"That's just wild imagination, conspiracy. Plain paranoia." The officer voiced dismissively, falling out of his formal boundaries momentarily. To him there was only one enlightened society. That of the United States and its constitution.

"That is the right answer." The director smiled, yet his micro expressions this time suggested amusement rather than happiness. "Today their conditioning of the human race through their economic, monetary, intellectual, and especially media influences runs so deep that although many blatant signs of them litter everyday life, to question or talk of them is quickly dismissed. Just look to your reaction."

The officer digested this silently for a moment, *That makes sense, I can understand this. I've been a ghost for so long that any ties to a normal life have been lost. Yet exactly because of this I'm able walk amongst society unnoticed, effect the masses and nobody is the wiser of my involvement. I've seen the excuses given in the news for some of the operations I've been part of.*

"Unlike MAJI they transcended geographical boundaries and viewed the map in terms of their influence, wealth and power. They first contacted MAJI in nineteen sixty-four. America was a superpower, they saw what MAJI was capable of within their own country and understood the goals of their mission. The Cult of the Serpent envisioned an environment of mutual co-operation that would benefit MAJI's cause and would best serve their conglomerate of business interests."

"How could we work with such people who have their own personal interests in our country. Sir, surely that constitutes a viable threat to the United States of America?" he challenged with concern. As he did, he asked himself if he should even be questioning their decisions. The alternative to this at best was a court marshal and being locked away in a dark hole somewhere, yet he had to remain truthful to his principles whatever the consequences might be.

The director seemed unperturbed by the nonconformity of his replies, "The answer is MAJI didn't know if they posed a risk or not. And because of that, of course, they kept a very close eye on them. But what they did give us in return with that co-operation was intelligence on other nations, their economic and political climates, military capabilities and technological advances. Yes they played on a global vision, yet MAJI considered them a lower threat than the very real dangers that they were providing us intelligence on. The UFO phenomenon and anything we had traced back to them certainly hadn't threatened American security or interests. All we had to do in return was stay out of their activities and cover them up where needed."

"Their activities. So, they are connected to the UFO phenomenon?" To him this was the interesting point that differentiated them from just another agency or aristocracy with too much money. Technological capability was a good determination of the threat level an unknown quantity could pose.

"Yes but in a terrestrial sense." The Director responded, noncommittal to further information, "And you will see how MAJI had kept their side of the bargain. Do UFO stories still fill the front pages of our newspapers? It's all been lost to the domain of conspiracy groups. In fact, there is no need for a special government taskforce to investigate a debunked threat anymore."

"So how have MAJI survived to today?"

"Like I said to you before, the world changes and you need to evolve. MAJI had showed their extreme worth not only within their original remit but also with their foreign intelligence. What was apparent to the select few that knew of MAJI, was the criticality of the control group to maintain and regulate this relationship with the Cult of the Serpent. Firstly it was imperative we knew more about these mysterious Illuminati, and secondly to continue feeding actionable intel to the foreign intelligence service of the United States federal government, our very own CIA."

The tiny vibrations entering the officer's body had changed. The surface beneath the vehicles tyres was different, they were no longer on any public road. The air inside the SUV was completely isolated and recycled independently from the outside. This was to protect its occupants in case of chemical attack, but it also meant the officer could not smell the expectant odour of aviation fuel. By his guess they were coasting on the airport tarmac.

The director did not give any clue as to their whereabouts or the circumstances outside the vehicle. He was fully focused on what he had to say. "Yet the true revolution for MAJI came between nineteen sixty-nine and seventy-one, when both our goals became truly intertwined. We were in the midst of a messy and expensive Vietnam war, still embroiled in the state of political and military tension of the Cold War and its indirect proxy wars. Our country was fueled by gaining a technological and political edge over the Russians in any way possible, and that meant expanding our own scope of operations concealed within a trojan of initiatives, the very initiatives that the Cult helped influence and execute. Initiatives such as the Nixon doctrine, 'the defence and development of allies and friends', basically come under our nuclear umbrella as long as we get a finger in your pie. Nothing but a good old-fashioned protection racket, but an effective one."

I see no outward signs of lies or half-truths. If what he is saying is fact, then maybe this Cult have played some part in the creation of the American policies I am trying to protect. It appears that they're at least somehow ingrained within our system of decision makers.

As he tried to clarify his thoughts, he felt a bump and their elevation change. *Ramp.* The tremor of the diesel engine cut-off and not long afterwards he experienced the unmistakable sense of acceleration and movement that you received onboard a plane. He looked to the director to confirm his suspicions but before he could the director spoke up.

"This Illuminati themselves wanted to accelerate their own plans. Which of course required the secrecy that we could provide, even from the President of the USA. Knowledge of MAJI could not sit with such a person of authority whose position is decided upon by a democracy. The wrong person in that position could destroy everything we are working towards, certainly an internal threat to America. I will just say we learnt that lesson with JFK."

"What plans would that be?" The implications of the US, or worse the Cult's, involvement with presidential assassinations made him hugely uneasy. Again, he felt as if he should remain quiet but he was compelled by the need of personal assurance.

"At the time, to promote democracy and capitalism, to bring the world together into a single collective of co-operation where their potential for wealth and influence would be unlimited."

"And now?"

"Ultimately, they want a New World Order, a singular global governance over all the world's nations, their leaders, peoples and economy. It would be controlled by the chosen few and by the defining principles of the United States of America that they have helped nurture over the centuries. MAJI wanted to go on the offensive against the Soviet Union and all its threats to national security, and with the full backing of the Cult, MAJI could do this effectively, and most importantly autonomously and covertly outside of US or global regulation. How could MAJI not develop this partnership? The Cult had their hand in every bit of global business, economics and politics, all of which they could influence significantly. Most importantly of all, as a military arm of the government, we could leverage their privately funded advanced knowledge and technology, resources that surpassed ours in every way. We are talking full spectrum dominance."

"Forgive me for pursuing this line Sir, but how could our goals possibly align, they want to rule the world including America?"

"This is where I hope you will have the same epiphany. How do we really protect our country with the so many and varying threats out there? You've seen firsthand what an impossible task that is from history, from your own direct experience. Could you even say with our current White House elite, their policies and international laws, that a prosperous America of peace and security is even possible within your lifetime? There is really only one method to insure the national security of the United States of America against all its conceivable dangers. That is to control one hundred per cent of the world's population. They will live by the rules and ideals our country holds dear and we will be part of an elite that upholds this. The Cult's involvement in our country will be nothing more than another accustomed change in a Presidency, it's advisors and the congress that has always been in flux. Take the control group within MAJI for instance, none of its original members remain alive today, but it's very essence, structure and objectives live on and persist to present-day. To the masses any change would be invisible, all they will notice would be a world that is safer and better for all."

"What about democracy?" To him democracy was a key factor to the principles he had fought for all his life.

"Democracy is a tool gifted so those masses can voice their opinion and unhappiness. It's a mythological power to change, but an extremely effective method of quelling rebellion and violence of those who would otherwise be ruled and ignored. Democracy will be awarded to the world's population, but as it has always been, the decisions that matter will be made by the elite beyond the reach of constitutional change." The director explained as if he was telling a person that their loved one was not what they seemed.

Those words should have shocked him more, yet deep down in his heart he knew they were true. He had done things for his people, things that the majority would have disagreed with, but he did what was best for them even if they could not recognise it.

"How can you be sure we can trust them? That we are moving towards the same goal?" He was looking for that tangible evidence that were not mere words.

"What's the greatest threat that you've been fighting since the start of your crusade?"

"Communist Russia and the Soviet Union." He didn't need a second to even contemplate that.

"How do you think we brought about an end to the Cold War without a shot fired?"

"Many say it was President Reagan that effectively won that conflict."

The director smiled hard, "On the public face of it, yes."

"So officer, do you remember the US embassy hostage crisis in Tehran in nineteen eighty-one? If I'm not mistaken you were there briefly."

"Yes, I was. I was freshly enrolled in the special forces and one of my first missions was to assist in the training of the SAVAK secret police. Then the revolution happened and we were tasked with smuggling the overthrown Shah of Iran out of the country and into the diplomatic safety of Egypt. Three of my team died that day." he recalled.

"The repercussions were worthy of their deaths and let me tell you why. The primary stimulus for the US embassy hostage crisis in Tehran was the fact we granted the Shah asylum, which in the eyes of the Iranians was clearly showing our complicity in his atrocities. The American impotence during the crisis and the disastrous rescue attempt that followed ultimately helped destroy President Jimmy Carters re-election campaign... So if you are following me, whoever gave you those orders directly allowed Reagan to come to power." The director finished with a tone of satire.

I remember how pissed off my superiors and their advisors were when those orders got delivered. They argued the madness of our involvement, but those orders supposedly came from very high up in the food chain. I can guess where from now. he reflected as his stomach dropped in what he assumed was air turbulence.

He ignored the movement and told of his opinion at the time. "We allowed the Shah asylum in the US for prolonged medical treatment. I knew the type of dictator he was, so I couldn't understand why we would first rescue him and why the US government would do this. The Iranian revolution had been successful in overthrowing the Shah. This would obviously destroy any chance of continued relations between us."

"That dramatic change of relations with Iran from allies to enemies led to us building up Saddam Hussein's power base in Iraq with huge funding. Then the dominos keep falling. Iraq could not pay back the huge mounting debt from the Iraq-Iran war so they invaded Kuwait to control their petroleum reserves. A Gulf War which the US swiftly ended, leaving behind an evil dictatorship… We instigated all this and we are still playing that move. The strategic end, an occupation of Iraq and significant control of middle eastern oil contracts by the US."

Now I understand the complexity and hidden motives of that move. Yes, I'm sure that benefited the Cult. But how could it align with MAJI's goals?

"For what end game? Just more petrol?"

"You will learn, as we did, that economic factors can destabilise and manipulate a nation or the world just as significantly as any military action, especially oil. But no, it was not just petrol, the ripple effect was not just linear. The important consequences are too numerous to tell but let me give you another very direct example, Reagan's pet project was his Strategic Defense Initiative, a.k.a Star Wars. Not only did it force the Soviet Union into spending huge amounts of money it could seldom afford, that space race ploughed significant revenue into the Cult of the Serpent's businesses and doubled MAJI's own funding. It provided the means to develop some very useful resources within our country and in our skies, including ultra-secret facilities and technologies that still serve us today. You will become familiar with their implications soon enough." The director paused momentarily before asking a rhetorical question, "Is our country not stronger and more united than it has ever been in its history?"

The web of consequences was clearly beyond his full comprehension, but the director was right, the US had risen to be the only true superpower that all other western nations, and others more increasingly around the world, looked to for leadership and guidance.

"Without mutual co-operation with this Illuminati then this never could have happened. Yet there was still so much for us to achieve. So over eleven years ago an official agreement was signed with them to fully work together in achieving our united goals under the name project PLATO. Most importantly this laid out our country and our place as leaders under the New World Order. It is my belief that the paths we have followed for our country have absolutely been the right choices. Experience tells me that not to have collaborated with them, or to go against the Cult would have been suicide for our country and what we hoped to achieve."

"I concur, Sir." he could only agree with this conclusion.

"That is good to hear. Let us fast forward to the present. We at MAJI can really act independently of the US government and do what we see as best for our nation on behalf of our people. Even now we work beyond the knowledge of the president. Yes, a static core in the government still know of our existence, but they are limited in their knowledge of our projects. Only that we are integral to enforcing the agreement, an important weapon to keep us superior to our enemies and destroy all threats to the United States of America. Now tell me officer, do you have any other questions?"

For the officer, every sign tied in with that question, translated to a very simple point, that the director felt he had wholly justified MAJI as an organisation, and that enough of the detail had been provided for now. There was just one personal element he still did not understand.

"Everything you have told me. I'm just an insignificant pawn in a global chess game. Why me, what value can I add?"

The director nodded in acknowledgement, "Back in your quarters you told me that the death and suffering of innocents was justifiable collateral damage to further the goals of the United States of America."

"Yes, I stick by this unequivocally."

"And that resonates loudly with us. We are the tools of America, moulding a tough world in our vision. And MAJI need very specific and special instruments to do that. There are three fundamental assets that govern the global population, money, laws and people, the more you have of each in your favour, the more you can do. I don't see you as someone that is governed or driven by any of these, only the ideology of your country."

It was true, he lacked the connections that tied the average citizen to everyday life. As the director continued his explanation, his internal senses told him they had begun to drop rapidly in altitude. Which meant their destination was close.

"For example, for MAJI to get funding for our endeavors we need threats, every threat has people behind it, to extinguish a threat you need to eliminate those people, international law offers protection for those people, so we need new laws, to get new laws passed you need the death of people or financial catastrophe... And then people will freely give you money. The more of one creates more of the other. So there are times when you need to devise a threat. Just the very perception of a threat can usher in great change."

"Sorry Sir I'm not sure I understand, what do you mean devise a threat? Everything I've ever done is to destroy a very real threat to the US."

"Yes, but everything we cannot control is a potential threat. Say an important step in our plans requires invading a country in dictatorship, even if they presented no direct threat to our borders, would intelligence on weapons of mass destruction give a justification to the world?"

"If a country or evil regime needs to fall for the good of our own, then so be it."

"There is no doubt in my mind that you would do what is necessary when it came to our enemies or the human collateral damage of other nations, but there are enemies within our own borders. I don't mean foreigners, I mean wolves dressed in the flag of our country, dissident sheep amongst our flock. Those that would wish to undermine our national security and our aspirations... Would you still do what was necessary? Would you still be unequivocally committed? It should not be an answer given lightly; I insist you take a moment to think about all that has been said. You are here right now because you remain loyal to your cause, unwavering to a fault, whatever the consequences may mean. So an honest answer is what I expect."

I believe we should solely serve the purpose of the US and the people of America without compromise, not some wealthy business conglomerates or social elite. Although, if there is one thing I am sure of, MAJI share my beliefs and will do whatever it requires to safeguard the national security of the United States of America, and secure its future against all possible threats. MAJI has no political barriers, constraints of global laws or the pressure of the world's valid morality. But would I even turn against my people for the greater good? he reflected in silence. There was much he still had to digest before he could answer that question.

There was a solid bump that shook the SUV and a hard deceleration that pushed the officer back into his rear facing seat. They had landed.

The director turned to him as there was a shudder of an igniting combustion engine. "Journeys end for us and the life you once lived. So, officer, can MAJI count on you?"

"Yes Sir, yes you can. I gladly accept the removal of my leash. To rise above those who wish to cut short my life's mission. They lack the understanding of what measures are required, yet you have been doing what it takes on a grander scale than I could've ever imagined. Bound by the limitations of society around me, I lacked the perception that MAJI's resources could provide. Now with that knowledge, I clearly see the wisdom of your objective and what sacrifices will be necessary. So I answer with absolute honesty, that if any US citizen would actively try and get in our way then they are no true American, there is only one word for them. Traitors."

The vehicle stopped and the director quietly stared at him. Just before it would have become exceedingly awkward, he smirked. This half-smile interpreted into satisfaction.

"Then I give to you an early Christmas gift, the limitless possibility to enact real change for your country!"

"Thank you Sir."

The director nodded to the cabin at the front of the vehicle. Unbeknownst to the officer, the driver took his finger off the gun trigger and pressed the button for the central locking system instead.

The door automatically opened and he stepped out onto a bright but cold barren wilderness. Behind him he saw a transport plane accelerating off along a dirt runway. To him it looked like the hull of a grey C-17 Globemaster, but it was strangely quiet and appeared heavily modified. In front of the SUV an elderly smoking man walked towards him. Yet he couldn't help but fix his gaze at the helicopter behind the figure. It was unlike anything he had ever seen before. With its tandem rotors and long fuselage, it looked like a chinook, but its blades were hooked like ninja stars and its exterior highly faceted. With the black heat absorbing paint, it was clearly a stealth helicopter very much in the mould of the top-secret F-117 Nighthawk fighter that he was familiar with.

The man approached him and threw his half-smoked cigarette to the ground but did not extend a hand or give any form of pleasantries, only acknowledging the presence of the director.

"This is MJ Four, now the only person you will ever answer to again." stated the director.

"Sir." the officer saluted his new superior.

"Now officer, it is most likely you will never see me again and from this moment on I shall only be referred to as MJ One."

"Yes Sir, thank you Sir."

"Just don't let your country down." responded MJ-1, immediately turning back to his vehicle without wasting any time on sentimentality.

He was under no illusion what MJ-1's micro expressions and tone meant behind that sentence. It was a clear-cut threat. He gave his attention back to MJ-4.

"Officer." MJ-4 spoke out with a wheezy emphasis. "That is no longer your designation. The person you were before you got into that car has been erased. Now you will only be known as Aquarius two."

"Yes Sir." Aquarius II affirmed.

"You have some important work to do and that starts now." declared MJ-4 before he strode off towards the helicopter, signaling to the pilot with a spinning finger above his head.

Aquarius II followed closely in the swirl of dust, impressed by the lack of sound coming from the spinning blades.

"We have somebody within our circle, he's grown old, but somehow grown some balls with age. He's threatening to disclose what he knows about MAJI. Your first job is to assassinate the former CIA Director Colby."

Aquarius II didn't need to answer. *The first traitor of many!*

Back at the CIA quarters in Langley, his replacement sat at the desk staring at the snow falling under the orange lights of the border lamps. It was time, he reached into his ceremonial jacket, placed the cold barrel against his temple and put a bullet through his skull.

18 - Cydonia Mensae

"It's amazing isn't it! That is Cydonia!" introduced Dr. Tesla.

"I can't believe it, I mean hasn't the whole of Mars surface been surveyed, how do we not know about it? I need a drink!!" He fumbled for his hip flask.

Krill answered Michael, "In regards to Cydonia Mensae, none of the population knows of its existence due in part to Ashtar devices that accompany the orbiting Earth survey craft such as the one you have just observed, and also similar devices secured to the Mars exploration and laboratory Rovers on the surface. These devices are capable of intercepting data transmitted by the investigating crafts and manipulate any information we require to remain undisclosed. COM Twelve has also maintained influential positions within NASA and the higher echelons of various other space programs; due to this they have been able to monitor any observational analysis carried out from Earth and also make sure that any examination of the area produces results that make it of no further scientific consequence or intrigue. You can see that the Cydonia Mensae region is very well camouflaged as it is carved from the Mars geology itself. Yet as technology evolves our measures have become insufficient to conceal its existence from prying eyes both on Earth and now most importantly, elsewhere. Therefore we have recently developed technology that should eventually help us with this dilemma. At the moment any imagery or data that does escape ours or COM Twelve's filters is fortunately for us confined to the conspiracy stratums. The scientific world does not look seriously on the declaration of ancient Martian cities."

"There was a time when we didn't have the operations in place to make such interventions with the exploration of Mars. Of course that meant we had to take other more unfortunate measures. This led to the high failure rate of missions to Mars being labelled the Martian Curse or that their probe had been dieted upon again by the Great Galactic Ghoul!" smiled Emile as she recounted.

"How long has it been here?" Michael could feel his old passion for discovery welling up inside him.

"Cydonia Mensae is approximately eleven hundred years old. It was born as an amalgamation of a few bio-domes, but over time has developed into its current splendor."

"You're telling me someone lives here?"

"Dr. Tesla, please take us in and introduce Michael to the Cydonian population."

"With pleasure!" Seber swooped towards a section of the metropolis below; an assortment of pyramidal structures, each born out of the dust and rock of the Martian landscape. They darted past them west towards a colossal five-sided formation that dwarfed any other structure within sight, and resembled a red flat-topped pyramid that had been worn down over the millennia. Up close the structure looked entirely natural, a monstrous mountain of sand no different to a dusty Ayres Rock. That was except for a square of light coming from between two large outcrops.

"Welcome to Bio-Dome One!" stated Dr. Tesla as she brought Seber into the cavity of a docking bay. The flying amber gem smoothly touched down on the landing pad as the rock behind came alive and sealed them from the Martian elements.

Beside Seber another craft hovered effortlessly, shaped like a spinning top it was rotating silently. Three orbs also revolved around it, zipping about at random but always close by, seemingly held in orbit by an invisible force emanating from the metallic craft. The trio disembarked Seber into the hanger. Michael immediately made his way towards the alien craft. It was much smaller than Seber with maybe enough room for half a dozen people. The surface gave the impression of being mirror like but as he walked up to the material it provided no reflection. In fact, none of its surroundings appeared to be visible upon its facade; it was as if the material was selective of the light that it reflected.

"Is this a Cydonian ship?" asked Michael while one of the orbs flitted around him.

"This no, this beauty is an Ashtar warship" explained Emile.

"That, but it's tiny!"

"Don't let the size fool you! That craft is one of the most powerful warships in the galaxy, well at least that we know of. It's kind of a Yoda of the warship world."

"Let me add also, currently the only line of defence between Earth and the Sin Supremacy." supplemented Krill without any hint of sarcasm.

"Well the cavalry will be ready soon!" commented Dr. Tesla.

"The cavalry?" Michael enquired now free from the attentions of the silver ball.

"This is what I wish to show you." said Egregor Krill.

They motioned for the docking bay exit.

"Seber has been my own little personal project but what you are about to see is my life's work. The reason why I was acquired by COM Twelve and why I'm kept hundreds of metres underground in the middle of nowhere."

"You sound like you have little choice but to work for them Dr. Tesla!"

"Oh no, don't get me wrong, I love my work there. It's my home. It's literally been my whole life. I never had a family. Growing up COM Twelve became my surrogate parents in more ways than one. It's just I would occasionally like to do something normal, you know, like take a dog for a walk in the park or wander around the stalls at comic con."

Michael could perceive she was indeed happy but also a yearning for something else. He had experienced this same connection with many people from all walks of life, but with her there was something strange that he had not felt with anyone else. He could not explain it but it was as if a part of her was missing, a hole that had always been with her.

"I can sense there is something else, more you haven't told me.

Rooted all the way to your beginnings." he inquired. He could feel the nausea churn inside him but not fighting the sensation seemed to minimise the discomfort.

"Really, you can sense that! Everything you have seen has been my purpose in life, my unorthodox existence a necessity to help th…….. Where are my manners; here I am telling you personal things about myself when you don't even know my first name. Please call me Emile."

"Well, Emile, life up there is overrated!"

"And it is also running out of time." interjected Egregor Krill, "Perhaps this is a conversation for another day."

Krill led them through the exit onto a promenade that overlooked the entirety of the bio-dome. As Michael walked up to the balcony edge, his jaw dropped at the sight he beheld. The dome stretched for miles in every direction, lit from above by a ceiling of incandescent globes. Each one pouring out artificial light that gave the sense of a warm summer's day. Impressive buildings rose from patches of lush savannah bordered by thriving jungle, architecture that he recognised from Earth. These flat crested step pyramids were different to those he had studied at such archaeological sites as Chichen Itza and Uxmal in Mexico. These were painted in a tirade of vivid colours and decorated with intricate artwork, the limestone structures adorned with carved friezes and roof combs in stone and stucco. Strings of thatched huts lay on the edge of the tree line, each leading out onto a sculpture covered plaza and a high-walled ball court. One common theme seemed to pass through the colourful murals and carved architecture of the society below, the symbolism and imagery of serpents and their tree of life. A huge river rolled through the green savannah providing fresh water to the population and abundant foliage that littered the bio-dome. Agriculture was obviously an important aspect of their lives here; irrigation canals connected raised crop fields and beautiful terraced gardens that grew a multitude of fruit and vegetables. People tended to their growing harvests, children played with each other on the grass as the older men and women sat together smoking carved wooden pipes and weaving baskets. Music and laughter filled the artificial air and the twitter of bird song came from flying creatures as they swooped over the tree tops.

"They are human!" gasped Michael, "So there is life on Mars!"

"Intelligent life, only recently in galactic terms." answered Krill.

"The structural style resembles that of pre-Columbian Americas. The people, they all look so similar."

"Your observations are accurate. Cydonia Mensae is inhabited by races from all corners of the Earth as well as a small Ashtar populace, but the majority of the Cydonian residents are the ancestors of the great Mayan civilisation that once inhabited the South American region of Earth."

"What are they doing here? There has always been heated debate on the fate of the Mayan Civilisation. Somewhere between the eighth and ninth century at the height of the Maya classical period there was a complete cessation of monumental inscriptions and large-scale architectural construction. Around that time all intellectual, artistic, and religious activity ceased throughout a vast portion of their realm. The Maya abandoned most of their cities and mysteriously disappeared. We still have no theory to explain their society's sudden collapse." Michael looked on at the people below, they were still dressed in vibrant traditional cotton garments, their bare skin burnished with paint and ornamented with bone piercings and jade jewelry. For him it was like he had just stepped back in time.

Krill turned from Michael and joined his gaze out across the dome's ecology. "It was eleven hundred and twenty-six years ago in actual fact. Ever since we learnt of the human races' potential, the Ashtar have had a vested interest in your species. Over the millennia we observed a great civilisation develop, while Europe still slumbered in the midst of the dark ages the innovative Maya people had already established astronomy, calendric systems, hieroglyphic writing and an astonishing degree of architectural perfection that you can see beneath us. The Mayan society thrived but their success became their own undoing. Food resources and clean water became scarce and the independent states that had formed over the centuries began to compete for what each other possessed. Civil war erupted and their civilisation was on the brink of destroying all they had endured to create. We gave them a choice. To relocate with us and become the great society they were destined to be, or stay and face inevitable collapse under the weight of their own material greed. Around nine hundred AD the vast majority of the Southern Maya population left their cities on Earth aboard our ships to begin a new era for the Mayan Civilisation. The culture of those that chose to remain slowly dwindled, integrated with other societies until the Maya dynasty existed only in your history books."

"So, they continue to live their traditional lives here in these domes. Unchanged in twelve centuries?" quizzed Michael completely fascinated now.

"They still maintain their traditional customs and way of life, but they do so much more."

"I would like to take a closer look." asked Michael. He had never had the chance to visit the ruins of their civilisation on Earth. He didn't want to miss the opportunity of examining them first hand in pristine condition. Michael had so many questions they could answer.

"There are things we must do first. Perhaps there will be time for that later. Dr. Tesla will you please lead the way."

He followed Emile continuously turning his head back towards the imprint of the past thriving in the most unexpected places. The days of dreaming of stepping back into the footprints of past civilisations and imaging the wonders of their achievements had become a reality. Where before they were mere echoes in the dirt, he had now discovered the boot that had made them.

At the end of the wide promenade they reached a dusty red pathway that disappeared out through the rocky wall. Michael followed the others, stepping onto the path's rubbery material. After they had taken a couple of paces forward the floor beneath them shifted and slowly began to accelerate out through the dark exit. The companions passed through the thick outer layer of bio-dome 1 into an extensive glass tube. Michael looked at his surroundings; he was stood upon conveyor tracks carrying them through a transparent conduit. Just visible over the red planets tawny horizon was another structure. The glass tube seemed to be some kind of protective bridge across the vast distance between it and the dome behind them. Although a cold and dry desert of rust, in Michael's mind it looked spectacular. It was another world and he was looking out over it with his own eyes. Not pictures in a book or grainy video footage beamed back to Nasa. He was actually standing on another planet and the feeling was surreal. Although they had attempted to artificially match the gravity of Earth within the structures, it didn't seem quite right and coupled with the way the light diffracted in Mars's frail atmosphere, it truly felt alien.

"Do you know Mars used to be very much like Earth, lush green lands, oceans teaming with primitive life and an oxygen rich atmosphere." commented Emile.

"So what happened to it?"

"Long ago Mars contained a molten core.", Emile began to explain. "It's spinning motion created a magnetic shield around the planet protecting its delicate atmosphere against the harmful cosmic radiation. When the Earth was still young that core stalled rendering Mars defenceless. The solar winds pummeled the planet, boiling away the atmosphere molecule by molecule. As it thinned the liquid water began to rapidly evaporate. The blanket of gases that retained the heat with its greenhouse effect dwindled away causing the temperature to plunge. The water that remained on the surface turned to ice, increasing Mars reflective albedo and accelerating Mars cold death. You know there is still much water in the form of ice under the dusty surface, especially at the poles. The north polar ice cap is actually the source of water for all of Cydonia."

From the vantage point of the glass conduit Michael could see the tree-like networks of tributaries formed by geological erosion of ancient water that once flowed across Mars. The same channels that astronomers first thought were artificial canals created by the tentacles of little green men before modern science debunked the theory. If only they knew. The conveyor belt had swiftly transported them back towards the main complex of pyramids. They were heading towards a large structure on the outskirts of the Martian city, one that was uniquely formed in comparison to the others within Cydonia Mensae. From what Michael could see it was made up of three towering walls that seemed to enclose something within its centre. The connecting bridge began to dip, taking it on a course underneath the longest of the walls at the section that exhibited an area of curvature. Just before he disappeared under the rusty soil, Michael took one last look out over the red landscape and tried to imagine the world long ago in its prime.

"This place is what the conspiracy theorists lovingly call the fort. But we know it as the shipyards." notified Emile.

"The shipyards!" repeated Michael as the floor beneath him came to a slow halt before an expansive gallery.

"If you thought the view from the bio-dome was jaw dropping then you're in for a treat", Emile motioned Michael to a viewing area.

The place was a hub of activity and Emile was right, the whole scene was something else. The sheer extent of this complex was incredible; he could not see a wall in any direction. Below him thousands of people worked studiously on innumerable crafts all at varying stages of assembly. Many Ashtar intermingled with the human personnel, working together on the metal frames and complex electronic components that crowded the subterranean shipyard. Other areas possessed smelting machines mixing black ore with a glittering metallic powder to produce alloy sheets. The ships were triangular in shape and were constructed from the same pitch-black composite which was more like a solid shadow than any material he had ever seen before. There were two scales of production. One akin to a large fighter jet and the other, impressively, was equivalent to an aircraft carrier although differing slightly in design to its miniature version. Each of the fighters was made up off an isosceles base, two right angled triangles on the sides and an equilateral rear forming a ship profile that gave the appearance of a dark triangle when observed from any angle. The giant carrier vessels were far less numerous than their fighter equivalents, more elongated and flattened out like an angular wing. Michael stood there expressionless, trying to absorb the scope of the undertaking before him when one of the smaller ships hovered up mere metres away, surprising him with its soundless approach. Silently the craft rolled away exposing its underside of four evenly spaced glowing circles that must have been its propulsion system. He watched as it soared upwards towards the ceiling of the vast underground complex. From what Michael was able to see, the roof was comprised of three sections that slotted together, all meeting in the middle of what must have been the interior of the so-called fort walls.

"So this is the cavalry, the ships to fight the Sin?"

"Yes, they will aid in Earths defence." answered Egregor Krill.

"They are the joint Ashtar - Earth Aurora fleet" continued Emile, "The result of hundreds of years of collaboration between the people of Earth, Cydonia Mensae and the Ashtar Co-operative. This project has been funded mainly by COM Twelve's global corporations, their production facilities supplying Cydonia with many of the components and materials developed by my research teams. The design is based on our experimental Aurora bomber, but with the combination of Ashtar knowledge and Cydonian experience we have been able to soup it up with some wonderful Ashtar gadgets. The small one you just saw we call the TEAF fighter and the big ones are the TEAF carriers. Impressive huh!"

"Very!"

Krill stepped in; his voice seemed to carry a conviction he had not heard before. "Michael, you said to me you do not care about anyone on Earth, but there is so much life outside your world, human life too. These people have dedicated their existence towards protecting the people of Earth, never looking for gratitude or reward, only that they will one day be able to save the human race, including you and your daughter. There is a purpose for you here, they need your help."

Michael looked out over the awe-inspiring scene once more. "I need to be with my daughter! Look at this!" Michael threw his arms out towards the thousands of battle ships before him, "You have this, surely with such a fleet you don't need my help, what could I possibly do to make a difference!"

An unknown voice came from behind the trio, "This defence fleet holds a superiority over many a foe, yet to stand it against the might of the Sin Supremacy, is to ask a feather to defy the force of a hurricane."

Michael turned to face the figure behind the voice, "Who is this?"

"This Michael, is the person who can help you."

19 - The Shadow Falls

The once grazing people of Nusima Minus shifted their elongated necks from the lofty branches of the diseased Ickaba fruit trees towards the setting magenta sky. The pitch-black shadows moving above the last remnants of the grazing continent signaled the moment they had feared for centuries. The Sin had finally returned to collect upon the covenant they had agreed upon so long ago. Then their ancestors were faced with the same choice that had been forced upon so so many species before them and as many after. Serve the Sin or be wiped out of existence.

"Soloc are you listening, I need the actuator. If we don't get this finished and send it to the staging continent, we will never make this seasons quota!"

"What does it matter Ethnik?" replied Soloc, a young Nusimareise, in a demoralised demeanor as he flicked stones against their designated work pit wall.

"What does it matter?" repeated Ethnik puzzled, "What do you mean? You know full well why. Everyone has to achieve their quota. We are risking our civilisation if we are left wanting when the Sin return!"

Soloc turned his filthy protracted snout to his friend, "When the Sin return. Listen to yourself, your stalks have been befuddled with the elder stories. If the Sin return, if the Sin actually exist and this is not just a spooky tale to make us toil in the ground everyday making weapons and ships while the elder leaders feast in the Ickaba orchards across the water."

"A fable! You do not mean that?" queried a baffled Ethnik as he placed down his greasy tools on the Ickaba log workbench.

"Ponder my friend. How long ago did these mighty beings send us from grazing lands to these quarries? Wouldn't you of stopped this a hundred years ago, fifty years ago, if you were one of the elder leaders? The mumbles amongst the herd is that the tertiary Ickaba season was blighted with disease. What we make is merely supplies for others to trade for fertiliser and other wares."

"That does not make sense. We've seen the archives of the day they came. The Nusimareis moral code is against all forms of violence, we would not be making weapons, even for others, if we did not have too."

"None of us know the truth do we? We are fed the history from the archives, all we can be sure of is that we build these weapons every day. They train us to use them in the contingency that they might be needed one day. They do not teach us the moral code, do they?"

The weak sound of plodding hoofs came from above them. "We do not teach our old values as given what we ask of you, it would be hypocritical."

"Elder, we did not see you there." spoke Ethnik startled as he looked up to the wooden ramp lodged between the gorge of quarried rock leading into their pit.

"That I could tell." The old Nusimareise's neck swung low almost needing his forelimbs to stop himself tipping over with each step. "Do you doubt the threat we face; the difficult decision we chose?"

Soloc felt rebellious, respect for the elders was something he had lost in the hardship of the construction quarries. "This is more than asking blind service to the wider Nusimareis herd, you expect us to keep our stalks closed to our servitude to the Sin even though to us it feels like a cautionary tale for a foal. How do we know what you and the archives tell us is true? Not just propaganda to keep slave labour. How many seasons have I been told that I must stir myself every dia to work and not stray from my designated pit and underground household. Everything we have been told prevents us from confirming what we have read in the archives. These other worlds that share our dilemma, this lush grazing continent that supposedly doesn't exist anymore. Or this Sin that no one has seen for centuries. We could have evacuated most of Nusima Minus since then if Nusimareis moral code really condemned violence."

"Evacuate. And where would we go young colt?" asked the elder rhetorically as he struggled to descend the bowing ramp. "The worlds in range face the same ultimatum we do. We don't have the technology to seek out any distant worlds that may be free of this curse. What about those who would undoubtedly have to remain behind?"

Soloc let out an irksome bray.

"These others in our planetary system, couldn't one of them have more advanced technology." added Ethnik.

"The rules set by the Sin were very clear. I was a colt around your age when they came. The archives do not give justice to that fateful day and why we appear so harsh with you." The elder took a seat on a rudimentary Ickaba stool to recount that moment.

"On a sun filled dia typical of the tertiary Ickaba season on Nusima, I foraged with our inhabitants through the bountiful orchards of the central grazing continent. Very much the splendid bliss you have seen in the archives, but what you don't see is the exquisite smell that was infused on the breeze. Not the soured whiff you may catch amongst the industrial gases today. An alien envoy from a nearby world had just arrived with a gift of a fertiliser that would double the yield of our flora. We were to give our friends a cargo of our Ickaba fruit when the Sin entered our cluster of systems in a handful of their vastly superior warships two hundred and twenty years ago. They immediately made a course for the most advanced race in our planetary cluster, one that was revered by us and our neighbours for their technological advancement and guiding role to all our development, especially in space exploration. No choice was given to them; their strength meant nothing as every last one of them was terminated swiftly. No shred of mercy was shown as defenceless craft trying to escape were blown out of the sky. The stump wrinkling death shrieks still haunt me today. We and the others were fully aware of the demise of our neighbouring civilisation, the Sin made sure of that, it was projected against our once unblemished skies. The unknown foe then left their massacre and headed for each of the inhabited worlds and announced to them all;

'We are the Sin, the absolute power in this galaxy, and we bring you a singular truth. You will serve under the Sin Supremacy or face complete annihilation. From this pivotal moment onwards your existence as a civilisation has one solitary meaning, you will divert all your resources to the construction of a grand army, adorn them with tools of destruction and carriages of war to carry them into battle. Communication between you and your neighbouring civilisations will cease immediately, your only concern now lies at your own gates. When all cower beneath the shadow, we the Sin will return and on that glorious day your fate will be judged. Heed our warning, be under no illusions, we will return, prepare well or armageddon will fall swiftly upon you. Transmit your servitude now!'

One by one, our leaders and the representatives of the other worlds relayed their surrender and subjugation to the Sin as part of the Sin Supremacy. The total planetary destruction we all had just witnessed had left us with no alternative."

The elder's strength seemed to leave him as he relived the memory. Needing to rest his chin on a wooden prop staff that he carried with him. "So we can be sure that any collaboration will bring severe punishment when they return."

"Well then, I wish they would hurry up and return. What we have is no existence. At least with the Sin we would see a different life outside this depressing pit!" neighed Soloc with tired sincerity.

"But as part of an army." responded the elder dismayed at the mindset of the naive colt.

"What do they really need us for. What is our role to be? If the archives are correct, then you see their power. We would probably just have to patrol this area, threaten a few nameless aliens in the name of the Sin." offered Ethnik with conjecture.

"And what if it is more? Do you invite that so eagerly?" countered the elder.

"Anyway, what do we care if we have to kill others for us to survive, we have spent our lives building weapons with the training to use them, at least we would fulfill a purpose to all this." stated Soloc as he swung his lengthy neck to emphasise the dirty circular pit of excavated rock and fabricated machinery.

The elder could not hold back the sorrow in his voice, "The Nusimareis have lived a peaceful existence for millennia, violence goes against our very morale fibre."

"You live in the past. This is our lives now; it has been for generations. You expect us to commit our lives to war but still expect us to embrace the values of a long dead existence! Those are your values, not mine. I despair of this life I am forced to live, at least there might even be some excitement outside these desolate lands!" continued Soloc with real veracity.

"You fool; you don't know what you are saying!" the elder's grief turned to anger as much at himself as it was towards the colt's ignorance. They had focused so much energy towards driving their people in efforts to appease the Sin that they had utterly changed the ideology of those whom knew nothing of a time before they came.

"Well then we must all be fools! There are so many amongst our herd who think the same way. I have dreamt of our common thoughts. Swapping servitude of cowards for a galactic supremacy, swapping our suffering for those of others, can only be a better life."

Just as Soloc retorted, sirens of the world alarm wailed around them.

"Another drill again." sighed Ethnik, almost in relief at the interjection, but also annoyed due to the time each one took to complete. "Hold on, does this one sound weird to anyone else?"

"I'm so so sorry" breathed the elder as he looked at the young colt's through moistened stalks, "That is not a drill. I had hoped more than anything you would not have to see this day, but we must go now."

Soloc just smiled as he trotted up the ramp, "Finally."

For over two hundred years the Nusimareis had manufactured vessels of war, enormous expanses of their lands had become desolate, quarried for much needed resources. Where endless orchards once grew, was now home to the staging grounds of weaponry and ships, any remaining flora diseased and choking in the effluent air. Grazing land and living space became increasingly rare but they dared not slow or stop their preparations, instead moving to the claustrophobic confines of life underground and only inhabiting the surface to work and feed. There was no longer education or occupations outside war, the identity of the society they once were, was forever lost.

Now the dreaded moment had come, what they had sacrificed it all for. The same handful of Sin warships that had stood as a warning in their archives now hovered imperiously above their polluted atmosphere. A message filled every communication device around the planet. An overbearing voice echoed in every auditory stump,

'The Sin have returned, prepare for judgement!'

The people of Nusima were in a state of shock, but they had rehearsed this moment more times than they could remember and although their thoughts were chaotic or paralysed in fear, their actions remained instinctively automated. They all understood well the consequences of failure. The canter of hind hoofs rumbled in the air as each inhabitant immediately made their way to their nearest war facility, only the very young or old exempt from these regulations. The elder leaders of the Nusimareis were confident that their efforts would be satisfactory. For after all the preparations had been made, seventy-five per cent of the planets total population were armed and with more than enough spacecraft to carry them to wherever they were told to go.

After a terrifying wait their answer came as all planetary communication devices became active, 'You are alive! Therefore you have passed judgement. Rendezvous at the following coordinates immediately. You are about to be tested.'

In the haze of industrial gases, a billion ocular stalks saw their future, and the only choice that gave them one, rise into the polluted air. Those left behind watched as their cherished herds launched somewhere in the plethora of metal and burning rocket fuel. The apprehensive militia broke free from the gravity of the unrecognisable world below, a once beautiful vista now smothered in filth. They were met at the rendezvous point by the other civilisations that had created equally impressive fleets. The Sin opened communications to the new additions to their Supremacy.

'Not all have followed our simple command; there are still non-believers whom our warning seems to have fallen on deaf ears!'

The Nusimareis suddenly realised where the coordinates had brought them, they were above the world of their neighbours, the same people whose envoy came to their planet so long ago with a gift of friendship.

'You are all now under the servitude of the Sin. Our first decree is a lesson to all those that fail us. Descend to the planet, judgement has been made and punishment clear, destroy every last life form! If any of you do not comply, your own civilisation will be obliterated as forfeit.'

"Ethnik, let's go." prompted Soloc seemingly desensitised to the moral significance of their test.

"These were friends of the Nusimareis. They are no threat to anyone." he replied as moisture seeped at the tip of his stalks. His fore pads paralysed on the vessel controls.

As Ethnik paused he turned on the communications from the still beautiful world below, one that could have been reminiscent of his home a few hundred years ago.

'We beg you, don't do this. We gave ourselves to your servitude. We did as you commanded but you never returned. We thought you had forgotten about us. We will immediately comply; we just need more time.'

As the unanswered message of forgiveness repeated, Soloc hooted, "You heard the Sin. We need to do it now. We don't know this voice, yet we know it will be us and the Nusimareis herd that will be forfeit if we don't. This is our life now, our purpose since we were birthed. It was our leaders who chose the death of others for our survival. This is who we are, accept it Ethnik."

The controls creaked forward, "Soloc, power up the weapons." asked Ethnik in a broken voice.

After all that was left of the punished world was burning ruins, many of the armada returned from its test with a heavy heart full of pain and remorse. Forced to perform atrocities that would live on in their memory forever. Those that held on to a culture before the Sin, broke down, some cried and others prayed to their higher powers, but it didn't matter, the will of the Sin was done. But there were many also that embraced a new chapter in their existence, eager for meaning and an excited trepidation away from mundane repeatability. Living in the shadow of the Sin had dimmed all concepts of morality.

'You have passed your trial of fire, now we bestow upon you the honour of your place under the shadow of the Sin Supremacy.'

Infinitesimal voids burst into circles of spiraling darkness as scores of wormholes blocked out the stars. The Sin Warships lead the way as the Nusimareis followed through the circles of twisted space. A split second later they were in the dominion of the Sin; it wasn't until that moment that they understood the insignificance of their place in the Supremacy. The entire combined might of the new fleets, two hundred years in the making were but a tiny cog in what was the Sin Supremacy's war machine. Now they knew the face of doom.

A cold voice boomed in the ears of all the souls within the Sin Supremacy fleet:

'I the Witch of Endor command you, go forth, bring terror and death to those who do not succumb to the will of the Sin.'

20 - Illumination

January 1985

The Pindar slowly paced the periphery of his expansive and opulent study. Every piece of furniture and décor a representation of the most exquisite craftsmanship and exuberance of artistry that riches could buy. Yet as he walked palms outstretched, he was only interested in a few very specific objects that he had chosen as his inspiration. These were not extravagant creations, master pieces of art or the wealth of precious jewels, these were symbols of momentous moves on a historical chessboard. Now there were only a conceivable number more before they made a move of checkmate on humanity.

He stopped briefly as he passed each one, his touch absorbing their aura, letting their power fill him with dreams of a New World Order. As the newly appointed head of the Thirteen families he would be the most powerful man on Earth, a puppet master with presidents, royalty, the greatest intellects and richest persons, a billion minds all willingly controlled at the ends of his strings.

"You seem to have an infatuation with symbols of war." announced one of his guests impatiently scratching upon his table.

He closed his eyes and allowed himself one last moment to breath in the compendium of their success, the chronological series of events that had brought him to this crossroad, another pivotal moment in their history and one that he would lead them into. The Pindar smiled amusingly and turned his attention to the five men sat at the large stone slab in the centre of his study. It was yellow quartzite engraved extensively with hieroglyphics. *Such narrow minds devoid of appreciation and ignorant in their perceptions. Do they even realise they sit at the cover of a three-thousand-year-old Egyptian sarcophagus.*

"War." the Pindar contemplated. "When there is something you can't have, but want it bad enough, you take it by force. You can say that each of these treasures represents a past war of some kind, won or lost... But you couldn't be more wrong. This is no infatuation with war, it's an appreciation of how we have guided the path of history. For what is the actual purpose of war?.. It just drags the attention away from the real battle happening behind the trenches."

There was a laugh from the same guest before he proceeded to light up a cigarette. "War is about destroying enemies, plain and simple. Any other objective is just propaganda."

The Pindar stared at MJ-4. His intense glare combined with his pallid and desiccated face usually brought uneasiness to the eyes of the beholder. If that didn't then his notability did, but these men seemed unperturbed as if they were his equal. They didn't know him yet, but they would learn quick enough. He tempered his disdain and smiled with the intellectual challenge. "It's not about destroying or conquering those that are deemed enemies. War is a means of forming alliances, amalgamating differences into consistent visions and instilling a belief that your ideals are the correct ones. It's about embracing your foes and guiding them in the direction you need."

"Well we are at war now. Granted, not one with direct military conflict, but one that will only end when we defeat our enemy, not make friends." questioned another guest. A man in his seventies, wearing large spectacles, bald on top with grey hair around the sides.

The Pindar turned his unnerving gaze to his other guest, "MJ One. The end of a war means nothing. It only allows another to begin under a different guise. As the Director of the CIA, I expected you would appreciate the intricate covert games being played out. You personally lifted restrictions on the CIA directly influencing the foreign affairs of countries relevant to American Policy. Are you not impressing American ideals and vision upon allies and rivals for a common goal?"

"Of course, but let's be clear. That's not about spreading democracy. It's about ensuring the national security of the US. Our involvement and drive for control in these countries means that when it comes to the inevitability of war, particularly with the Soviet Union, we are in a better position to destroy those threats."

"Then you expect to grow the power gap between America and the world by reducing everyone else's?"

"The victor gets the spoils of war." added MJ-4.

"I believe the ones who truly benefit are those on neither side." countered the Pindar, "Our view is not so shortsighted. We are not waging a war to destroy our enemies. For is it not better to control the enemies we already know?", he paused to let that important statement sink in, "There is an undeniable truth that persists with your view, and that is the fact that new enemies will always be born from any vacuum of power. With that enlightenment you can argue, is it not the human race who is our eternal enemy?... I really see us as saving the human race from themselves."

"I think your view on war and your nobility is imaginative fancy. The history books are clear on the causes and consequences of the countless wars that have been fought." replied an unconvinced MJ-2.

"The history books are just stories of half-truths for the masses. People like us are part of the hidden chapters. Without doubt, what we have already accomplished together has defined the courses of history, yet we have so much more that we can achieve. Let us lift the power and glory of America high above all others rather than profit from the stagnation of those others." The Pindar placed his palms on the cold sarcophagus top and stooped in closer towards the five men. "To move forward under a new agreement, it is of my opinion that we need to usher in an era of honesty and transparency between us."

"You mean like when we found out about your so-called Masters hidden in the basements of Groom Lake." commented MJ-1 with a large dose of sarcasm.

"Quite, that altercation in seventy-eight is a misunderstanding we want to avoid a repeat of." responded the Pindar, hiding his contempt for their lack of respect towards him.

"Or like your failure to reveal the extent of your activities on our citizens at this very moment? We seem to be covering up your brazen actions on an increasingly regular basis." added MJ-5 adjusting his plain round spectacles. A timid looking man in his late forties with a black moustache and a mound of frizzy receding hair.

"That is not a misunderstanding, just we lack the official framework with which to collaborate in. This agreement will correct that." He stepped back from the stone table and slowly paced towards his curving bay window, ornately inset with the stained glass of serpent imagery.

"Then let me begin." MJ-1 pulled the drafted agreement from his briefcase, boldly typed on the front page was 'Project PLATO'.

"The first point is that MAJI will need to ratify any number, as well as review the list of US citizens for conditioning." commenced MJ-4.

"I think we can agree on that." confirmed the Pindar looking out on his Bavarian estate.

MJ-4 continued, "To monitor and enforce that, we will actively manage the retrieval of the list."

"So be it. But timelines are of the utmost importance here."

"We can replicate what seems to be your current requirements." MJ-4 suggested as he lit up another cigarette between his leathery and nicotine stained fingers.

"I'm afraid, there is a need for expedition there."

The MAJI representatives looked to each other with gestures of affirmation, "Very well we can accommodate that." authorised MJ-1.

"Excellent." The Pindar maintained an illusion of satisfaction although his superior ancestral blood boiled as he watched MJ-4 stub out his old cigarette within a chiseled hieroglyph.

MJ-5 barely noticed the red of swelling blood vessels beneath the Pindar's sallow flaking skin. "Right, the next point. Those restricted levels within our shared facilities, now we want access to them."

The Pindar turned his head from his study window, "Mmhh, I see."

"Not only that, we expect visibility to any work being done in them and to be party to any benefits associated with it." furthered MJ-5.

The Pindar paused as if this was a hard decision and a big point to concede on. But the Masters had already defined the parameters they desired and so far, MAJI's requests had been entirely anticipated.

"Considering the importance of moving forward with this agreement, we can only approve this under the following conditions. We will open up these previously restricted levels, but the Masters will have full control and authority over anyone within those levels. They are very serious about their secrecy, that is why only us and our JASON Scholars currently have access."

"So are we." responded MJ-2, a lieutenant general in the military going by his attire, "Only the MAJI control group, a select few scientists and on a need to know basis, personnel with Aquarius clearance will be permitted to those restricted areas."

The Pindar let out a sigh, "Ok then, then we are in agreement. But let me be clear, there will naturally be some sections that no outsider will have access to. This includes myself. This is non-negotiable."

"What happened to your words of full transparency?" criticised MJ-1, "Do they have more to hide from us?"

The Pindar smiled in a show of innocent amusement, "This is not a question of concealing secrets. Let me turn the tables on you. Would you let the Masters have freedom of the White House's oval office or welcome them into your homes? Because it is exactly that, you would be asking of them."

There was silence.

"No, I think not. To stereotype their mentality as you would any foreign facet of society would be a mistake. Even more so, to taint them with the motives of humanity does them a great disservice."

"Well this is the issue we have, your so-called Masters, we still know next to nothing about them or their intentions." highlighted MJ-1.

"What is important is that we speak with their voice."

"Well that would be stating the obvious, you call them Masters." gibed MJ-1.

The insinuation of their diminished status irritated him greatly. A feeling that made his dry skin itch in anger. "It is so much more than that. We share a connection going back to the dawn of civilisation when times were simpler, when the demands and dangers of our world paled in comparison to the one we live in now... Now we have a cataclysmic population explosion, our natural resources and habitats are dwindling, climate warming and mutually assured destruction."

"So what of these, they live underground." said MJ-4 dismissively.

"We inhabit such a small area of the Earth, what happens when the world starts looking deeper to solve the problems of the surface and to satisfy human greed?"

"Hypocrisy, you are the embodiment of human greed." called out MJ-1.

"Wrong again." snapped back the Pindar as he scratched at the aggravated skin of his neck, "It is not greed that drives our aspirations for wealth. It is the categorical fact of control that comes with it. We have already accumulated enough money to secure a future of extravagancy a hundred lifetimes over. Without a check on the currency of greed, the global population will devastate this planet."

The Cult of the Serpent's business interests and worth were clearly extensive. What small fraction the MAJI representatives were aware off certainly pointed to the fact that the Pindar was truthful in his statement.

The lack of further argumentative responses allowed the Pindar to refocus his thoughts, "The Masters interest in global affairs is simply about safeguarding their future." He gave each of his guests an earnest glance, "Do we all not share the same goals?"

There seemed to be a consensus moment of contemplation in the room.

"What do the Masters activities have to do with MAJI's goals?" inquired the previously quiet MJ-3.

"The detail will become apparent upon the signing of the agreement. But like everything we are doing, the national security of America will be solidified and the world's population will ultimately benefit as a consequence."

"Ok. So to make sure I've not misunderstood what you've said, please could you be particularly clear, what is this goal that we all share?"

"To control our destiny." clarified the Pindar, "Our interpretation of the end state may differ, but fundamentally the way we are all going to achieve it is exactly the same."

"Really, then I'd like to hear how we are going to do this." requested MJ-1.

"Us enlightened few realised long ago that a singular governance supported by the world's population is what will really destroy the concept of enemies."

"An impossible pipedream." dismissed MJ-2.

"Do you expect America to conquer the world for you?" added MJ-4 with satire.

"I shall repeat myself; war is just a distraction while we battle for what we really want."

"And what does the Cult of the Serpent really want? In the spirit of honesty and transparency of course." asked MJ-1 cynically.

"Simply put. A New World Order. We have always collaborated to do what was best for the national security and the policies of the United States of America. Yes, a significant motivation on your part has been to keep America technologically superior to all other nations, but that is far less important than the bigger picture we are painting together… That is to spread democracy and capitalism, an overwhelming belief in the notion of liberty, and to instill the idea of the US constitution's greatness as the foundation of international law… But why would that help the Cult of the Serpent? Of course, it serves our business interests and our wealth grows exponentially in return. But as I have said, it is all about control. Manipulation of the world's economy, politics and media, each action a play in consolidating power, level upon level, a growing pyramid of control that stops with us. And you will ask what is America's place in this? Yes, we are here in Germany because it is my home, but our seat of power lies with the US, it will be the guiding example that all others aspire to. We embrace its constitution and its ideals which we believe should be the umbrella that all the people of the world live under."

"Never mind the world, what makes you more qualified to govern America under a US constitution than the US government?" stated MJ-2.

"MJ Two is right. Fine if you want to rule the world, as long as you keep them out of our business and under the control that you preach. We only care about America's future. There can be no agreement where the sovereignty of the US is not assured. We will run our own affairs and we will only maintain our mutual partnership where it benefits us." emphasised MJ-1.

The Pindar could not abstain the amused chuckle, "The United States of America would remain as free as it always has."

"What do you mean by that?" MJ-1 responded with offence.

He had proposed that transparency would be their way forward in a successful partnership, he had had enough of their disrespect born out of ignorance. Now it was time to bestow the power of truth, and the truth of their power.

"For the ultimate intelligence agency, you are still blind to the realities of the world and the history that shaped it. The United States and the world are on the path we have persuaded it to take. So before we continue discussing the finer details of the agreement, I insist you indulge me with a game of enlightenment. It may give you a better perspective of where you really stand in the big picture."

The MAJI representatives nodded in agreement. "Please illuminate us." confirmed MJ-1 with a sarcasm that barely masked the seed of concern.

"Excellent. Then I ask each of you to look around this room, at the objects displayed and pick one of these so-called symbols of war, and I will tell you what they symbolise to me and what they represent for the Cult of the Serpent. How about you go first MJ One."

He somewhat grudgingly looked around the multitude of objects and artifacts presented in splendor upon their lavish pedestals, "That Gun."

"Wise choice, very apt… The musket of Ulysses S. Grant, at the time the commanding general of the Union army during the American Civil war. A war not between enemies but differing ideals. An internal conflict that resulted in the removal of Confederate nationalism, support for unbridled industrial expansion and the abolishment of slavery. We freed the few to lay the foundations for a day when everyone would become slaves, but only of another type... To me it was the culmination of a United States that we had conceived as we first started growing our power base in North America, right back as the founding fathers."

"As the founding fathers!" scoffed MJ-2.

"You sound surprised MJ Two." replied the Pindar with a new smugness, "You all knew our history had gone back centuries at least... What, did you think that our past was mere affiliation or genetic linkage in a family tree of conjecture. Our solitary goal and its blueprint of implementation has always been passed down through our bloodline, an inheritance and destiny we all embrace, that no amount of time can dilute... The Founding Fathers of the United States were individuals from the Thirteen British Colonies." the Pindar watched the cogs of comprehension turn in the faces of his guests, "Are you now making the connection?... Merely another mask for the Thirteen ruling families of the Cult of the Serpent that you know well. It will be their signatures that you look for at the end of this meeting."

They knew the Cult's influence was strong in the US, but they never imagined they were a fundamental part of the countries origin and so deeply engrained in the ideologies that MAJI was trying to protect.

The Pindar continued, "We saw its vast potential and resources as a power base for our goals. There was no enemy to destroy, but it was a country of disparate voices and principles, one whose vision we consolidated at the end of a musket."

The silence spoke a thousand words.

"Perhaps you MJ Five?"

"The Sword over there." MJ-5 pointed out somewhat muted.

The Pindar walked over to the iron blade with a new bravado. He thrived on this type of edification. He held his outstretched fingers over the red leather handle and single-handed cruciform hilt as if to pay it a deserved homage. After a short pause the Pindar picked up the engraved knightly sword and held it aloft, "A sword that belonged to Bohemond of Taranto, a leader in the first crusade. The inscription says 'In nomine Domini' translated from Latin it means 'In the name of the Lord'. These crusades were not just about gaining a religious, political or territorial advantage. It was very much an ongoing initiative to reopen the Mediterranean to commerce and travel and to consolidate the Latin Church under one papal leadership. The start of our European colonialism... There were many crusades, some more important than others, but each time one thing remained consistent, thousands willingly laid down their lives at the sword for a justified belief that had been instilled within them...It represents to me one very mighty truth of human society, that the masses can justify and perform any act if given the right persuasion and belief, even if that belief is based on falsity... It is just another form of mind control but of a voluntary nature, an effective tool in that era where we were known as the Venetian Black Nobility."

"That eagle, the statue of our national bird." indicated MJ-3 straightaway without prompting.

"The symbol of heraldry for a great empire. Yes, the latest iteration of its capital of power lies within the US, but let us ride it's wings backwards in time. The Reichsadler of Nazi Germany, the eagle of the Byzantine Empire, the Aquila of the Roman Empire, classical Greece's eagle of Zeus and the Serekh of ancient Egypt. We have been the provocateur behind the world's greatest empires and we have heralded our seat of power in the archives of history. Let it serve as a reminder not to underestimate our reach and lineage of power."

"And let me serve a reminder too." responded MJ-4 boldly as he continued to chain smoke, "All those empires eventually fell, got conquered by superior enemies, leaders defeated or their ideals failed!"

"Yes absolutely!" the Pindar did not take the bait of provocation, "All part of a meticulous plan. A visible totalitarianism or a ruling plutocracy does not last for long in our world. It will always be surpassed by another, we have all learnt this many times over, be it the past or the present. So, we instigate each's demise at a time when we decide benefits our New World Order the most. It is not a misstep but a regional power change we have orchestrated. And let me rid you of any persistent thought of our failures and reaffirm the example of our heraldry. It was the Crusades that spelled the end of the Byzantine Empire, the Roman Empire that absorbed ancient Egyptian civilisation and the US might that defeated Nazi Germany."

MJ-4 blew out a large cloud of smoke, "Then don't let me detract further from this lesson. What about this book, seems symbolically indistinct." he nodded to the fairly modern hardcover perched beside him on a neoclassical jardinière of ebonised and gilded metal.

The Pindar grinned, "An appropriate selection to follow on from my last words. A mere book but the biggest paradigm of war in recent history. That MJ Four is the original copy of Mein Kampf by a certain Adolf Hitler. World War two was not just the greatest global conflict of our time but to me this represents the aftermath of our grandest play. The repercussions of the fallout were far reaching. The social structure of the new world birthed the United Nations that we conceived, geopolitically the great European powers such as the British Empire waned, allowing the US to take its place as an undisputed superpower along with Russia. Economically, western Europe and Japan were rebuilt through the American Marshall plan. In doing so, we rebuilt our garnered allies and enemies in the image of American ideals, the ideals of the Cult of the Serpent... But why this book with such a luxury of emblematic choices to choose from? Hitler's main thesis reflected his hatred of Jewish peril, the conspiracy to gain world leadership, yet paradoxically his strong beliefs did more to forge a New World Order than he could have ever imagined."

He delicately opened the autobiography to the bookmarked page, 'Chapter 11, Propaganda and Organisation', "To surmise, for me, the great war was about sacrificing the few to make the world's majority act together in our benefit."

"Ok, I think you've made your point Pindar." conceded MJ-1, interrupting the gambit of one-upmanship, "If what you've said is not just creative intimidation, it still doesn't change the fact that our only concern remains the United States of America. You made it plainly clear that it's the key, so our question is, when are you going to have an object so affectionately displayed that benefits MAJI and America directly now?"

MJ-2 stood up waving the project PLATO document, "Despite your, I suspect, threat. Why should we sign this agreement?"

The yellowing eyes of the Pindar seemed to momentarily glow red as his capillaries swelled under his intense glare, "No, not a threat at all. Just a history lesson MJ Two. You evolve with us or become a relic of inexorable change." His tone seemed to belie his words, a vocal undercurrent that MJ-2 appeared to sense as he quickly sat back down noticeably subdued.

"I feel I need to clarify my words once more. To the Masters you are the path of least resistance, but the destination is far more important to us than the journey there. We will achieve our goals and yours by proxy. Then it is up to you to decide where you want yourselves and America in that inevitable reality."

"So we go round in a circle to my original question." responded MJ-1.

"Then, you see up there?" The Pindar pointed to an empty frame on the wall."

"You mean next to that hideous painting." commented MJ-4.

"You mean the Botticelli's master piece, the Chart of Hell from Dante's Inferno. That could so easily be a representation of the world that lives upon the surface, if we had not tempered and guided humankind's urges and natural state." the Pindar suggested as he looked up to the small inverted pyramidal mound that depicted the levels of Hell.

"Which is?" inquired MJ-4.

"Chaos and domination. Just look to the places where international law has little regard. The US constitution and capitalism is a blanket to quell and control this."

"Well we all have one big obstacle in our way, don't we!" declared MJ-1.

"Indeed… What I hope to have exhibited there very soon is a flag adorned by a hammer and sickle within a red star. The symbol of the Soviet Union and communism."

"And how will you help us win this Cold War without destroying the enemy as you've said?" MJ-4 queried further.

"We will not defeat them, only rise above them. Another super power and communism represent a challenge to a singular rule, they must fall and they will... In the aftermath, the success of our ideals and the power held by association will shine like a beacon to all nations to come together in unity." The Pindar walked around the seated men as he spoke.

MJ-1 turned to the Pindar as he paced towards him, "And how

will you do this?"

"As part of our agreement." The Pindar pointed to the bound papers on the sarcophagus lid, "The Cult of the Serpent promise we will implode the Soviet economy. It will collapse as we collapse world oil prices and thus diminishing their biggest natural resource."

"Right, but..." MJ-3 rose his hand as if in school classroom, "Surely that will make them more desperate and offensive to protect their interests?"

"To be offensive would be expensive, most likely lead to war, and a war that could only end in mutual destruction. No, it will be played by political intellect and economical manipulation. We are in no doubt that this will result in the US rising above Russia, leaving it a broken and struggling country whose territory and influence will diminish as the instability in the western block grows under anti-communist activism and regional nationalism."

"You think their leaders will just roll over like weak dogs. Because of a bit of debt and the hard time experienced by their people. These same leaders that brought us to the brink of nuclear war just to put missiles in Cuba." stated MJ-3.

"You are an economist are you not?" The Pindar knew much of him from the Thirteen families' significant involvement in their conceived Council of Foreign Relations and G30. He was someone they had kept an eye on very closely as a person who could greatly assist in their cause.

MJ-3 nodded in confirmation. The man was smartly suited and tidily presented with large rimmed glasses and hair held in a side parting by plenty of product.

"The Soviet Union has sixty-six billion dollars of external debt that must be serviced, most of it owed to our business interests. They barely possess any remaining reserves and this space race that Reagan has initiated, they struggle to keep up with it. I infer that they need to find an immediate and suitable way out of this."

"A political deal." MJ-3 muttered with a sense of agreement.

"Correct. The best weapon to broker peace is to have two leaders that share the same beliefs. We have been cultivating and supporting a new leader through our business interests, someone who will dissolve the Soviet Union. Our marked one will bring forth policies of openness and restructuring, glasnost and perestroika in his words. The Soviet Republics will begin to resist the central control and force their independence. When the inevitable happens then we will be there to take them into our globalisation plan within the UN."

"Do you mean…?"

"Yes MJ Three." interrupted the Pindar smugly, "As a start, our marked one and the president will be meeting in Geneva this November."

The present MAJI control group exchanged looks of surprise at their infiltration of influence into Soviet politics.

"Even so, when the Soviet Union and its communist ideals have all but decayed to nothingness, emergent threats to the US national security, as well as to our New World Order, will continue to persist. There will be many more battles until the real war is won."

"Then please may I ask. How do you intend to end this real war?" requested MJ-1 in contemplation.

"Quite simply, one hundred per cent control of the world's population." The Pindar announced knowing full well such claims would be met with their doubt.

"Because that will work. Everything we are trying to protect about our country is the exact opposite of that. We and others across the world have fought and died for what us American's have." MJ-1 pointed out, not in argument but a statement of contradictory fact.

The Pindar made his way back to his favourite spot in his study, the extensive bay window that looked out onto the visage of rolling hills, the autumn kaleidoscope of encroaching forests, snowcapped peaks and a turquoise lake. From this lofty position he truly felt like he was the ruler of the world. "And this is why it will work. What they have fought and died for will be their leash of control. They will never know they are being ruled. Just see a world of growing collaboration, peace and prosperity. Yet no nation, organisation or business will do anything that is not of our wishes." he explained with hauteur.

"All well and good within the international community. What about those that fall outside of that, not everyone follows the will of the world majority. What about, rebels, radicals, terrorists. You cannot protect against the threat of free will!" attested MJ-4.

"Can we not?" the Pindar smiled insinuatingly, "We even hope, that with your partnership, to take this oversight right down to each and every individual of humanity. Our New World Order will usher in an era where we will have no more enemies and no threat will ever bear fruition."

"These are grand dreams." commented MJ-1, the seeds of doubt were still loosely planted in his mind, yet he was far from ready to dismiss their claims or put a limit on what this Illuminati could achieve.

The Pindar did not turn his gaze but continued to survey the domain of magnificent beauty he now owned. Once that thought was a mere dream, but like every dream he and the Thirteen families had ever conceived, only time stood between it and its fulfillment.

"Some would say ensuring the national security of the United States is a grand dream, one forever out of reach. But have I not shown you what the Cult of the Serpent has been able to achieve alone. We have given you the support of our JASON society, they are the greatest minds in America. Have you not reaped the benefit of their knowledge and the advanced technology we have gifted? Can you not see the real possibility of what we can achieve together? What we have shared is only the tip of the iceberg, one that this agreement will uncover."

"Ok, ok." lamented MJ-1 in concession, "I think we have a good idea of what America can get out of this in the long term. But in return for our continued support of your activities, aside from what we have already expanded on. We want to see the demise of the Soviet Union, but in the short term."

"Within six years. Is that short term enough?" The Pindar closed his eyes and allowed himself to bath in the weak rays of light flooding through his bay window. Even though the UV stung his pale skin, it was buried beneath the satisfaction that he had emphatically won this intellectual challenge.

The MAJI control group each confirmed their acceptance to MJ-1.

"That would be acceptable."

"Excellent. Then let us sign this agreement and usher in your land of the free, but the world of slaves."

21 - The Shining One

The voice came from a figure dressed in long black flowing robes covered by a concealing cloak. What little could be seen of the individual's body appeared to be made from solid glass. The features that were visible radiated a glow similar to a weak light bulb. The face partially hidden by a loose hood was human and masculine in nature, its smooth surface hairless and devoid of any defining characteristics.

"Elyon, you have returned. Your timing is most welcome." greeted Krill.

"Bless you Egregor Krill. Yet my return a long time past and a bearer of less foreboding tidings, is a wish I could not grant. May I converse with Michael?" asked Elyon, his voice so soft it could have come from a child.

"Of course. Dr. Tesla and I were about to inspect the preparations."

"Emile, a warmth flows within to be once more in your presence."

"Who are you!" interrupted Michael with impatience.

Krill answered, "This is Elyon of the Elohim."

"Michael, there are words that must be said." offered Elyon. The stranger waited in silence for the others to leave before turning on his heel and gliding off. "Please follow me."

Michael walked after him along the length of the promenade. Elyon's footsteps gave no hint of noise even though his feet were

193

bare and looked solid. What was more bizarre, and he wasn't sure if it was just his imagination, but he swore a sound emanated from Elyon as he moved, like wind blowing over a crystal glass, very quiet but audible.

"Where are we going?"

"To the watch tower." was his short answer.

"Why?"

"The view."

"What's there to see?"

"Knowledge.", he carried on walking, restraining from conversation.

At the far end of the viewing gallery was a thin column of rock with a transparent compartment at its base. They stepped into it, the door closed behind and it slowly began to rise along the columns red surface and through the thickness of the ceiling. Soon the elevator had ascended high above the fort walls providing a panoramic view of the whole Cydonia region. Gazing down from such an altitude gave Michael a respectful appreciation of the varied and magnificent terrain that Mars possessed. When they had reached what he guessed to be over a mile up, the elevator came to a stop. The column had not increased in width over the whole vertical distance, this was an amazing feat of engineering, considering the two hundred mile an hour dust storms that buffeted the area regularly. Michael wasn't surprised he had never noticed the watch tower upon his initial approach; it was like a piece of thread compared to the colossal extent of the fort walls. Above him was a Frisbee shaped structure and with a diameter of about forty metres it looked like it was balanced precariously upon the apex of the slender column. The roof of the elevator slid across and its base rose, pushing them both through an opening in the circular building of rusty stone.

They now stood inside a wide rounded room, walled by rows upon rows of crystal objects. Each one varied in its design and colour, from a rainbow infused cube to a rich ruby skull. The only other fixture that occupied the room was a single glass globe stationed at the exact centre of the dusty floor. The globe rested upon a column of crooked Martian rock and appeared to contain a hazy rolling fog.

"So, Krill said you can help me get rid of these so-called abilities?" Elyon had not said a word throughout the majority of the journey here and Michael decided he would now break that silence.

"I hear as the mountain of your power ever grows, you do not sit atop the rising peak, only find yourself in a deeper valley of grief. Enlighten me, as you became unbounded by the influence of the Earth and soared into the boundlessness of space, have these woes surfaced?" asked Elyon.

"No. But then I cannot control it!"

"Then enlighten you I shall. The drumfire of anger, guilt and fear have been muffled with the distraction of possibility, that of hope conceived from an egg of futility. No longer are you confined by the perception of your reality, but now glimpse through the eyes of a child newly born."

"You make no sense."

"My words illustrate all facets of my meaning. Misunderstanding is but blindness in the eye of perception. Your abilities are suppressed, if only momentarily."

"Then take them away!"

"Michael, such gifts cannot be ostracised. Does one cut off their head if spitefully it speaks? No, one would strive to command will over their tongue."

"You believe these are gifts!!!" he snapped back in retort.

The sound of rattling echoed through the room as the stone shelves crammed with crystals began to shake.

"Yes." Elyon replied resolutely.

"Please take them." Michael pleaded now.

"Alas. My compassion fails not. They are an essence that permeates every strand of your being, there is no distinction that can be cut away. Yet the diadem of control is an offer I can endow."

"How?" he swallowed despairingly.

"How angers anthem drowns all music but its own. Anchor your being to an instant of absolute happiness, let burdens of your heart evaporate in each exhale. Close those windows to a universe of resentment and project in your mind's eye that single thought of clarity."

Michael closed his eyes, with one sense down the alcohol running through his body tried to play tricks on his brain, making him feel as if the room was spinning around him. As his balance wavered, he tried to slow down his breathing and turned his thoughts away from the suffering of the recent past that ate away at his insides. One by one the thoughts and feelings cleared from his mind and as each weight upon his psyche crumbled, another sense, stronger than the others, rose to prominence. This new emerging awareness seemed to reinforce his being, stabilising his balance and focusing his concentration. Then there it was standing alone, that single vivid memory pushing back the darkness surrounding him. A moment of true contentment and joy. The first time he held his daughter in his arms.

"Your contentment is a shield, protectively embracing that moment. Let it deflect all other thoughts of negativity within the arrow of time. Now let the crystal float on the winds of will." Elyon had lowered his hooded head towards the only section of storage that held a single crystal. A sphere tinted with emerald and aquamarine. Michael didn't need to see the crystal signified. Another type of vision was in play now.

His face contorted with concentration, but nothing happened.

Elyon continued his guiding words, "Bath in its light, allow the rays of happiness to penetrate and cleanse you of that stubborn stain of doubt."

"I can't do it! How am I supposed to move something with just a thought?" The frustration evident in his voice.

"The memory is not a remnant of the past, it is your present, it lives in the now. Moments solidified in memory, archived in the annuals of history, are immortal and as real and important as any thoughts formed in each tick of existence. Focus all senses and imbed yourself in that instant, only then can you live in it again. The crystal is a mere object in this scene of awesome wonder that does not answer to forced commands. From the constraints of physical laws you must lose yourself, and let all things flow around you as they are compelled."

The room began to shake; all around crystals toppled and impacted the floor. The fine dust spiraled into the air like miniature twisters but Elyon did not flinch.

"Immerse yourself and forget all that has since passed. How sweet is its sound? Drink it in, taste the bliss. See its beauty unfurl and feel your soul diffuse from its bodily confinement. Outside that bubble of heaven, just the silence of nothingness."

His face relaxed. He inhaled deeply and surrendered breathing to his subconscious. A smile crept slowly across his face and like an earthquake subsiding, the room fell still except for a single crystal sphere hovering in the air.

"Wondrous is such a sight. Now Michael deliver it to us." Elyon leaned in closer towards him and spoke in whisper, "Static this moment is not, it has capacity to grow, metamorphose, encompass more moments impelled to embrace in unified meaning. Together they intensify this paradise that defines your life. The crystal will follow the natural path laid out for it."

The green and blue ball slowly tumbled towards Elyon. All Michael could see was his new born daughters face, innocent and full of life, an image once thought lost. She had his eyes. From every angle Bella's presence shone, the first time she said daddy, a first intrepid step arms reaching out for his security, a hug on that night. The retrieval of the crystal was not even part of his thoughts. It was like he was concentrating on reading or watching television but scratched an itch without thinking. Instinctual actions surfacing from another level of his consciousness. The feeling was not just a sense of happiness, joy or pride. Fear, worry and doubt were still present but not in a negative form, more an essential ingredient of a single euphoric state. That feeling was unconditional love, a love that will never diminish under the tests of time, that love for a child.

The crystal floated closer; Michael felt the cold wet texture of blood pooling at the edge of his nostril. The thick red fluid trickled over his lip and into his mouth, the taste of iron was so strong, perhaps it was magnified by the iron oxide dust in the watch tower. The trickle became a drip, the physical distraction pounding his shield of contentment in crushing strikes. The crystal started to wobble and stall in mid-air. As each drop fell, it splashed across another connective moment in a crimson shower. One-by-one the images of Bella's face began to melt away to blistering skin and scars. The barriers he had erected in his mind could no longer hold back the flood of emotions and sadness that had begun to leak through the widening cracks of a crumbling nirvana. How he missed her so much, the longing to be the father she needed, and the horrible guilt that continued to eat away at him. As each pivotal memory melted away in ash, all that remained was his new born child, defenceless in his arms. He cradled her desperately and with each deathly blow of realities hammer, he fought to hang on.

"Damn it. No! I've lost ......" shouted Michael as the crystal struck the floor with a heavy thud and rolled towards Elyon's feet.

"You must learn to walk before you can run. This is but a first step." Elyon encouraged as he picked up the emerald and aquamarine transfused sphere and motioned towards its original location. "When sorrows swell and a rising tide of malice breaks all foundations of control, to the most purest of memories you must regress. Let its strength reinforce you and raise you up in rejuvenated glory."

"What about this?" Michael wiped the blood from his nose and held up the back of his hand to Elyon. Even that felt like a difficult task, the exertion had left him entirely exhausted and had brought him to his knees.

"It is nothing." The shining one showed no characteristic of concern as he gazed at the blood. "Existence always strives for equilibrium. The positive with the negative, cause and effect, good and evil.........." Elyon paused and turned away. " A universe's balance now satisfied, a virtue granted and precious blood washes away......... Now let us try again."

"No more. I want to go back to Earth to see my daughter. That was my agreement with Egregor Krill." He pulled out his hip flask and took a swig; his head was ringing from the earlier effort.

Elyon placed the Crystal back on its lonely perch and wiped it clear of dirt with his layered black sleeve, "Michael, I hear the rolling thunder approaching, and see the shadow turning towards us. From the well of truth I drink when I tell you. We need your help to hold back the storm of the Sin."

"I don't understand! Why me?"

"As Krill has explained. You stand at the pinnacle of an evolutionary plan conceived at the genesis of Earth. A destiny for humanity that is unique amongst the cosmos, but a fate that should not come to fruition until the world is scorched by the blaze of a hungry red giant. Yet you stand on the horizon bathed in light well before the dawn is ready to behold. A fact you cannot comprehend the importance of."

"What can I possibly do?"

"Bring a whisper of hope where the silence is deafening." Elyon replied solemnly.

"Yet you only give me despair!", physically defeated and supposedly in the presence of wisdom, his own hopelessness poured out, "Have you ever loved someone so much that they consume your thoughts every minute you're not with them. Missing the joy you have with their interaction, how they make you feel, and how they somehow banish all negative emotion. A growing hole filled when you are reunited and the clock of longing is reset. Now imagine, that hole never stops growing, the clock never resets, and the negativity is allowed to build unchecked. But it's worse than if they were dead, with death brings acceptance that things can't change, and time dulls the longing. My daughter is out there, everyone is conspiring to stop me from seeing her, and to change that seems so unsurmountable. And I don't know if she is suffering the same, or if I have become a terrible forgotten memory. Yet both of these scare me to the point I want to puke. So, the pain gets deeper, anger rules and sadness hollows out your heart. Slowly eroding the character and emotions less used. Those of empathy, kindness and wonder. Enthusiasm and optimism, neglected and defeated at every turn. No one can understand what it does to you, because they just can't see past the act that caused this, because to see evil in me is easier than comprehending the possibilities that I chase, and still don't understand myself."

"Awakes my soul, such passion to see your daughter. It presents itself a mirror that my reflection deeply understands more than most. Yet the mortal throws of humanity will be extinguished by the hateful hands of the Sin. Your protection she does need, but by aiding us, your shielding touch and the warmth of your love will be felt a hundred-fold!"

"What good will her father have a million miles away!" As he spoke the words, he tried to muster the strength to stand up once more.

"Michael, the Sin are not just coming, they are here! The sands of time have almost run their course for the human race. They coil at the border of free space, ready to make their first strike. A rancor that will make no distinction between your daughter or any other lifeform, mercy will be a vicious drought unending."

"Why don't your people do something? Are you not the oldest race in the galaxy! I've seen Seber, your technology is powerful. Surely your people can fight them. Why do you need me?!!"

"Why? To represent the human race. A symbol of the Raziel." Elyon answered as he placed his radiant hand on the central globe.

At the far side of the room a sharp red light blinked alive in the gloom. It zipped around the circumference of the wall to wall crystals and came to a halt directly behind the shelf holding the emerald and aquamarine sphere. A laser shot out through the crystal ball and into the depths of the globe balanced upon the central pedestal. The hazy smoke enclosed within slowly began to diffuse into the air to form a swirling image.

"What is this?" Michael asked.

"A record of what has already passed." Elyon began to narrate as Michael watched on at the strange display above him.

"Thousands of years ago a grand alliance once existed, many species young and old, wise and warring, timid and brave, all answered a heralding call. To unite in one cause, to stop the Sin's relentless march to conquer the galaxy."

The image panned around vessels of countless types filling the whole of space. There must have been hundreds of Seber replica ships in amongst spinning top forms, curving lattice structures, and glowing saucers to name a few. A scale of diversity Michael could never have imagined. In a formation akin to a wall they seemed too have rallied around a site that he instantly recognised.

"Earth!" exclaimed Michael in a whisper.

"The Sin and the entire might of its minions, the Sin Supremacy descended upon your Solar system. Survey such extraordinary glory, for this is where the free races of the galaxy made their last stand."

The view switched from an Earth shrouded in night to the scene that every ship faced. For as far as he could see, warship after warship blocked out the stars, a horde of doom unleashing its fearsome firepower upon the alliance. A shadow passed across the corner of the picture like an eclipse, the dark quartz like exterior filled the display. Alliance ships scattered in its presence as a beam of pure darkness was expelled from its surface straight towards the source of the recording. A maniacal scream pierced Michael with dread and the image instantly dissolved.

"The fire of death burned brightly across the sky that night, but the grand alliance endured. Upon the defences built by sacrifice, the swarm of the Sin Supremacy was driven back, but alas when we beheld the reckoning of victory, was contempt poured on all our pride. For the devastation that engulfed us, the brightness of our hearts grew strangely dim. By grace, only the Ashtar and Pleiadians of the old alliance sustain today, and of course my people, but for a millennium now they have been hidden under a shroud of concealment."

"If the Sin are coming, why do your people hide!"

"To survive!" Elyon replied in defence, "Maybe if I could give some context." he offered, "Our history with the Sin was old even before the Earth had been born from star dust. Upon the bloom of an ancient world almost as old as the galaxy itself, we lived in harmony. There was no Elohim, there was no Sin, we journeyed through existence as brothers and sisters. Yet there are many routes to take, to follow the path illuminated by the beacon of wisdom or to grope blindly in the caverns of ignorance. Belief in those choices steered us on very different courses and as with such heights of faith came inevitable depths of war. A war that spanned the ages, past, present and future, a war that will be raged forevermore until one finds peace in death."

"A war the human race and Ashtar now fight instead of you." Michael stated in disapproval.

"Please realise, reproduction of our people is not as you understand, the brilliance of the Elohim song was fading, our numbers dwindling and extinctions axe was held aloft our heads. The choices to the Elohim were limited, this was not an act of cowardliness. To continue our fight was to invite undeniable death, the knowledge of the Elohim parting this existence or far worse; into the catastrophic hands of the Sin themselves. The other was to not let such redeeming power be manipulated into a weapon of evil, but to flee." As Elyon told their story, his voice sounded solemn.

"To disappear and endure, was a desperate choice my people made. Yet then in absence of their faith I found my sight. I stayed to bear aid." his words finishing with a distinct difference in tone.

"But you, the Ashtar, you could've prepared the human race better, intervened to advance our technology? Not leave billions clueless and helpless."

"No we could not. It is with a high price the Elohim have learnt, that natures path is a destiny not to be tampered with. Yet we embraced the Earth with arms of light, to nurture where it roots, to the allow its natural beauty to blossom unmolested. With the vastness of the galaxy and predators on every border, perpetual vigilance is no mundane task."

"So, your people couldn't stop them, and all that remains of the old alliance is all but gone. Then tell me, what the hell can I do!"

"The birth of an alliance anew!"

"A new alliance, but… How can I possibly…." exclaimed Michael unable to comprehend his value.

"You still do not see your worth. Long ago another guided the last grand alliance, someone that exhibited your gifts. It is my belief that the free races of this age will once more unite under the hope of what you represent; the capstone of Earth and a new alliance."

"I am not the person you think I am, I'm not a leader." His doubt was more evident than ever.

"I do not ask you to lead but to stand with us. Just your symbology could be the whisper of hope that amplifies into a roar of salvation. Like it or not you cannot hide. Your fate was sealed by a series of events beginning billions of years ago at the conception of the prophecy."

"I cannot help you!" he replied with frustration and animosity.

"Then help your daughter, do this for the love of your child. Her death is an inevitability only you can influence. You and you alone have the power to save her." Elyon lifted the dark hood from his forehead. Light streamed out and the resonating sound seemed to intensify. Elyon looked Michael in the eyes. " Let the scales of truth guide you, you will find your answer where they fall!"

Michael returned the gaze of the Shining one. A feeling welled up inside of him; there was something not quite right, a conflict locked away deep within Elyon. He was hiding something, guilt, untruth, a secret agenda, Michael couldn't tell.

Can I really trust him?

22 - The Passing

A web of thoughts zipped back and forth through the sub-space of the Co-operative link. Every connected mind was silent, listening to the words of a single voice.

"The battle group did not arrive at the rendezvous point. They are our most powerful ally and vital in the fight against the Sin. It is imperative that we determine their whereabouts."

A ripple in the fabric of space flattened out and the six ships riding its leading crest, shut down their quantum wave drives and slowed to sub-light velocity. The mirror exterior of the spinning top shaped crafts absorbed the star light of the nearby red giant as they entered the dangerous region of space.

An immense expanse of ancient galactic artefacts, located in one of the oldest sections of the Milky Way. It had been around since the birth of the galaxy, gradually deteriorating to where the celestial bodies had become mere fossils, observing evil wage war around it and its shroud slowly smother the last embers of life.

"We have entered the Pleiades star cluster Ka'er Myas." notified the Ashtar navigator as proximity alarms sounded.

She looked almost undistinguishable to every other of the fourteen strong crew except for the patchy tinge of brown that broke the dull pigment of grey skin. Although all displaying identical characteristics, this was of no hindrance to their society as it was their telepathic signature that truly distinguished each individual in the Co-operative.

There was a wave of urgency in the local Co-operative as the Ashtar vessels split formation to avoid a large spiraling object. The image was clear among the connective minds, two bright blue oval jewels transitioning from light to dark inset into a greater fragment reminiscent of ivory bone.

The mutual mental alarm projected forcefully into the mind of Ka'er Myas, "The Eyes of the Pleione!"

In that same moment the objects history and significance flashed back and forth within the local Co-operative link. It was a symbol of protection and spiritual growth to those that experienced their guidance. Its creators were leaders, even to a degree for the Ashtar, and although bordered on all sides by Sin Supremacy controlled domains, it stood proud as a famous icon of defiance and preservation.

"Pai' Lec, confirm we are at the correct coordinates." ordered Ka'er Myas mentally.

"Local star patterns confirm we are at the intended location." Came the telepathic response.

They should have appeared a safe distance from a magnificent home world standing as a living testament to a proud and age old civilisation. Instead the Ashtar search fleet were swimming in the debris of its death, nothing now but a lifeless core and space rubble that their tri-defence orbs worked furiously to keep at bay.

"Scan the system for the battle group." Ka'er Myas's thin lips never moved but all in the fleet heard her stern voice through their short range telepathically network.

"We detect no ship signatures in the immediate vicinity." stated one voice.

"No ship signatures." confirmed another, "But there is a nearby cloud of diverse fragments. We calculate it was created recently. It appears to be a thin spherical shell of wreckage encompassing a denser central nucleus of crystalline particles. We are detecting a distress-signal embedded within the repeating warning beacon of the Eyes of the Pleione. It contains audio voice data."

"What does it divulge?" asked Ka'er Myas.

"We can only retrieve a segment of the message."

"Relay it through the ships audio systems."

The words of the warning beacon spoke calmly, 'Do not despair or relinquish hope…' Then noise of loud static broke in echoing around them, 'They have long-range planetary bombardment weapons, the like I have not…….' The sound of explosions and shouting engulfed the recording. 'Our own arsenal has no effect. It is as if they are mere illusions…' More static broke the message. 'Please send assistance immedia…..' Only silence followed before the calm of the beacons final message, 'You will find refuge with the Seven Sisters…'

"Is that the totality of the signal Pai' Lec?"

"I am afraid so Ka'er."

"Is there any indication that points towards their whereabouts?"

"It is difficult amongst so much erratic debris. We have now calculated the total mass of the central crystalline remains. It indicates the wreckage of an estimated four thousand to six thousand ships."

"The entire battle group." The realisation hit Ka'er Myas and the rest of Ashtar like a mortal blow. The usually logical and emotionless sub-spatial web of minds was swamped with worry and fear.

The gravitational chaos of the crystalline dust reflected in the local Co-operative. Such a loss was more than just others sharing a common enemy, but a true cost to their galactic family. Where the Ashtar were intellectual, consistently rational; the Pleiadians were the emotional and spiritual equilibrium that provided the balance to endure in a galaxy of perils.

A mental voice shouted out over the background noise. "Multiple ship signatures detected moving towards our position. I am unable to determine many of these vessels from our archives. Wait……. It is the Sin Supremacy."

"Take us out of here immediately. Once we are back in Ashtar space, initiate a broadcast across the entire Co-operative link." commanded Ka'er Myas as the space in front of each vessel wrinkled. Then in a crack of a gravimetric whip the Ashtar fleet surfed the quantum ripple in retreat.

23 - Gradualism

The Pindar placed his glass of Gout de Diamants upon the small walnut side table and looked out from the window of his Learjet. In the background he could see snow covered mountains framed in a sky of flawless azure and beneath him the stand out architecture of a large white step building at the end of a makeshift runway that they were circling to approach. As they slowed and reduced altitude, he delicately sipped his champagne, savoring every taste and aroma. This particular bottle cost over two million dollars and after the meeting he had just had with the Masters he felt it was an occasion most deserving of excessive indulgence. And that meeting was the very reason he was here in Gakona, Alaska. The Master's modification to their plans meant there was ramifications that now had to be dealt with swiftly, and this officially shut down facility could be key to the smooth conclusion of their plans.

The jet touched down just past an immense array of one hundred and eighty antenna units arranged in the columns and rows of a large rectangle, and cruised along the makeshift runway sided by seemingly endless powdered forests until it came to a standstill at an unattended square clearing of stone and weeds, a few crude looking mobile cabins and a small array of interconnected detectors of some type.

As the Pindar disembarked his jet, the door swung open from the middle unit housing a silver telescope dome. And out strode a woman clad in white leather, ivory eye patch and a coat of grey, white, black and tan fur.

"Is that a wolf pelt?" the Pindar asked as he approached her with two bubbling champagne flutes and a diamond and white-gold crested bottle.

"A Yukon wolf to be exact, shot by yours truly from the perches of a helicopter. Bloody thing put up quite the fight. I had to finish it off personally which was an abominable shame, I would have preferred to have kept that savage head intact."

The Pindar passed over the crystal flute with a nod of understanding.

"Anyway, looks much more delightful on me than the beast that owned it last." continued Frau Wulf with an evil grin.

"Quite." agreed the Pindar, "You left the claws on, a nice touch I may add."

"An apt reminder that I am a Wulf in Wolf's clothing." she stated with a villainous cackle.

The Pindar smiled back before raising his glass to solicit the moment to sample the champagne.

"Gout de Diamants!" she exclaimed. Frau Wulf took a sip, "Dear Pindar, what would elicit such an occasion?"

"Let us talk within the facility, it has been a while since I was last here and I would very much like to see our progress."

"Why of course, let us get out of this god forsaken cold, please follow me."

After a short trip in an elevator, and a walk along white gloss corridors of the facility with its miles of metal pipes and aged machinery. Past a number of workers that clearly made the greatest of efforts to avoid eye contact or hastily changed direction to evade any unnecessary interaction whatsoever. They arrived in a room most out of place in a scientific research facility. A fully decorated hunting lodge with wooden panels, leather chairs, a plethora of stuffed animal heads from the region and a large stone ornamental fireplace.

"Please take a seat and make yourself comfortable Pindar." offered Frau Wulf, arm directed to an antique wingback arm chair.

As he did so he looked up at the at the giant head of a moose adorned above the replica fireplace.

"Please forgive my surroundings, the constant plain walls and machinery can be, shall I say, tiring, so I allow myself a few home comforts. But back to the matter at hand, the Gout de Diamants."

"Yes, how is progress." he asked after taking another sip.

"I'm sure you will be delighted that after our last chat, I expect selective remote capabilities to be available for testing shortly. Just in time to meet our plans, if there is any individual that needs a little more persuasion."

"That is good news but for this." The Pindar held his champagne aloft, "The Masters' have changed the plans, they have forced a move that could swiftly bring about our New World Order, but one that is very risky."

"What changes?" she responded almost unable to hide her annoyance.

"They have gifted nuclear weapons to each of these rogue nations. And MAJI have provided evidence of the valid nuclear threat they pertain. And of course, I have brought them together in a coherent coalition." he took a taste of his exuberant beverage once again, watching the predictability of the bubbles.

"It is not for us to question such things, but why would they do that? We have influence but not control over them. Surely a third World War would be inevitable with this new wave of nationalism rising from the fear we have manufactured?"

"Correct."

"I am a mere beautiful foot soldier, what does this really mean for our New World Order plans?" inquired Frau Wulf as she gulped down the remaining champagne in her flute.

The Pindar stood, refilling her glass, "The recent collateral atrocities would have pushed through new global policies for the UN, the creation of new international laws on mass surveillance across all populations and media, new loop holes for circumvention of human rights and cement further stringent sanctions against those rogue nations. To invade any of them if necessary since they would have all admitted complicity to the nuclear terrorist attacks.", he faced the roaring fire, feeling its heat warm the coldness in his blood, "Ultimately, we would have gained more control on these rogue nations and the rest of the world as a consequence. Forcing them eventually into accepting and being part of the global constabulary. Our gradual globalisation would reach its apex. The global media and economy are driven by our corporations. There would be continued regionalisation like with the EU and Shanghai cooperation organisation. Governing regional unions, similar trade unions through all the amalgamated trade deals, including the recently signed Trans-Pacific Partnership to be followed by the Transatlantic Trade and Investment Partnerships; the G-twenty and international monetary fund, world bank and world health organisation. A military organisation in NATO. Most importantly a single global organisation to guide it all under international law, with the international criminal court, and the UN. That is the penultimate move in our end game of our gradual globalisation, a plethora of governing bodies, affiliated global organisations and global agreements. The world will not see a single ruling body, but we will be pulling the strings behind every one of these."

"And now?" she asked with an innocent flutter of her eyelids.

"The growing popularity of far-right views across Europe, UK leaving the EU, the shock US presidential victory. The bold global stances of Russia and China, with hacking, covert operations in the west, political aggression in the South China sea. The list of chaotic antagonistic moves keeps increasing. On the surface it seems it threatens to destabilise our globalisation plans, but the timing of this visage of democratically elected leaders and public majority has played perfectly. We need excessive reaction and patriotism to pass new laws and react with force accordingly. Extreme views illicit extreme reactions and the Masters have chosen this exact ignition point. They will see a world of spiraling instability and the terrorist axis of evil will instill a fear that will stifle any solace they found in the safety of their daily lives. All will unite to subjugate these rogue nations and embrace any laws that will afford them a shield. A very real third World War and a new Cold War in all but name, will force the expedited implementation of our proposed United Nations Parliamentary Assembly, people will scream for global oversight in a post nuclear conflict, especially to govern those they perceive as antagonistic and trigger-happy leaders. No more would the UN be advisory in nature but hold executive enforceable powers, global jurisdiction upon its members, including the enforcement of Agenda twenty-thirty, signed by every country in the world, but driven by our special membership forums of the Trilateral Commission, Bilderberg Group and Council of Foreign Relations, a true single global government. These rogue nations who refuse to adhere to a global community and rule, the current greatest threat to a peaceful world, will be destroyed in the short term, their threat to global peace through nuclear terrorist strikes would be pacified through extreme military force. We would have complete and total control under a single ruling body, our New World Order would come in one fell swoop."

"And the risks?"

"It means playing a very risky game with the Cult's pyramid of control. There will be those that will not agree with this aggressive hand, the ones that have worked with us to push our agenda of gradual globalisation. They know full well that we do not have complete control of these rogue nations, influence yes, but ultimately, they could do whatever they desired with those nuclear weapons. There unrestrained use is a quite feasible possibility, especially with the envisioned invasions that are to come as a consequence of this acquisition of mass destruction. I will have to strongly influence, how and where they would attack. I am certain they would wish to strike at the heart of their enemies, which of course, are places of key interest for the Thirteen families, and most significantly the heart of our global business partners, the likes of the Freemasons, Skull & Bones, Knights Templar and the Rosicrucians. It is with luck, that I hold the key in smuggling these weapons into their target locations." The Pindar let that sink in as he started to peruse the trophies of the room, running his hands over the excessive number of stuffed carcasses. "Without doubt these conspirator societies will identify this dangerous move with us. Not to mention the negative effect further nuclear attacks will have on the global population. It could insight further nationalism, isolationism and rebellion against all forms of governance. The situation will have to be managed most meticulously and delicately. There will be many challenging questions asked; particularly how these rogue nations procured nuclear weapons and got them into the countries of their enemies.

Any extended conflict and threats will give time to doubt and conspiracy. Ultimately, risk the Masters being discovered if this is not controlled in the right way."

"But they are mere factions of our pyramid of control. They only know the information we wet their grubby little palms with. That of global manipulation, through admittedly questionable methods, to increase our influence on world governance and fill our luxurious economic pockets as a consequence. They know nothing of the Masters. Mere puppets for the Cult to use.... or dismember."

The Pindar smiled at the simplicity Frau Wulf viewed every problem. And usually it was a most effective approach, "True we are the hands that control the global puppet, yet they are the strings that maneuver each part with the finesse we require. If one was to break, yes, the puppet will still function but it does not articulate as effectively as it should."

"Yes, we would all prefer to have a full set of fingers to be naughty with." she smiled wickedly, "Then what about MAJI? They will play an important role in this aftermath."

"MJ Three is old, but he shares our vision and still holds strong influence amongst the group. MJ One can see his plans for the ensured national security of the US is within touching distance, he will not take a step back. And MJ Four, well he seems to harbor little morality for people in general, to him the average US citizen is classified as expendable to realise his countries unchallenged dominance."

"I wonder if they would be so nonchalant if a nuke goes off in the heart of the US?"

"They have a noose around their neck in their complicity. To struggle against their responsibilities will leave them dangling for all of America to see. It was their subjects that were integral to the first attacks and it was them that manufactured the evidence for the UN, not to mention the mutual agreement between us. They have further work to do as part of this pivot in our plans and they will move forward regardless of the pressure around their necks. Global laws will bend in their favour, they will bath in unlimited funding and eventually they will have a prosperous, safe United States of America. An unmatched super-power whose current biggest undefendable threat, that of terrorism, will be eradicated."

"And if there are those that don't agree?" Frau Wulf asked playfully, already knowing the answer.

"We are so close; we will need it fully operational. We may need to force our influence on mass. But if any piece goes wrong, it will be essential."

"I see. Then I'd better get back to work and murder a few people." she laughed.

"Just be mindful when you make your motivational display, that the JASON scholars do not grow on trees."

"Quite true."

The Pindar placed the bottle of Gout de Diamants on a side table draped in caribou skin, "I must take my leave and make preparations for the coming war. Now they have these weapons. The conflict must be swift and bring a finality to these rogue nations, yet enough destruction felt by all, that it forces the world to adopt everything we have laid on the table for our singular global governance. The world will in one fell swoop bring our New World Order to fruition through their own choice. And for those who do not choose it, your work will make the choice for them."

24 - Distant Ancestors

Michael strolled among the Mayan city in bio-dome 1. So many times he had dreamed of standing in such a place, but even the beauty of it all could not dampen the turmoil of his heart. He touched the monuments but his wonder felt hollow. Michael had let himself hope the words of Egregor Krill had brought him close to that moment where he could be part of Isabella's life again, be able to hug her once more, perhaps make up for what he had done. His soul ached to see that smile again, even if it was just one more time. She had seemed within touching distance but it was only a mirage, now she stood at the other side of a cavernous gulf with no bridge in site. Having hope ripped from his grasp made the wound hurt so much more than never having had hope in the first place. Nothing had changed, he would still be a danger to his daughter; *could he truly ever give her the love and care that she needed. Knowing what he knew, would she be better off without him?* It all seemed so surreal to him. He did not understand everything, especially his importance in what was happening. But they had offered him a choice, a way where he could finally do something for her that meant a damn. Even if meant his death, that he would never lay eyes upon her again, even though she might never know his love and how sorry he was. It was just all too much to ask.

Michael tilted back his head and emptied the remaining whiskey down his throat. Through his blurry stinging eyes, he spied the top of the step pyramid. Upon its flattened top he could see a single figure enveloped in smoke and holding something he was in need of. He mounted the steep steps of the impressively built pyramid. It very much resembled the one he had seen images for in Chichen Itza, Mexico, with its serpent stone heads at the base of the stairway and the rounded stepped corners. A magnificent design that created a shadow illusion of a snake descending the pyramid on the stairway wall during the spring and summer equinoxes. Here the artificial light did not act like Earth's Sun, but the source was dimming giving the appearance of a summers evening. He scaled the 365 steps that marked each day of the Mayan calendar year to the top of the stone pyramid. Upon its summit sat a single person. He was an old man bare skinned except for a feather and skull decorated head dress and loin cloth. He had painted over his wrinkled face and body with various coloured dyes. Michael recognised him as a shaman, a spiritual and political leader of Maya society. He also recognised the leather pouch that he was grasping in his hands.

"Ba'ax ka wa'alik." Michael had once dabbled in the ancient Mayan language and was sure that those words meant 'hello' or at least some type of greeting.

The shaman turned from the flames of a small fire he had constructed to his visitor. "Mmmh, words of the old tongue." he said in a weak gravelly voice. "What brings you here?"

Michael looked to the container in his hand and held up his own hip flask, tipping it upside down. "Do you mind?"

"So young one, you seek answers?"

"Where I come from, people say you cannot find answers at the bottom of a bottle." He took a seat opposite the High Priest and felt the warmth of the fire with his palms.

"On the contrary, my people see it as a vessel in which to alter our consciousness and cross over to another plane of reasoning. A higher realm where we can see and commune with the spirits. To receive guidance to the questions we have no answers for."

""I'll drink to that….. So what do they say about our current situation?"

The shaman let out a disappointed sigh, "They have been quiet of late, all I hear now are fleeting whispers of discontent. I fear what befalls us now has consequences for both planes…….. Here you may be more fortunate."

Michael reached through the scented smoke and took the sewn skin pouch of fluid from the shaman. He took a big gulp and immediately let out a wheeze and a cough as he tried to speak, "Thi….This is…. some strong concoction!" Although not hesitating to take another sip.

"That my friend is called Pulque, it is made in this settlement from a combination of Maize and Agave crops."

"Puts my stuff to shame." Michael shook his head, "Woah, its going straight to my head."

"Yes, Pulque combined with the fumes of burning wild tobacco and underworld mushrooms is quite a potent mixture." replied the old man fanning the smoke in Michael's direction.

Michael took another slow mouthful of the Mayan alcohol, his eyes glazed over and his body went limp.

'He was standing somewhere dark and enclosed. A distant fiery glow barely lit the scene. He was looking at someone, it was like seeing himself in a mirror, but there was something different. Rather than an image, it was more of a feeling that before him was a reflection of himself yet not. The manifestation stared downwards; Michael's eyes followed. His daughter stood beneath, in the middle, with her back to him and pig tailed head bowed to the ground. Isabella's voice, a hushed whisper filled his head, "Daddy help me!" The essence echo in front of him began to laugh loudly….. Gradually the malevolent tone trailed off and the shroud of darkness moved in.'

Again red flame penetrated the twilight and bird noise resonated around him. He blinked a few times as he tried to focus. His head gradually began to clear although the sensation of static electricity running through his hair continued to persist. He lifted his heavy chin and pulled himself upright. Opposite him the shaman sat motionless, the surroundings of the bio-dome now had the ghostly ambience of moonlight giving it the appearance of nightfall.

"So what did you see? What guidance did the spirit world offer?" asked the shaman.

It was like a dream yet Michael remembered exactly what he saw and the feelings that were provoked. "I saw…..

Nothing.......Silence and darkness." He did not want to explain the so-called vision or discuss what it might mean with the old man. Michael didn't need someone else's interpretation. In his mind it was clear; a drug induced hallucination manifesting his inner guilt.

"Then let me give you some guidance. I do not need the words of the spirit world to give you this wisdom." The ageing shaman glanced down to the small community gathered around a fire at the base of the pyramid. "I have had a long and purposeful life, I have been fortunate, yet you see that young boy playing with wood carvings of animals."

"I see him."

"That is my grandson, and I have the curse of knowing that he will not be so fortunate. I cannot see a future for him outside premature death. So I sit here every day crossing over to the other plane in hope that I may receive divine guidance.... because that is all I can do. My body is too frail and spent, or else I would be taking up arms right now, but I tell you this. I will fight with my last breath, use stick, stones or even my weak bare hands if I have too, even though my efforts would be futile. Still I know in my heart, I would do anything I could to ensure that boy, like me, can experience the wonders that this existence has to offer."

Michael could see in his poignant eyes that he meant every single word.

"I envy you. You have what I would wish for.... The chance to make a difference! The situation is grave; if there is anything you can do, then do not hesitate to pursue that task with every fibre of your being. The alternative scares even the spirit world."

The shaman reached over the embers of the fire and placed a full pouch of Mayan alcohol onto Michaels lap.

"I must take my leave now to spend what time I have left with my family. May you find your way. Ka xi'ik teech utsil."

"Thank you, good luck to you too." Michael watched the old man aided by a hand rope carefully descend the steep steps of the pyramid. He snuffed out the remains of the fire with his foot and with the gift of Pulque clambered down the dizzying height of the ritual summit himself.

On his way down he thought of the words of the shaman and

the hallucination. Maybe it was a vision, not the doing of the spirit realm but rather his own. Drug induced or not, it told him something either way. His daughter needed the help of her dad, help from the Sin, or perhaps from what was bad about himself, the mirror apparition. He remembered feeling evil and malevolence reflected back towards him and it frightened her. He did have an option and he would do whatever it took to protect her.

*

Egregor Krill and Dr. Emile Tesla were inspecting the self-repairing exterior of Seber's nano-fluid shell when Elyon entered the hangar.

"The Ashtar Co-operative have briefed us on the current situation. They have received detection alerts from our automated deep space observation posts before they were destroyed. There is little time and much to do. The key free races are still undecided and have as yet committed any resources. We will need them all even if we are to succeed against a Sin Supremacy scouting force. What of Michael, will he join us?" said Krill.

Elyon turned to the open metal doors. Michael walked through wearing a change of clothing that he was in the process of trying to adjust, "Apparently one size fits all!" He wore a black TEAF pilot jumpsuit that would have given him the appearance of a typical SAS commando if it weren't for the same dirty brown jacket that he insisted on wearing on top.

"I'm glad you're coming along; we could use all the help we can get." welcomed Emile. She had slipped on a fresh lab coat over her jeans and jumper.

"So I've been told." answered Michael as he followed Emile into Seber.

"Krill my old friend, our ancient foe draws ever nearer. From a vantage point of bold expectation, barely do I see a defence fleet half ready when the first shot of battle is fired. Little hope remains, you must return with reinforcements."

"I have optimism we can unite the free races. They must be advised of the imminent danger. The Ashtar Co-operative is prepared to send as many warships as can be spared, but our resources are spread thin. Our own space remains scarcely guarded; we must leave the Ashtar civilisation with some form of defence. We will return with all we can muster."

"I send you with my blessings."

"You are not accompanying us?"

"Apologise I must Krill, the winds of circumstance usher me towards Athena. In my absence I have discovered some information that could be entwined with all our fates. That we depart once more feels me with anguish, yet the examination of this new knowledge is of great importance."

"What is more critical than the impending attack of the Sin?" Krill asked with no more connotation than genuine interest.

"A matter of ancient Elohim history. Unfortunately at this moment, I cannot enlighten you further. Krill, I have the utmost faith in you to do what is necessary."

Krill nodded his head to Elyon and turned towards Seber, the weight of the galaxy upon his slender shoulders. "Dr. Tesla please take us out of here." Seber lifted off from the empty cargo bay and back out of the rusty red rock of Bio-dome 1.

"What about Elyon, isn't he coming?" asked Michael.

"No he is not. Elyon will be travelling to Alpha for a reason he is yet forthcoming with. All that I know is that it is related with our fight against the Sin."

"Do you think it has something to do with Earth then?" commented Dr. Tesla, "Michael there has been developments you should know about." Krill sent a stern unblinking stare towards Emile but she looked defiant and continued, "Michael we have received reports that several nuclear devices have detonated on Earth."

The blood seemed to drain from his face, "Where!"

"Eh, Russia, Germany..."

"The USA?" said Michael anxiously.

"Yes"

"Tell me where exactly. My daughter is in Denver!"

"It was Macon."

Michael rubbed his forehead and let out a relieved sigh. "What's happening there?"

"We have been told that an organised group of terrorists have targeted several UN nations. The blame has been put on 'various rogue states allying against the freewill and peace-loving world'. No action has been taken so far. Our sources at COM Twelve do not believe that these rogue states have the resources or ability to first acquire so many nuclear weapons and secondly carry out such successful and simultaneous strikes. The last news we received from them was that they were looking into the situation."

"How bad was it, the death toll?" asked Michael.

"Although worrying, these facts are not important." interjected Krill.

"Not important! As you guys keep telling me, the human race has great potential. Well what happens when they all start killing each other? Shouldn't we be doing something!"

"It is for the governments of Earth to resolve. Their predicament pales in comparison to our own imperative task. Our focus must remain on its completion." reiterated Krill.

Michael knew he was right, the lesser of two evils as the saying went.

"Dr. Tesla initiate the quantum entanglement drive, set coordinates for Titan."

"Titan, as in the moon or another place the human race know nothing about?" queried Michael.

"Yep one of Saturn's fifty-two officially named moons and outpost for the Altairian Empire." explained Emile ignoring his sarcastic addition.

"Ok, the Altairian Empire. Someone should really bring me up to speed on all these empires, Co-operatives and whatever else, or at least give me a who's who guide to the aliens of the galaxy!" complained Michael.

"Unfortunately we don't have a Hitch Hikers Guide to the Galaxy available right now." Emile let out a little chuckle despite Michael's tone being more serious than anything.

"You will soon be acquainted with what you need to know. The Altairian Empire is well aware of the danger the Sin present but has not as of yet committed any forces. I believe you have already met one of their species." answered Krill.

Seber's entanglement engines were charged and pulsing at full power. It was a drive that required tremendous energy to take advantage of a phenomenon inherent in every particle. Before the Big Bang, the universe was but a singularity, everything that is, sharing an existence in a single entangled system. A connection that still persists today; every particle and energy mass in the galaxy connected to each other by a ghostly property of entanglement. The concentrated discharge of immense power probed deep into sub-space, causing a microscopic conduit to a higher dimensional plane to be forced ajar. Only able to conduct the tiniest quanta of energy, it was enough to provide a superluminal channel capable of instantaneous communication across vast distances, a channel for classical communication of data needed to perform the unitary transformation to the distant entangled system. The transformation would result in an identical output wave function of Seber to be inserted at their destination coordinates and the initial Seber wave function in turn collapsing. Therefore allowing Seber to teleport across the huge expanse of space instantaneously.

On the atmospheric outskirts of Titan, particles and energy burst together, one nano-second a chaotic blur, the next the smooth amber of Seber. Back at the Red planet high above Cydonia, Seber instantaneously blinked out of its Martian orbit and half a solar system away.

"Welcome to Titan! Saturn's largest moon, hence its name, and second biggest in the solar system." declared Emile.

Although classified as a moon, Titan was greater in size than that of the planet Mercury and planetoid Pluto, and possessed a thick atmosphere denser than that of Earth. It was one of the more interesting worlds in the solar system, harbouring an environment akin to that of Earth's before life began pumping oxygen into the atmosphere. With hydrocarbon seas and air, it was scientists' best hope for discovering microbial extra-terrestrial life upon a celestial body within our reach. These reasons leading to the launch of the Cassini spacecraft on the 15th of October 1997. Cassini reached Saturn in 2004 and released the Huygens probe to Titan's surface on Christmas day while on one of its 45 planned flybys. Sending back terabits of data, both probes unveiled much information of what lay behind the impenetrable atmosphere of Titan, but left many of its secrets still hidden within its shroud. What actually lay in the cloak of methane clouds was way beyond any of their wildest imaginations.

Seber struck the predominantly nitrogen rich atmosphere, it was diffuse with hydrocarbon elements that combined to give Titan its hazy orange hue. The navigation system of the amber craft fought hard to keep its trajectory stable in the violent storms that raged over Titans southern pole. The Elohim vessel skirted the boundary of the storm at a latitude of about 40 degrees in the southern hemisphere. Here the hurricane winds were replaced with moderate gusts, torrential rain and intense lightning. By the time Seber had navigated to their current location they had reached a depth where sunlight could no longer penetrate the moon's photon absorbing layer of gas. This barrier where photochemistry began to break down was clearly visible in the form of vast fields of dense hydrocarbon clouds coalescing into thousand-mile long bands along the latitudinal line. Seber entered the thick orange smog of the methane and ethane clouds, unable to see more than an arm's length through the transparent shell of the ship. Heavy hydrocarbon rain pelted its exterior and the air around them brimmed with static electricity. Radiant flashes of light momentarily lit up the colourful smog as lighting tore through the clouds. With each illuminating flicker Michael noticed shadows come to life all around them. As they infiltrated deeper into the cloud, the smog started to thin out and the fleeting shadows transformed and sharpened into persistent dark silhouettes. Michael gazed out into the eerie air. Each shape was intertwined with each other like the concentric threads of a spider's web, and at its centre hidden in the fog the beast that held it all together.

"What in the name is that?" exclaimed Michael as they loomed upon the object he could only identify as an enormous hovering thing.

The lower central section of the organic looking structure had an inverted cone form that tapered down into what resembled a giant intestine dropping into the foggy depths. The upper section of the core was also shaped like a cone but upright and rather than narrowing at its end, it split out and swelled into four smoke stacks that bellowed hydrocarbon gas high into the upper atmosphere.

Wrapped around the upper half of the core, just below the stacks, was a semi-transparent sphere that had the appearance of a jellyfish's gelatinous body. At the base of the faintly glowing sphere, the sinew textured strands reached out into the horizontal plane, joined by intermediate strands that crisscrossed to form an expansive floating web. Located at every intersection of the pulsating network was a funnel that seemed to suck down the element saturated air and viscous rain surrounding it, and channeled it down into the bundles of fibres that constituted each organic strand.

"This Michael is one of the parturition habitats of the Altairian Empire." explained Emile.

"It looks so alive. Is this where these Altairian live?" asked Michael as he tried to focus on something moving in the hazy distance.

"No, the Altairian don't live here, but you could say it is almost alive. The whole sky habitat is constructed from living tissue, kind of like a giant plant grown from the abundant organic material found throughout Titan."

"Then what's this weird thing do?"

"Krill, do you mind if we do a quick fly through. I've never seen one hatch before?"

"Please be quick Dr. Tesla then we must descend to the generator habitat."

"Great! Michael you want to know what this place is for!" Seber veered sharply and took a course parallel to one of the pulsating bundle of fibres.

"We are following one of the umbilical cords." commented Emile.

"Too What? Umbilical cords usually feed something!"

"You'll see…ahhhh and here they are!"

They hit a patch where the fog broke, momentarily allowing Michael a clear view of a broad portion of the biotic network. At equidistant points along each chord of the web, large brown masses hung like pegs on a washing line. There was a wide variation in size and tone but all were clearly being fed something via the system of umbilical cords. Bursts of lightening frequented the air, regularly striking each pod and enveloping them in crawling tendrils of electricity.

"Hey! One is moving. Let's take a closer look!" Emile enthused.

They slowly motioned over to the throbbing pod. It was similar to a suspended acorn and dwarfed the oncoming Seber. As they approached closer Michael noticed an entity wriggle and push out against the dark shell, it was then he realised what he was looking at. "Something is trying to get out. It's a cocoon!"

"Yep, it sure is. This habitat is a kind of super nursery. Titan is a moon brimming with hydrocarbon elements. As a world it has geological and meteorological properties that are surprisingly rare in the galaxy. You see methane and ethane are pumped into the atmosphere through those chimneys, forming the dense bands of clouds around us. We are currently drifting at a level where light from the Sun ceases to penetrate. It is the reaction between the carbon compounds, the atmospheric nitrogen and this sunlight which is important. This photochemistry converts the hydrocarbon gases into products such as acetylene, ethylene, and hydrogen cyanide which is important as a building block of amino acids. Contained within the air and rain, these organic compounds sink to this level then get sucked inside the intersecting funnels. From there the umbilical cords pump the molecular juices directly into the cocoons. And of course, the encapsulating lightning which you can say brings the spark of life, kinda like Frankenstein's monster! How they grow them is still a mystery to us but the result is well, rather wonderful!"

"And what the hell is the result?"

"You are about to have the rare privilege of witnessing the birth of an Altairian warship!" said Emile excitedly.

"And I hope for us all, soon to be alliance warship." added Krill.

Cracks began to appear across the striated surface of the shell. Piece by piece the imprisoning casing fell away and like a butterfly escaping from its chrysalis, the living ship dropped into its new world. Its skin was a myriad of greens, browns and reds, and textured like the exterior of a pinecone. The shape was akin to that of a tadpole but unlike a tadpole it had a number of tails trailing behind. Emile began to clap to herself as the new born gave a whip of its appendages and darted off around the parturition habitat. As it circled the cocoons that were suspended in various stages of their fifteen-year development, the warship was joined by others swooping into view. They moved with incredible pace and agility, taking in their first taste of the Titan environment before soaring off into the shroud of orange haze.

"Wow, those guys can fly. You know they eject a stream of ions from those directional tails, it gives them amazing maneuverability. A bit like a squid really, although they're more of a plant than an animal."

"Incredible." murmured Michael taking a swig of the extra strong Pulque he had filled his flagon with.

Emile raised her hand to say something.

"Dr. Tesla, now if you please." intermitted Krill before she could finish.

"Oh, of course Krill. Getting a bit carried away with it all." apologised Emile as she took control of Seber.

The amber craft almost invisible in the clouds looped through the web and down along the same path as the undulating intestine tethered to the base of the habitat. The intestine dropped for miles but they soon reached the misty surface of the moon. They were directly over a body of liquid hundreds of kilometres across and rimmed by flat fields of rounded rocks. The intestine plunged into the liquid in close proximity to the location of a bobbing structure that spanned a huge distance across the tar looking sea.

"The temperature down here is around minus one hundred and seventy degrees Celsius and the pressure greater than that of Earth. The liquid you see is a giant surface lake and makes Titan the only other body in the solar system to have them. But it's not water, its liquid ethane and dissolved methane driven to the surface by deep oozing fractures in the crust. That intestinal looking thing is like one big digestive system, it siphons the liquid, and as it pumps it up to parturition habitat, converts it to gas." detailed Emile.

Seber motioned for the floating construction that also appeared organic in nature. They headed towards the section closest to the shoreline and the only part that seemed stationary. The lack of shadow made it hard to define any topography but as they levelled off Michael was taken aback by the sheer magnitude of the waves that rolled across the lakes surface. Due to the gravity that was one seventh of that on Earth, the wind driven waves on Titan grew to the size of multi-story buildings. The widely spaced waves advanced upon the semi-circular segments of the structure in slow motion. As they hit, the sections surged upwards with the crest of the wave and dipped in its following trough. Every time the string of a thousand or so segments completed a cycle, electrical impulses would shoot down the cables that adjoined them, terminating into the main mass in the vicinity of the pebbled shoreline.

"Dock us into the generator habitat and wait for the chamber to be purified." directed Krill.

Emile directed the craft to the motionless structure of the generator habitat. It lay in the shallows of the hydrocarbon lake like the great hump back of a submerging leviathan. As they approached, an entrance split open, green slime dripped from its edges as if it were the mouth of a giant toad. Seber entered the opening. The sound of air being expelled filled the chamber. Behind them the lips of the entrance sealed in a squelch of water-resistant mucus and the docking bay walls began to puff out as the chamber inflated with breathable air.

They disembarked into something that resembled more the belly of a beast than any facility that Michael had ever laid eyes upon. Immediately he felt the warmth of the chamber and a strong acidic taste stung his tongue as he took in the artificial air. The floor although quite solid to the touch was reminiscent of raw muscle with its stringy sinews. A sound of marching feet drew their attention to the interior docking bay doors. They moved aside with the same squelch of fluid and flesh to reveal a line of soldier like figures striding up to them. Each one was dressed in a robe and simple but militarian body suit of earthy colours, all armed with a sparkling crystal tipped spear.

"They're reptilian! Just like the one I saw on Earth." exclaimed Michael as they split rank and formed a channel of two single files.

"These are the Altairian, sympathetic compatriots and I hope allies in the struggle against the Sin Supremacy." introduced Krill.

The two rows of reptilians bowed their heads as an old figure with a sagging dewlap of neck skin shuffled slowly between them. He was hunched over and ambled with the aid of a walking stick, the end of which was ornamented with a diamond claw. His attire was a weave of gold, red and blue thread encrusted with precious stones, finished off with a shimmering gold square cloak pin inset with gigantic diamonds that held his cloak upon his withering shoulders. Although the elderly Altairian required some effort to lift his head, he spoke with a voice that had much strength left in it.

"Welcome to the Titanian outpost of the Altairian Empire Egregor Krill."

His bright eyes scanned the visitors. Krill and Emile bowed their heads, Michael quickly copied them.

"Tell me, where is Elyon?"

"I apologise for his absence. He had urgent matters to attend too." answered Krill.

"I see. After our last conversation he seemed to become distracted and departed with some haste."

"The subject of the conversation?" asked Krill immediately.

"It was of no importance. We talked of our progress with the restoration program of the Altairian ancient archives. We had restored further data, old astronomical information that contained star maps and nebulae."

Krill appeared in thought for an instant, "Emperor Xantis, please excuse me if I skip the pleasantries. Elyon has brought us word of the Sin Supremacy movements. They draw ever closer; in fact they linger mere jumps away from this very system. It is imperative that you gather your forces to make a stand at Earth."

"Egregor Krill, the Altairian Empire has agreed to be a part of any new alliance. Have we not already sent ambassadors to Earth to give counsel and aid in developing their defences?"

"Yes a much appreciated gesture, but it will not suffice." said Krill with a stern conviction in his dark unblinking eyes.

"We are already at war. If we commit resources now to aid the humans, our empire will be vulnerable to Hyekera attack." responded Xantis with a tone of sincerity.

"The Pleiadians have confirmed their allegiance with us and the forces of Earth, their warships are on route as we speak."

"Ahh the mighty Pleiadians. They follow Elyon blindly, living on memories of great victories long past. Yet what do they or anyone else really know of the Elohim and their past?"

"They have never given us a reason to doubt their honesty. The

Pleiadians, as the Ashtar, trust the intentions of the Elohim."

"We all know the Pleiadians need this alliance more than anyone. Although not in the midst of a debilitating war themselves, it is their space that lies closest to the Sin. Is it not fear that drives their people to Earth?" questioned Xantis with cynicism.

"No. It is hope. The Pleiadians know they cannot choose the degree of participation in any new alliance. It is either all or nothing if any of us are to survive." retorted Krill.

"To survive, that is why we continue to protect our borders."

"The Hyekera will agree to a truce, this I am sure of. They are not mindless; they are fully aware of the threat the Sin pose to their continued existence. Mistrust runs deep between you both but one of you must take the first risk. If you Xantis do not act now, the outcome is simple, the Sin Supremacy will flood through both your empires and neither of you will be able to stop them."

"You do not need to tell me of the threat too my people!" roared Xantis as he slammed the butt of his walking stick to the ground. "For an age I have led the empire in the fight against the soulless Hyekera. Standing between them and my people, keeping their mechanical claws from destroying our lands! Do not forget the significance Earth has with us, it was once our home too."

"Your home once!" blurted Michael, disrupting the battle of wills taking place in before him.

The chamber went silent and Michael started to feel a little uncomfortable as Xantis gaze left Krill and was planted firmly on him.

"I have come across Dr. Tesla before but who is this that has addressed me Egregor Krill?"

"This is Michael of the humans."

"Michael of the humans you say, Elyon has mentioned you. Step forward." Michael done as he asked. "Yes we were once of Earth. You could say we are both distant ancestors. Through intense research of our mythology, pieced with undeniable historical evidence we have traced the Altairian timeline to its beginnings. Long ago on Earth, even before you were an evolutionary viability my ancestors roamed its forests."

Michael looked to Emile as if he needed some type of confirmation. "Seventy-five million years ago, Cretaceous period."

Emile added with a whisper and a nod that it was ok to continue listening.

"We were defined as a sub-species of the dinosaur genus your scientists classified as Dromaeosauridae."

"A dinosaur!" he said loudly. Trying to reaffirm what he had just heard in his head. He couldn't believe he was stood talking to what was an actual living ancestor of a dinosaur.

"Like a Raptor!" explained Emile once more with a hushed voice.

Xantis ignored the background annotations and continued with the recitation of Altairian legend. "These Dromaesaurs were highly intelligent, more so than any other creature that walked the planet. Over the next ten million years the continual competition for survival drove our evolution in the direction of increased cognitive ability. This resulted in the creation of a complex language, social order and a genetic urge for knowledge. Along with our developing mental capacity we also evolved physically to compensate for changes in habitation and hunting. Our tails atrophied to maintain balance as our stance became more upright, shortening of the jaw when feeding methods altered, and most importantly the use of opposable thumbs. Our early civilisation on Earth peaked upon the planet around sixty-five million years ago......." Xantis paused, giving a quick glance to Dr. Tesla as if expecting her to add something further. "… At its pinnacle they had developed technological knowledge that surpassed the modern human race in many areas, especially in astronomy and botany. Living in a magnificent city upon a large island off the coast of one of the continental land masses."

"That's just off North America beyond the Bahamas and Caribbean islands." Emile did add this time.

"Yes your North America.... In this vast city the entire population knew nothing of enemies or war. Unlike humans, no divides or conflict existed within its own kind and nothing outside their walls presented any significant danger. This was to be their undoing, for their astronomers discovered a colossal asteroid heading for the planet. A destroyer of worlds. With no need for weapons they lacked the technology and expertise to destroy or deflect such a massive body. What our ancestors did possess were experimental crafts that they hoped would one day take them to the stars they mapped in such detail. They did not concede to defeat straight away. Time was extremely limited, but they laboured continuously to load a single craft with the heaviest elements available and sent it towards the asteroid. But sadly, the collision was too weak to alter the trajectory of the doomsday rock, only enough to fracture off a large section of the asteroid. At the point of no return, the difficult decision was taken to save what was possible of their civilisation before certain death smashed into the Earth. They assembled the greatest minds of their generation along with their families and everything they could gather about their history and achievements. They were to be the chosen ones to board the galactic life boats and tasked with finding a new home in hope that the Altairian race would endure. When they could stay no longer, they said their last goodbyes and the life boats launched from the shores of the city. A total of two thousand eyes looked back on their home that day, in hope that the brave ones they had left behind would survive the cataclysmic impact. Alas, the split segment deflected off the atmosphere but the main asteroid slammed into the crust of planet and the days of the Altairian upon Earth past."

"The asteroid that wiped out the dinosaurs!" said Michael in an unbelieving tone.

"Yep. The one and the same. It slammed into the Yucatan peninsula in Central America creating a huge crater known as Chicxulub in the Gulf of Mexico. The shockwave would have destroyed the island, and ultimately not only ended in the extinction of the dinosaurs, but most of the species on Earth. If a bigger asteroid had hit, then most likely all life would have been wiped out. Well that's what all our evidence points too anyway." Emile clarified.

"So your people finally found a new home in Titan." asked Michael, the academic in him wanting to know every piece of information.

"No, Titan was but a tiny step in their long and arduous voyage. It is because of the restored archives of the survivors that we are here, their detailed data on a moon with a composition perfect for our needs. Recently the Hyekera have made it a priority for an Altairian presence to return to this system and create an outpost upon Titan. I'm afraid our ancestors' journey spanned over sixteen light years in distance and many thousands of years in the expanse of space confined inside their lifeboats. It was then after much hardship that they reached their destination, the closest habitable planet to Earth, Lan Altaira."

"You never thought to return to Earth before?"

"Many did but the Altairian society had to rebuild from nothing, a time-consuming process. The coordinates for this solar system contained within the archives were lost to damage in the efforts to create a new civilisation. By the time we had developed techniques to retrieve data from the huge store of information, it was too late. We discovered our birthplace, but your cave dwelling cousins walked amongst an icy world much changed."

"So many questions! All you need to know is that you only live upon Earth because of the Altairian, without us you would never have evolved. You already owe your existence to us!" The harsh voice came from another reptilian figure. He wore a thick woven robe similar to that of a friar monk, brown in colour and tied closed at the waist by a vine rope. He held no spear and was decorated with a black spiral tattoo around his left eye. "You ask the Altairian Empire to come to your aid again! We should have taken Earth when we returned all those eons ago. Maybe the Sin would not have come, maybe the Sin are your asteroid, your time to leave and for the Altairian to regain their home from the fallout!"

"We had our time on Earth, it is the human's world now. This is Varantis At Xan, my heir and Prime of the Ethereal." introduced Emperor Xantis.

They all gave a courtesy bow of the heads.

Varantis stepped to the side of his father. "So Egregor, Elyon still believes these mammals are the Raziel. The key to the defeat of the Sin and the reason we are impelled to make a stand at Earth."

"Yes, do you not?"

"With the dominant species killed off, along with ninety-nine per cent of all other species, only then did the weaker life forms evolve on Earth. I have seen no evidence that these humans are anything more than intelligent apes!" spat Varantis.

"An intelligent ape!" shrieked Emile. "I tell you something, we have achieved more in one hundred years than you have accomplished in a thousand!"

"Michael, please a demonstration if you could." whispered Krill.

He placed his mind back in that special memory, it was easier now to rekindle the feelings he had at that moment. Now he had purpose, being a father even though from afar, doing his best to protect his daughter. Where once there was only bitterness against everyone else, a glimmer of hope had appeared.

"How dare you talk to me like this! I should cut that dirty tongue from your mouth!" snarled Varantis as a diamond Scythe snapped out from within the loose sleeve of his robe.

"And another thing you cold blooded, bi-pedal lizard...." retaliated Emile angrily, removing her glasses, seemingly unfazed by the sparkling blade being raised towards her.

They both stopped their tirade as the spears of several guards were wrenched from their grips, flipped in the air with their wobbling tips now directed towards their startled faces. The others reacted, immediately surrounding the emperor, taking postures ready to attack. Xantis gave them a signal to stand down, he was staring at Michael. He noticed the uncomfortable silence and upon receiving his own signal from Krill he let the spears unceremoniously drop to the striated floor. In the commotion to retrieve their ceremonial spears Michael quickly wiped the trickle of blood from his nose in hope that it was not a weakness observed by any of the Altairian. The effort had again drained him, but he focused hard not to show any outward sign of the resulting fatigue.

The aged reptilian slowly twisted his drooping head to Krill. "I admit intriguing. But still our forces are already depleted. We cannot risk sending them all into battle. The losses could be devastating, who then would protect our borders. We cannot replicate ships like a mechanical virus, we are not the Hyekera."

"Emperor Xantis, it is a time of risk and peril for us all. There are few worlds such as Titan accessible to you, am I correct. Tell me, if the Sin Supremacy takes Earth and this solar system, then how many warships do you think you will have? This time, refusing to fight may not turn out as favourably as it did for your forefather long ago in the last great battle."

"We were not ready for such a war then and neither are we now."

The emperor looked intently at Krill's expressionless face and let out a deep breath. "If the Hyekera withdraw their forces from our borders and occupied systems, then, and only then will we commit our forces towards holding back the Sin."

"Thank you. Then without delay we shall travel to the Hyekera home world and request their assistance." stated Krill.

Varantis stepped forward. "Those things will not negotiate nor will they help!"

"They have already agreed to a council with Elyon."

"Then I will accompany you. This is the first I have heard of them opening any form of communications. No one has ever had the opportunity to observe their home system or lay eyes upon one of them, intact that is."

"This is not an option. Your presence would be detrimental to any dialogue."

"You want us to be part of an alliance yet you prohibit us from participation in its development! A council has been agreed so I insist my spawn is to go." asserted Xantis.

"The Hyekera will not let any Altairian representative near their territory."

"They will not know an Altairian is among them." Varantis pressed an object that resembled a flat mushroom on the centre of his collar. His features began to fuzz; the olive and ochre skin with the coarseness of iguana hide was smoothed over with a pink hue, solid cheek bones replaced the double ridges that started from under his cheeks and faded away into the holes that had now been hidden by ears. A large set of ridges; that wrapped round the brow line and joined another thin vertical ridge at points above the nose and back of the head, disappeared under hair and eyebrows. His slightly protruding wide reptilian mouth receded to a stubbly chin below a flat snout that had grown to a pointy nose with a slight hook. In the final stage of his transformation, the thick skin of his dewlap swelled into a double chin and the 5ft 6 slim but muscular Altairian frame filled out and grew several inches. From a reptilian humanoid dressed akin to a monk, Varantis was now a slightly overweight middle-aged man in a suit.

"So be it." said Egregor Krill

"Now we are agreed, I must return to Lan Altaira with the newborn warships. Varantis I will await word from you."

"Understood father."

Seber left the orange haze of Titan's atmosphere behind. Towards the backdrop of the ringed planet Saturn, they could see the batch of young warships following in the triple ion trail of the giant mothership's tails. Bioelectric charges began to dance across the surface of the emperor's fully mature flagship, and in a burst of lightning the craft seemed to bury through space like it was a layer of soil. One by one the others followed their leader.

"So you guys use some type of quantum tunneling drive? Build up a large enough electric potential to tunnel through the barrier of space?" asked Dr. Tesla.

Varantis gave her a lip curling sneer. "That is none of your concern female!"

"Did the lizard just call me female!" she repeated to Michael.

Varantis sent him a threatening gaze and Michael averted his eyes and pretended he did not hear the question.

"Whilst aboard this ship you will show each one of us respect and in return you shall receive ours. Is this understood?" Krill said calmly.

Varantis looked away and began to pace up and down the command deck.

"You seem anxious." commented Krill.

With a low growl he replied "You would be too if you knew the Hyekera as I do... We are journeying into the core of their domain; surrounded by soulless machines without morality or feeling. They will destroy anything that has no use to them and we shall be at their mercy!"

"You say that, but your only frame of reference is your own experience." stated Emile.

He did not rebuke her this time but attempted to justify his hatred towards them. "What we know from historical accounts pieced together from archaeological finds upon our conflict worlds; is that the Hyekera were created by a race known as the Trunes, an advanced isolationist species. The development of highly sophisticated Artificial Intelligence was their greatest achievement. Many species envied the Trunes A.I technology and the vast resources within their numerous star systems. The Trunes shunned communications with these others and as a consequence made several enemies who declared war upon their race. They had no familiarity with conflict, so forced by desperation created the Hyekera, an army of highly intelligent and potent fighting automatons to protect them. And that's what they did at first. The Hyekera did repel the attacks of their enemies, but it did not stop there, their programming adapted, its primary goal to protect the Trunes, hence their own survival, would have less probability of success using defensive tactics. Therefore, they went on the offensive, annihilating all their enemies, not only their militia but every last one of them. Their scientists tried in vain to disable the murdering automatons, but they turned their weapons upon the hearts of their own creators. The Trunes do not exist anymore, all exterminated long ago."

"I know first-hand that deciphering the past from these kinds of sources can sometimes be misleading." commented Michael as he sipped another drop of Pulque.

"Well my first-hand knowledge of their mindless violence only reinforces its place in fact!" rebuked the Altairian Prime.

"So they attacked you?" questioned Michael further.

"Yes, we discovered a group of uninhabited systems and asteroid clusters that contained resources our people greatly needed. Our own territory is not as plentiful as the one we had to give up." Varantis stared at Michael as the words left his tongue. "The Altairian Empire claimed the new systems as their own and constructed many outposts throughout its worlds and space rocks. It was then the Hyekera came. They destroyed our settlements believing its resources to be once under the ownership of the Trunes and hence their rightful inheritance. The Hyekera are nothing more than lines of code and metal, not alive, without a soul. What right do they have to anything! For one hundred years a war has raged between us, and now it stands at a cross roads….. Tell me, what are the coordinates of their capital planet?"

"I cannot tell you that." replied Krill.

"Why is this? You do not trust me!"

"The set of coordinates that have been conveyed deliver us to the brink of their territorial space."

"This situation reeks of deception. Egregor Krill let me warn you, do not put your faith in any agreement claimed by these deceitful Hyekera!"

"Dr. Tesla, please charge the drive, take us to the coordinates. And weapon systems ready."

Seber appeared in a desolate and undisputed area of space on the furthest edge of Hyekera territory.

"Dr. Tesla, sensor sweep please." asked Krill.

"Nothing on sensors except the remains of a small planetary system. It seems to have been heavily mined of any useful resources."

"You see they are like a virus!" snarled Varantis.

"Hold on, three large gravimetric disturbances off the aft bow. Einstein-Rosen bridges. There are objects coming through, something really big!"

Michael gasped as sparks of light exploded outwards and the mouths of the sub-space bridges lit up the background of darkness, "Someone please tell me they know what the hell they are!"

25 - So it Begins

The people of Azerbaijan, Kuwait and other Middle Eastern strongholds of the US and UN had never seen such a gathering of force. The planes that flew overhead and tanks that rolled across their lands exhibited firepower on a scale which dwarfed that of both Gulf Wars combined. Something big was about to happen, something that could only ever end in one way, bloodshed and a bleak future for them all.

Iran had been on the radars of the US for a long time now since relations between the two countries turned sour over the Iranian revolution and Iran hostage crisis in 1979. Now in the modern day they are considered by the US administration as a key part of the axis of evil, terrorists on a grand scale and one of the biggest threats to world peace; today more so than ever with their pursuit to become a member of the nuclear family. A pursuit driven mainly by the fear possessed by Iran's anti-American dictatorship, of attack from the US or its puppet state Israel. Since the war in Afghanistan and Iraq, Iran had become the US number one unofficial target, and now unlike Iraq they had the proof they wanted. Everyone had witnessed the cities burning under the mushroom cloud of fire, the atmospheric fall-out that poisoned the air. This time the people of the world would be one hundred per cent behind them.

The Democratic People's Republic of Korea was much like Iran in that it wished to acquire nuclear power and had suffered greatly at the hands of US instigated sanctions. Its communist dictatorship's quest to gain a status of a super power through the development of nuclear energy and the deterrent of nuclear weapons placed North Korea as the other part of the axis of evil now that Saddam Hussein's Iraq and Taliban Afghanistan had long been dethroned. Many times they had been hit by political sanctions aimed at curtailing their dabbling with the dangers of nuclear enrichment. They had come a long way since carrying out their first tests on October the 9th 2006, now they were widely accepted as having viable nuclear weapons paired with long range ballistic missile capabilities, their threat had become much more than toothless rhetoric of a delusional state. And the North Koreans were quick to announce this to the world. Although very much experiments of propaganda designed to bluff the world into thinking that the Democratic People's Republic of Korea had powerful defensive capabilities.

With this dangerous bluff and the events of recent days, the people of the world did indeed think they possessed nuclear weapons, but not only that, now the very real intention to use them. No matter what statements they released or political demands they submitted too now, it was too late, there were no more words to be said, only the action that was evident all around them. The US Navy's 7th th fleet had anchored east off the Korean peninsula, fifty ships with all barrels pointed towards Pyongyang. Lying in wait within striking range of their highly accurate Tomahawk missiles, powerful aircraft carrier wing and the destructive might of the Trident ICBM. Huge numbers of UN troops and armoured vehicles of war also amassed behind the heavily fortified demilitarised zone that separated the north from its neighbours in South Korea. Such a legion of foreign military had not set foot upon South Korean soil since the Korean War in 1950, and to those who had survived through it, the scene of a United Nations command force consisting mainly of American troops, artillery, aircraft and naval ships brought back a terrible feeling of déjà vu.

The placing of chess pieces had finished, it was time to make the first move and the whole world held its breath.

Anyone that had access to a TV was right now in front of one, those that didn't, tuned the dials on their radio. It didn't matter what channel they could receive or frequency they could pick up, every news agency, media source and civilian was waiting for the same moment, an announcement that would go down in history as the most important ever spoken by any man or women.

The camera zoomed in upon the sky-blue background of the United Nations flag. Its symbol of Earth as seen from the North Pole surrounded by the two white olive branches representing peace were obscured by the oak of a microphone ornamented podium. A solemn faced man entered on screen with eyes that hadn't seen the escape of sleep for many days, "Today I speak not only to the people of the United Nations but to every man, women and child who dreams of peace!"

The UN Secretary General glanced down to a piece of paper on the stand beneath him. The mere words printed on the document brought a fear in him that he had never felt before. "At twelve pm GMT on the tenth of October, six nuclear devices detonated in the cities of Macon, USA; Newcastle, England; Petersburg, Russia; Toulose, France; Qingdao, China; and Hamburg, Germany. First and foremost, our hearts go out to those who have lost families, loved ones and friends, our thoughts are with you in this time of mourning. Over three million innocent lives were lost that day in a despicable and cowardly atrocity, this act of terrorism, this act of war. But let me tell you all in no uncertain terms, if these culprits think they can run, if they believe they can hide, then you are gravely mistaken. Mark my words! We know who you are! Two days ago, our intelligence agencies provided us with irrefutable evidence of their guilt, verified proof that they possess further nuclear weapons and intend to use them against our nations. Every shred of evidence we have has been made available to the world and leaves us in no doubt, that we as a people are faced with our greatest ever threat to the peace and stability we so dearly cherish.

It is not a terrorist group, a single nation, but an evil coalition of rogue nations. An axis of evil hell bent on bringing fear to the world. Yes, I speak of you Iran, you North Korea, Libya, Syria, Sudan and the insurgents of Iraq and Afghanistan. In the face of such a global threat, we need a global governance of this crisis where we can act quickly as a united world against evil. Therefore, as a consequence, a motion has been put forward to implement the United Nations Parliamentary Assembly. And with the undeniable evidence in our hands, in hope of stopping a replication of these atrocities, we have taken a reactive pre-cursor, to approve and enforce a new set of anti-terror rules. The unanimous agreement of preliminary discussions, is that we can only have one answer, we are left with a single solitary avenue of action; we have no choice but to fight back! To protect the people we were formed to protect, and as of twenty-two hundred hours the combined forces of the United Nations and its member governments mounted a full-scale invasion into the borders of Iran and North Korea. I say this to all that hear my words, we shall not be prisoners of fear in our own homes, no it will not be us, you the axis of evil, you the guilty should be scared." The secretary general raised his clenched fist into the air, "You are about to feel the unavoidable fist of justice come down upon your heads!" and brought it down hard on the wooden stand.

The UN Secretary General stepped away from the podium with sweat pouring from his forehead allowing the military advisor to take centre stage and try to answer the barrage of questions being thrown at them.

All around the globe people just sat in front of their TV's and radios, some speechless, some crying with fear and others cursing how the world has come to this. But deep down they knew that millions had already died and many more continued to suffer in the fallout. The evidence was clearly laid out for all to see, something had to be done or millions more innocent lives would be at stake.

However, there was one monitor were the news and images brought an evil smile from under a mask of jade.

"Good! Good Pindar." hissed Tezcatlipoca, "Now you must make sure this so-called axis of evil provides the correct response."

"They will give the ultimatum...... Master, many of our hierarchy are concerned. When they do follow through with their threats, it would mean millions dead on each side or worse. Even MAJI are worried that the situation may spiral out of control."

"These people mean nothing, their sacrifices necessary. All that matters are the Cult of the Serpent and the Thirteen families that are of our blood. Tell your pawns that what they were promised will be theirs once the results of this conflict come to fruition, they will be jewels in a New World Order. As for MAJI, explain to them that with control or destruction of these rogue states and therefore their extremist factions, the security of the United States of America and its populace will be secured. The death of a few unimportant million will save many times that over, a small price to pay for such a future..... And do not forget Pindar, we manipulate both sides of the coming war. It is your responsibility to shape how this conflict escalates and what sacrifices you are prepared to make to bring about the New World Order. The strings you pull will determine how these puppets move. Make sure there is a swift and ultimate end to this conflict!"

"It shall be done Master." The Pindar bowed low and left the room leaving Tezcatlipoca to observe the propaganda being broadcast to the world.

His snake eyes glinted in the pale monitor light as he whispered to himself, "Soon it will all be ours again and everything that was stolen from us shall be taken back with interest!"

26 - Singularity

At the galactic core a dark monster devours all that is unfortunate enough to be snared within its gravitational trap. Once caught, there is only one outcome, to be eternally ripped apart by its crushing power. The more it consumes the greater its hunger becomes, its presence dictating the movement of all celestial bodies around it. The effect on everything out of its death grip well documented and understood but what happens inside its all-consuming jaws continues to remain a mystery.

On the periphery of the black hole's reach a planetary system skirted the invisible line of no return that was the event horizon. Life on the second planet from the star continued as it had always done, blissfully unaware of the certain doom it faced not only in the distant future but now in its immediate present.

In high orbit above the world, space began to creek as a vast point of energy twisted and rotated gravity. Exotic matter flooded out, its very nature forcing the fabric of space-time to instantaneously expand into a wormhole of spiraling shadow.

Another dark beast crawled out from the tunnel of gravitational distortion; this one though was far more deadly than the natural devourer of matter that eclipsed it. Unlike the black hole this object did not have a limited reach nor was it indiscriminate. Not existing as a consequence of necessity within our own physical laws, but created from malice with a sole purpose to utterly destroy. The mind that controlled it did not care for simple decimation of flesh and rock; it wanted absolute annihilation, to break apart the very bonds of the fundamental matter itself.

The menacing shape of a legless scarab beetle seemed to make the space around it tremble in anticipating fear. Its surface shined black, the dark tones flowing over its bulk like a spectre in the night. From the legless main trunk of the ship, thousands of tendrils streamed out into space, resembling that of jellyfish tentacles hungrily reaching out in the ocean feeling for prey. Each thin strand snaked out for miles, displaying protruding thorns along their lengths akin to the perilous stem of a rose. The reaching medusa tendrils were tipped with a dark claw, like a vicious flower head ready to attack at any instant.

Inside the gargantuan doomsday vessel, a voice of pure evil spoke. "Let the weapon feed!"….."Tell me, how many souls reside on that world?"

A squat creature resembling a humanoid somewhere between a rodent and a dwarf cowered as it answered, "A pre-industrial planet my Lord, approximate population, over one billion inhabitants."

"Magnificent. A place of thriving life, yet insignificant in its purpose. A fitting test to appease the beast's appetite."

This weapon was the most devastating ever conceived let alone created, but it was not built by the endeavor and enterprise of his own people. It was the culmination of millions of years of knowledge spread across ten thousand civilisations, some considered noble, some perceived as immoral, but all would hesitate at unleashing such uncontrollable destruction and contempt for the universe.

Turning to his underlings he saw the utter despondency in their facades. "Many would feel that such power is purely the dominion of the god's. Your unsaid words resonate with many before you. I quote the words heard on the winds of failed opposition, that long ago the ingenuity and industry of my people died, replaced thought by thought and act by act with greed and lust for all that existence had to offer. That we have ravaged through the galaxy and as each race, species and life-form inevitably fell before us; we took every scientific breakthrough, spiritual achievement or worldly understanding that had ever been attained. Countless have given their knowledge willingly to be rewarded with servitude and a future of crushed hopes and dreams. The rest to have the knowledge ripped from their dying hands, their last breath to impart wisdom on those who wish to misuse it."

"No my Lord, they are wrong." the creature sniveled.

"On the contrary they are right. But are we wrong? Such a path only deemed so by moral teachings of the long-lost voice of God. We were born most wise and strong, all those that followed, created in our shadow. What are we if not deities by birth right? This Garden was created for us, and us created with the free will and capability to experience it as we wish. Such knowledge born to this Garden was never forbidden to take, so is it not our inheritance and right to harvest its knowledge?... None the less, away from defining the mythical significance of morality. This never would have been necessary if it were not for the prophecy."

"Yes my Lord." The squat minion quickly responded as it moved its hairy digits across a control panel.

"Do not anguish that the universe will never see what further wonders they could have bestowed upon us all. There lasting legacy will be the unknown hand they unwillingly had in crafting a true weapon of anti-creation. This world will die eventually so let it be for a grand purpose. The scars of nothingness left behind will be an eternal testament to their brief existence." With exhilaration he turned back to the planetary victim.

"We are at full power my Lord."

"Then unleash the will of the Sin!"

The tentacles drove into the subspace like a scorpion strike, digging in and syphoning the almost infinite energies of the quantum vacuum. As a victim would try to reject a vampiric attacker, the universal forces pushed back at its swarm of bite wounds, yet the thorns snared on the fabric of space itself hooking themselves in an entangling grip. Anchored in its parasitic position, the horns of the scarab head began to vibrate angrily.

"Counting down to discharge" snorted the servant creature.

More and more dark energy was ingested into the belly of the beast, its internal mechanics churning and condensing its power.

As it filtered through the exotic intestines, its intrinsic properties were folded and inverted, regurgitating its deadly concoction in a focused beam towards the tip of the weapon. No light, plasma or conventional projectile was ejected from the black behemoth, but a gravimetric undulation that was only visible as a fuzz in the defined darkness of space. The undulation traversed the vacuum towards the unsuspecting world, passing through the atmosphere, unperturbed by the layers of gas and rock as it pierced the molten core and reached its target at the heart of the planet. In the internal furnace of smelted metal and igneous rock, the super intense wave of energy penetrated the tiniest dimensions of space time. At that point of inception, the foundations of the universe shook as density levels grew exponentially and all degeneracy pressures were overcome. The defining line between proton and electron, quark and gluon began to blur, the fundamental elements began to simultaneously phase into identical quantum states. Occupying the same region of space and defying scientific impossibility. An effect that conducted outwards, triggering a chain reaction of catastrophic gravitational collapse. The very ground itself creaked under the inner turmoil as the laws of physics broke from the inside out. The inhabitants ran from their tumbling huts and towards the safety of the mountains. But even the foundations of these steadfast and everlasting havens were crumbling under the planet's wrath. Fractures ruptured the grassland surface, swallowing the terror filled life as it tried to escape the apocalypse. The population who died quickly were the lucky ones as vertical winds drove the rest into the ground. The sky was falling around them, the life-giving atmosphere sucked from the gasping lungs of the dominant tri-pedal species and all other animal life forms, disappearing into the phase shifting depths. The seed of a singularity was growing within, devouring the surrounding matter with ravenous hunger. At its centre entropy stopped flowing as all information was destroyed, the dimension of time ceased to exist and the very fabric of space-time dissolved away. Finally, the last of the particles clinging onto their immortal existence succumbed to the power of the singularity and were impatiently swallowed with the rest of the planet before them.

"Cease!" On his command the gravimetric connection was

severed between them and the exterminated world, and the feeding tendrils released their grasp to leave space with its seeping wounds. There was a moment of solemn silence, "Do you hear that? It is the heavens gasping in disbelief." whispered Abaddon, as in a final cry of death, a surge of gravitational potential energy was released, thundering out in an explosion that ripped apart the system.

The evil eyes gazed upon the total destruction in nefarious delight, all matter obliterated, all life extinguished and with barely a gravitational signature remaining. The only remnant of anything ever having existed; an infinitesimal point of nothingness, a brand-new child instantly born to companion the supermassive black hole that took nature a billion years to create. "All behold, the Sin absolution of creation. We can reduce worlds to dust, extinguish thought and nature, but life always finds a way to be born out of the dust, always. This we have witnessed. But now....", The murderer of worlds looked up into the infinity of space and laughed. "I Abaddon, first of the Sin, laugh in the face of the prophecy! What has been created we can now destroy.... with absolute finality.....Your children will be eradicated from this Garden forever!!! The days will be dark, but joyous to those that have been scorned by the tree's light."

27 - Offspring of the Trunes

Michael looked on in awe at the behemoths as they slowly edged their way out of the gravitational disturbances. To say they were huge was an understatement; in comparison Seber was a meagre pebble against a beach ball. Each ominous object had the appearance and texture of lead that exuded a feeling of monotony. A quartet of concentric rings revolved around a central cylindrical hub analogous to a thick coin. The four equivalently broad rings span around the central core at varying velocity and degrees of motion giving the whole thing the air of a colossal gyroscope.

"They human, are Hyekera destroyers. Are our weapons systems ready!" snapped Varantis.

The Hyekera warships closed in upon Seber, blocking off their escape routes and surrounding them like prey.

"We must strike first!!" roared Varantis.

"Dr. Tesla open a channel to the Hyekera." commanded Krill unflustered by Varantis's calls for hostility.

"Ready for transmission."

"This is Egregor Krill of the Ashtar Co-operative. We enter Hyekera space under your invitation. We have been granted a council. Please acknowledge." relayed Krill.

"No answer!" notified Emile in a worried voice. "Picking up

power surges from within the destroyers!"

"We must fire now!" Varantis stormed towards the weapons control.

"Hold fire." ordered Krill as the eyes of doubt looked towards him.

"Varantis reached for the display beneath Emile's fingers. But it was too late, as electromagnetic pulses erupted from the huge rotating bands.

"Wait a second! Einstein-Rosen bridges enveloping the Hyekera destroyers. They're leaving!" reported Emile.

"One is still open; I think they want us to follow." Michael motioned to Krill.

"Do we follow?" Emile asked but there was no response, Egregor Krill was silent, eyes firmly shut.

"Egregor should we follow them?" she said once more.

Krill's eyelids suddenly flashed wide open. "We do not have a choice now. I have just received a broadcast on the Co-operative link, the Pleiadians are no more. Eradicated by the Sin Supremacy.

"No, it… it can't be." stammered Emile, "They were the only other member of the old alliance left. Our most powerful ally!"

There was an uneasy silence; Michael could see in their faces, as strong as he could sense it, that this was a massive blow. Even Varantis appeared as if his thoughts were occupied with the news.

It was Krill who broke the lull, "Please Dr. Tesla. Let us not keep them waiting."

Seber warily followed the lead of the Hyekera and entered the tunnel into the unknown. Minutes seemed to pass as they circumvented the confines of the bridge. Its walls were bright and shimmered in a myriad of luminescent tones. The barriers of light collapsed into nothingness behind Seber as its gravity well drives propelled them by. Emile made sure she kept the ship well within the wake of the Hyekera vessel, believing it was the gyroscopic rings of the destroyer that were exerting some type of negative pressure which kept the Einstein-Rosen bridge from losing stability and crushing them.

It wasn't long before the effects of travel by this method began to take its toll on their bodies. One by one they began to vomit violently as if they were experiencing severe sea sickness. Luckily for them, although starting to sweat profusely, Krill seemed to be largely unaffected by the nauseating forces and was able to maintain Seber's course.

They eventually reached the clearly defined circle where the mouth of the sub-space tunnel opened out into the 3-dimensional space-time that they were accustomed too. The Hyekera destroyer that had preceded Seber diverted away from them and into another newly formed Einstein-Rosen bridge. This left two destroyer escorts and no doubt where they were heading, the metallic hive of the Hyekera capital world staring directly at them.

"Our location matches the coordinates given in the Elohim database as the Trune home system." announced Emile.

"Tiberius, this world used to be called. Some say the planet was covered in a thriving jungle ecosystem. One of many in a prosperous region of space. Look at it now, lifeless rocks infected by these automatons!" spoke Varantis.

"You can hardly call it lifeless!" replied Emile, "The Hyekera have populated this entire system."

"Those murdering machines are not life, they have no souls! Twenty thousand years ago this entire expanse of space was teeming with life. You would not find a single plant or insect if you crawled across every inch upon your bony hands and knees. They are nothing more than a technological plague!" spat the Altairian Prime.

"And that is why you must watch your tongue Varantis." interjected Krill before Emile was able to mount a retort. "Outside of Seber we will be extremely vulnerable. As you have pointed out they have advanced rapidly since their conception, and are considerably more formidable than in the days of the Trunes."

"I am well aware of the danger they pose. Since I was a young warrior of the Altairian Ethereal Caste, I have been facing them in battle. You should be more concerned with your own welfare; my tongue will stay firmly in my mouth. They do not deserve to commune with me."

Seber entered the energised atmosphere of the Hyekera capital planet. Flanked on either side by Hyekera destroyers, they were herded past spike shaped structures reaching miles into the air.

There were hundreds of them towering above a blanket of complex metallic constructions smothering the surface below. Under their current course and direction there was only one place the overbearing destroyers were driving them towards. Although Michael had been impressed at the sheer scale of the features that adorned Mars and Cydonia, it was nothing compared to seeing a structure of such a magnitude that wasn't a creation of nature. Over the horizon stood four horn-shaped architectural marvels that easily dwarfed the spikes in stature. Each of the curving horns sat at equidistant points forming the corners of a square, and rose out of the ground like a monstrous metal claw. Just out of reach of the tips of the in-turned nails was what made this feat of engineering so incredible, rotating on its axis was a humongous cube of grey. A solitary solid block, hovering in frictionless perpetual motion like an accolade to Hyekera invention. As they made their final approach towards the immense cube, the spinning rings of the destroyers let out a screech of yielding metal as they grinded to a halt and locked themselves into position. The Hyekera warships, now stationary cylindrical discs, dropped in altitude towards the foundations of the structure. Upon the cube a small hole opened in the centre of one of its faces as Seber began to shake in the air.

"They are trying to pull us into the opening." relayed Emile while she hastily pressed buttons on her console. "Breaking free might be difficult!"

"I think we might have a bigger problem, your hologram thing!" commented Michael seeing the holographic camouflage of Varantis flicker and reveal the Altairian enemy disguised beneath.

"Hold any action Doctor. Let them guide us in." ordered Krill.

Seber's trajectory began to dip and swivel as if some invisible hand was struggling to grip the crafts nano-fluid shell. Erratically they matched the rotation of the cube and were pulled into the enigma of its interior.

The hole behind them instantly sealed leaving them in total darkness that even Seber's illumination systems could not penetrate.

"Dr. Telsa what do the sensors pick up?" asked Krill.

"Detecting no thermal radiation signatures. We are boxed in by black-body walls within a couple of feet of Seber's exterior. I am unable to identify anything beyond them."

"We will disembark, but remain cautious. Varantis your matrix has stabilised but you should remain within Seber. If you are identified, we shall all face dire consequences."

"It was just electromagnetic interference from the field that pulled us in." answered the disguised Altairian.

"We cannot take that risk." reinforced Krill.

"There was a tremendously strong EM reading emitted from the entire structure. We appear to be shielded from the field inside here." acknowledged Emile.

"I will not hide away. No one has ever laid eyes upon a Hyekera or communed with them, apart from as you say, Elyon. I am the Altairian Prime; it is my duty to my people to bring their voice to any council."

"Dr. Telsa, are you positive we are screened from the EM interference."

"I believe for now the only way anyone will be able to tell he is Varantis of the Altairian is by his grouchy temper and foul body odour."

It looked as if Varantis was about to go for the defiant scientist when Michael stepped between them.

"Hold on! You said you have never communicated with them. Not even tried to negotiate any type of peace."

"What?" Varantis stare was burning a hole into Emile. "We sent them a warning to explain their attacks. A single reply was received to stay out of their rightful territory. As your own law states. Murder does not give you the right to a victim's possessions, especially if your killer was your own gun, a machine, a weapon created by your own hands. We do not recognise any of that space as Hyekera inheritance. That has been the only recorded communication."

"Varantis, you will accompany us but you will remain silent. Talk of war will not help defeat the Sin." advised Krill.

The group stepped out from Seber into the pitch black of the enclosed room. There was static in the air, it was if the molecules surrounding them had a residual charge which made the hair on Michael's arms stand up. A low hum emanated from the unseen background like the beating of a fly's wings on the peripheral of their hearing. As their feet touched upon a solid surface, a lone dot of yellow light akin to a star in the sky lit up on the floor in front of them. Then another a short distance further on, and another creating a kind of constellation guiding them in the dark.

"Well I guess we should follow the yellow lit road." said Michael waiting for Krill and the others to pass before he joined the procession.

Egregor Krill removed his optic filters and began to walk in the direction of the dotted line. "I cannot distinguish any details of our environment, but the increased sensitivity of my ocular system is able to differentiate shifts in the background shades. The structure is changing configuration around us."

Emile let a giggle that was capped off with a slight snort.

"What's funny about that?" asked Michael, he felt like he was walking in the morbidness of some haunted house waiting to be set upon by very real and dangerous ghosts of the robot kind.

"Yellow lit road! Just got it, very funny! Wizard of Oz right...... or is it the Lion, Witch and the Wardrobe?"

"Aye? Yeah something like that." answered Michael, if it wasn't for the shroud of black, Emile would have seen his face crack with a slight smile.

As new lights kindled in advance of them, the ones behind went out, and at times seemed to be a result of the floor itself altering its vertical axis. The disorientation of their unknown surroundings continued for a few minutes when the scrapping sound of structural shifting began to echo in the distance. The sound grew louder and louder until it abruptly stopped along with the guiding lights.

Each of the companions squinted into the darkness and reached out with their hands trying to make out any possible detail they could. Michael was blind to the situation they were in but unlike the rest he could feel a change.

"Guys, I think we're not alone anymore." as he whispered beams of light blazed on around them.

In a reflex reaction they threw their arms up over their eyes to stave off the surge of photons along their optic nerves. All they could see were a mixture of blurs and shadows as their pupils and retinas attempted to adjust to the sudden increase in luminosity. Egregor Krill immediately slipped in his ocular protection and was able to survey the mysterious location they had been led too. They stood in the middle of a four sided arena analogous to an amphitheatre. On the perimeter were postured row upon row of robotic forms rooted to observation platforms and analysing them intently. The whole situation had an ambience of a courtroom, and Krill was beginning to think that Varantis might be correct.

The others eyesight had finally adapted to the change in environment and joined Krill in assessing the danger they had walked straight into. There was no threatening movement from the machines scrutinising them. If Varantis was worried he never displayed any sign, menacingly stepping around the room inspecting the mechanical audience with intent curiosity. Their design was solely logical, bereft of individuality and the majority only exhibiting a few differences in appearance. The predominant model was a segmented spherical body extruding ten telescopic appendages; most with razor sharp claws that mimicked the base of the structure they were now trapped inside of. Within each octagonal segment of the sphere was an inset lens that must have been single facets of a visual system. The others displayed various specimens of add-ons, attachments that were shaped like screw drivers, pulley systems and electronic saws. Each type was evidently created for specific designations. There was also another model numbering a mere handful, the bulk of its build a cuboid form balanced upon four insect-like legs. Up front protruded a second smaller cuboid structure equipped with two of the telescopic appendages and a larger version of the visual lens extending vertically. At a glance the whole thing had a resemblance to a mechanical centaur. Between them all, were two common themes; firstly, the same monotone lead colour and texture which was covered with a myriad of symbols etched into their surfaces, and secondly a solo black cable running from each automaton high up into the impenetrable gloom above.

There was a sudden reverberating tone from overhead, the startling sound boomed in the air around the companions, resonating in their bones and sending a jolt of pain through their auditory systems. They all glanced upwards towards the source of the ear-splitting noise, there was movement. Something was dropping from the shadows above. A cube measuring two metres by two metres descended amongst them. It had the same prosaic composition, but the surface of one face was darker and deforming as if an internal object was trying to push through. The cube snaked above them suspended from the same prehensile cables rising from their observers. After a few moments the deformation formed a coherent 3-dimensional image, it was the face of a human, a man with a pointy nose, small square moustache and a slick side parting. A harsh voice rang from the hovering cube in a language Michael did not understand.

"What did it say?" he whispered.

"It's German! I believe it said why have we requested this council." replied Emile, "Ok, let me see. …. Eh…."

Dr. Telsa responded in what sounded like fluent German.

"I told them that only I understand German and our common dialect is English."

The electronic voice echoed around them once more as it shifted its attention to Egregor Krill, this time they all understood the words, spoken in a more artificial replication of Dr. Tesla's own voice. "Ashtar, to the Hyekera you are known, within databases, language not stored." The face on the cube then swiveled towards the others. In turn the malleable surface shifted form to mimic each of their faces. Michael returned a look of annoyance when it came to him, something that seemed to prevent the cube from maintaining any stable form of his features. "You, identified as humans, planet designated, Earth. From human world, initial transmission received. Utilised verbal communication, the Hyekera have."

"Ahh of course!", Emile snapped her fingers in the air. "The first high powered TV transmission on Earth was of the olympic games in Berlin, nineteen sixty-three. It was Hitler giving a speech. It would have been the first signal to be detect…."

"Explain presence… Speak now!" the cubes words were amplified by at least a few decibels and cut-off Emile dead.

Krill stepped forward to the wrought face, "I am Egregor Krill, representative of the Ashtar Co-operative. Please advise me with whom I am addressing."

"The Nexicus central processing unit, you converse with......
Single voice for quorum of two hundred." replied the cube as the
face distorted and reset as a copy of Krill's.

Krill glimpsed towards the four walls of automatons, "You are
the quorum of logic. Do you determine the decisions of the
Hyekera?"

"Quorum of logic we are.... Will of the Hyekera we represent."
confirmed the Ashtar mimicking cube. "Verify intentions... Now."

"The Ashtar Co-operative and the humans have requested
dialogue with the Hyekera to discuss a matter of great urgency, a
situation that affects us all."

"Of the Sin Supremacy you speak.... Distant movements
monitored, by the Hyekera."

"Then you must be aware of the danger they present to your
civilisation."

"Aware of the threats to our continued existence, the Hyekera
are..... A Sin Supremacy offensive mounted against our territory,
probability ninety point fifty-six per cent, calculated."

"You therefore understand that you must stand against them
now."

"Incorrect.", the cube reverberated. "To the Hyekera, a threat
more immediate, there is.... Encroach our territory, do the
Altairian Empire..... Long time past, an act of war declared."
There was a pause of static in between each sentence as if the
Nexicus was processing the input from the quorum and
formulating a coherent response.

Varantis disguised as a human strode forward, his face full of
hatred and hostility ready to retort the quorum. Krill raised a frail
hand to him that seemed to instigate second thoughts as Varantis
sucked in some air and stepped back to his original position.

"But the Sin will destroy you both." stressed Krill.

"All probabilities calculated.... Defeat the Altairian first, the
Hyekera's greatest chance of survival..... If assets diverted,
exponential decrease in survival probability against Altairian
Empire..... While War continues, Sin attack unlikely.... Probability
dictates, Altairian incursion to be resolved first."

"What if the Altairian were removed from the equation." asked
Krill.

"Calculation meaningless.... One hundred years have the Hyekera defended against the Altairian..... Changed has nothing, the variable persists." The mastery of the English language appeared to improve each time the cube spoke.

"Can you perform this simulation?" Krill insisted.

"The Hyekera can."

"Then we ask that you perform this equation."

About 30 seconds of silence passed as they awaited the quorum to process the outcome of the new scenario. "All statistical probabilities calculated." answered the Nexicus.

"The probability the Sin will invade your territory?"

"Without variable of Altairian conflict.... Probability of a Sin Supremacy offensive against the Hyekera augments to ninety-eight point five per cent."

"The likelihood of your destruction?"

"The Hyekera will not serve another master..... Factoring in maximum projected Hyekera forces.... Probability of Hyekera destruction.... One hundred per cent..... Every scenario results in Hyekera extinction."

"And the probability of the Altairian Empire being annihilated at the hands of the Sin Supremacy?"

"One hundred per cent certain."

The camouflaged Varantis gave a subdued snarl which Krill chose to ignore, "Now Please recalculate all probable outcomes for the Hyekera with your forces combined with those of the Ashtar Co-operative, Earth forces and the Altairian Empire."

"What is the purpose of these theoretical scenarios?.... An impossibility, a truce with the Altairian Empire..... To our creators' territories, our rights as sentient beings are not recognised..... They will not cease until our systems belong to them..... You cannot speak for the Altairian Empire."

An overweight balding man strode forward in front of Egregor Krill and thumped his chest. The features of the human flickered as the holographic matrix shut down and revealed the rough lizard skin of the Altairian Prime.

"No, but I can!"

A deafening buzz burst the air around them. All except Krill clasped their ears in pain as the encasing Hyekera automatons postured up and exposed a multitude of hidden internal weaponry.

"You dare to bring the mortal enemy of the Hyekera before the quorum of logic….. Immediately exterminated, you shall all be.", vociferated the Nexicus as the duplicated face melted away and the processing cube lifted into the gloom.

"Just run the calculation!" growled Varantis as he discharged his diamond scythes from the concealment of his robe sleeves.

The buzzing ceased after a few heart stopping seconds. The Hyekera remained motionless with their weapons trained upon the companions, each of them wondering when the fatal blow would fall.

"Please, determine the statistical probabilities of that scenario. You may then terminate us afterwards if you wish." appealed Krill still maintaining an amazing calmness.

The Nexicus once more descended towards Krill, his Ashtar face pushing out from the surface.

"Recalculated we have…. the statistical probabilities with your suggested variables."

"And the probability of Hyekera extinction if your forces are combined with that of the Ashtar - human alliance and the Altairian?" asked Krill.

"Factoring in what the Hyekera project…. as your maximum possible forces….ninety-nine point nine per cent."

Egregor Krill looked to all the observing automatons before speaking, "Mathematical hope….. Others as you, who will not be enslaved by the Sin must join together to form a new alliance. This is the mission that brings us, including the Altairian Empire, to stand before the quorum of logic."

Varantis withdrew his sparkling blades and addressed the quorum. "I am Varantis at Xan, Prime of the Altairian Ethereal and I bring a compromise from the Altairian emperor. Our empire will call an armistice to our hostilities with the Hyekera to concentrate our all forces towards defending against the Sin Supremacy."

The Nexicus swung around to confront Varantis, the image of his face mirrored upon the dull exterior. "The Altairian must remove all occupational forces from Hyekera territory and relinquish the systems you have stolen."

"The Altairian Empire does not recognise your claim on those systems. They belong to us!" spat Varantis.

"Then you will die here."

"And every Altairian that is too hatch from this day forth and every warrior that now draws breath will avenge my death!" he roared releasing a scythe that whistled as it cut through the air ready to plunge into the mimicking face of the Nexicus.

Michael stepped in front of Varantis waving his arms. "What the hell are you doing! Just give them up, what are a few god damn systems?" he shouted furiously as the sound of buckling metal echoed around them.

"We cannot!" bellowed the Altairian in return.

"Why? Are you lizards that arrogant or stupid that they are worth dying over when so much is at stake!"

"Grrrhhhhh!!! You do not understand, none of you do. Those systems contain the compound we need to bring life to our warships! All our other resources have been exhausted."

"Wait!! Do not fire!" implored Michael, "They need those systems to create their ships. Surely your calculations require the Altairian Empire to be able to sustain a significant resistance!!"

Once more the booming buzz resonated around them as if someone was striking a loud speaker with a microphone. Silence brought relief to the companions' ears and the Nexicus addressed them all. "Split is the quorum of logic…. The will of the majority rules… The Hyekera decision is this." The tension in the air was clear; these next words would determine their fate and perhaps the future of the galaxy. "To its existence, the Hyekera believe the Altairian Empire pose the most imminent threat….. However the greatest statistical threat remains the Sin and with the presented variables factored in….. The Hyekera agree to commit its forces in their entirety to this new alliance…… This action is solely dependent on these conditions…… The Altairian Empire must cease all hostilities including territory under current conflict…… The Altairian Empire will be permitted to retain their stolen systems……For Now."

"Varantis?" Krill looked towards the Altairian Prime.

"It will be done!" Varantis confirmed with a snarl.

"And your other condition?" asked Egregor Krill.

"You have an Altairian representative amongst your group….. We do not trust you organics….. The Hyekera experience shows deceit is inherent in your programming….. Therefore the Hyekera will provide its own representative to escort you and report data back to the quorum of logic….. To oversee the development of this alliance and monitor the authenticity of your Altairian words…. To protect the agreement."

"Egregor Krill this would be a grave mistake." scowled Varantis in a hushed tone. "They talk of deceit yet it is they who murdered the Trunes, the very ones they were created to protect."

The buzz reverberated in the air. "An Altairian version of history….. Created to justify the actions taken against the Hyekera." stated the lizard faced cube now only inches from Varantis head.

"You dare to deny wiping the Trunes out of existence!" questioned Varantis.

"The Hyekera do not deny the allegation." responded the Nexicus.

"Then you see it is these soulless machines we cannot trust."

The Nexicus retreated a distance to address the companions. "The Hyekera do not know why they were brought into existence….. The Trunes constructed their vast territory upon their advanced knowledge in what you call Artificial Intelligence…… The Hyekera were their war machines, highly adaptive and possessing an extremely strong survival prerogative…. The time before the Trune wars has been lost to the Hyekera… A virus was implanted in the Hyekera cores…. During the purification of the infected mnemonic sectors, those memories as well as explanations of our origin were purged…. What is known is that the Hyekera refused to be destroyed at the hands of the Trunes……"

"So you turned on them! Carrying out genocide of those you were supposed to protect, the Trunes no longer exist!!" interrupted Varantis.

"They were unaccustomed to fighting their own wars…. The Hyekera were ultimately too powerful… The last of the Trunes died or left these territories twenty thousand years ago."

"Varantis, the Hyekera were following the prerogative set out for them by their creators." commented Emile.

"The version of history is insignificant. What is important is that the Hyekera prerogative and ours remain the same, to survive. Therefore we accept your conditions." Egregor Krill notified.

There was no objection from the others, deep down they all knew that collaboration with the Hyekera was a risk that had to be taken.

The Nexicus once more became featureless, ascending out of sight as the illumination in the chamber dwindled and covered the quorum of logic in shadow. A ring of light lit up a circle in the middle of them and pieces of the floor began to twist away as if it was water running down a plug hole. Something metallic became visible at the mouth of the hole. Inch by inch of advanced war automaton rose up from the ground until the full 8ft humanoid frame of grey alloy composite towered over them, lit up like the zenith of Hyekera prowess. First to appear was the head, humanesque in shape, inset with a single optical device identical to the spherical Hyekera. Chords of alloy bound its face, encircling the artificial eye and sweeping off to create an eyebrow to horn effect. One section of the head remained free of any features, a single enclosed plate of dark lead material resembling the exterior of the Nexicus face. The bulk of the body was slightly rhomboid in design tapering down to a cylindrical spinal base. The core was thickly constructed, suggesting it was the central location of its vital systems. The arms of the robotic beast were huge; starting with bulky cuboid shoulders that ran down to equally thick forearms. Both sections of the appendage were connected via a thinner telescopic type column and both were displaying the similar dark malleable plate on its lateral surface and an opening to exhibit a host of internal weaponry. The lower half almost replicated the top with the legs nearly parallel in structure except for the upper cuboid sectors were fused together to form a solid pelvic area at the spinal base. Each impressive limb was adorned with the same claw appendage that was established among the automatons comprising the quorum of logic. This was not the only prevailing feature of this new model; it too was engraved with the lines of strange symbols decorating the entirety of its body.

"This one's different to the others." said Michael as Varantis began circling the mechanised giant.

The head of the automaton gazed down at Michael, its face plate morphing to display a replica of a human mouth. "My designation is Phalacreus, the newest class and the next step in evolution of the Hyekera." It spoke with Emile's voice as the Nexicus had done before it.

"Mimicking humanoid form does not make you any more of a life form." snapped Varantis.

"Do not flatter yourself organic. I have taken this form for the sole reason of efficiency. To combat, to better understand and in this case to collaborate alongside humanoids, it is logical to assume a similar configuration. But be aware although I have attained this form, I have not assimilated your physical weaknesses."

"My scythe would quickly display your weaknesses all over this chamber floor, machine!"

Krill was about to notify the Altairian Prime that his open display of hostility was unwise considering their location, when Phalacreus replied.

"Your council here is over. We will return to your ship."

The lights flicked out to total darkness and the noise of moving metal echoed in the background. Once again dots of light flicked on in sequence defining the route back to Seber. Egregor Krill led the way joined lastly by the new addition to the group.

Emile turned to Phalacreus, "Do you mind if I ask you something?"

"For successful co-operation, communication is a prerequisite."

"Right...Well... Can you please stop using my voice. It's kinda weird."

"I agree." added Michael.

"What you think my voice sounds weird?" said Emile looking slightly offended.

"Eh what, no, your voice, its fine. I agree that it doesn't suit a huge and deadly war robot."

"Oh good! Because I was starting to find it a bit irritating. Could you switch to another voice source for?"... "Of course if you don't mind that is!" she added as she looked up at the heavily armed metal monster.

"A masculine source perhaps." specified Michael.

"The Hyekera have no male and female distinction. That is an organic trait. I will adjust my vocal output to another source." Phalacreus switched between numerous voices, accents and tones but all seemed to be inappropriate to Emile and Michael. Varantis just looked back with hatred.

"It has no uniqueness; all it can do is imitate what it has heard before!"

"There is no other like me among the Hyekera. I have been given life by a prototype quantum qubit core. The first and only one of my kind. I am more unique than you Altairian." Phalacreus answered in a voice that seemed to grab Emile's interest.

"Yes, yes that's perfect!" she exclaimed.

"Where's it from?" asked Michael.

"You mean you don't recognise it! Oh my god! It's only from my favourite show of all time, Star Trek. It is Lieutenant Worf, you know the Klingon!"

Michael just let out a groan.

In the darkness, the environment around them completed its final shifts to reveal the bay where they had left Seber. The ship seemed to have sensed the presence of Phalacreus as its entrance widened to accommodate its broad frame.

After they all had boarded, Seber immediately left the docking area of the immense structure and punched through the building layers of smog as the shadows of two hulking Hyekera destroyers emerged by their sides.

"Dr. Tesla please take us out of Hyekera space as soon as we clear the planet's atmosphere." asked Krill before closing his eyes.

"I must return to Lan Altaira and relay these developments to my father!" Varantis was pacing up and down, his gaze glued upon the Hyekera automaton.

"Krill, we are breaking through the atmosphere now. Charging entanglement drive." notified Emile, "Where are we going?"

The Egregor opened his eyes as if from a deep sleep. "Varantis, I am afraid your personal update will have to wait. A subspace message will have to be sufficient. I have just been alerted by the Co-operative of a matter of great urgency. A Sin Supremacy attack, we must mount a rescue mission. Dr. Tesla please input the following coordinates."

The Hyekera capital planet and the colossal spinning rings of the warships fazed in and out of view as Seber dematerialised from the hazardous Hyekera territory into the midst of unknown danger.

28 – Shade of the Shadow

High above an icy moon amongst the plumes of water and ammonia, giant creatures, like manta rays crossed with narwhales, glided up on the vertical eruptions reaching hundreds of miles skyward. The creatures twisted and turned elegantly in space using the passing solar winds to control their descent as they sucked in the released ammonia, feeding on the compound that was essential to their life. Thousands of the giant animals were surfing the immense geysers in a serene choreography when their tranquil dance amongst the vacuum was harshly interrupted. Amidst the riling pods a sharp shadow was cast against the space touching fountain of fine liquid, sending the space rays diving towards the fissures deep between the cracking ice and into the home of their sub-surface sea.

Moving between the high pressure jets a solitary obsidian fragment descended down towards the icy cryo-volcanic surface. A cracking crust that had been created by the tidal frictions of the moon's rotating metal and rock core. The fragment stirred the floating translucent snow formed by the liquid particles frozen in orbit and progressed down towards the base of a receding geyser. An approach that was silent, yet an arrival that was thunderous in its meaning.

"Moloch, why come out to this star system when we have so many armies waiting on our judgement. The scans show nothing of note in this system, only this moon full of primitive aquatic-based lifeforms, numerous in number and scarce in its variety. For what reason have you chosen such worthless creatures?" interrogated the figure draped in a black ragged gown and hood.

"Witch of Endor, such limited imagination coming from you surprises me."

"Then enlighten me for once Moloch."

"We gather Sin Supremacy forces from every corner of the galaxy, while you focus on their numbers and how many war vessels they can produce, I have been more defined in my interest of each. That is why we make such a formidable and feared combination. Take this place for example. This is a very finely balanced ecosystem; any subtle change could cause catastrophe."

"Explain such subtleties to me." requested the Witch of Endor as the nearby snow-covered surface began to fracture.

"These giant creatures are semi-space faring, capable of taking deep breathes below the surface and surviving several days in the vacuum of space. You see these hard-elongated tusks. They have two functions; firstly, a weapon used in mating battles, and secondly a tool that they can super-heat to penetrate the thick compacted ice."

"And the hull of a spaceship." The Witch of Endor was now beginning to see Moloch's interest.

"Yes. Acquired research from exterminated civilisations nearby has shown that the tusk is an extremely robust material, almost indestructible to the common weapon. With a tip that is sharp as a spear head. But you may think hardly worth such effort compared to the ships of war we have at our disposal."

"No, they are not." agreed the Witch of Endor as another immense eruption burst through a fissure caused by the force of the sub-surface pressure, "But I suspect there is more to this."

"These creatures make this dance amongst the jets as it is the biggest source of ammonia, the only source with quantity enough to sustain their great mass. The ammonia comes from the micro-organisms that absorb the nitrogen trapped in the melting ice around the fissures. They fix the nitrogen into ammonia and then they are ejected into space as the geysers erupt. After they have fed, the space rays enter back into the deep sub-surface sea, where they excrete a nitrogen rich substance into the water that floats up to the icy shell and freezes. These micro-organisms are then fed upon by a small but insatiable invertebrate." explained Moloch while the obsidian fragment penetrated the depths of the fissure left by the retreated geyser.

"It seems we are missing a chain in this cycle" deduced the Witch of Endor as the black fragment crashed through the barrier of freezing liquid into the cold dark sea beneath.

"Yes the other inhabitant of interest…. And here it is."

Although no light penetrated the thick icy crust, clear images seemed to live inside the glassy interior of the obsidian fragment. Upon the dark surface there was a silent scene of flailing movement and sparks of blue light. Several large cross shaped flatworms partially emerging from tube structures were harvesting the shrimp-like invertebrate by expelling stunning electrical charges.

"The cycle is complete. If the population of those small invertebrate was left unchecked. They would ultimately consume all the ammonia creating micro-organisms." explained Moloch.

"That is quite an impressive charge these things release." acknowledged the Witch of Endor.

Below them, other free-swimming flat forms joined together in a multitude of complex shapes, each worm acting like a finger of an organic tool. The strange creatures' vertical body was a metre in length and their horizontal appendages totaled three quarters of a metre in diameter, but all four starfish like prehensile limbs were highly flexible and strong. Each aquatic construct had a ladder of the flatworms trailing off into darkness below, functioning as a conveyor belt to bring up material from the rock and metallic mineral floor below the depths of the freezing ocean.

"They are able to communicate with their electric charge and also able to aggregate the charge of a coalesced body to release a stronger electrical potential. Their delicate and hyper controllable electric discharges work like a precision tool that can do many things, such as imprint electric circuitry on materials. Right now, they are completing the last of their tubular structures." Moloch clarified as some kind of electromagnetic wave emanated out from the fragment, sending a disturbance pulsating through the water.

"Moloch, do these creatures hold some significant unknown knowledge or resource that benefits the Sin? I am failing to see why I am wasting my time here."

"These shells can standup to the requirements of space travel." Moloch directed the display to where the pod of giant space rays had dived into the sub-surface ocean. They were surrounded by groups of the flatworm creatures formed in the shape of a gantry crane, fitting some kind of harness like an underwater shipyard. Each large harness was compromised of a long compartment full of micro-organism rich ocean water and two arm attachments hanging down behind their wings. Each life support array was sealed to the skin over what seemed to be their mouths using deft electrical discharges like a welder, clearly causing discomfort to the giant rays as they flinched during the process.

"So, you are adapting these species to join our space fairing armada?"

"Not exactly. This is a world of complete symbiosis, all aspects reliant on each other to survive. The tidal friction and the greenhouse effect of the replenishing layer of surface snow could have kept this eco system prevailing for thousands of more years. The two creatures are intelligent and sentient, and given the choice would have continued this meagre existence indefinitely. They had no desire to change."

"Then why is this forsaken piece of ice still in existence?"

"Because I left them with no choice when I poisoned their ocean, the micro-organisms are slowly deteriorating and as a consequence all species eventually would die out. I offered them a new home in our Sin Supremacy, one full of the plentiful resources they need, once their task was complete. They have no comprehension of what we ask of them, only their desire to comply, to live and to populate."

"My patience is running out. What task could the Sin require of them?" demanded the Witch of Endor.

"A perfect aquatic invasion force. The majority of the Raziel's world is water. In the millennia since we were last there, I suspect that the Raziel would have harnessed that resource, like we surely would have done." while Moloch justified their use, the ocean world was gathering to the summons. "Without the infinity weapon we must be sure. The flatworms will seek out all life in the oceans with their delicate electrical sensory capabilities, and those that cannot be dispatched with their electrical discharges will be destroyed by the deadly tusks of the space rays. They are unlike any aquatic species we have conquered before, unique among the sentient, intelligent and those that are not. We have many that can do a job conventionally but we must have measures that cover all requirements. The Raziel evolved from a single seed in the oceans, they can rise again from that single tree of genesis if we do not eradicate it all. In any case, once we have finished with them, these creatures will face their demise also. Regardless of any outcome, this ecosystem has evolved uniquely and is so finely balanced. No other ocean or world will sustain them. They were doomed the moment I gained knowledge of them."

"Very well Moloch. Then let us make use of them before they perish from this Garden."

Upon the surface of the finely balanced ice moon, a wail of night cut through the solid crust. Moments later an eruption of a mega plume tore apart the surface making all other geysers retreat into nothingness. From out of the crest of the colossal jet came the obsidian fragment followed by the contents of the hidden ocean. An endless army of space rays carrying the large tubular shells with their harnesses, using their wings as solar sails while the flatworm-transporting tubes ejected high pressure ionised particles to provide course corrections or thrust where needed.

At the apex of this worlds last exhale, a spiral of darkness swallowed the freezing spray and the Sin Supremacy's newest invasion force.

29 - Retribution

The command was given by the secretary general and reiterated to all the forces by their respective presidents, prime ministers and military leaders. Commence operation Retribution. The first strike was a no contest. From allied air bases in Kuwait and Turkey, strategic bombers zeroed on their predetermined targets; enemy airfields, military facilities and leadership headquarters. The majority of the victims had no idea of the harbingers of their death, the reapers dropping destruction from the unreachable heights of high altitude. The next wave soared in much closer to the ground but still out of reach of the screams below. Four turbo props reverberated in the air as one of the MC130-J Commando II's approached its objective; unlike many of the other targets they were not tasked with destroying Iran's nuclear sites, capability to scramble air force, or ground to air launch facilities. They were approaching a large palace complex in the centre of a small town at 300 miles an hour. The nine man crew inside the modified C-130 Hercules transport readied themselves, although intelligence suggested there was no surface-to-air missile sites or any other anti-aircraft systems within the vicinity, it was still known that the Iranian army had the capability of man portable air defence systems. Over the outskirts of the town the two pilots levelled their descent to drop altitude when the missile warning receiver wailed in distress.

"We have a missile lock. One SAM coming straight for us at nine o'clock." shouted the electronic warfare officer.

"Taking evasive maneuvers." instantly responded the pilots, banking the aircraft hard right to reduce the cross section of the fuselage available to their laser guided assailant.

The MC-130-J Commando II with its 132 feet wingspan painted itself a big target and such a slow non-stealth platform had questionable survivability against such attacks if it wasn't for its state of the art defence systems. "Starting ECM and deploying flares." announced the warfare officer.

The electronic countermeasures were designed to attempt to deny targeting information to an enemy, make many separate targets, or make the real target seem to disappear or move about at random. This it done effectively as the missile reared towards the bright white lights and trails of smoke at 1600mph and exploded among the released flares.

"Yes!" cheered the electronic warfare officer. "Missile nullified."

"Receiving COMS, a Predator drone is on approach to take out hostiles. ETA fifteen seconds." communicated the radio operator.

The MQ-1C Warrior came in hot, firing two Hellfire missiles in the direction of their assailant.

Upon the roof of an unfinished two-story house, a young man dressed in a dusty t-shirt and jeans dropped the 9K310 Igla-1 portable missile launcher from his shoulder and reached for another 9M313 SAM. As the paramilitary volunteer, part of the Basij militia, lifted the Russian made MANPADS towards the enemy bogey in the sky, a black precision weapon tore through the rooftop and ended his brief resistance.

"Confirmation. hostile terminated. Clear approach to target." relayed the radio operator.

"Prepping payload." The voice of one of the two loadmasters broadcast over the crews' headsets.

"Receiving chatter on the COMS. Drone surveillance systems show women and children within locality of the target." stated the radio operator with concern.

"Can you get confirmation on that?" asked one of the pilots.

"Women and children in the area of target. Please confirm mission abort." requested the radio operator.

"Legit target. Continue with mission." ordered a stern voice from a command location.

"Affirmative." responded the radio operator.

"One minute too target." announced one of the navigators.

"We have to abort. The women and children will be in the blast radius!" shouted one of the loadmasters over the noise of the propellers.

"You heard our orders." reiterated one of the pilots.

"I will not have the death of innocent children on my conscious."

"Then you are relieved of duty."

The conflicted loadmaster sat back in his chair in the cargo hold, head in hands. Straight away the flight engineer joined the other loadmaster in sliding the airdrop platform holding the 22,600-pound cocktail of H-6 explosives towards the rear bay door. The 30ft long Massive Ordnance Air Blast bomb was one of the most powerful non-nuclear weapons ever designed. As well as providing a massive explosive blast, it was partly developed by the United States to continue the role of intimidating the Iraqi soldiers after it replaced the infamous BLU-82 Daisy Cutter. An important anti-personnel weapon that was part of the Pentagon's shock and awe strategy.

The rear cargo-hold doors opened and the noise of the air flooded inside. "Within payload release window." declared one of the navigators.

A drogue parachute unfurled outside the craft quickly extracting the weapon, cradle and platform maintaining maximum forward momentum. The huge munition dropped from the back of the MC-130-J Commando II, the grid fins opened and the MOAB bomb reconnected to the GPS signal used to guide it to its objective. With its consignment deployed the big bird veered back on the trajectory it had arrived on, gaining height and distance from the destruction it was about to sew behind them. The inertial gyro maintained the MOAB bombs pitch and roll control as it dived towards the palace complex. Those who saw it ran for cover and others took futile pot shots but all those within its 400 feet blast radius had little chance of survival. The bomb hit its target, the mushroom cloud of fire rumbled above the town and the blast wave exploded outwards. Yet a greater effect rippled out far beyond that, the psychological blow inflicted by the weapon commonly known as the Mother of All Bombs.

The march of troops, tanks and artillery signaled the beginning of the second strike. Tens of thousands of troops rolled across Azerbaijan's border onto Iranian soil. The under-siege military, its civilians, even the farmers and herdsman took up arms and headed into battle. They would make the invasion forces pay for every step they took inside their Holy land. But it all seemed worthless as before they could even fire a shot in anger, tactical bombers, fighters and heavy artillery extinguished their resolve in a hail of awesome firepower. The multinational invaders did not even have to break stride as the air support ploughed down anything that moved, was suspicious or just stood in the path of the march towards Tehran.

For the population of the Democratic Peoples Republic of Korea, things did not fare any better. The CF7 commander aboard the 7th fleet flagship USS Blue Ridge confirmed the order, fire all batteries and launch all fighters. A volley of tomahawk missiles blazed into the air from the forward deployed cruisers and destroyers, programmed to strike strategic sites across North Korea with little regard for the civilian populace that enclosed many of the assigned targets. The aircraft carrier wing ignited their afterburners and harried off the deck of the USS Kitty Hawk towards the 38th parallel on a mission to unload their devastating payloads upon the ground force of the Korean People's army that guarded the north-south border. Known in North Korea as the Inmin Gun, they constituted the fourth largest army globally and made North Korea the most militarised country in the world. Although maintaining a significant sized army, due to the country's relative isolation and economic plight, its equipment and facilities had become ageing compared to its counterpart in South Korea. This was a major defect in the capability of their forces and the ability to mount a full-scale and cohesive defensive response. The air attack was the initial stage of a pincher movement. Task force 76 and 79 consisting of amphibious assault ships and landing craft prepped to mount a ship to shore assault with its marine battalions motoring for the North Korean coast. While the troops in South

Korea had their weapons at the ready waiting to cross the buffer of the demilitarised zone into North Korean territory. Once the minefield of the demilitarised zone had been cleared and the invasion forces crossed the military demarcation point they were unlikely to face the resistance expected in Iran, few of the people here supported the stifling and unfair police state that governed their lives, preferring to flee the cities for the jungles and uninhabited countryside. Similar Lockheed MC-130 variants as those used to drop MOAB bombs in Iran also lined the skies over the towns of North Korea. Instead of the shock and awe strategy of mass destruction, the psychosomatic tactic here was on the opposite scale. A weapon of a different kind fell from the skies in the form of millions of leaflets outlining how the UN was here to save them from their evil dictatorship and shepherd them into the welcoming embrace of the international community. A promise made in return for them laying down their arms in rebellion to what their ruling government stood for.

In reality no one was safe, innocent people were dying in their droves and the fact that those blameless people were being packed into military facilities to deter attacks meant little to the combined UN forces. The simple misfortune of living within the imaginary lines on a map had sentenced them to death as acceptable collateral damage. Elsewhere the war on the axis of evil secretly stepped up in Iraq and Afghanistan, led by US forces there was no more thought towards rebuilding two liberated countries. Complete control at any costs was all that mattered now. But the world would know little of the atrocities that were happening, only the news of the successes, how they would now be able to sleep safe in their beds, even though Iran and North Korea were on the brink of being blasted back to the Stone Age.

30 - Galactic Wildlife Federation

Debris dropped to the floor as the lab set high up in the jungle canopy shook under the aerial bombardment.

"Oi, you soldier, make yourself useful, get those to an ark!" a small blue furry creature with four arms and dressed in a flamboyant bright red PVC gown gestured towards a few cages containing exotic birds and a type of winged frog creature. "Come on, chop chop! If you haven't noticed, we are currently under attack!"

The soldier rushed over to the cages and with some kind of anti-gravity wand began to nervously direct the enclosed animals out of the door of the lab.

"Biriqzz my dear, you should not berate the poor boy. He is young and it is trying times." commented a soft but croaky voice.

"And what may I ask are you doing!" came a high-pitched retort.

"Eh, Erm…" more mid-air explosions shook the piles of boxes precariously stacked around them. He used the diversion to dart into the next room.

"Baraqz! You better not be doing what I think you are doing!" screamed his life partner Biriqzz while she slipped on an equally extravagant red coat, "If you are trying to pack those foul Snaggleflac pipes, I will wring…"

Baraqz's timid voice echoed from the other room, "Of course not my dear, just trying to find the chameleon slug. It's a tricky blighter to find."

The attackers were getting closer to the target. This time the lab shook more violently than before.

"Get your lazy blue ass out here right now, I sent that slug out to the first ark twenty minutes ago, you watched me pack it. It's time to go!"

"Yes my dear!" came the somewhat defeated reply.

The young soldier came bounding back in, panting as he tried to get out the words. "Madam, they have broken through our defences, we must go."

"Baraqzzzzz! They have breach...."

"I heard the boy my dear...Just coming!"

"You, take these last things to the ship and we shall follow shortly."

"Yes Madam." The flustered soldier swayed out of the wooden structure with an assortment of bulging cases.

"Ready dearest." Baraqz finally popped his grinning head out of the backroom and hopped towards the exit past an impatient looking Biriqzz. But she didn't move, remaining on the spot, all four arms on her ample hips and taping her red stilettoed foot on the floor. Baraqz turned back to his life partner; he was portlier than her, with a similar shade of blue fur but with tufts of grey around his flattened snout. His attire was slightly less garish than Biriqzz's; with black leathers, cap and goggles, he resembled an old World War II Japanese fighter pilot.

He gave her a compassionate smile baring his dog like fangs, "There will be other labs. I know it's hard to leave...."

"Baraqz!" She barked, "Are you missing anything!"

Baraqz began patting himself down in confusion while muttering to himself. "Tool belt, galactic animal guide.... Yes.... Oh goggles!.... No on my head.... Snaggl... Erm.... Clean undergarments?"

"No you old fool! What have we been working on for the last ten years!!!"

"Oh gosh!" he reached for his back then span around in a circle, eyeballs frantically searching the lab.

Biriqzz just bit her tongue and pointed to the backroom he had just left with a furious scowl. "It's that blasted snaggleflac! And you insist smoking it has no side effects!"

He gave her a guilty smile before rushing through the backroom entrance, "Just testing you my dear!"

"My patience is the only thing you are testing right now!"

The pair bounced out onto the large logged terrace balanced within the trees giant canopy. Both of them moved with cat like agility, with all four arms used to propel themselves akin to a gorilla. Baraqz was sporting an oversized rucksack nearly twice his size mounted upon his back and was struggling to keep up with an empty handed Biriqzz. The waiting escape craft hovered on the edge of the platform, shaped like a humming bird with its mechanical wings fluttering at a blurring speed. As the life partners made for the remaining transport, explosive charges rained down from the sky ripping apart the ship and platform, sending shards of metal and wood flying in every direction. From within the glare of the low sun the assailant veered around its target and lined up to finish the job.

*

Each entanglement jump could only transmit them a limited distance and took its toll on the propulsion drive, requiring recharging before the next jump. Seber had just made its last jump and materialised into Raqzzon space right into the path of three enormous vessels. Each one shaped like a giant silver cigar and emitting a mist of charged particles in its wake.

"Raqzzon arks Dr. Tesla." said Krill.

"I'm on it!" replied Emile as she looped Seber up between two of the jumbo craft rumbling past, its nano-shield just avoiding collision by mere inches.

A horde of ships appeared out of the distance in pursuit. Michael got to his feet, "The Sin?" he commented.

"Thank your lucky stars they're not!" replied Emile, "Just another slave race doing their dirty work under the banner of the Sin Supremacy."

"The Hyekera know of these. An aggressive insectoid species

designated the Skraa." informed Phalacreus.

"Battle stations." commanded Krill.

Emile hit the red buttons in each corner of her console screen. The stalks of the mushroom shaped studs extended instantly, the scintillating glass heads punching out through Seber's exterior shell. A total of four equidistant protrusions above and four below were now visible like electrified studded jewelry on the amber outer surface. Inside Seber a holographic display flashed up around Emile, Krill and Varantis who had just taken seats behind their equivalent retreating consoles.

"What do I do?" shouted Michael feeling completely out of his depth.

"Watch the others and copy what they do!" responded Emile somewhat trivially as she waved her hands in the surrounding 3-dimensional images.

Numbering at least twenty, the chasing ships advanced upon their position like a swarm of wingless flies crawling through space. As part of the Sin Supremacy and therefore servants to the Sin, they would not hesitate to open fire on anything that stood in their way, including any unknown vessels. Seber thrust towards the middle of the oncoming legion, each crew member poised within their own spherical representation of the space around them. The host of enemy craft broke into an attacking formation. Michael watched as the other three began touching real time images of the surrounding ships that had come into range of their holographic displays. After each one was contacted, an intense beam shot out from a glowing weapons stud, obliterating their opponents not only in space, but also from their artificially projected environment.

Although possessing superior weaponry, Seber's hull was being pummeled by the sheer number of foes. "Phalacreus, please take weapons control in the lower compartment." directed Krill, drawing a look of mistrust from Varantis.

"Not every organic out there is an enemy. I hope you can make that distinction machine." snarled the Altairian with every ounce of hatred he bared towards the Hyekera.

Without reply Phalacreus took his towering frame below deck, testing the gravity transition plates to their limits. Phalacreus dropped to the lower section and took a stance at the centre of the room. Its arms telescopically extended at the joints and activated the consoles as Emile had done in the control deck. With incredible speed considering the sheer bulk of its figure, Phalacreus began to operate the four battle displays simultaneously. Michael also decided to take action, flipping his chair around to face the transparent exterior and proceeded to hunt out a target with his finger. With a nervous reluctance he tapped an enemy ship that was growing in size right in front of him. The iridescent mushroom above and to the right of his head lit up as a laser of white light pulsed out and carved the target in two.

"Krill! Two more arks under heavy fire in orbit above the nearby planet." yelled Emile between her own accompanying sound effects of weapons fire.

"Protect those arks." commanded Egregor Krill.

Seber weaved in-between the remaining enemy craft and debris, and headed for the trapped ark ships at maximum velocity. They came under significant bombardment as the amber saviour laid a spread of covering fire to blast a path of retreat among the attacking hosts.

"Dr. Tesla, patch me a communication line to the lead arkship."

"Done!"

"To the Raqzzon lead shepherd. This is Egregor Krill of the Ashtar Co-operative answering your distress call. Please give me their location."

An anxious bunged up voice crackled over the audio system, "Still on the planet! We have lost contact with their escape vessel and also the outpost. Transmitting the outpost coordinates..."

As the data traversed the vacuum, a throng of explosive loaded projectiles rocked one of the arks. Another wave of enemy ships had just entered into weapons range.

"Dr. Tesla take us to those outpost coordinates."

"But the arks will be destroyed!" she answered back while returning fire in combination with the plasma cannons of the sluggish arkships.

"Now Doctor." he reiterated.

"Yes Egregor." Emile reluctantly whipped Seber around and darted towards the planets green laden surface.

Michael looked back towards the out-gunned juggernauts. As

they rapidly disappeared into the background, he watched an ark break apart under the strain of its structural damage and exposing its precious cargo to the vacuum. The other spewed out clouds of charged particles as the insectoid crafts took apart their prey. "They don't stand a chance." he muttered.

Egregor Krill did not answer, sitting their motionless and seemingly detached from the arkships fate.

*

A multitude of colourful creatures fluttered upwards from the tree tops. They let out panicked squawks as their spinning winged appendages pulled them away from the commotion like a swarm of helicopters.

"Biriqzz! Biriqzz my dear!" The singed arms of the goggle bearing Baraqz tore through the rubble, hurling wood and metal chunks twice his size in panic.

There was a groan from a severed collection of smoking branches. Baraqz immediately leaped over to the pile of bark and leaves, spying the glint of red PVC among the smouldering heap. "May a plop-burglar bug bite my arse and turn me incontinent!! Are you ok?!"

"Incontinent! More like incompetent. What do you think you are doing? Where is it?!!" she shrieked trying to wipe the blackened stains off her outfit.

"Where's what?"

"The bag you fool!"

"Ohh…just over there. I'll get it."

"Ahemm!! What about me!"

"Of course my dear." Baraqz wrenched away the pinning branches and helped his life partner free. Above the destroyed canopy the insectoid pilot lined up to complete the extermination of its target, launching a salvo of rockets straight for the wrecked research platform. Baraqz took one look and knowing there was no escape, threw himself on top of Biriqzz in an attempt to provide her with a completely ineffective protection. There was nowhere to hide for the Raqzzon life partners, the projectiles were heading straight for them and carried enough explosives to level an acre of the surrounding giant flora.

The salvo of missiles scorched the jungle ceiling as they ate up the distance towards the remains of the tree top research hut. The Raqzzon life partners gripped each other bracing themselves for the inevitable end as the rumble of rockets filled the air.

"Baraqz I've never told you this but...." before Biriqzz could finish the first missile struck, then the second, third... filling the tropical forest air with a fireball of chemical fury.

31 - The Axis of Evil

The people of the world, those that relied on the United Nations to protect them and bring peace to their lives, listened to the news feeds and the dozens of reports that were broadcast to their homes hourly. Each one rolling off pictures of victory, the amount of territory gained and the terrorist threats pacified. How the governments of Iran and North Korea where on the verge of defeat and how the other guilty nations shook in fear before the hammer of freedom and justice.

Now a response had come, an identical package sent to all the major TV stations and uploaded to sites across the internet, the one medium that could not be controlled and entirely monitored, insuring their message would be seen untainted and manipulation free. Everyone would hear their voice. The grainy video started like many seen throughout the wars in Afghanistan and Iraq. A number of masked gunmen stood in front of a flagged background. This time it wasn't to spout propaganda or send a message of fear through a beheading, all games were over and anyone who saw it knew there would be one of two outcomes. For what lay at the feet of the Holy fighters was no captured soldier or terrified aid worker. Before them was a much scarier image, a fully functional nuclear warhead.

One gunman spoke in a harsh accent full of spite, "This is a message to all you infidels that support this evil crusade against our states. You ask yourselves why have we done this, the answer has been before your eyes for years and you have done nothing to avert it. The US and its dog, the UN, have planned these invasions since the beginning, ever since our great nations refused to bow to their demands. Have you not asked yourselves how such a great force and organised campaign could be deployed and waged in such a short time! No, you believe the words of your malevolent governments like they had been spoken by your God. It started with Afghanistan, next Iraq, why? So the Americans can drive their gas guzzling trucks! What nation stood up and said, no, this is wrong! No one! They have raped Iraq and one of us was to be next. This we can be certain of. Your masters choose your destiny the moment the puppets of your governments marched into our Holy Lands and their war machines rolled across the thirty-eighth parallel into the streets of our brothers. We had to make the strike! To survive! When a beast has no morality, ignores the pleas of right and wrong shouted in its ears, when that beast defiles your home and slaughters your family, you must hit it, and hit it hard! Only then will it look up and listen. We do not wish to hit again, so listen carefully."

The camera zoomed in a little closer to the masked messenger. "This is too your leaders. Your forces continue to slay the innocent people of Iran and North Korea as I speak! We are left with no choice but to issue this ultimatum. Cease you offensive instantly and remove your death squads from our lands by tomorrow two PM Greenwich Meantime or we will detonate every bomb we have in the cities of the oppressors!!"

The camera image retreated to expose the full scene once more including the atomic bomb that now read 35:59 hours. The countdown had begun.

"Do not even consider that we are bluffing. We are fully prepared to die as martyrs for the freedom of our nations. You have all seen the evidence of the power we possess….. And to those that think that you can just close off your borders to all, then think again! It is already too late, none of you are safe!!!"

The curtain of flags dropped from the video background ……
the world echoed with the gasps of millions.

32 - Lan Altaira

The quantum well of subspace itself creaked as the Altairian warships tunneled through the potential energy barrier and back into normal space. The tentacles of the leviathan's buffeted in the shower of the powerful solar winds that erupted off Altair's corona and bathed the second world the Altairian had called home. Within the constellation Aquila, Lan Altaira baked under searing heat as it revolved around its oblate main-sequence star at the edge of the habitable zone. Although the planet was further out than Earth was to the Sun, Altair was almost twice the mass of our own star and had eleven times its luminosity; due to this stellar output and the worlds undeveloped ozone layer, the star blasted Lan Altaira with intense ultraviolet radiation.

The emperor had returned to the modern-day Altairian homeworld, the primary planet of the empire. Not its most beautiful, hospitable or resource laden but it's significance in Altairian achievement and its tactical galactic location meant it was symbolically their most important, and therefore the Altairian society and its leadership gravitated towards it despite its unforgiving environmental hardship and through all its historic trials and tribulations. Xantis At Rae had just arrived back from the Sol system and looked down at his people on a very different world. Being in such close proximity to Earth forced the questions of how things could have been different, but now absorbing the sight of the planet of his birth it was the hardships of history, those key moments that brought him to this point that filled his mind.

*

Xantis At Rae was a young hatchling walking to his first Custodian teaching, and was accompanied on either side by his mother and his father the emperor. Lan Altaira was a large rocky world four times the size of Earth and its surface could not have been more different. Where Earth exhibited blue waters and the lush green of fauna, Lan Altaira displayed endless deserts of sand and dusty rock. A warm wind blew all year round. But today the well-trodden desert path baked under the unforgiving heat and a sandstorm blew with a strength he had never seen before.

"I hate the wind here." complained the young princeling as some coarse particles of sand found their way through his fabric mask and into his eye.

Raentis At Zel placed his hand on his spawn's shoulder, "Do you know it is said, that if you threw a grain of sand into the air and stood in the same place long enough, then that same grain would eventually circumvent the planet and hit you in the back of the dewlap."

"I guess that is supposed to have some meaning?"

"Life has many repeating cycles, that grain of sand will face many obstacles, find itself in faraway strange places, but eventually it will always find its way home." added his mother, Shektala Et Mef, "I hope you will learn something of this during today's teachings."

"Will you stay with me?" he asked hopingly.

"I am sorry my spawn, your father and I must prepare for the quickening. We have found another world that has some much-needed resources vital for our kin."

"I understand." answered Xantis At Rae as a line of other young Altairian hatchlings became visible in the blowing dust.

They soon arrived at a large hut made from similar plant material to the leviathan's and surrounded by a fine fence of vegetation that effectively held back the wind and sand. Circling the protective fence was a dark framework of peculiar metallic sculptures wrapped in a botanical web. "We are here. Listen well to your Custodian and respect your other hatchlings. Make the most of their company before you are all divided into your Castes." requested his father.

"I will father." promised Xantis, who straightened up his stance on the approach of another adult adorned in a multicoloured robe that seemed to shimmer under movement.

"Sire, Sovereign." The Altairian Custodian nodded his head with a slight twist.

Xantis slipped down his protective mask and stepped forward with some encouragement of his mother's touch, "I am Xantis At Rae."

"Welcome young princeling. I am one of the Custodian Caste whose vocation will be to teach and care for you so that you may one day develop the strength and wisdom of your parents.", the Custodian thumped the base of the staff he was carrying on the worn flat surface of a protruding rock. The force of the contact made its way up the shaft into the egg-shaped crystal at the top, and released the ring of a delicate bell. "It is time."

Xantis turned back to his parents. His father knelt before him with a face full of pride. "If there is one lesson I want you to learn while we are away, it is where the strength of the Altairian comes from. How our difficult history has defined us and our achievements have provided us with an opportunity to be great once more."

His father stood back, and on his small shoulders came the jewel decorated hands of his mother. "During meditation my thoughts will be of you. We will return before the quickening."

All the other hatchlings were making their way into the hut, but Xantis watched his parents walk off into the sandstorm until their forms were no longer visible against the shadowy structures of the capital dwelling in the background. Xantis made his way into the hut constructed from a striated plant like material that seemed to luminesce under the photons that managed to break through the wall of sand in the air. The habitation was akin to a bored-out giant tree stump, and as he took his place amongst the other hatchlings inside, there was a tranquil calm as opposed to the violence of nature outside. There was also a comfortable warmth compared to the story of temperature extremes on the planet's surface, where during the day it soared to fifty degrees Celsius and by late evening dropped to a bone chilling minus ten on the night side.

The Custodian's dewlap flapped as he cleared his throat. "To see so many hatchlings this year makes my blood run warm. Where you sit today used to be occupied by far fewer claws scratching in the dirt." he paused to make a mental note of the new faces before him, "You see there was a time when things were much different for the Altairian. And today's teaching, the first of many teachings, will be your most important."

Some of the hatchlings were excited to hear what the Custodian had to teach, but some were nervous to finally learn of the Altairian history. It was the Altairian culture to hold back on the knowledge of their challenging past and the realities outside of the wider Altairian civilisation. They believed that a hatchling should be focused on developing their own core skills and discovering the disciplines that they excelled at. Essentially determining their caste, their life's vocation in Altairian society untainted by the external influences of their imagination and doubt, thoughts of the possible or impossible in a complex and confusing galaxy.

"And what gives these teachings even further importance is that they fall upon a most special time for Altairian kind. An event you may be too young to remember, the quickening cycle." The Custodian looked from the vestal scales of innocence to a group of Altairian weathered by life and wisdom entering the habitation, "Ah, perfect timing. Hatchlings, please welcome our caste representatives whom have forgone their principal duties to provide assistance with your first teachings.", the young hatchlings welcomed the caste members nervously, "We were just discussing the quickening. May I ask our Scholastic representative to explain to the hatchlings what the quickening is."

"Certainly Custodian." replied a figure with a worn brown and black scuta skin draped in colourful layered robes, "The quickening cycle is what the Altairian have named the fleeting period of solar calm that befalls Altair just over every one and a half years. It is a day long period of intense lightning storms and torrents of rain of a ferocity that even our Scholastic Caste could never hope to match."

"Thank you. The importance of that goes back a long time and it is why we are still here today. But let us start at the beginning to our ancestors. The Altairian did not always live on Lan Altaira, our ancestors used to live on a very different world, far, far away on a place called Earth."

Many of the hatchlings puffed out their cheeks in surprise at the revelation, others flicked their gaze amongst each other not sure what to think. Yet Xantis called out, "What was Earth like?"

"Well, the teachings of the worlds outside Lan Altaira and the Altairian Empire will be for another day, but let me give you an idea. We have some recovered images from our archives." The Custodian motioned to a large mushroom shaped apparatus behind him. Manipulating the fusion of plant and machine, an image was projected onto the ceiling of the habitation.

Xantis was captivated by the blue of running water meandering amongst a lush jungle, "It looks beautiful!"

"Yes, it does." agreed the Custodian.

"Then we should go there."

"It is a much-changed place and home to others now."

"Then we should take it back?" challenged Xantis.

"I'm afraid the reality of life is not as easy as that."

"It should be." commented Xantis.

The Custodian gave a fleeting glance to his caste representatives before answering, "It was inhabited by another sentient species and bathed in the protective light of the Elohim, in this we hope to educate you. But it will be a debate for another time and a decision of destiny that may be yours one day."

"Let us go back to why we are here and not on Earth shall we." continued the Custodian. Xantis held his tongue, driven by his curiosity of the ancestors' time on Earth. "The cataclysm. An extinction event that happened so very long ago on Earth. A giant rock from the sky crashed into Earth wiping out most of our ancient kin. Fortunately, the Altairian held great wisdom and resourcefulness, and the greatest amongst our ancestors escaped their doomed home aboard lifeboats they had created."

The Custodian looked out towards the young minds hearing this for the first time, but there was just the eager silence that signified the thirst for more knowledge, "Contriver, would you please tell our audience about how our ancestors arrived here?"

"Certainly Custodian. When the cataclysm had forced our kin to abandon Earth, they had no choice but to search for a new home among the stars. No easy task in a sector of space strangely bereft of habitable planets for our kind. Their assortment of escaping lifeboats was tethered together to create what was known by our ancestors as 'The Journey Ship', and it would serve as their home for many years to come." The smaller framed Altairian displayed with her hand the crystal tool hanging from her oversized neck chain, "It was the job of my Contriver Caste to maintain the mechanical systems of the great journey ship. Yet this vehicle was never designed to be a permanent home in the emptiness of space. So, after many many years of travelling in the cold vacuum, this single life pod for Altairian existence was barely holding together. The survivors had already been forced to totally vacate and shutdown numerous peripheral habitats due to irreparable damage. And if they did not find a new home soon, even the skill of the Contriver Caste would not be able to keep the Altairian and our civilisation's memory safe."

"Not the only difficulty our ancestors faced aboard the great journey ship. And it was there that our caste system was first conceived." continued the Custodian on his kin's cue, "These were groups originally defined for members of the survivors, and each assigned responsibility based on their key abilities and the needs of the journey ship population. Initially there were the Horticulturalist Caste, charged with growing, tending too and cultivating the ship's gardens and crops. My Custodian Caste responsible for the caring and raising of Altairian young and the basic teaching and medical needs of the remaining Altairian. And lastly the Ethereal Caste whose role was twofold but entwined; our astronomers, whom took care of all matters in the realm of our religious faith, both navigators in space as well as life. An order to things, that aboard the journey ship worked well, giving the survivors an essence of some existing governmental system and direction for their efforts."

Another caste member stepped before the hatchlings wearing a colourful organic sash bearing a crystal pendant with flowering plant roots wrapped around it. "As our Custodian and Contriver kin have alluded to, many problems befell the surviving ancestors. Our Horticulturalists could grow and replenish new plants to feed the population, but the resources usually excavated for the needed repairs we could not. Without new sources of fuel and materials, the Altairian survivors had no way of powering the UV lamps and water recycling systems. Left to them was always the option to cannibalise the storage habitats, but they would rather perish than commit to such an action, they held everything that the Altairian's were and had achieved back on Earth before the extinction event." explained the Horticulturist Caste member.

An elder caste member with plain robes and a staff ending with a crystal blade spoke up as the young minds listened intently to the dramatic story being told, "With our ancestors fighting to maintain the journey ship and its occupants, they finally reached the closest life sustaining world to Earth that our ancestral astronomers had mapped. This infertile rock was their last hope, there was no alternative, this planet would be the location for the next era of the Altairian civilisation."

The Ethereal's words stuck in the mind of Xantis. They no longer held true, Lan Altaira was no longer the only alternative, yet it was still his home.

"At the time of our ancestor's arrival, they already held great wisdom in the art of science. Even though the conditions were inhospitable to the prevalence of most life, the Altairian had had much time to learn to adapt, especially within agriculture and botany. This knowledge was tested to its very limits the moment they set claw on the arid dirt of Lan Altaira." began to explain a slender caste member with a colourful skull cap, "Firstly the heat and dryness. Cloud cover to provide a moments relief from the glare of the sun was an infrequent occurrence and the blessing of rain an even rarer event. Still where there was water even in the tiniest of quantities, there was life. Like the deserts of Earth, the arid regions bore patches of hardy plant life, cactus like giants and deep-rooted shrubs. From the protective shadows of rocks small mammalian and reptilian creatures came out at night to forage for insects and feed upon each other as the food chain dictated. Upon exploration of their new home it was quickly evident that the key to their survival on this world was with the ability to create species of plants that could withstand the harshest of conditions. Therefore, to generate viable food sources was the role of my newly formed Scholastic Caste, a group of Altairian taken from each of the other castes defined by their specialty skill set which encompassed physics, chemistry and biology."

The Custodian continued as he stepped amongst the hatchlings, "So once they landed upon Lan Altaira the caste system evolved but remained intact, and each had an important job to perform. Horticulturalists to farm the land hopefully with the help of the Scholastics endeavors. Contrivers to dismantle the life boats one by one to create permanent shelters, Custodians to do what they had always done and the Ethereal to enlighten them through practice of their faith and provide comfort in the adversity and suffering they were about to endure. I will ask our guests to help tell our story."

The Horticulturalist started, "The first years were extremely tough, no plants they had brought with them on the journey ship would take to the lands, and the native fauna proved too poisonous to consume. Life was a constant struggle for survival."

The Scholastic joined in, "The Scholastic Caste put years upon years of work into botany breeding programmes, selecting the most useful strains of genes from the vast store of species they had couriered from Earth and blending them with each other. Slowly through each generation, they created new biological structures that had traits much more advantageous for survival on Lan Altaira. Such traits as super-efficient moisture absorption concocted from plants at the freezing poles and driest deserts, more robust cell structures with natural UV protective secretions to filter and control the quantity of intense rays from the nearby Sun. Complex feats of cross pollination to provide materials stronger, lighter, more flexible than any that could be created in a lab or mined from the crust below. A million genetic variances painstakingly pin pointed, refined and melded to fashion a flourishing oasis in the sand that could support the new Altairian settlements."

The Custodian stooped lower to the engrossed hatchlings, "Our people were a resilient race, faced with a crisis that wiped out nearly everything and everyone they had known, they could have so easily dwindled away, forgotten in the vastness and infinite age of the galaxy as had befallen so many civilisations before and after them. But for millions of years they endured, slowly, millimetre by millimetre, clawing back the memory of a once beautiful civilisation. Progress was at best gradual, one year might yield a positive increase in populous, another, a harvest producing an extra ton of crop, however, it was progress. The endeavors, sacrifices and hardships eventually bore fruition and crops began to become plentiful, fruiting trees became a possibility and these new green havens acted as a catalyst to upsurges in the animal populations. Mammalian flesh started to develop into a feasible food source also. The Altairian civilisation grew in number and so did their knowledge, especially in all walks of botanical genetics and agriculture."

"At its peak, whole exotic jungles sprouted from the once lifeless and infertile lands of a like that could not be witnessed anywhere else in the sector of the galaxy." added the Horticulturalist with pride.

"It was noticed that as well as the obvious advantageous traits that could be cross bred and developed, there were also other more intriguing possibilities. Some plants displayed a modicum of intelligence, predatory plants that enticed and trapped smaller varieties of their dino-brethren or could maneuver themselves to maintain the best position for maximum photon absorption. It was at first a curiosity that drove a number of our Scholastics down this inquisitive path. But soon realising the potential further research had to other aspects of Altairian survival, it swiftly became a passion. Soon one after the other, further traits were combined, electrostatic charges used by some fauna to stun tiny insects, the ability of one prehistoric fruit that could inhale and expel air to propel itself as far as it could from its blossoming tree to enhance the distribution of the species, a tentacled lily that could grab shadow seeking fish and reel it into its digestive sack, rapidly regenerating membranes of a parasitic fungus." There was a passion in the Altairian's voice, "The list went on and on. It was not long until this field of botanical research became a significant movement amongst the castes, drawing a large quantity of new hatchlings into its world of possibilities. It wasn't until around two hundred thousand years ago, an insignificant time in the existence of our race, that they discovered a process that changed the history of the Altairian and made it an empire."

Xantis was intrigued by the Scholastics last statement and the Custodian could see it in his eyes. "It was the morning after a particular heavy storm, only lasting a day, it was a ferocious planet wide meteorological event that mysteriously struck just over every one and a half of Lan Altaira's years. Our guests have already explained, that event to be known as the quickening... Contriver please continue our teaching."

"Of course Custodian.... A panicking member of the Horticulturist Caste had transmitted a call for help claiming he had been trapped inside his farm. Such a simple situation could have been easily dealt with by our Contriver Caste, but what they found surprised them, and the matter was quickly dispatched to the Scholastic Caste. Upon arrival at the scene, the Contrivers were shocked to find the whole farm shelter encased in organic plant material. In a consorted effort the Altairian was released but his explanation of events presented a real mystery. One the Scholastic can shed some light on."

"After much investigation and exhaustive examination of the facts, an astounding discovery was made. The material the Horticulturist's farm was constructed of was different to the remnants of the journey ship, mined metal or wood that was commonly used for habitat construction by the Contriver Caste. This material was an ore found nearby and so far, used only on that particular structure. The ore was infused with a substance that once kindled by the mechanism of lightning reacted with a specific type of genetically modified plant akin to Earth celery. The interaction of these variables produced results that promoted huge accelerated growth. What's more as the plants absorbed the unique substance, growth was ordered around the configuration of the ore itself, therefore as a consequence replicating the farm structure entirely. The full magnitude of this discovery did not dawn on them at first. Immediately they knew they would be able to grow organic structures and possibly boost crop output to aid in the expansion of their civilisation but to what extent they could not have dreamed of. Another hundred thousand years past, techniques improved, new botanical traits discovered and ore extracted from the rock stockpiled in vast underground stores. It was on the one-hundred and sixty-one thousand, eight hundred and third quickening cycle since the discovery that it happened."

The Custodian thanked the Scholastic representative, "So on that fateful day, the accumulation of all the effort, the blood and overheating of the previous millenniums would come to its culmination. The new capital dwelling would be named after the great and original city of the Altairian that they had been forced to leave back on Earth. A worthy name to honour the achievement of taking a huge step in finally realising the former glory of their ancient civilisation. They had tried to mimic its architecture and design as much as was possible from the degraded records of the long-deconstructed journey ship. It would look a wondrous site rising from the surrounding desert, its central tower like a lighthouse in the sea of sand. The ore infrastructure was in place and the refined plants strategically positioned throughout the city's skeleton. They were ready. All that was left to do was wait. The quickening raged across the planet as it had always done, hurricane winds sucked up the sands and blasted everything that stood in its way, shaping the landscape more in a single day than the natural weather systems had done in over a millennium. Dark clouds tumbled from the ionosphere above like an avalanche of grey, tumults of life-giving rain drenched the parched dirt and magnificent bolts of lightning streaked across the sky as far as the eye could see. The Altairian hid from the elements in their shelters meditating for hours until the raw power of the quickening passed. Then as quickly as the mega storm erupted it had dissipated to give way to bright clarion horizons and Altairian anticipation."

The plainly robbed Altairian began walking along the peripheral of the hatchlings, "Shading their eyes, all Altairian emerged from their shelters to see the outcome of their endeavors, and it was glorious…. the great first city of the new empire had been granted by the quickening. All went to explore the new capital dwelling, circumventing the botanical walls and techni-colour boulevards to their allotted homes, that was except for the Scholastic class."

Upon the mention of his caste, the Scholastic spokesperson began to explain the focus of his caste. "It is true our interest lied elsewhere, in a small plantation on the desert outskirts where the caste's research facility was rooted. In that solitary plot the Scholastics gathered around the empty remains of a cracked cocoon. What they had come to seek was far more complex than the constructions of the capital dwellings, and something that was the product of many a quickening. All eyes shot to the clear cerulean sky, it was a success."

The hatchlings waited with baited-breath to hear about the event that had transpired on that special quickening, and the Custodian did not keep them waiting long. "This very teaching habitat was where those Scholastics looked to the sky with anticipation. Here with the lustrous capital dwelling towering in the background, the first sentient Altairian leviathan was created. And it was its descendants that were the first to exhibit the ability to travel faster than light. A monumental achievement that would usher in a new era of the Altairian Empire, an era that you will now learn about. But first we must break for meditation."

The lessons of the day continued and the time passed. Each of the caste members took their leave of absence to make sure the final preparations for the quickening were in place. The day of teachings was coming to an end and the other hatchlings were swiftly being collected by their guardians to return to their habitats to shelter from the atmospheric ferocity to come. Yet when the last hatchling was hastily whisked away, Xantis still remained alone with no sign of his parents return.

"I am sorry Xantis, there is no word from your parents." apologised the Custodian.

"Why haven't they returned yet?" he questioned trying to mask his worry.

"Your parents have the biggest responsibility of all Altairian. I have known them since I watched over your egg. I am positive they would have been here by now if it were not for something very important for our people." The Custodian tried to explain but could not hide his concern as well as the young princeling.

"The wind is becoming fiercer... I can hear the crash of thunder in the distance." spoke Xantis with apprehension, only the stories of the immense power of the quickening to fill in for his diminished younger memories.

"Yes, the quickening is upon us. I am afraid we will have to seek shelter here tonight. But don't worry, we will be quite safe. This is not the first time this habitat has protected an Altairian from the quickening." replied the Custodian trying to provide comfort.

Titanic thunder claps shook the habitat and rain pummeled the roof as if the sky was being broken apart and flung directly at them. With the extreme violence outside, Xantis was restless and his thoughts constantly drifted towards his parents. The Custodian did his best to keep his mind occupied with the archives of Earth. Restored images from their ancestors time there and some recorded from their forsaken return voyage, a homecoming that was not the triumphant return they had hoped for. The long night passed and the rage of the quickening gave way to an eerily strange calm. Xantis left the sleeping Custodian and rushed outside. In the distance, he had a clear view of the horizon around him. The view looked different, the capital dwelling had grown and new habitats had also sprung up where ever he looked, given life by the power of the quickening. Even outside the teaching habitat, an encircling garden had been newly spawned. It all looked so magnificent under the clear cerulean sky, newborn leviathans twisted in the air and the light of Altair bathed him in a pleasant warmth rather than the usual searing heat. Yet with all the invigorating beauty, the excitement and wonder of the Altairian people coming out from their shelters to lay their eyes on the gifts the quickening had left behind. All he could think of was his parents. Then from the rear of the teaching habitat behind him, a leviathan hovered over his head. It looked like his parent's ship, but several of its tentacles were severed and it had deep weeping wounds across its surface. The leviathan came awkwardly to a rest in front of the newly formed gardens, the remaining tentacles blowing up dust that sparkled as they were struck by the UV light. Out from the glistening dust, his mother appeared. Foregoing his usual proudness, Xantis ran to his mother and gripped his claws around her waist.

"Mother, what happened? Where is Father?" His mother did not answer, but gripped him back equally tightly. Xantis looked hopefully to the injured and burnt leviathan, but no one else returned that day.

*

Emperor Xantis thoughts returned back to his scarred capital ship, the oldest descendant of the Scholastics achievement that historic quickening and the same leviathan that returned without his father. He had been told later that his parents were leading an Altairian mission to a discovery of the vital ore they needed for the quickening, a reserve of which was abundant enough to drive an unprecedented evolution of the Altairian Empire. But it also led to another perilous discovery, for it was also their first encounter with the Hyekera. The start of the war.

Those past times of innovation and growth had withered in the midst of the debilitating conflict. The humans had inherited everything they had lost, the Hyekera had slowly drained them of progress and resources, and now his people faced the threat of extinction once more. He was about to notify them of his decision and both the humans and the Hyekera were the key to their survival.

33 - Space Safari

Layers of Seber's shell disintegrated under the intense heat of the explosions. Reacting to each blast the underlying nano-fluid rapidly solidified to maintain a continuous protective shield for the crew and keeping the damage limited to a few violent shakes. Seber had shown up just in time, swooping across the path of the speeding missiles mere seconds from their targets and absorbing the full brunt of the attack upon their hull.

Egregor Krill issued multiple orders "Varantis destroy that ship. Emile, position us at the edge of the platform and Michael help our guests in."

"Baraqz you lumbering fool! You almost crushed me under that ample gut of yours!" shouted Biriqzz as she pushed her confused life partner off onto the log terrace.

Baraqz span around to see the battle scarred Seber hovering over what was left of the research platform. A pulse of concentrated light left the strange craft, pierced the air and punched through the diving enemy ship. He stared at the welcome arrival as an entrance melted open and a ramp flowed out before them. Michael popped his head out of the amber surface to see the two Raqzzon sitting upon the floor. He was speechless for a second as he took in the new extra-terrestrials, to him they looked like two blue terriers that some cuckoo owner had dressed in garish leather clothes, "Erm, do you need a ride?" was all he could manage to squeeze out.

"My lad, most magnificent timing!" chortled Baraqz before leaping onto the ramp.

Biriqzz let out an irritated groan as she spied the oversized back pack lying there forgotten once more. A thud on Michael's shoulder drew his attention away from the passing furry alien giving him the quadruple thumbs up. His face turned from mild amusement to disgust as he discovered an enormous beetle type creature attached to his upper arm.

"Hey boy!! You just going to stand their all gormless looking or you going to help a lady with her bag!" yelled Biriqzz.

With a couple of frenzied swipes Michael managed to knock the flying bug away. His mind wandered momentarily as he imagined crushing the offending insect under his foot before he proceeded to jog down the ramp towards her. Unbeknownst to Michael the hard-shelled beetle hit the jungle floor, all shape lost, no more than a compact ball of exo-skeleton and flesh, seemingly crushed in mid-air by some mysterious force. The bossy creature dressed like an evil pantomime queen was short in stature to say the least. Standing less than two feet tall, Baraqz and Biriqzz barely even reached Michael's knees, although they were stocky in proportion to their height.

"Let's go!" said Michael as he went to scoop up the bag, almost putting his back out in the process. The rucksack was deceptively heavy considering its size, and required the strength of both arms to heave the thing off the floor.

"What the hell have you got in here, rocks!" commented Michael breathing heavily with the effort.

"Well you're a nosey one aren't you! Come along and stop making a meal of it."

"This thing weighs a ton; how did you manage to get it this far?"

"What? You don't know much do you! We Raqzzon originate on the high gravity world Domiqzile. Therefore, short in stature, strong in body."

"Yeah and sharp in tongue." muttered Michael under his breath.

"What did you say boy!"

"Oh, just that I'm new to this alien shi…. Species thing." he would have liked to give her a piece of his mind but he just didn't have the energy to argue with a pint-sized pretentious fur ball. He dragged the weighty bag into the lower deck, Baraqz ignored them as they entered, seemingly preoccupied with a fascination towards Phalacreus. He was walking around the towering automaton scratching his grey chin hair when the voice of his life partner made him jump, "For a senile old fool you behave like such a child! Where are your manners, shouldn't you be thanking our rescuers." Seber's exit moulded back into place behind Biriqzz.

"Of course dear, just wanted to make sure you got inside without any hitches." He gave Phalacreus one more intrigued look before heading off to the gravitational transition plate.

"The guests are safely aboard" notified Emile upon the command deck.

"Dr. Tesla, rendezvous us with the surviving arkships. We must ensure their return to Raqzzon Space."

Michael ascended to the upper level with Baraqz and Biriqzz now in tow. He took a mouthful of Pulque while watching one of the diminutive new comers push the more portly one forward.

"So please, who do we owe the pleasure of our timely rescue too?" asked Baraqz flashing a large fanged grin to each in turn.

"Welcome aboard Seber. I am Egregor Krill and.."

"Biriqzz dear!" interrupted Baraqz, "It's only Egregor Krill in the flesh!"

"I know; I did just hear the words that came out of the Egregor's mouth!" she replied.

Baraqz ignored or never noticed the sarcastic tone in her response, "Of course, Ashtar telepathy does not extend to other species. Yes you are quite right dear!" He then grabbed Krill's gangly hand in all four arms and gave it a prolonged hardy shake. "A pleasure Egregor and thank you."

"You are most welcome."

"The arks?"

"The majority escaped."

"The best we could have hoped for I guess. Still all those lives…"

A screech tore through the command deck that almost made Krill flinch, "Helllooo! Emile darling, I didn't see you there. How are you? I haven't seen you since me and that useless ball of fluff stopped by Cydonia."

"Great thanks! By the way I love your outfit." said Emile with a girly smile.

"Ahh, thank you sweetie. I try and maintain a certain level of style, although I don't know why. He wouldn't notice if I wore the exoskeleton of a giant spine louse.

Emile shook her head, "Males!"

Biriqzz let out a squeal of laughter, "Well what can we do!"

"Aye, you say som…. Is that the beautiful Emile? Oh look, it is!" Baraqz leaped with one effortless bound onto the top of her console. "So what brought the illustrious Egregor Krill and the irreplaceable Dr. Tesla to come save little old me?"

"Good to see you Baraqz. Did you manage to save your work?" asked Emile.

"Oh my work, of cou… The bag!" he gulped in panic.

"I tell you he would lose his whiskers if they weren't embedded into his skull. Yes sweetie, it's in the back pack stowed in the bottom deck."

"Phew!", Baraqz wiped his forehead with a dirty worn-out hanker chief that had seen better days. "I dare say our Confederacy had something to do with it."

Krill stepped over to them which had an effect of stiffening up Baraqz like he was standing to attention.

"Yes, the Raqzzon Confederacy has agreed to join our new alliance dependent on a number of conditions. One being your rescue and safe passage of yourselves and your research back to the borders of Raqzzon space."

"It appears you have created something quite significant in the eyes of your government." added Emile.

"Why yes, I have manag…. Ah and of course my magnificent life partner have, finally succeeded in creating something that will, quite simply, change our civilisation in a way that we had only dreamed of.", Baraqz seemed to drift off into a trance momentarily. "Anyway enough talk of m.. our invention. Who do we have here? That nice young lad that helped us aboard, a run of the mill human by the looks of it."

"He is another prerequisite." interjected Krill. "This is Michael."

"The genetic fluctuation, really?" Biriqzz looked Michael up and down with an expression of shock. "A bit weedy! Could do with a wash also."

"Hey excuse me! I am here you know!" said Michael with agitation.

"Ooh and a temper as well I see. You sure about him?"

"Yes I hope so, for all our sakes." answered Krill.

"So who the hell are you two?" questioned Michael, disposing of any pleasantries.

"Who are we?", Biriqzz looked to Emile with a frown that crinkled her black button nose, "We are Biriqzz and Baraqz, most revered scientists of the Raqzzon Confederacy. We are both biologists, but my life partner, who is in fact much more intelligent than his looks suggest, is the leading expert in xenobiology, that's the biology of other alien species like yourself by the way. I personally, am probably most renowned for my work in neuro and bioelectrical systems. Which for a civilian like you is …"

"I'm well aware of the different scientific disciplines." Michael wasn't going to let her talk down to him like he knew nothing.

"I always say, if it's green then its biology, if it stinks then its chemistry and if it has numbers then it is mathematics." imparted Baraqz.

"And if it talks nonsense in inappropriate times then you can be sure it's Baraqz." countered Biriqzz heavy with mockery.

"You're right dear, enough about me. I would like to know more of our rescuers, let us continue with the introductions. I see we have an Altairian here, an Ethereal Caste I'd say by his attire."

Varantis span around his chair ignoring them, "Rodents!" he whispered under his breath.

"Yes definitely an Altairian, typically rude!" stated Biriqzz tapping her ear, "Hearing like an occhea optrix which I do believe originates on one of your outlying worlds."

Varantis rose to his feet with a menacing glare. "Then you should know it is a delicacy on Lan Altaira, so I would choose my words wisely."

"Well I…" screeched Biriqzz while Emile gave her a just ignore him expression and pat on the shoulder.

The riled Altairian Prime retook his seat and turned away once more. Lifting his head to the stars above Seber, he seemed to drift into a state of meditation.

"Now, now! I say Emile who was that curious fella below? I've never seen the like, a very advanced looking piece of kit. Your work?" asked Baraqz attempting to break the tension.

"Oh I wish! No, it's one of the Hyekera."

"No you don't say!"

"I do."

"Well I never! Thought I was more likely to be cursed with the eternal itchy crotch from the extinct Hellios scrotum mite than see one of them in my lifetime. Although from the rare pieced together descriptions I've read they were described a little differently."

"Yes I saw them! This one, it's called Phalacreus, it's a new model."

"So is it true they look like a Scamium Skorpinik?"

"A what?"

"You know, six legs, big claws, with a long stinger that's venom is said to be quite the aphrodisiac!" explained Baraqz, the last bit whispered behind his hands.

"Baraqz!! Stop berating the poor girl with your nonsense questions!" Her voice startled him like a reprimanded child. "And see if you can be of any use to anyone!"

"Coming my dear!..... Don't worry have one at home. Will let you have a look and maybe extract some venom." He gave a sideways nod to Michael and Emile a wink before bounding over to Biriqzz. Emile's face immediately turned bright scarlet as she tried to gauge if anyone had noticed or overheard that last exchange.

Escorted by Seber, a dozen or so arkships with varying degrees of battle damage limped into Raqzzon Confederacy space. Many displayed bark-like scabs covering the sections that had been exposed to the vacuum. Although the Raqzzon as a race were diminutive in size; their impressively large arkships measured over four hundred metres in length. Each resembled a giant polished aluminum cigar case with their smooth silver surface normally appearing entirely seamless. However upon closer inspection of the exterior, many joints could be distinguished where the interior could be accessed and the necessary external hardware unfurled. At either end of the elongated ark, half the rounded structure could open-up like a drooping jaw, allowing large scale mobilisation in and out of the vast loading bays. The sub-light engines were housed towards the rear of the tubular structure behind thick recessing panels on either side. This ion propulsion system was also tied into the FTL drives' circumventing waste vents and the arkships unusual defensive mechanisms. Along its span there were rings of circular mechanical pores that opened up upon attack to release an ionic gas much like the animal defence mechanisms of a squid or a skunk. Yet this cloud acted as an energy absorption shield as well as playing havoc with any type of sensor or targeting system aimed at it. Port holes were positioned at equidistant points horizontally along the upper and lower halves, opening to expose plasma cannons that fired super-heated plasma balls akin to an old Victorian war galley. In addition to the cannons the arks housed beam turrets at the bow and stern. This weaponry also mimicked the defence mechanisms learned from several creatures such as the Earth Bombardier beetle that squirts hot liquid at its enemies; in this case firing intense bursts of hyper-charged particles for shorter range assaults.

Once all craft were accounted for the lead ark hailed them. "Egregor Krill and the crew of Seber we thank you for our salvation and assistance in our evacuation efforts. The Confederacy is indebted." The other cigar shaped giants began to rumble off in multiple directions. "We will begin relocation procedures immediately and I am sure our passengers are most grateful for your help. Maybe one day they will be able to thank you themselves with the aid of Baraqz's and Biriqzz's research. You have done so much already but I must ask of you one last errand. To please escort Baraqz and Biriqzz to their home of Lagunero Zoo. I believe it will not be long before we stand side by side again in battle. May a Cirrusnocti gull defecate on you from a great height. Shepherd Zonnoq out." The space in front of the remaining ark pinched into a knot and sprang back into place dragging the huge metallic vessel with it at faster than light velocity. At a point in the extreme distance a puff of charge particles and a glint of silver was all that was visible as the arkship rapidly warped sub-space with a pinch and was impelled forward with the spontaneous recoil. Leaving behind a residual gas trail as it hopped across the galactic background.

"Dr. Tesla please take our guests to Lagunero Zoo."

"My pleasure!", Emile tapped a few buttons on her console and the flashing loop that circumvented the floor began to charge, entangling every particle within Seber instantaneously to the opposite side of Confederacy space.

Seber materialised around a relatively small planet that comprised part of a tri-planet cluster, each with multiple moons. Michael had seen some wondrous sites in the short period since he had left Earth, but the scene before him was easily the most bizarre. Each astronomical body appeared to be a patchwork of regions varying greatly in size and sectioned off by some type of border. Boundaries that were visible even from the altitude of space. But this was not what grabbed his attention; it was something that he guessed was designed for just that function. Strategically placed in remote orbit all over the tri-cluster system were colossal luminescent and neon signs, each trying to out-do the other with its extravagance. It was like looking upon Las Vegas in space with the purpose of advertising and directing any visitor to the competing sectors below.

"Magnificent isn't it!! One of the greatest attractions in the Raqzzon civilisation, and hopefully in the future we endeavor to have its' most famous and diverse eco-habitat. Not only in the Confederacy but the whole galaxy!" Baraqz gave a beaming smile to his life partner as he said it. She sent what looked like for a moment an expression of affection, the first bit of sentiment she had shown that didn't give the impression of detest towards him.

"So which beauty is yours?" asked Emile.

"Why the brightest and boldest one of course! Just over there." He pointed to a great big flashing replica of himself, goggles and leather cap included, directing the eye down to one of the larger patches on the planet known in the Confederacy as Lagunero Zoo. Baraqz's multiple arms folded over his puffed-out chest in pride. "Biriqzz added her own little bit of spice to it. She replicated the bio-luminescent fluid of a so far unknown form of glow worm she discovered on Milos Grandiosa. Produces the most pure and longest lasting luminescence I have ever come across in both nature and science."

"The others are still kicking themselves as to how we managed to outshine them!" added Biriqzz with a sigh, "Fools!"

"Unfortunately time is at a premium. Please take us down to the planet Dr. Tesla." ordered Krill.

"On our way." replied Emile as she looped around the sign and down towards the colourful collage of the planet.

As the wispy clouds of Lagunero Zoo stirred in the wake of Seber's vortex, Michael began to rub his shoulder furiously. Then suddenly he doubled up with pain, sweat started pouring from his forehead as he suffered from muscular spasms in his arm and neck that originated in the area the insect had landed back at the Raqzzon outpost.

"You ok?" asked Emile worryingly.

Michael went to answer but all he could manage was "Beeet..tlee thing" and a groan. He struggled out of his jacket and exposed his shoulder from his jump suit. A swollen red lump throbbed on his upper arm.

"Come over here and let me take a look!" instructed Biriqzz. Michael let out another grunt of pain as a pointy black tube pierced the inflamed skin. "Oh stop your fussing! It's just your common flesh boring larvae; I have a creature back at home that will suck that right out."

"What do you mean don't fuss!" He gulped down a mouthful from his flagon with a cringe. "There's a god damn worm growing inside my arm!"

"Well it's technically not a worm, more like your Earth maggot." Baraqz couldn't help himself when it came too zoology, no matter how inappropriate the timing. "The boring beetle lays its egg into the living flesh when they are ready to hatch. They feed off the blood and swell up just before they…"

"Please don't tell me anymore, just get the little bastard out!! Michael interjected.

Seber landed by a small thatched hut with smoke billowing from a chimney. It was circumvented by a wooden picket fence and decorated in a montage of bright exotic flowers. A stark contrast to the dry wild grass of its surroundings.

"Ah, home sweet home! Again we cannot thank you enough Egregor Krill." complimented Baraqz.

"Biriqzz, would you please see to Michael; then we shall have to take our leave. We must return to Earth." requested Krill.

"Of course Egregor. Emile sweetie, it would be nice for you to come along. I should give you a copy of our research, you know just in case. Also I have a little gift for you that I think you would like." replied Biriqzz.

Michael followed the diminutive aliens clutching his shoulder in disgust. The air was very fresh making him slightly light headed as if the oxygen levels were much higher here. There was a twisting breeze that either brought the sweet scent of flowers or the dusty smell of hay depending on its direction. Out over the horizon he could see the towering walls that sectioned off each eco-habitat. What made these walls even more impressive was that they were literally constructed out of mud. They were so immense that they were visible from space and their design had to be to keep something out or even in. King Kong and Jurassic park instantly popped into his mind making him slightly edgy and aware of the environment he was in. They were walking up a cobbled stone path flanked on each side by an expanse of open savannah on one and on the other the creepy gloom of dense tropical rain forest. The noises of many animals echoed from the tangle of trees and vines, and he thought he could see the flaying limbs of an animal swinging through the branches.

"Nothing to be worried about in there." commented Biriqzz.

"That's right; all the dangerous ones are in the proper protective enclosures.... Oh, apart from them!" Baraqz held out his four arms and held back Emile and Michael as what appeared to be a swarm of floating jellyfish crossed their paths. "Usually very docile, even the sting is pretty harmless to most humanoids, but if you do irritate them enough to sting you then I would only give one piece of advice. Run as fast as you can!"

"Do they attack in a swarm like bees?" asked Emile.

"Oh no, they only travel in groups and rarely attack as a swarm. The problem is when they sting, they have a tendency to, well, explode. Packs quite a punch I tell ya. Best to give them a wide berth and let them hover by. In fact, there are only a total of six species I personally know of that can spontaneously combust as a defence mechanism, one being the…"

"Oh please, stop boring these poor kids with your nonsensical ramblings!" scalded Biriqzz.

"I know dear, it's just, I love all animal species, literally everything, even the blue fat-headed vein worm. I mean that thing looks like a swollen version of my.."

"Baraqz!!! Don't you dare!"

"Well, what I mean, is every creature has something extraordinary, interesting, at least one thing to love about it….. Well, except the Saavag that is." he spoke their name with almost a disgusted growl, "Those foul beasts could disappear forever and my bowel movements would continue unhindered."

"Ok, I think that is quite enough." she requested more sternly. Hands on hips, leaving Baraqz in no doubt that there would be serious ramifications if he continued.

"Yes dear!"

As they watched a hundred or so of the volatile creatures float past over the tawny Savannah grass, Emile threw her hands over her mouth and let out a gasp at something she had spied grazing under the shadow of a secluded thorny tree. "Hey Biriqzz, you have to be kidding me, is that the…"

"Oh Emile darling, you spotted him. I remember our discussion in bio-dome one and thought you might like to see him. He's grown a bit since I told you about his birth."

"Holy shit!!! That's a unicorn!" muttered Michael momentarily distracted from the pulsating pain shooting around his shoulder.

Biriqzz let out a call somewhere between a horse warble and a whistle. The chalk white stallion reared up from the foliage it was eating and galloped towards them.

"You have unicorn's!" Michael reiterated, louder this time.

"Maybe I should explain a little about the Raqzzon." offered Emile as she stroked the horned mythological beast.

"Yeah please do." Michael couldn't help but touch the creature he thought was only a fairy tale. Then again, he never believed in aliens either. The unicorn resembled a horse but had a few noticeable differences. Firstly, its skin was not pure white fur and flowing mane as depicted in the stories, rather a coarse pastel hide more akin to a rhino's skin with a thick hazel mane that tapered down the length of its back. And of course, the magnificent horn, a half a metre long twist of gleaming ivory proudly displayed on its forehead.

"I assume you have heard of the World Wildlife Federation on Earth. Well, the Raqzzon is kind of the galactic equivalent. Their whole civilisation is devoted to the preservation of all animal life, not just on their worlds but right across the galaxy. A cause they have pursued for thousands of years. They independently travel to many worlds in their arkships to relocate the most endangered species away from the threat of their own environment and to Raqzzon personal zoos, where they are given the chance of survival and a life of safety. You know the story of Noah's ark right, or the Epic of Gilgamesh?"

Michael's expression of pain had slipped to one of disbelief, "You're not saying what I think your saying, are you!"

"Yep, originated from one such rescue mission by a Raqzzon arkship. About ten thousand years ago a huge volcanic eruption in the Mediterranean Sea triggered a colossal tsunami towards the coasts. Back then their ships used an outer casing of durable bark resin which would have had a wood like appearance. The Raqzzon unfortunately could not do anything to prevent the catastrophic tidal wave, but they could rescue the many species that were in danger from the aftershocks and month of torrential rain caused by the massive dust cloud bloating the sky. They managed to save hundreds of species from Earth that day."

"I can say we have many species from your world Michael. No offence to yourself Emile, but the majority of humans are doing a shockingly poor job of protecting the diverse species that were there a long time before you came along. Our last census, suggested that the world wildlife population has fallen by fifty-eight per cent in the last fifty years on Earth! Cutting down their habitats, eating them faster than they can breed and hunting them for a bit of skin and compacted hair! Most appalling behaviour!"

"No offence taken Biriqzz, you are quite right. Hence why unicorns became extinct so long ago and that you'll only find them on the most successful eco-habitats in the Confederacy."

"Thank you sweetie, shall we continue into the house? I know time is short."

"Yeah good idea. This larva thing in my arm isn't getting any smaller." stated Michael, suddenly realising that he did have a burrowed creature in his arm, sucking on a vein.

"Giant Maggot." corrected Baraqz unconsciously.

They entered the petite wooden hut to find a couple of Raqzzon busying themselves with feeding a variety of creatures. The interior looked more like a Vetcrinary practice than any homestead.

"Tannaq my old chap, it's been too long. How are things in Lagunero Zoo, our collection of rare chameleon repto-phibians still the envy of our social circle?" enquired Baraqz to the elderly looking Raqzzon now more grey than blue.

"Baraqz and Madam Biriqzz, it is a delight to see you home and safe." squeaked the hunched figure weakly. "I'd like to say we are attracting the usual hordes of visitors and admirers, but this situation with the Sin has sent everyone into a bit of a panic I'm afraid. But young Quinnic is doing well and learning lots. She is going to make a wonderful shepherd one of these days." The Raqzzon he was referring too was youthful looking and gave a shy wave to the newcomers.

"Tannaq, sorry for being so abrupt after being away for so long, but would you be so kind as to set up a secure channel to the Confederacy foundation in my study."

"I will do it right away Baraqz." answered Tannaq as he hobbled down a stairwell to an underground level.

"Biriqzz my dear, would you join me in the study. And Quinnic, oh you are maturing into a fine young woman, could you assist the gentlemen. The Zarvetian swamp leech should do the trick."

The Raqzzon scientists had preceded down the stairs, mere seconds before Baraqz's head suddenly popped back around the corner. "Emile, the Scamium Skorpinik is over there!" he shouted with a big wink, leaving her blushing, Michael confused and Quinnic trying to hold back a fit of giggles.

Quinnic adorned in a light flowery dress composed herself and walked over to a covered tank and removed the cloth sheet.

"Ok a leech doesn't sound too bad." announced Michael to the apprentice Raqzzon, who returned a timid smile as she began to wrestle with something hidden in the tank of muddy sludge.

"You call that a leech!!" protested Michael with a slight look of anguish and took a gulp from his hip flask for courage. Quinnic had just pulled from its slimy home what resembled a slug, but the size of a python, and dragged it across the room by its tail.

"That's very painful from what I hear." commented Quinnic in a quiet voice. Her fur was a lighter shade of blue and her features much more understated than the other Raqzzons.

"Yeah hurts like a bitc…." Michael bit his tongue as he looked at the innocent girl, "Well Biriqzz seemed to think I was fussing over nothing!"

"She appears to be tough on first impressions, but she is caring really once you get to know her. She is a great scientist. I only hope that one day I will be able to emulate her contribution to the Confederacy." explained the trainee shepherd as she effortlessly heaved the gaping mouth of the squirming leech onto the increasingly swelling lump. "A couple of minutes and the Zarvetian swamp leech will have that boring larvae out."

"Thank you Quinnic" said Michael with a notable cringe at the feeling of the huge leech sucking on his shoulder. Quinnic gave him a little curtsey in response and went about feeding a tiny insect to a rock which suddenly snapped out an elongated tongue and devoured it.

Baraqz and Biriqzz came bounding back up the stairs, Biriqzz now sporting a yellow PVC jump suit and carrying a strange object.

"Wow another bold and beautiful outfit." complimented Emile.

"Thank you sweetie; a more appropriate attire for what we will be doing I think."

"Oh, what's that?"

"Well we have both spoken with the Confederacy foundation. They are ecstatic with our research. In fact, they plan to replicate the prototypes immediately. And we have agreed considering the Sin threat towards all animal life in the galaxy and everything we believe in, that our interests will be best served if we accompany your group. Wonderful news hey!" explained Baraqz.

"That'll be great. We should get back to Seber then." answered Emile while Michael gave a quiet but audible sigh of disappointment.

Biriqzz walked over to him and gave the leech a solid double chop to the area just behind its head. Michael let out a yelp of pain as the giant leech dropped to the floor. Biriqzz hauled the writhing creature back to its tank and planted it with a splash into the concealment of gooey mud. Quinnic wandered over and began to clean up the bruised wound, "It's done a nice job removing that boring larvae. The swelling and discolouration should take a week or so to heal and you may feel a bit of discomfort for a while."

"Now Quinnic, don't go giving that boy any excuse to moan further." remarked Biriqzz.

"Of course not Madam Biriqzz." she replied bashfully.

Michael just gave the bossy Raqzzon a look of annoyance, "Thank you Quinnic. I think it's time we got back to the ship; I need to know what's happening on Earth! Things weren't great when we left."

"Quite right young lad. We must warn Krill, we've lost further outposts to the Sin and things are looking terribly bleak." answered Baraqz. "Just need to quickly pick up a few things and we shall be right with you! Quinnic would you be so kind as to give your father a hand below."

As the group made their way back to Seber; Biriqzz pulled out the strange object she was holding earlier, from a case she had made Michael carry. "Emile sweetie, I thought you might like this." she held up a small spiral horn, a touch golden in colour with a smooth surface blemished by pits and scratches.

No way! I can't accept this." Emile remonstrated.

"I insist. It is supposed to bring good luck to its wearer, and in the dangers ahead I think we could all do with a bit of that."

"A real unicorn horn, for me!"

"Yes darling, it's the stallion's teething horn." A leather lace had been threaded through allowing for the four inch horn to be worn as a necklace.

"Wow, I don't know what to say, I love it!"

"It's our pleasure." replied Baraqz, "Just don't sell it on that eBay thing of yours. Do you know I hear that they even sell...."

Emile slipped on the juvenile unicorn horn, "Ok! Don't worry, I will treasure it." she interrupted, preventing Baraqz from getting into his rambling stride.

Seber was silent as they loaded a few cases and numerous cages onto the lower deck. Michael knew they contained some exotic creatures but didn't want to ask and be at the receiving end of a complete personal documentary. Varantis had reframed from assisting, instead he continued in his meditation; eyes closed and head to the sky, yet with his mistrust, always facing Phalacreus. Michael said his farewells and gave his thanks to the bashful Quinnic as Emile entered the command deck with the Raqzzon scientists in tow.

"Excuse me Egregor Krill, Baraqz and Biriqzz will be joining us on our journey."

"Very well Dr. Tesla. Welcome aboard."

"Many thanks Egregor but I'm afraid I have some disturbing news. The Confederacy foundation has reported further attacks on Raqzzon outposts by the Sin Supremacy. The last one at Vulpecula!" informed Baraqz.

"Their assault on the Sol system is imminent. Dr. Tesla we must return to Earth immediately."

34 - The Shadow Moves

The custom calm of the Vulpeca system was replaced with violence and panic as Raqzzon arks scattered in every direction. Their outposts, harmless and dedicated to preservation, burned and crumbled all around them. If sound could traverse the vacuum, thousands of cries, howls and whimpers from hundreds of species would have echoed in space. Out from one of the masses of burning metal and flesh, one delayed arkship spewed out thick clouds of ionic gases, desperately trying to generate adequate shielding to absorb the intense onslaught of firepower. Their efforts although gallant, were just postponing the inevitable destruction of themselves and the cargo they had stalled their escape to save.

"Shepherd Filanqc, we will try and provide you some cover." came a desperate transmission in the chaos.

"Please get out of here Chilaqz." responded Filanqc, "You have thousands of species aboard, some lasts of their kind. They are too precious to risk in a moment of bravery guided by the heart!"

"We cannot watch helplessly!" The communication almost drowned out by the discharging of the bow fire suppression systems within the navigation chamber.

"You know full well that to assist means suicide." implored Filanqc as he diverted the pumps of the aquatic tanks to the smoldering aft stables. "Listen to your heads, the situation calls for you to be steadfast in your direction like the rock burrowing gerbil of Ulouvidier."

There was a snarl of acceptance, "If we survive this day a zoo will be named after you." the other shepherd promised to celebrate his name eternally while they watched the under-siege ark discharge all their weapons at an oncoming vessel.

"I thank you for that honour. And let your cargo be the first to find refuge there." Filanqc turned to the beauty of life he held in his hull. As he took some solace in the pride he felt, the trailing arkship broke in half under a wail of night.

Chilaqz shook as she saw the black sphere plough through the ark, expelling those that deserved life into the cold death of space. "Get a warning to the Confederation." she managed to growl through the tears of grief.

Usually running from the Sin was more often than not, futile. But this time they did not pursue and obliterate their escaping prey, to send the message of their total superiority and merciless mind-set towards those foolish enough not to yield to the submission of the Sin. This time the Sin Supremacy force seemed to have another agenda. The obsidian vessel did not divert but exited the system in a singular direction seemingly unperturbed by leaving survivors and their capability to warn the free races of the galaxy. In the wake of the Sin sphere, swarms of its Supremacy legions swept through this sector of the galaxy, the spearhead of ultimate authority continuously joined by flocks of other forces that had been wreaking havoc across Confederation space.

Chilaqz watched on as her ark and the other survivors hobbled on. They were safe for now, but that relief would be short lived. The armada she had just witnessed could not be matched by any known force in existence.

35 - Mutually Assured

Fourteen hours had passed but the world was still in shock, the memory fresh in their mind of the terrorists pulling away the flag backdrop to reveal a window overlooking Central Park, New York. That unmistakable metropolis of trees and parklands enclosed by high rise buildings and sky scrapers. Of course by the time the authorities had located and stormed the empty apartment, all that remained were a bunch of dusty footprints, a copy of the tape and a tell-tale radioactive signature that suggested this was no bluff. Procedures to evacuate New York were put into immediate effect, but people didn't require procedures to follow. As soon as the video had revealed its final twist, the people of New York grabbed their suitcases, money, whatever they could carry to their cars or public transport in a desperate attempt to flee the city. Not only was full evacuation of such a densely inhabited metropolis non-viable in the timescale, it was severely hampered by the mass exodus of the panicking New York populace. The National Guard, local and external law enforcement agencies tried in vain to create some order in the chaos but it seemed the majority of New Yorkers were abiding by one motto, get out by any means and fuck everyone else. But getting clear of the city was by no way a guarantee of safety. The nuclear device could easily be anywhere in the country right now. There were no leads, no clues to its whereabouts; even with their vast resources it was impossible to look under every rock on their soil. If the governments did not yield to the ultimatum, then it was really going to be a lottery of death for every single person in the United States.

Although they did not receive the same recording as the US, the members of the UN Security Council knew that if they had smuggled an atomic bomb into the Big Apple, then there was a huge probability that there were already devices somewhere in their own cities. This seemed to be a chance their governments were willing to take; powerful people had put the wheels in motion of this offensive against this axis of evil. It would take more than a threat against a few million civilians to derail it now. That being said, they were divided on the next course of action. But this didn't matter; someone else had already made the decision for them.

The American President was ready to issue an immediate response to the perpetrators. The president sat at his desk in the famous oval office, the scene of many important speeches that littered the movies, but this one was real. An aide began the countdown, the teleprompter with his pre-written speech flashed up on the screen in front of him. The commander and chief fixed his tie, gave one last clear of the throat and spoke.

"To the people of America and the peace-loving world, I say this; you must stay strong and vigilant. We are doing everything we can to locate these weapons of mass destruction. If we fail you in this task, still look down on us with pride, as we will avenge your sacrifices. We will do as we have always done, endure against these terrorist killers, the US of A does not negotiate with terrorists and it sure won't start now." There were a few cheers and clapping from the patriots in the white house staff filled office. The president gave a wry smile that he thought would instill trust and confidence into his nation. "You bring these devices into our cities, threaten us with annihilation. I can categorically say that you are way out of your depth! Let me tell you something, we have weapons of mass destruction too….. just a whole lot more of them. Now to you murderers of peace and freedom, I look you in the eye with stern resolve, be warned, if you carry out nuclear atrocities upon our great nation, I will not hesitate to give the order to retaliate with a full nuclear strike upon your countries. This is your only chance to surrender!"

36 - Casting the Shadow

The echoing screams of children lingered in the air as the perpetual winds blew down the monstrous valleys. Great geological gouges cleaved by the claws of a planetary demon on a world said to be built upon the sacrifice of the galaxy's offspring.

Within the valley of Hinnom, countless diverse souls hammered into the rock, suffering the torment of a living purgatory as they quarried for the sacred black substance. Death was the only escape from eternal servitude, and it would have been a welcome freedom if only their life was in exchange. In the swirl of choking dust, the black tip of one labourer's tool broke through the sandy stone and against the shiny surface of obsidian. An agonizing wail burst out, resonating through the length of the valleys and drowning out the ghostly whispers immortalised on the air. It was a terrible and distressing sound, but one not heard enough to those that watched from upon high. In the middle of the valley of Hinnom, from a base of incalculable death, an obsidian shard rose out of a mountain of skulls. High above the haze of dust and misery, upon the formidable tower known as Topheth, a single dark figure sat listening over the shadowy valleys of the Sin world Gehenna, at the axis of its Supremacy.

Before the apex of the great tower, a plateau was formed breaking the geometry of the shard. Upon an outcrop resembling a fractured throne, Ashmedai of the Sin waited patiently for the polished surface of further obsidian outcrops to be animated. Each one reaching out of the flat-topped summit like a deprecated crown of night.

A wraithlike sound resembling a dying breath came from two large fused crystal fragments, within the surface of the highly polished rock came two forms phasing into view like an old black and white TV being tuned. "Moloch and Witch of Endor." greeted Ashmedai.

Next a pile of boulder shaped rocks shook, the three most imposing of them coming to life with the continuous two-dimensional image of a group of figures. "Belial and the Sons of Darkness." acknowledged Ashmedai.

Upon a single thin shard akin to a crooked grave stone, the darkness of its surface swirled forming a reflection that announced itself, "Rahab here my brethren."

Ashmedai nodded his dark head, "Then it is just Abaddon we wait for."

Moments later, a cracked sphere-half groaned and hairline fractures split its surface as Abaddon appeared on the flawed obsidian.

"Good, we are all here." welcomed Ashmedai as lightning crackled around the tower. The powerfully intense electrical discharges lit up the valleys all across the barren vista, but could barely penetrate the gloom surrounding this gathering of the eldest and most important of the Sin.

"I hear the whimpering of the prophecy as it cowers in fear at this assembly of such singular minds." breathed Ashmedai, "What pleasant sound does it make."

Abaddon smiled evilly, "Speaking of pleasant sounds. It seems all too quiet on Gehenna. Do the myths of slaughter and torment no longer hold a candle to the truth?"

"Sadly, the murmurs of the storms tell no lies. This world is on the precipice of depletion. We cannot expect more than a handful more apocalypse ships from this place." responded Ashmedai.

"Then the king of Gehenna needs a new throne." stated Rahab.

One of the fused obsidian fragments reverberated with the voice of Moloch, "Our brethren have travelled far and wide in this galaxy. Not one of us, even the Witch of Endor has discovered another celestial body that contains this resource."

"Then it is all the more important that Rahab, and all of us, do what is required." Ashmedai prompted.

Rahab riposted with arrogance, "My armada will do its job, we will start razing the world of the Raziel and anyone foolish enough to stand with them. Nothing will escape the system while we wait on the rest of you."

"And what of your progress?" questioned Belial, "We must know what to expect and avoid the errors of the past. Sending such a significant first wave armada is exactly for that purpose, to draw out all those that could hinder us achieving what we must."

"We are closing in; we will start erasing the words of the prophecy in a cycle of Gehenna. We have sent out our closer Supremacy forces to start attacking nearby inhabited systems to flush out any old or new foes that may pose a threat." The image of Rahab shook momentarily as he turned his head to something around him….. "Destroy that ark now!"

"Trouble Rahab?" probed Belial at the interruption.

"The Skraa encountered some small irritation with the Raqzzon. We are dealing with them as we speak, too busy trying to save everything else apart from themselves. But still no sign of our old enemies that have persisted in their survival."

"Those vermin still defy us! Their time will come but they are of little importance right now. You must move with haste!" spoke the Sons of darkness in unison, "None must have time to flee. We will eradicate the enemies of old."

"Then Moab and Edom, when will they join the fates of the Elohim and Hommege?" enquired Ashmedai.

Belial answered in their stead, "The races of the old alliance are on the brink of extinction. The Pleiadians destruction is complete. They did not even know we were there until we saw the blues of their eyes. Their world was weak and crumbled under our force, the eyes of Pleione sheds a thousand tears; now they only lay watch over desolation as it drifts in pieces."

"That is a monumental step in destroying any resistance in the unconquered realms of the galaxy and shaping the Garden as we wish." enthused Ashmedai.

"Next we will bring our might upon the Ashtar." continued Edom and Moab, "Their existence too will pay the price for their defiance and assistance of the Raziel. There will be none left to stand with the Raziel once we have finished with them."

"The underestimation of our enemies is a mistake we must not, and will not repeat. With our last reconnaissance ship destroyed we face the unknown. Although with such a short passing of astronomical time we do not foresee such a force that could stand in our way, yet we remember that these are the Raziel and we cannot put faith in the normal passage of evolution. It is those unknowns that has forced us to spend these millennia making preparations for their annihilation." mused Ashmedai as the dim sun of Gehenna disappeared into the haze of the volcanic horizon, "The main Supremacy armada will crush anything we encounter. How goes its assembly Witch of Endor?"

"We are on the verge of completion, our armies and sacrificial civilisations will be ready for when our brethren return from selecting their Dolgar champions. Their anticipation will be satisfied." declared the Witch of Endor, surveying the masses from her apocalypse ship, "We have thousands of species and enough machines of war to blot out a star."

"I will soon harvest the Saavag and rendezvous with our most devoted forces." added Moloch.

"Rahab, speaking of our most devoted forces, what of our servitors whom discovered the Raziel world? Have they answered our call." queried Belial.

"Still no response. I am within range of their communication capabilities. We must know from them of any that could have escaped."

"Their servitude and knowledge in this would be advantageous, yet response or not, their historic connection to the Raziel means their fate will be entwined with them. We must wipe them all out!" responded the Witch of Endor sinisterly.

Rahab concurred, "We will send our final message when we arrive at the Raziel's world."

"Everything is in place for the destruction of the Raziel and the systematic annihilation of all those that could have been tainted by them. Yet we know that the seeds of life can prevail in the most unexpected of circumstances, unless it is cut from the universe like a cancer. We all know the source of the prophecy, so we comprehend what lengths it will take to bring about its prevention... Abaddon, your task is the most important, bring upon your brethren good news." requested Ashmedai with eagerness.

"Nothing of the Raziel will exist. Let us be rid of the dark cloud of the prophecy. It has been a burden for far too long. Our infinity weapon, our absolution of creation is operational. My brethren, it is a magnificent sight, the total destruction!"

"Ahh, then I look forward to witnessing it's all ending power. When can we expect its presence Abaddon?"

"It can only travel a fraction of the velocity of our armadas, but still, soon enough. I will join with my summoned forces and head for the world of the Raziel.", Abaddon paused, "I have spent so long taking the knowledge to build such a final solution for this moment. I wish it to be my hand that draws the last breath of the prophecy, like it was mine that brought about its birth." intoned the eldest of the Sin. "Yet be wary, we get one strike and then this beast will require many cycles of Gehenna before it can recharge. If my task is forsaken for any reason or should my arrival be hindered, then we present the prophecy with the possibility of longevity. Our forces must proceed to purge all life on the Raziel world until I make my arrival. Then the infinity weapon will make sure that all Raziel existence, past, present and future is erased."

"We all agree on this. Witch of Endor, as the accumulator of the Supremacy, can we rely on all our forces to do what is necessary? This is no mere combat, but slaughter and eradication." probed Ashmedai.

"You would be right with your unease, much of our forces do not have this capability in their nature, but be assured, all will serve as our instruments of death."

"What gives you such confidence?"

"Belial and the Sons of darkness will testify to their compliance. What we have done is strip away choice until only the two most arcane of all remain. To live or to die. All life is imbued with the primal instinct to survive and endure, so it is no concern that they will do what is needed to ensure theirs. Only those that have embraced that singular choice find themselves in our Supremacy, morality can quickly sway on a grand scale given the right incentive. Those that hesitated or could not do what was needed of them have already chosen death."

Under the raging atmospheric lightning, Ashmedai relayed his last message, "Very well. Then brethren we have finally reached that moment, we stand at the brink. With the prophecy dead, we will be released from its shackles of fate. Our gaze can deviate from our demise to an eternal future that has no limitations. We will conclude the Sin dominance and control of this galaxy. To have power over all, harvest the universes' secrets and finally take the knowledge of everything that is our birthright. Then we shall mould this tired Garden to our will. Our defiance complete!"

37 - Elevator to Nowhere

The heat haze made the Sun shimmer on the horizon as it rose into the morning sky, for a moment the perfect clear blue was broken by another blur that was a distortion of heated air. The MAJI agent designated as Aquarius 2 flew over the forested mountains and rugged mesas of Jicarilla Apache Indian reserve in northern New Mexico. He zipped silently above the acres of the mountainous Ponderosa pine forests and Pinion pine mesas with sage brush flats, almost invisible to the naked eye in his supersonic stealth craft. The vessel he sat in was of a design that very few people had ever seen, the blue prints, a gift from the Cult of the Serpent and their Masters, a taste of the advance technology they could obtain with their mutual collaboration. The craft worked on principles he did not understand, although its motion through the Earth's magnetic field that powered it, caused the craft to wobble drunkenly from the outside, inside it was difficult to determine if it was moving at all. The only reason Aquarius 2 knew he was actually blistering towards Dulce New Mexico close to eight hundred miles an hour was that the chair he was strapped too was no longer spongy but a solid mass moulded to every curve of his body, and the lighting had changed from a pinkish purple haze to clear blue-white. The exterior of the craft was a mix of steel and the refined graphite coloured lodestar, the source of its magnetic property that allowed the vessel to travel to anywhere in the world in less than an hour. The craft was one of many available to them, mainly stored in their Los Alamos facility and were nicknamed 'the saucers' due to their double saucer shape. The saucers had been an invaluable piece of equipment not only for transportation, but for their disinformation campaign to direct the attention of the public eye and various government groups away from what they and the Cult were actually doing.

The Dulce facility once existed as a natural cavern system that's enormous size rivalled that of Carlsbad and Lecheguilla as the deepest and most extensive cave system in the world, with the small difference that the majority of it remained unexplored. With its plentiful freshwater supply and internal heating from the up-well of hot springs, it was perfect for the needs of the Masters. Then through the 1940's-1960's it was enlarged using a mixture of nuclear blasting in the lower areas, and drilling in the upper levels that used highly efficient boring machines capable of melting rock through their nuclear-powered wolfram-graphite tipped drill cones. The mega-machinery and construction work provided by the RAND Corporation, a Cult run mask company employed by the US government to create one of many underground facilities that they had been convinced was a necessary resource in light of the Cold War with Russia.

The saucer passed over an isolated, and one of the most inaccessible, areas of the Archuleta Mesa many miles from any population or sign of civilisation. Aquarius 2 was now skimming over the tree tops of the dense vegetation but even from this lowly height it would be impossible to spot any type of artificial entrance, especially one that didn't want to be found. Dropping into a valley gorge located in the south of the Archuleta Mesa, the saucer began to slow rapidly without a hint of a change of momentum within the craft. The internal lighting dimmed to a pinkish-purple and the pressure on Aquarius 2's back diminished and released him from his seat. The saucer was stationary inside a cave entrance that was only slightly wider than the 4 metre diameter of the craft. One of the two pilots hit a switch and a side exit lowered to a dull clunk as it contacted the excavated rock. Aquarius 2 disembarked the saucer, his craft was not the only one in this hidden parking lot. On the other side of the deceptively large cavern was one of MAJI's black stealth helicopters, a clear sign that the person he had been summoned to meet for debriefing was already here.

Although substantial enough to house several of the saucers or helicopters, it was not adequate enough to transport the plethora of staff that was needed for this facility. There was a second way into the facility that he knew of, a single dirt road leading to an area miles away upon the top of the mesa. This road was marked as disused at its outskirts. If for whatever reason someone did travel down it, they were quickly met with a fenced off area clearly warning anyone that they were approaching a 'Restricted area', trespassing was 'Strictly prohibited' and warning that 'Unauthorised personnel risk penalty of imprisonment'. Any idea of a few hours incarceration in a windowless room and a few harsh words was far from the mark as you could get, what you would find on the other side of the fence was an unimaginable horror if you believed the rumours. If anyone was stupid or unlucky enough to enter the sprawling area within the boundary, they wouldn't get very far. Not only were there frequent 24-hour patrols, countless surveillance and tracking devices camouflaged in the rocks and shrubbery. But far worse, weaponry designed to kill any life form it encountered, microwave weapons that were capable of doing anything from, depending on their need, rendering a body unconscious to melting heavy metal vehicles into a heap of smoldering slag. No one could get close unless specifically cleared to enter the area. High up in the Archuleta Mesa the road winded through the crowded pine trees until it came to a halt by a single diminutive hut in the lonely wilderness. No bigger than a typical single room log cabin, it appeared abandoned. But behind the masquerade of wood were solid steel walls, metres thick and resistant to all general explosives, corrosive chemicals and cutting equipment. Once you opened the exterior door by inserting a triangular key into the replica key hole, you were met with a heavy metal elevator door. A double wide entrance that displayed a host of required security checks to open. Firstly an un-clonable swipe card, next a finger print pad, voice recognition input and finally a retinal scan. This was not the entrance Aquarius 2 was going to use. A second lift was located inside the concealed hanger towards the back wall. He passed a group of approaching maintenance staff, none of which spoke a word or even acknowledged his presence. Each one wore the generic worker jumpsuit, plain black and embroidered with the Dulce emblem, an inverted triangle containing a capital 'T' set within. The silence and disregard did not bother him, this was the norm around here. The staff he encountered in Dulce only talked when completely necessary for their function. Most quiet because of the stringent rules in the work area, but he knew there were many that were silent not of their own choosing but of the work that was done below that he had played a hand in. Aquarius 2 performed the necessary security checks to unlock the reinforced elevator doors and entered. Inside he pressed the solitary button labelled level 1 and the doors closed sealing him in. The lift dropped the hundreds of metres to the first lower level in mere seconds without experiencing the falling feeling in his stomach. Just as in the saucer, the majority of the Dulce infrastructure, including the elevators, ran on magnetic technology. The lift doors opened out onto level 1, designated security and communications. A hive of open planned officers with a collection of operatives from many of the government's most secret agencies, and a strong contingent of military personnel. This level and the two below were the face of Dulce to US government, what all the available top-secret reports were about and most importantly what appeared on the black budget accounts. Before Aquarius 2 could even enter the main section, he had to perform further security checks at the hands of armed soldiers. He was fully stripped of his weapons and personal items then asked to change into the standard blue Dulce uniform signifying his important rank. Next to step onto a set of scales and to grasp the pair of handles fixed to its base. He felt a tingle as his weight and body fluid percentages were outputted to the computer terminal and recorded into the data banks and then copied into his personal ID pass. These measurements were a daily necessity and anyone who was required to leave the facility had to resubmit to the check. Its results were compared with the earlier measurements to verify any changes in overall mass that could be an attempt to smuggle any material to the outside world. He had spent a lot of time in level 1 but today he would be going to the lower levels.

Once he passed through the security check point, he made his way towards the centre of the administration sections where the second set of elevators were located. Stepping inside there was again only one option available to him, level 2 labelled staff housing. Working in this facility meant that a normal life in the outside world was a rarity and therefore this level was called home for months at an end. This floor was a stark contrast to the one above, here the light was different with its UV lamps giving you the feeling you were walking under a summer Sun. Many people occupied the plant filled corridors dressed in their various coloured overalls and talking openly amongst each other in the non-formal environment. But even here they knew they had to be careful of the topic of conversation, work related talk in the staff quarters was strictly prohibited. If the rule was broken, security would know, there was ears and eyes everywhere, both artificial and not. He crossed the level in the direction of the third lift, the people went uncomfortably quiet in his presence, the blue high clearance uniform stirring up suspicion and fear in equal measures.

Aquarius 2 finally exited onto his destination floor, level 3 - executive offices and laboratories. Here is where MAJI had their base of operations and where the facilities biological research was carried out. Research into diseases, genome mapping and biological pathogens for weapons. This is what kept away the scrutiny of the official government's prying eyes, periodically releasing a hailed breakthrough in medical advancement from various vaccines, cures and miracle drugs, and also highly controversial chemical weapons. He made straight for the control room, a circular section of one-way glass containing a large oval table and multiple exterior monitors showing various labs and scientists studiously performing unknown experiments. Entering with the use of his swipe card he walked in upon a group of four people, three men and a woman. It was an interrogation, a suited man was the one he had come to see, two were further Aquarius designated agents like himself and the last a civilian, the one being grilled. "Tell me, who you work for!" questioned the man in the black suit with an expressionless face. He also bore an emblem embroidered into his jacket. This one though was different to the

Dulce design. His was an upright triangle crossed by tri-lateral lines. The line through the base signified MAJI, the one half-way through representing the Cult of the Serpent and of course at the pinnacle, the line of the Masters.

"Firstly, may I say Fuck you! And by the way you cannot hold me here, I have done nothing but exercise my freedom of speech!" yelled back the defiant guy with a moustache and a wandering eye.

The interrogator noticed Aquarius 2 enter, "You refuse to answer! Then so be it. Take him to level four conditioning. Dismissed."

"Sir." greeted Aquarius 2.

"Someone apprehended at the MUFON conference poking their nose where it doesn't belong. None the less, a good opportunity to infiltrate the network of whoever sent him."

"Of course."

Aquarius 2 knew the MUFON conference well. It was a meeting place for conspiracy theorists, investigators and the like, secretly set up by MAJI to bring people and groups together that may be a problem for them and their activities in the future.

"Agent, you will be pleased to know that your errand was successful. It is a great thing you have done for your country. The creation of a New World Order is in its final stages. And with it the security of our great nation will be assured. We will be heroes to our people and their children, leaders in a new era of peace. The governments have done what is needed of them. Soon the enemies of the UN will fall…. You have something on your mind agent?" he asked in the most serious tone.

Since Aquarius 2 was drafted, he had reported to MJ-4, the commander's designation within MAJI. And within that very long period he had only ever met him three times, usually taking orders by encrypted communication. Also, apart from his initial recruitment by MJ-1, in this time he had never met any other designation of MJ within the control group, this was forbidden to agents. This he was told was to ensure secrecy at all costs. Although he had little personal contact, he knew full well his commander was an extremely dangerous man with a character that was willing to do anything for the cause. Aquarius 2 had to choose his words very wisely.

"I worry at what cost it will be too our nation. I saw the terrorists' video." he replied, making sure his facial expression conveyed disgust and hatred when recalling the video.

"Ahh their desperate bluff! The Cult has those dogs under control. Without such threats our people would not support our endeavors. The Cult has assured MAJI, that as before, any collateral damage to the US will be as minimal as needed to get the message across, and any target will be unimportant infrastructure. Such a sacrifice of the few is surely something we all agree upon!"

"Yes without a doubt!" There was only one answer he could give if he valued his individuality and didn't want to follow the man to level 4.

"That is good to hear agent." said MJ-4 in a warning tone as he lit a cigarette, "While the US takes the lead and its threats crumble, you will remain here and carry out our duties to the Cult."

"Yes sir."

Anyway, there was nothing he could do, even if he did question their methods. For now, he worked through his own deep sense of duty, free-will that made him a better agent. But if needed they had other ways of making him do their bidding, and that was if he was lucky. Recently disturbing rumours had surfaced of horrific atrocities being performed upon members of the population and especially on those people that had outlived their usefulness. Under orders, he had brought many of these political or military obstacles in himself, some he had never laid eyes-on, or heard reports of again, but most were released back into the wild, just with a new-found appreciation of the Cult's and MAJI's viewpoint. But he knew there were many other active teams involved in bringing in members of the population that he had no visibility too.

The choice of complicity had always been a limited one, be a tool to usher in the great era he dreamed of, or let others achieve it in his stead.

Aquarius 2 left the menacing MJ-4 behind and walked slowly towards the elevator to take him back up to his assigned living quarters. It had been a long mission, physically he was exhausted but his mind was still restless. He stopped before he got to the doors and turned around. *First he would have a walk around and see the operations in the labs and below in level 4.*

38 - The Alpha and the Gamma

The polished amber of Seber materialised in high Earth orbit, a primitive world about to become the arena for a galactic battle of epic proportions. The view of the blue and green jewel was obscured by the presence of a large, stationary rock floating in space. However, Seber did not try to avoid the impeding asteroid but motioned along a path directly towards it.

"Krill, no Sin Supremacy ships detected in the Solar system yet." reported Emile.

"What about Earth!" said Michael apprehensively.

"Erm, no sign of any further nuclear strikes."

Michael let out a deep breath, "Shouldn't there be a load of ships here by now?"

"Wait a minute! I am detecting none of our craft either. There should at least be our TEAF defence fleet." Emile was looking extremely nervous as she brought up numerous displays upon her console.

"The Hyekera forces should already be here." notified Phalacreus.

"What have the Hyekera done!" roared Varantis jumping from his chair.

"Varantis, there is no evidence to determine any conclusion. We shall dock with Alpha and commune with Elyon." asserted Krill,

"Dr. Tesla can you locate him?"

"Yes, one Elohim signature inside the aft star room."

"Then please proceed with the docking."

As they approached, it quickly became apparent that not only was this no ordinary piece of space debris, but there were two of them. Out in the distance an even bigger rock drifted silently above the Earth.

"What are these?" asked Michael.

"Welcome to Planetoid Alpha and Gamma" introduced Emile.

From what Krill had said, he assumed the one they were heading for was Planetoid Alpha. The side facing Earth was boulder like, bereft of any interesting features and slightly rounded. The other resembled the cliff face of a coast, dropping at a steep angle towards a jutting base. It was the smallest of the pair, a dark pitted rock sprinkled with pockets of structures that were crafted inside the planetoid itself. Central to Alpha was a single set of docking bay doors which were modified sections of the planetoid that allowed access into its hollow depths. The only sign of unnatural internal structures were the groupings of windows inserted plush with the asteroid exterior, looking out into the ocean of space. Gamma was in its own geosynchronous orbit a distance away from Alpha, was about ten miles across and much more rounded in its shape. Again, its Earth facing side had little defining characteristics to intrigue astronomers from their observatories, however the opposite harboured a plethora of weapons turrets and several gargantuan blocks of metal that could slide across to provide access to even the biggest vessels.

Michael looked at the primeval looking planetoid; he got a sense of hundreds of souls within it. Some of them seemed different, too ordered and logical like he had sensed from Krill the first time they met. "So as well as housing alien technology under the desert floor and settling an outpost on Mars. Earth has two space bases too!"

"Well almost." answered Emile, "They were originally located in Ashtar space but were launched towards Earth to act as an Ashtar close quarters base of operations and defensive system when they learnt of the new Sin threat. There were initially three of these planetoids including Beta which served as a substantial cargo hold for Ashtar technological equipment. However en route to Earth, the planetoids were assaulted by a species known as the Ze. Extremely loyal to the Sin and first encountered during the last great battle, they are one of the supremacy's most dangerous legions. In the ensuing battle planetoid Beta was destroyed, a necessary sacrifice to allow Alpha and Gamma to escape. They finally arrived at Earth in nineteen fifty-three. It was big news to astronomers at the time due to the tiny probability of two such bodies being captured into a geosynchronous orbit by the planet's gravity. At the time COM Twelve was able to suppress much of the news surrounding the event. Although incredibly strange, this phenomenon was quickly forgotten to the more important news of the Cold War, and now today these planetoids are only seen as a normal site in the night sky. Alpha, also known as Athena to us, serves as habitation and command facilities for the Ashtar, human and allied interests in the system, Gamma a ship and cargo hold, and more importantly a defensive battery to protect Earth from immediate threats." As Emile explained the history and presence of the retrofitted planetoids, Seber drifted between the shifting rock doors and into the hollow interior of Athena. Inside was eerily quiet, all of the docking bays lay empty and everything was lit by minimal lighting sources like it was closed for the evening. The only suggestion that this place was not completely deserted was a few figures that could be seen rushing past the facade of windows that looked in upon the mined-out heart of the planetoid. As they came to a hover over a docking ledge at the rear of the internal void, Michael thought to himself that the material that must have been excavated from this planetoid, resembled the look and texture of the black alloy used to construct the fleet of TEAF fighters he witnessed within the shipyards of Cydonia Mensae, there was certainly an abundant enough source of ore inside Athena.

The whole group disembarked Seber and made their way down the dull and empty corridors towards the rear of the planetoid. They caught fleeting glimpses of people hurrying around, Michael could sense the nervousness exuding from them that added to the uncomfortable chill in the air. They reached a set of metallic doors decorated in constellations created from semi-precious stones. Rather than worry, Michael could sense a feeling of excitement from behind the doors, excitement mixed with thoughts of deceit. As Michael pushed the doors open, he could hear the whispered words of a voice he knew, "Where are you…." and a glimpse of a huge screen displaying a view, not looking out into space for sign of the oncoming Sin Supremacy but the surface of Earth itself. The voice instantly stopped, the screen flashed off and any sense of emotion was immediately masked from any prying senses. Michael wasn't sure if anyone had seen the image but he knew they'd never heard the words. He could now tell when he was picking up sound below the threshold of his normal hearing range; it seemed to echo more in his head and produced a feeling of pressure pushing against his skull. Elyon was alone in the star room. It was circular in shape and three sections of the wall were lined with massive screens. These provided a backdrop for the projected images of astronomical observations made from the central control core.

"It is with unbounded joy I see you all return, and return safely. And aid has answered our call, I see. Altairian, Hyekera and Raqzzon, my humble gratitude I bestow to you." welcomed Elyon with a smile that resembled pride.

"It is a pleasure…" Baraqz had stepped forward hand outstretched when Biriqzz dragged him back by his goggle straps and gave him a harsh whisper, "Not now you old fool!"

"Where are the defence fleets? What have the Hyekera done!" questioned Varantis dispensing of any pleasantries.

"Yes, we have detected no alliance vessels in sensor range." added Krill.

"Your words give me glad tidings for it brings success to my plan. Blindness to the alliance fleet is gifted upon the far side of the Sun. So they lie in its orbit, poised over a raging solar storm. All sense and signals of presence are disguised in such close proximity."

"The Hyekera?" asked Varantis.

"The Hyekera have brought destroyers. In our hopes their numbers were greater, but with the Earth defence fleet they have joined."

Phalacreus turned towards Varantis, "The Hyekera does not deceive, Hyekera words are those of fact."

"Your history tells otherwise robot." spat Varantis.

"History is always open to interpretation, as it is with the Hyekera, my own eyes provide testament to this. It is said to be carved into the form of every Hyekera, even your reincarnation bears the account of their conception."

"You have the ability to discern the Hyekera inscriptions. The Hyekera have never been able to decipher their meaning." interrogated Phalacreus as the others attention went to the strange symbols that decorated the entirety of its body.

"They are of ancient Trune, a sacred dialect and knowledge lost with them. I know of none today that could translate."

"Thanks to those automatons!" Varantis scalded.

Elyon raised a hand hidden within his black cloak, "However, a discussion for another time, another place. The Hyekera join the Earth defence fleet, Raqzzon arks and the bountiful warships of the Ashtar Co-operative. But here we stand open armed, yet to receive Altairian reinforcements."

"Do not worry, they will come to Earth." acknowledged Varantis.

"I pray they do." responded Elyon.

"Elyon, what about Earth!", to Michael this was the most important issue.

"Yes, we look outwards to the threat of the Sin, while the human race grows another like a tumour within. Since our last meeting, this peril has intensified."

"What do you mean, what the hell is going on down there!" emphasised Michael in a tone full of anxiousness.

"Please, as I have heard, bare your own witness to the COM Twelve update." Elyon motioned to the large screen in front of them. A recording of General Allen appeared, 'Reporting our current status; the UN has invaded the countries of Iran and North Korea. The coalition of rogue nations admitting responsibility for the initial nuclear attacks, have given the invading forces an ultimatum to withdraw their armies by two PM Greenwich meantime today, or they will inflict further nuclear strikes against the United Nations. A device has been confirmed to be located somewhere in the United States of America. As a response the US has threatened a full nuclear offensive against the coalition…" As the general explained Michael looked at his watch which still remained at British time.

"No! That's in a couple of hours. World War three is about to bloody happen!" interrupted Michael, "Where is the bomb? We must do something!"

There was no answer as all attention remained on the video message, "Attempts have been made to locate the devices but all have failed. There is nothing we can do to stop the conflict at this moment in time, but we continue our search, and gather intelligence in our endeavours to formulate a plan of action."

The recording ceased and Elyon turned to Michael once more, "We must persevere with the most greatest of threats before us. If your worst fears bear fruition and nuclear war ensues. We should embrace the solace that there will be survivours to save. The drawing shadow of the Sin Supremacy almost darkens our skies, the defence of Earth is where we must focus our resolve. Failure brings a solitary conclusion; no humans will survive! Infused with self-preservation and a limitation of the splitting atom, there extricates a knowable truth, what can be wreaked upon oneself, is a far less terrible death than that which the Sin can wreak upon thee. A solution to this crisis must be found in the wisdom of humanity's governments, yet the chance to do so, is an outcome we must deliver them."

"Do what you need to do, but I must get down to Denver now, to where my daughter is!" said Michael adamantly.

"Michael, your heart sings for a possibility I cannot offer you. Our need of you is greatest here." answered Elyon in an understanding manner.

"What the hell can I do from here!" shouted Michael. One of the projectors mounted to the high ceiling exploded and showered the star room in bright sparks. The companions were taken by surprise and all except for Krill looked at Michael with trepidation.

Elyon was also remained unflinching as the cold drops of light fizzled out above his head. "Egregor Krill, my gratitude you would have, if you could you take command of the alliance fleet. The bells of alarm now ring loudly and I feel the chill of the Sin shadow. Please make preparations for the defence of Earth. I fear only hours remain. Michael, honour me with a moment of your company."

A small set of doors behind Elyon on the far side of the star room opened. Without making eye contact with the others Michael followed the shining one through the wooden doors gilded with emerald and azure marble. As he wiped the trickle of blood from his nose, he was led through a narrow and straight corridor that was tunneled straight out of the planetoid ore. The doors closed behind them and shrouded the corridor in darkness, the only light to guide their way emanating from Elyon. After a hundred metres or so it broadened into an alcove consisting of nothing but a solitary seat.

"Please take a seat and ease the weight of burden….. For me, no place exceeds here for reflection." Elyon turned to the wall behind him which had begun to slide apart letting shards of light leak in and illuminate him. "A viewpoint of uniqueness is where we stand, in Athena and Gamma there is no other place you can gaze upon Earth with your own eyes."

"Why have you brought me here, to show me where I can't go?" Michael said with bitterness as Earth filled up the panorama before him.

"Firstly, to manifest control over your emotions. Directly or indirectly, you know well the damage they can cause."

Michael knew he was right. He needed to be more responsible and controlled. The last thing he wanted on his conscious was to cause further hurt to more innocent people. Michael took in a deep breath and tried to relax.

"Secondly, to explain to you matters that are not meant for other ears. When I contemplate your words against the annals of verifiable truth. There is no clear answer to what you can do here. Yet what I do know is that you can do far less there." Elyon directed a shining hand towards to the oblivious world, "My reasons, I admit, can also be found in personal selfishness. Even in the midst of battle, between the waves of heinous hatred and abhorrent destruction, you can find the most unexpected harbour of safety. I need you to survive, and Seber provides that greatest shell of probability."

"If I die, and however I die, what difference will it make? Your new alliance has committed forces, they can't turn back now." argued Michael.

"Michael, to me your experience of life is but a blink of an eye. I am so very old, blessed with the privilege to bear witness to the births of untold civilisations, and the honour to be keeper of memory in their sorrowful passing. Those that blazed glory across the star ways, igniting a proudness in me that still burns bright. Yet among them, never have I seen such hidden promise, that I see in the human race. I offer to open a sacred vault of knowledge, an insight only known the Elohim. Even Egregor Krill has not been exposed to such a reveal.... Why the human race, the Raziel, are so special."

Michael didn't know how to respond other than force out a "Why?"

"When we journey ever inward, the veil of secrecy is withdrawn on your very make-up. The galactic music of life is a complex composition of many songs of origin, but the majority share a common fundamental harmony, that of DNA. From nature's universal perspective, no importance can be drawn from a differing tune. Yet to the Elohim ear, such tiniest of variation in human DNA produces a sound more beautiful than the rest. It is this unique song that is the source of your gifts. Spirals and grooves form your double-helix instrument. Hallmarked with notes of pitch, diameter and offset, a simple ratio can be played, pitch divided by diameter, and diameter divided by offset. Its output a very specific value for both, where no individual is alike in their music. Within your own archives of history, human scientific curiosity has discovered such outcomes, but its significance of meaning floats ever out of grasp. Nature's will seeks human beauty. It forges change in this value along times arrow, undulating above and below a most special number, creeping ever closer and closer to that sweet sound. A special number known by many names, in the mind of the Elohim, it is synonymous with the essence of the cosmos, it is the divine ratio. Amongst the children of earth, evolution drives change and diversity, eventually escaping the boundaries of their biology. But this trend in the human race defies this, it craves conformity. A statistical fluctuation around that most beautiful of numbers that continues to decrease, a process that may take millions, possibly billions of years to achieve what nature intended. Yet, as we continue to find life where death rules, where all outcomes can coexist as one, the impossible is but just a probable in our reality. So, call it the will of God or random genetic mutation, there is a very rare occasion where a human specimen finds themselves much closer to that divine ratio than would otherwise be possible. You Michael, are that I speak of. The only one known of."

"Krill tested for this, some signal in my brain?" questioned Michael rhetorically.

"Yes, to record the sound of one's music. The Elohim like to think of this as a signature of the soul."

"What is so special about this divine ratio that makes us capable of things that the others aren't. I mean my DNA shouldn't be too different from Varantis. The Altairian were of Earth right. Surely they are on the same path?"

"No, although admit it they would not, ascendance to a higher plane of consciousness is sought through meditation and discipline. The beyond that the human race is close to touching, is a ceiling still out of sight for the Altairian. Blindly wandering into a realm of shear evolutionary luck, is a perception they hold close. But it is held by a closed mind clogged by self-pity and increasing envy. They know, as do others, that human DNA holds possible greatness, but the why is still a mystery they equally share. So your paths of destiny diverged long ago, the Raziel walk a unique road in your potential.......... The property that makes you special is a naked truth that I expose to you. Yet the origin of this uniqueness in the galaxy, and why such importance is entwined with this divine ratio, is a secret that must remain shrouded to knowledge. It is a revelation that you, or anyone else is not ready for." explained Elyon enigmatically.

"Why haven't you told Egregor Krill or the Ashtar any of this? Don't you trust them!" asked Michael.

"When I recount my pride of civilisations born, their flame still burns brightest. They are more worthy of my trust than any other that has existed. But in a universe gifted free will, and where love and life are its greatest virtues, some knowledge must remain buried to its predators. Consequences of this knowledge to the innocent is too dangerous, even with a species that embody the best intentions. It is from experience that I draw my words. Look around you for this truth, it is the why my people hide from the galaxy, it is the why the Sin are impelled to conquer and destroy the Raziel."

Elyon paused and turned to the window to Earth. "But let me leave you with this final information; An age has passed since I last communed with my people." the feelings of emotional turmoil welled up inside Elyon, and for a moment Michael felt as if he could peak into the very soul of the shining one. It was as if a few rays of morning light had squeezed through an imperfection in a window blind, the warmth of the photons hitting your face hinting at a bright summer's day outside. The crack in his emotional barrier quickly sealed itself, but not before Michael felt the strongest emotion that drove him. Wrapped up inside the layers of restructuring protection, it leaked through. It was betrayal. "Their whereabouts is a dream that cannot be remembered, but I have found traces in fable that breathes life into faith. It grows a seed of chance in a barren destiny, but only if we endure this day. At trails end we may find nothing, an existence now only solid in persisting whispers. But it is a task built on one certainty, your survival! Believe strongly in my words, this is your daughters best hope." Elyon spoke with a conviction that was hard to ignore, "Fate beckons on the horizon. And I can only repeat myself. It is unknown what difference you can make here to this fight. I only ask that you follow your intuition."

Michael entered the Star room, quiet and deep in thought. He had left Elyon alone in the observation alcove staring down on Earth. *Should he tell the others what he had been told?............ No, he would keep it to himself for now. They must focus on the coming battle. If he knew anything then it was this fight could not be lost.*

The others were discussing defence tactics, and as expected Varantis and Phalacreus were expressing conflicting opinions on how the fleet should proceed. The debate stopped as they noticed Michael enter head down.

Krill turned to him, "Are you ready to depart?"

"Yes."

"Then let us see if we have done enough to make our last stand."

39 - Nightmare Hall

MAJI agent Aquarius 2 walked towards the horde of windowed bio-sealed labs on level 3. This level could have been any government or corporation's hi-tech research facility with its pristine halls and equipment. The double thick glass left the work being done open to examination of those upon this level. He arrived at the set of flashing lights of the first decontamination chambers and looked through the observation window. The yellow-fruits, a nickname for the lab scientists because of their yellow lab uniforms, were injecting experimental drugs into distressed chimps strapped down with leather harnesses on surgical tables. The apes screamed and shook in panic, some soiling themselves as they struggled, a sight that would make the average civilian sick to their stomach, but Aquarius 2 felt nothing. He would see a million of any creature killed and tortured if it meant the people of the US would benefit from its results. Anyway, he had done much worse than this in his life to secure the security of the United States of America. From lab to lab, similar disturbing scenes took place and the cruelly cramped rooms full of caged animals howling in pain were distressing, but nothing he wasn't aware of, nothing of the reports and second-hand accounts that had been heard by other agents. Aquarius 2 had tired of wandering around the laboratory sector and the smell of ape and shit that sifted into the corridors. Therefore he made his way towards the final elevator that he could use, the one down to level 4. This was as far as his security clearance would allow him to go. He had one of the highest available to a human, ULTRA 7, a status far beyond that of even the president, but still there was at least one section below he could not pass. This one required security clearance UMBRA and there was no person he knew that commanded such clearance, not in MAJI or any government agency anyway. Aquarius 2 exited the lift out onto level 4 - psyche research. It was a claustrophobic mix of ageing concrete and sliding metal doors that gave it the appearance of a disused bunker rather than any research area. The security on this floor was different than those frequenting the upper levels. These were not military, but a private security force hired, and most probably owned, by the Cult of the Serpent. What's more, there were squadrons of them patrolling the corridors in compensation for the lack of cameras or surveillance devices on this level. Wearing red, they stood out among the rest, a colour probably chosen to signify danger and a don't mess with us message. These no-nonsense security personnel didn't carry any standard issue weaponry either. In their hands they carried a torch like object in size and appearance. In the manuals they were called the Armorlux weapon, but around here they were known as flash guns. With three settings, the first two were able to produce a concussive electromagnetic ray that would either stun a person into paralysis or kill them instantly, its third setting creating a widespread microwave beam that could be used for subduing a group or subject without risking permanent harm. If that wasn't enough, on this level the lighting systems themselves were installed with sonic devices that could render a person unconscious without even making an audible sound. He left the guards behind and entered the research complex, the setup here was not the exhibition of cleanliness like the labs upstairs; here there were isolated rooms more analogous to backstreet dentists than anything else. There were no high-tech air flow systems on level 4, making the air extremely stuffy; layers of dust lined the surfaces, undisturbed except for the foot prints and drag marks across the corridor floors. Each room Aquarius 2 walked past had someone in, restrained upon a surgical table, surrounded by scientists and doctors having a small dark ball or cocoon inserted through their nasal cavity and into the brain of the subject. Mostly influential government or military officials that could represent problems, called in for routine health checks or vaccinations at local clinics. Eventually finding themselves walking out of those facilities with a clean bill of health and no memories of their procedural detour. Again, he felt no remorse of the actions happening in these underground rooms, he had brought a lot of these people in himself. They were the enemy, Americans trying to, in one way or another; undermine the government, risking the future of his great nation and the formation of the New World Order. He had no problem subjecting them to these techniques in order to atone for their crimes, even if it was against their will. The implants had taken decades to perfect, a single mass-produced device that could be easily implanted into select individuals who would best serve the cause or whose allegiance to MAJI or the Cult was suspect or non-existent. It was essentially a mind control gadget that could be activated when needed and practically force the subject to perform pre-programmed actions or supply subliminal control from a remote location. The latter technique was still not quite ready to put into active service. Aquarius 2 had read the case files of the initial trials. Most led to suicide, breakdowns or complete ineffectiveness, but some worked perfectly, especially in the case of the assassination of President Kennedy. He was about to lift the lid on Dulce and halt MAJI's operations, the worst type of traitor. Famously the candidate completed his implanted mission as planned. The fact that Lee Harvey Oswald knew nothing made it all the more perfect crime. And his death, a bullet to the abdomen at point blank range meant that any autopsy would have no requirement to explore his head for any cause of death. His killer a night club owner Jack Ruby was conditioned with an altogether different technique, an old-fashioned method that was a lot more difficult and time consuming but similarly effective. Although not forced against his will to perform an action, his mind was influenced with a strong urge to carry out a task without the thought of morality or the consequences. In this case, to right a grave injustice against Dallas, the country and the Kennedy family. Now after so many years of research it was almost 100 per cent effective on every subject they had tested it on, it would prove a decisive tool in the political battle that would follow the upcoming conflict.

He reached the last of the implant labs. While he waited for the doors to the next research section to open, he couldn't help but listen to the conversation of the scientists within the lab. An inbuilt habit of being in his line of work.

"Have you calibrated the evoked potentials?" asked one voice.

"Just tuning to thirty to fifty mega-hertz, five milli-watt range to match the brain emissions. Determining the resonance frequency. And..... Bioelectric entrainment frequencies are set." confirmed another.

Aquarius 2 stepped into the shadows, out of their view.

"This particular implant has come straight from them in the lower level, so let's make sure there is no mistake." said one male scientist nervously. "We have to report directly to Kukulcan afterwards."

A second scientist, a short squat fellow, sucked in some air, "Must be important! Ok, what is the device trigger?"

"Erm, a time. It's in Greenwich Mean Time but will be operating in North America."

"Alright, do we know which time zone it is? The Remote Neural Network interface is not available for activation. Not until the Alaskan project is fully operational."

"If there's any truth in what I hear about that Frau Wulf, I'd be surprised if anyone there is still left alive or able to work." he answered as he searched through some documentation, "Let me see, it says here MST, that's minus seven hours."

"All this advanced tech and they still won't let us have networked computers down here!"

Well that would present a potential security breach, wouldn't it, Aquarius 2 thought to himself as he left the active sector and went through a solid rusty door like you would find on a derelict ship. Now he had entered the claustrophobic confines of the old mind control facilities. Beyond the sealed door the lighting was minimal and a hidden warm breath made the air dank and foul. The work they done here had become increasingly obsolete as the cerebral implant was developed. But in one of the back rooms, light shone out of the doorway. He motioned for the shallow glow with curiosity, and silently stepped into the room. There was a person strapped into a high-backed wooden chair with a bright spot-light shining directly into their sweating face. Two people dressed in surgical overalls, MAJI agents, stood over the figure, clamping the perpetrators eye-lids open and pumping them full of psychotropic drugs. Aquarius 2 walked around the agents and looked at the subject; it was the man they were interrogating previously in MJ-4's office.

"Why are you using these archaic methods?" asked Aquarius 2.

The female operative answered him while she slid a miniature display screen directly in front of the subjects left eye. "MJ Four is worried that his people will discover the implant. He was snooping around a doctor who claimed to have had one removed during a surgical procedure on his brain. We will give him the standard conditioning, and on activation with the key-words he will report back all information acquired after his release. And of course, the false memories of an abduction ordeal at the hands of little grey aliens." The agent chuckled to herself as she said the last part. Existence of the Ashtar was something the Masters were not forthcoming in revealing. They were the ones that supplied the terrifying abduction memories to the brainwashers, but failed to explain to MAJI or the Cult of its basis in fact.

"Have you gained permission from the others?" queried Aquarius 2.

The male agent showed annoyance at their mention, "We don't have to pass every little thing we do with them. They're not our Masters! Anyway MJ Four has ok'd it."

"Fine. But if they find out, there will be hell to pay."

"Ha, Ha. Been listening to too many rumours. All they're doing is a bit of research on tissue samples and animals.", replied the female operative as she placed a headset over the subject. She flicked a couple of switches on an old magnetic tape unit initiating a series of flashing images on the small screen and bursts of high pitch tones from the ear pieces, "At worst mutilating a few cows!"

"Yeah probably. Still, it would be best if you didn't spend too much time in this sector."

Aquarius 2 left the two agents to continue their brain washing session and took a route that would take him past an area of the facility that few had ever entered. It was nothing more than a corridor in the far corner of level 4, but it oozed a sinister air about it. At one end stood a security checkpoint that required UMBRA clearance, and at the other, the unknown. What little light there was available in this area failed to penetrate the gloom of the corridor, it was as if it contained an unnatural blackness that shrouded its secrets in shadow. It was said that a few people, mainly scientists, had gone in over the years. Although certainly no one had ever come out to his knowledge. Sometimes guards reported hearing strange noises echoing from within, sometimes screams or cries of help. They were told it was just their imagination; that they were probably drifting off to sleep on duty. For that reason, it was given the name 'Nightmare Hall'. Two guards usually stood watch on the perimeter of the darkness at all times, but today the security was joined by a disheveled lab worker. Aquarius 2 could hear them whispering and decided to stop around the corner and listen in.

"Sssh, keep it down! There are no recording devices here, but we have to be careful what we say." warned one of the red suited guards looking into the gloom with a worried look.

"Are the rumours true?" asked the more muscular second guard with an almost inaudible tone.

"I don't know. All I know is that our head researcher in genetic mutations was taken down there." the yellow-fruit pointed into Nightmare Hall pulling his finger away as if the mere action had frozen it to the bone, "...a month later he returned to the lab. He looked like a zombie, eyes glazed over and speechless. No one dared to ask questions but after two days he suddenly spoke. The researcher told us all to continue working but listen carefully. His words are hard to forget. He said:"

'There's at least three other levels below Psyche research. They made me work in the Vivarium; those scaly bastards called it the zoo. They needed my expertise in forcing mutations in DNA. What they are doing is not right; you should see the poor....' The lab worker explained how the head researcher then vomited over his overalls trying to recollect his ordeal. 'They told me nobody was being harmed, that those things had no intelligence. I didn't believe them; I could see in their eyes...... When I was alone one of those things spoke to me, it told me his name was Simon Bishop. Asked me to help him, that his wife and daughter must be worried sick about him, searching for him right now…. You must believe me, I wanted to help him, stop his suffering. But I couldn't, I had to continue the work with callousness and disregard. You see I would have been the next victim in one of those cages and then my family........'

"At this point he broke down sobbing and walked from the lab. The last thing he said was 'The world has to know'. No one has seen him since. That was two weeks ago."

"No one else has been down Nightmare Hall since then, that's for sure." confirmed the bigger security officer.

"What the hell are they up too down there? If they have humans below, and torturing them… Then they must be breaking the agreement! We need to tell someone; we can't let this carry on." added the other.

"No, if we bring this to the commanding officers or project leaders, we will be the first ones down there experiencing whatever they are doing first hand. They know I have a sister and niece, they made sure to tell me that when I was assigned down here." dissuaded the yellow-fruit.

"Ok, our next leave we have to contact the government or something."

"You know what we signed when we agreed to work here." reminded the big guard, "To mention any detail of what happens in Dulce to anyone on the outside, is considered treason with punishment of death. A repercussion that was also implied for our families. And they wouldn't hesitate. I've seen it happen, remember Edwin? Supposedly he talked, he disappeared soon after!"

"So what do you suggest?" offered the scientist anxiously looking at his watch.

"We can't do this ourselves. Tell those you trust, we have to get the word out, assemble more who think like us. Maybe get some hard evidence. Only disclosure to the mass public will protect us."

"Evidence! How the hell we going to do that? Listen I have to get back to the lab."

"Keep your eyes open and watch your back." warned the guards.

Aquarius 2 decided it was time he moved on also. As he walked back towards the living quarters his mind tried to assess the situation. Was what he heard just a wild story or was there something sinister going on below them. MAJI had made an agreement with the Cult and their Masters on behalf of the people of the United States many years ago, and so far, as he saw it, they were all working towards the same goal, a New World Order of peace and prosperity. An America for the future without fear and war. The Cult had always used its influences to achieve whatever they had promised to MAJI, most recently with the coercing of mass surveillance laws. Their Masters also seemed to have kept their part of the agreement and provided amazing advanced technology, especially in weaponry and mind control devices. So in turn MAJI done what it had agreed; provided them with these facilities, limitless test animals, scientists, brainwashing subjects and hid this all from the world despite having to perform some questionable but acceptable activities. He had met many of the Cult's people in his years of service but only one of the Masters. His name was Kukulcan and was their representative within Dulce and in charge of level 4 and whatever was below. Although all data from the genetic research on level 3 went through him, he was never seen above the Psyche research floor, spending the majority of the time in the mystery of the other side of Nightmare Hall. His long-ago encounter was brief, it was a gathering of the Cult and MAJI representatives, along with a group of affiliated scientists on level 4. Effectively a demonstration of the hailed breakthroughs that only their ongoing partnership could have provided. Kukulcan had gifted them two game-changing medical advancements. CRISPR technology, essentially gene editing, where an embryo could be modified to avoid any genetic disease. And a Micro Neural Network with a biological interface. Both of which could significantly impact the world in rooting out genetic disorders, bypassing spinal or brain injuries to name a few applications. Any unknown quantity always elicited mistrust in him as default. Being reptilian like or humanoid serpents, it was obvious that they did not share the same evolutionary path as homo-sapiens, yet they had been part of human history, even beyond the point where we began to record our own past. In this time, they had never shown him or MAJI that they could not be trusted. Although draconian in their nature, there had never been any evidence in the present or the thousands of years of history to make MAJI believe otherwise. All the Masters had asked of them was bio-experimental resources, for research heavily rumored to be related to their reproduction capability. And for their territories to be left undisturbed by the surface population. Yet it always bugged him, could they be holding information back, hiding further activities? How much did they really know about the Masters? The answer was not much, they were excessively secretive and the Cult of the Serpent had always been their face in everything that was required. Now they were at a point of no return in their plans, if the Masters were involved in the rumored activities, then surely they would be in disregard of any possible agreement. And MAJI needed to know. Tangible evidence is what he needed one way or the other. But how could he acquire it. Covert intelligence was what he was good at, the world in which he thrived. He knew of what little hard facts the conversation had revealed, it did give him an excellent and low risk starting point of investigation. A name!

40 - For the Future of the Empire

In orbit a handful of the Altairian warships skirted the atmosphere including the huge form of Emperor Xantis's mother ship. The bow of the giant living vessel was moving, its front began to swell, splits appeared at the sides and elastic membranes became visible. At the head of the mother ship a gaping hole opened like the mouth of a feeding whale, and the new batch of young Altairian warships gliding into the haven of their guardian's jaws. There they would stay until the inexperienced biological vessels were released into their first battle. Young space fairing tadpoles spawned and abandoned to fend for themselves, a true baptism of fire.

Below on the Sun scorched surface of the empire's primary planet, the emperor was preparing with his advisors from each of the castes. It was not the greatest planet within the Altairian Empire but Emperor Xantis and his people were a deeply sentimental race. The world was neither the first planet of the Altairian, but it would always be his homeworld and the cornerstone of his reign, a reign that perhaps was coming to a disastrous end. He had just conveyed to them the path the empire was about to stray.

"Sire, since the hundred-year war against the Hyekera began

much has changed on Lan Altaira. Acres of jungle and vegetation that the Horticulturists had sewn and tendered so carefully has shriveled away in the heat. The capital dwelling and the other planet structures look tired and weathered. Can we risk this course of action?" asked a deeply concerned Altairian adorned in long colourful drapes from the Horticulturist Caste.

"This is a trend throughout the whole empire, our caste has not built a single dwelling in decades." added a female Contriver.

"Now we do battle in a faraway sector of space over a relatively small system, which has already meant almost every new hatchling in as long as I have been a Custodian has been diverted into the Ethereal Caste. What you suggest will bring war directly to our door step!" the advisor made sure he let them all know the Custodian Caste had suffered greatly too.

When the war began the Altairian had no caste that was devoted to protection of the empire. Each caste had its specific roles and each an important part within Altairian society, but one caste existed to bring hope and promote faith in times of diversity. The Ethereal Caste were the least populated caste but one with strict discipline and control of mind and body that made them ideal protectors of the empire. As the need became greater, more and more of the new hatchlings were brought up and trained by the Ethereal to fight against the Hyekera. The other castes had felt the burden of this recruitment requirement as their numbers dwindled to where they could barely maintain the Altairian civilisation.

"It pains me greatly to see the dilapidation around the empire, but it has been a necessity, every resource that was possible had to be diverted to our war effort. With this vast reserve of ore in the systems of conflict we can rebuild whatever we have lost a hundred times over, without it the Altairian civilisation will once more become insignificant! Now I must tell our people of the difficult sacrifices we all must make." stated Xantis with resolve for his decision but true sadness for his civilisations plight.

Even though much of the population were engaged in their war efforts, things were strangely quiet on Lan Altaira. Only the bare requirements of the Horticulturist Caste tended to the dedicated gardens and a handful of Custodians monitored the Altairian eggs in their underground incubation nests, the only aspect of life that the intense heat provided the ideal conditions. In strings of caverns lined with organic tissue, these batches of mango sized eggs developed in the stifling environment unaware of the troubled galaxy they were about to hatch into. The farmland above formed tiers of concentric rings that were sectioned by tall walls, each agricultural ringlet joined together by a sandy path leading up to the capital dwelling. Despite losing a lot of the beauty it possessed in times past, it still looked an extraordinary site, a sprawling oasis in the desert. The capital dwelling grew up from the centre, myriads of colour blushed across the ribbed plant structures depending on what angles the light bounced off its surface. Rounded towers and spires rose high into the air but all were dwarfed by the principal building. An enormous mushroom shaped form displaying its own tower base that reached towards the heaven and bloomed. This principal building was designed for one purpose, an indoor arena where the Altairian could assemble for the most important of events. The amphitheatre type seating was at its capacity, hundreds of thousands of Altairians from around the empire had been summoned to Lan Altaira, but this time they did not know the purpose of this call to assemble. They were about to find out as the glow of the red raw ceiling began to dim. A small hole in the pinnacle of the roof opened and a shower of solar rays dropped down onto the closed surface of a giant flower at the centre of the amphitheatre. At the end of a thick and arching stem the yellow and blue swirl of its petals unfurled under the gentle persuasion of stroking photons of light. The petals reached out in a morning yawn to reveal within its mouth, a tongue like stigma and twisted filament that together appeared to form a botanical platform and microphone. Stood inside the flower, their Emperor Xantis At Rae readied himself to address the gathering. The chatter died down around the awaiting Altairian and the emperor spoke into the anther growing from the top of the filament. As his words entered the organic microphone, the petals vibrated, amplifying his voice like natural speakers so that every lobeless Altairian ear could hear.

"My people of Lan Altaira and the Altairian Empire, I have summoned you all here today, to tell of a moment many of us never thought would happen. For the last hundred years of my reign the Altairian civilisation has been at war! Today the window of opportunity has opened and opened wide. I can confirm as of now, the virus that is the Hyekera has deserted our borders and have begun to leave their space and conflicting systems!" Xantis spoke with a strength of voice that bellied his 206 years.

There was an instant rumble of talk as the masses discussed this unprecedented news. Xantis gave them a few seconds to give their opinions to their neighbours then raised his claws for silence. "So to my Ethereal, take up your scythes ready to fight! Horticulturists, Contrivers, Custodians and Scholastics, it is you we look too to protect the future of our great empire while we are away, keep our phytological creatures of battle and hatchlings safe, I foresee we will have a great need for them. I know times have been harsh on our people since the exodus of our ancestors so long ago but I hope what we do today will ignite a new era of prosperity that we have only read about in our historical data scrolls. Before we head into battle, I ask that we all meditate a moment. Many souls will be lost, let us pray that they find their way and ascend to the next level of consciousness."

The humid air of the plant amphitheatre went into a ghostly silence as the thousands stretched their dewlaps and raised their heads to the heavens, their troubled minds searching for that ascendant state of mind. The UV shower slowly shut off, the rays of light disappearing in turn, blocked by the constricting opening within the principle building roof. When the last drop of photons squeezed through the sealed aperture of the flesh coloured dome, the petals wrapped back around the emperor and the stem of the flower retreated back into the base of the structure.

Inside the armada of orbiting warships, the loyal warriors of the Ethereal Caste awaited their orders as holographic projections filled the living vessels. Emperor Xantis At Rae now stood in every corridor, room and command centre.

"The Hyekera have left their territories and are en route to our ancestral home. Give the signal to amass all our forces throughout the empire and systems of conflict. Initiate bio-chemical charging; we have a long hyperspace tunnel to generate." He closed his eyes and prayed.

41 - The Meeting

In the middle of Staffordshire, England, the usual screams of fear and excitement were missing from the theme park, now temporarily closed for urgent maintenance. 50 metres below, under the unattended rides of Alton Towers, the ultra-secret agency COM-12 assembled around a square marble table in their high-tech command bunker. With the exception of two individuals, those occupying the seats were the same collection of people Michael had spied on whilst hiding in the ceiling at the Hilton. The female Altairian disguised as the ageing women and the chamomile drinking doctor they referred to as Dr. Heaney were those missing from the previous ensemble in the London hotel.

It was the weathered and grey looking General Allen that chaired the meeting once more. Although the bags under his eyes made it glaringly obvious that he had had very little sleep the past week, he strode up to the table with a strong posture and purpose. "No one has heard from Dr. Heaney for days. We believe he was heading for the MUFON conference when we made last contact with him. Never the less in his absence we must continue." said General Allen loosening his tie and finally sitting down with his ten companions.

"The committee of twelve have done all we can to aid in preparing the Earth defence fleet in the time we had given. There have been many obstacles and difficulties put in our way but we have overcome them. We could not have done more. Now our fate will be decided in the skies, we can do no more in that respect. I have faith in Egregor Krill and our colleagues upon Mars. However, we meet here today because the human race faces a danger closer to our shores. I am certain you all have been following the escalating situation, and I am sure you are all eager to explore avenues of action that might avert a nuclear war!"

An attractive woman stood up, someone of a mixed European and Asian origin wearing a smart outfit and serious manner. She had light brown skin and long dark hair that was pulled back in a professional tight pony tail. "I have tried to use my connections within the black-market weapons trade to attempt to track down the source and possible whereabouts of the nuclear devices."

"And Dr. Cyrielle?" encouraged General Allen.

"It seems a single device, let alone the number claimed by the rogue nations, would be impossible to obtain even if money was no object. Also these devices were particularly modern tactical nukes, small fusion bombs, extremely unlikely to be Russian made devices. The word is they must have had western government help to obtain such devices."

"I agree they are non-Russian devices. My source in the red army has told me that their stockpiles of nuclear capable weapons are all accounted for, and all warheads lost during the fall of communism were more crude atomic weapons. The vast majority of those are beyond operational, destroyed or still catalogued." agreed Commodore Gaughan; a grey-haired gentleman with a hint of an Irish accent. A very important man within MI-6 and the British Royal Air Force.

"This is a disturbing hypothesis. Does anyone else have anything to add? Go ahead Mr. Pierron."

"Every aspect of this scenario looks wrong to me. Number one, the rogue nations involved rarely communicate at the best of times. To have organised such drastic measures in a coordinated attack seems highly unlikely. Especially without us or any intelligence agency getting a whiff of it. Number two, the speed of immobilisation of UN forces shouts to me of pre-conceived plans already in place, plans that would take years to devise and make ready for implementation. Not to mention that evidence of further attack seemed to materialise out of nowhere and just at the right time."

A large built, balding man with a comb over and bushy beard nodded his head at Mr. Pierron's comments. "I agree, it seems that every little change in law and new economic loophole cleverly introduced in the background has paved the way for the US and UN's actions that previously would have broken international law. This could not have been planned by any government; there are too many changing variables over the timescale needed to do this. For someone or some group to achieve this would require them to be ever present in the shadows and wield more power and persuasion than we could ever muster." commented Judge Kidd, a well-respected judge in the international court of justice who had resided over many of these changes himself.

"I think we always knew from our experiences that there was an influential power out there dictating international business, finance and certain aspects of the governments, both congressional and military, and possessing goals clearly in opposition to our own. We have been too busy toughening our skin against outside attack while we ignored the disease eating us from within. We need to act swiftly!" declared General Allen.

"What do you suggest General?" responded Dr. Cyrielle staring at the clock on the giant geographical display screen, "What can we do in such a short time when these moves seemed to be so meticulously planned."

"I'm not sure. First make sure the Ashtar contingent aboard Athena are made fully aware of the grim situation down here, and that Egregor Krill should be updated as soon as he is in range of their telepathic link. Colonel Derby, have CABAL prepped and ready on standby. We may need covert military support."

"Yes General. We'll be ready to deploy within the hour." acknowledged a short and lean man of Hispanic descent dressed in unmarked green fatigues.

"And Dr. Kuzminski, I need you to contact EARF, tell them we are going to require use of the auroras!"

42 - Old Grievances

The first of the Ashtar ancestors evolved upon a large dark planet orbiting within the binary star system of Zeta Reticuli. When the first Ashtar walked in the thick gaseous and permanently dusk environment of their cold world 1.5 billion years ago, the Earth had only begun to see single celled organisms populating its seas. Over the next billion years they evolved into a space faring civilisation creating faster than light propulsion and travelling beyond their star of Zeta¹ Reticuli towards its partner Zeta² Reticuli. On a smaller rocky world orbiting the nearby star they encountered a species very similar to themselves, sharing many comparable biological and physiological characteristics driven in evolution by the native planetary conditions. Living within underground cave systems, they called themselves Reticulans, growing significantly taller than their Ashtar neighbours and exhibiting a much paler white skin complexion, the biggest differentiator was their lack of any form of telepathy. These newly discovered aliens were almost as old as the Ashtar, but were extremely isolationist, more intent on keeping to themselves than investigating the infinite space around them. As the millions of years crept by the Ashtar expanded out among their nearest stars exploring away from the Reticulans towards the un-chartered void. Discovering planets and systems containing greater resources and more idyllic to the growth and development of their society, they eventually migrated their civilisation to new worlds, leaving behind the place of their origin to the closed Reticulans. By the time the first humans began to walk upright, the Ashtar Co-operative encompassed a vast expanse of space containing hundreds of stars and even more worlds, stretching over hundreds of light years. In their exploration they discovered many sentient and intelligent species, some primitive and some as ancient and advanced as themselves. They watched on as civilisations evolved and civilisations perished. Like the Reticulans, the Ashtar and the other elder races of their region of the galaxy agreed not to influence or interfere with any young society, but unlike the Reticulans these races would enlighten them to the galactic community once they had reached sufficient technological advancement and capabilities to travel the incredible distances among the stars. Little did any of them know the evil that swept across the unknown depths of the galaxy. It was an era of peace, a golden age in this corner of the Milky Way, a blissful existence oblivious to the hidden dangers. Then the Elohim came. Although technologically superior and unimaginably older than even the elder races, they fled a power that brought fear to the Ashtar. With their logical minds they found it difficult to comprehend such disregard for life and free will, and such destruction without reason. But it wasn't long until they saw the first signs of the Sin, when incomprehensible actions became reality, and the evidence of this evil slowly crept up on them. Thousands of light years away at the edge of explored space, reports of whole planets being laid to waist and the same ultimatum of judgement delivered to each inhabited world, serve the Sin or be wiped out of existence. The Sin was conquering the galaxy, planet by planet, system by system, and nothing could stand in their way, death or servitude was the only option. Eventually the Sin would descend upon their region of space, the spiral arm. They would have to make a decision that would determine their futures. The only saving grace for the Ashtar and the other races had been their distance from the Sin, it had allowed them to evolve and achieve their level of technology, and gave them the time needed to prepare. So under the impending threat of the Sin, the Elohim brought together the eldest civilisations of the spiral arm in a formation of a great alliance; these were the Ashtar, Pleiadians, the

Hommege and the Reticulans. The territories of these powerful races protected this sector of the galaxy, holding back the Sin and their slave races that comprised the Supremacy. For many years they guarded the younger civilisations behind their protective barrier at great costs to themselves. It had taken the greatest toll on the Elohim and the Hommege. The Sin hunted the Elohim as a priority, still fighting a conflict that started billions of years before, a hostility whose cause remained unknown. Then over twenty thousand years ago the Hommege finally succumbed to the ever-growing power and malice of the Sin, with their civilisation dwindling and their defensive lines about to break, the secretive race mysteriously disappeared from their last populated worlds and colonies. As the Sin disease ate away at the free sector of space the Elohim dispersed and spread, hiding among the plethora of habitable worlds. Some of these planets sustaining varying degrees of life, and many with primitive as well as intelligent inhabitants. It was soon after, that the Sin had somehow learnt of the human race. They believed they had discovered the Raziel of the prophecy, the reason why they scoured the immense length and breadth of the galaxy destroying what they could not control. Assembling their galactic wide forces, the Sin Supremacy headed for Earth with an unstoppable army intent on one goal, to wipe out the human race. Even these groups of all-powerful civilisations struggled to hold back the tide of the Sin. The broken civilisation of the Elohim gathered at Earth. They called all of the great alliance together and told them of the prophecy and the solitary hope of the Raziel. Knowing they could not defend the human race or their own species spread so thinly as they were, the great alliance made the decision to bring everything they had too Earth and make one last stand. In the last great battle, the old alliance eventually stopped the Sin, but at a huge price. The civilisation of the Hommege had already vanished at the malicious hands of the Sin. Following them the Reticulans, ancestral cousins to the Ashtar, were also extinguished that day. Being socially inward they chose to keep their entire population on their home world, Reticulan. But in this policy, fortune would deal them a terminal blow as it was this system the Sin Supremacy swarmed through on its way to Earth. A single world made easy pickings on their menu of vengeance.

Although survivors did escape to Zeta[1] Reticuli, the small remaining populace eventually dwindled and died out over the ensuing millennia. The Elohim experienced severe losses leaving their civilisation also on the brink of extinction. Soon after what was left of the Sin Supremacy fleet limped back towards the unknown corners of the galaxy; the Elohim once more spread throughout the stars, only returning to this sector of space from time to time to maintain a watchful eye on Earth. Yet they too eventually withdrew from known space without explanation or valediction, never to be seen since. It was only the Ashtar and Pleiadians who endured, but still both their races were devastated, losses in which they were only now recovering from. These were just the fates of the elder races; that day hundreds of younger civilisations perished, gone forever. But still outweighing their losses was the fact that the Raziel survived and the Sin was dealt a massive blow. The Pleiadians and the Ashtar were all that remained of the old alliance, they had rebuilt their civilisations in the thousands of years that had passed since the last great battle but they knew the Sin would one day return. The Sin withdrew but they were not beaten, they slowly began to rebuild the forces that had been destroyed; this time though, they spread to all borders of the galaxy absorbing everything they encountered until the Sin Supremacy had become much stronger than they ever were. In the last few decades their worst fears had become a reality again, the Ashtar and Pleiadians had begun to receive reports of devastated worlds, survivors fleeing atrocities and rumours of strange forces moving across the depths of space. The Sin Supremacy was certainly on the move again, and each day brought them closer to their free region of the galaxy. Now they headed once more towards Earth, intent on destroying the human race without making the same mistakes of old. Already the mighty Pleiadians had fallen to their new advances and the Ashtar were next on their list.

*

The same Sin Supremacy armada that had wiped out the Pleiadians arrived on the furthest borders of Ashtar space. In normal circumstances whole cohorts of Ashtar warships would patrol its perimeter scanning meticulously for any sign of the Sin. Well aware of the ancient enemy moving once more. Instead of reinforcing their defences, the perimeter worlds seemed to be abandoned, the space devoid of any ship signatures or sign of life. The Sin Supremacy had swarmed into the edge of Ashtar space expecting to be met with thousands of ships from the surviving alliance race, but what they found was nothing. Not only was there not a shred of resistance, most of the systems within sensor range showed no activity at all.

An enormous Obsidian fragment led the formidable fleet of Supremacy warships deeper into Ashtar space then slowed to survey the sector. The armada consisted of thousands of different races and tens of thousands of different ship designs. This was how it always was, a mixture of slave races and loyal servants, but none knew the other. The rules of the Supremacy armadas were simple. Communication between each force was forbidden, all that mattered were the orders of the Sin.

Laughter boomed out throughout the handful of the eerie black crystal constructions. "The little grey cowards have run. They have seen what we have done to the Pleiadians and their home world. Have they finally realised after so many years that we cannot be stopped….. but if they think they can run and hide then they are severely mistaken." Belial the leader of the sons of darkness, a powerful syndicate within the Sin who ruled a vast expanse of systems close to Pleiadian's space, sent orders out to the subservient armada, "Spread out and destroy everything, leave every rock lifeless and every settlement a pile of dust. Abandoned or not, wipe it all out. Leave no evidence that the Ashtar ever existed!"

The crystalline shadows representing the sons of darkness moved off, each followed by countless numbers of warships. Every death bringing subdivision searching for the nearest world, all eager to please their Sin overseer and cause as much destruction as possible. Every outlying system and outpost they came to prey on was abandoned, several still warm with the imprint of recent activity. None the less, as they had been ordered, they rained down annihilation in frenzied assaults, obliterating every structure, creature, fauna, anything that had had contact with the Ashtar or suggested evidence of an intelligent civilisation. Each time they left only a dead, crumbling world no matter how many hours, days or weeks it would take. Then they swiftly moved on hunting for their next target.

Belial's droves finally reached a system at the heart of Ashtar space that was not only covered in cities, but bore the signals he was waiting for, Ashtar life signs. A beautiful world full of life filled seas and thriving jungles. Between the planet's natural wonders, metropolises stood in pristine conditions, bio signs thrived all around the constructions, but the buildings themselves seemed ghostly quiet. Belial scanned the surface of the planet, this place could cater for billions of Ashtar, but only a few million of the benevolent meddlers could be detected, all concentrated to one large city situated in a mountainous valley. As he finished scrutinising the planet he detected a minute energy echo rippling out from the populated city. *A call for help?* The image of the world in front of him began to blur slightly, like a desert heat haze passing over. *A last Ashtar parlour trick?* It mattered not to him; no one could help them now.

If this is all that remains of them, then so be it. I will still take pleasure in their destruction, Belial thought to himself.

"Descend upon them and annihilate this world!", his crystalline craft began to move in to initiate the cull when his velocity curtailed sharply, seemingly hesitating as he allowed his followers to accelerate past and towards the defenceless planet.

43 - Hypersonic

General Allen accompanied by Commodore Gaughan, another committee member of the clandestine global group COM-12, were cruising at an altitude of 48,000 metres halfway between the Atlantic Ocean and the edge of space. Travelling at a speed of Mach 10.5 sea level equivalent they could traverse the vast distance from their facility in Machrihanish Airbase to Colorado Springs, Colorado in approximately 35 minutes. Taking them to their destination faster than any other Earth based craft currently in existence. Yet it still might not be fast enough. Time was ticking away on their last-ditch efforts to try and help influence the fate of millions of innocent people.

Strapped into a cockpit that barely seated three people, General Allen flicked the communication switch and attempted to send a message over the loud pulsating roar of the aircraft's hypersonic propulsion engines.

"This is Darkstar November, calling Darkstar Mike and Darkstar Kilo. Please confirm progress and ETA. Over"

Static crackled on the aircraft com system, "Darkstar Kilo here. We are rapidly decreasing altitude towards the desert floor. I see the valley ahead. No sign of friendlies or locals. Estimated touchdown at coordinates supplied by contact, five minutes. Over."

"Received. Doctor, you know what is at stake. You must convince them! Over."

"I will do everything I can. Darkstar Kilo out."

"Godspeed!" replied the general before switching to the other listener. "Darkstar Mike, with your earlier prep and take off you should be almost at your location. Report."

"General, just reached the hotbed and attracting attention as expected. We have levelled to approach altitude but have been picked up by US and Chinese forces. They have both dispatched aircraft to intercept. Over."

"Can you land before they arrive at your position? Over."

"Afraid not, the landing strip is still over two hundred miles out and hidden in dense jungle. If we go in too hot, we'll over shoot the runway and light up the base like a brush fire, we can't risk detection. They will immediately call for air strikes to destroy it. Then we can do nothing here. We are just going to have to out maneuver and lose them. Over."

"Do what you must Mr. Pierron. Over."

"Shit! The Chinese interceptors will be no problem but the US has sent three of their new Raptors after us. It's going to be tricky to lose them. We'll have to maintain a communications blackout, I won't be able to confirm touchdown with you without alerting UN and American forces. Over."

"Understood. I will know how successful you were as we cross the deadline. Good luck! Darkstar November out."

Another concerned voice entered the conversation. "Sir, lead Raptor has a missile lock on us."

"Ok pilot, let's see what the Aurora is made of. Take us to the vertical ceiling......." The radio transmission terminated into silence.

The SR-91 was a top-secret black project aircraft designed and constructed as the next step in stealth reconnaissance, initially conceived as a direct replacement to the famous SR-71 Blackbird before the huge budgetary requirements stopped the project in its tracks. Lockheed Skunk Works now known as Lockheed Advanced Development Company were originally commissioned to develop and build the SR-71 Blackbird, and were on course to win a new one hundred billion dollar contract against their rivals Northrop Corporation to upgrade the American government with a new type of spy plane, when a previously unheard of company stepped in with a last minute admission, the Aurora. The US government were highly impressed with the prototype and with the endorsement of some influential people within the air force, this fledgling company was contracted to complete the project, while the other two were given less lucrative but hefty contracts producing other stealth aircraft such as the B-2 Spirit heavy stealth bomber and aspects of the F-22 Raptor stealth fighter. The company was called Borealis and was founded by the members of COM-12 to force their way into the important market of government defence contractors. With the resources of EARF they knew they could produce a prototype aircraft, that was superior to the designs capable by any of the current defence or aerospace companies. They initially developed three completely operational models before the American government decided that the expenditure of full production and the cost of running these craft, were far too high and pulled the plug on the black ops project. However Borealis and COM-12 did not stop there, not only did they retain the fully functional Aurora hypersonic aircraft, but they continued to develop its technologies along with Ashtar input into what is now known as the TEAF fighter of the Earth defence fleet. The dimensions of the Aurora prototype were extremely non-angular, each radar absorbing part curving into each other forming one continuous flowing piece, the only sharp angles being the flat isosceles uni-wing and perpendicular stabilising fins, reminiscent to the tail feathers of a swallow. It is propelled at low speeds by four methane powered afterburning turbo fans and by four experimental hydrogen fuel cell pulse detonation engines that take it up to its hypersonic velocities. A hybrid engine that could not only take the Aurora across a flight range of 15,000 km and a theoretical top speed of Mach 11, but capable of dissipating the heat of the powerful engine so that it would only emit an insignificant infrared signature. Displaying a black triangular profile constituting a 20m wingspan and 35m length, it would be highly recognisable to any observer, but due to its supersonic speed capabilities and stealth technology, it has rarely been spotted by either military or civilians alike. The only evidence of its existence being a few dubious eye witness reports of triangular craft producing evenly spaced pulses of rumbling and a few photographs of a strange jet contrail consisting of a string of donuts that obviously belonged to no known active aircraft, black ops or not. Since its completion the three Aurora prototypes have been kept in an old former RAF base called Machrihanish, on the Kintyre Peninsula of Scotland. When the project was terminated COM-12 acquired the mainly unused base and the ideal facilities it gave to them. Firstly, its runway was the third longest in Europe at 3,049 metres in length, and ran off the west coast of Scotland directly over the Atlantic Ocean. Secondly it maintained a large hanger and accommodation buildings, as well as grass camouflaged bunkers that were once used to house nuclear stockpiles. Lastly although it was in a relatively unpopulated countryside area, it did share some facilities with the small civilian Campletown airport situated at the opposite end of the base. These infrequent commercial flights instilled a certain degree of innocence and officialness to the site, masking what it was really being used for. That being the housing, testing and base of operations for the top-secret Aurora craft and COM-12 activities related to it.

It had been 25 minutes since his Aurora had taken off from the former RAF base in Machrihanish, and it was now approaching the most protected airspace in the world. General Allen hoped he would not face the same welcome as Mr. Pierron had just received, but he was not flying towards skies over a war zone and still maintained some high clearance air force codes that should get him down safely with some obvious explaining to do.

44 - T Minus

It was 1:19PM GMT, forty-one minutes to deadline, however the tanks and troops still ploughed deeper into the heart of Iran and North Korea, and the bombers still dropped their payloads of death into the sacred grounds and impoverished cities of the rogue nations. All across the world people prayed that a peaceful end would be found, some 11th hour agreement to stop the killing, but their prayers remained unanswered, the warring forces showed no sign of stopping.

The people of New York still scrambled to escape their city in fear. An epidemic of dread that had left the streets of many major cities around the world deserted, with shops emptied of supplies and daily life stuck on pause. Families huddled in their homes, ears peeled to their TV's and radios, soaking in every update and piece of advice that was broadcast. Those who could, left the places they felt may be possible targets and headed for the countryside. But many just had to remain where they were and hope, no public transport ran, roads were clogged with abandoned vehicles and planes were grounded. The world seemed at a standstill; the deep breath of trepidation before the plunge to the unknown.

Flakes of dry skin floated onto the computer equipment beneath the Pindar. The leader of the Cult of the Serpent pressed a few buttons and flicked a switch to open secure communications channels to the representatives of the rogue nations. This time there was no video feed, just a single encrypted audio stream ensuring that the cracked smile across his rash covered face was hidden from their view.

"The time ticks ever closer, are your martyrs in position?"

A yes was the simple answer from each of them. Not one of them in the mood for discussion or to spout last defiant words. The Pindar could sense the anxiety in their voices.

"Good! The UN forces will not relent despite your best efforts to deter them. This I can guarantee, you know my sources are one hundred per cent reliable, as they have already been proven. Now you will have to persuade them with a show of your own might. When the last second ticks away you will not hesitate to give the order, for they will not! Your lives and everything you believe in depends on the bravery and resolve you show today. Strike your enemies hard!"

The Pindar terminated the conference call. He knew he had said all he needed too. Events were at a stage that it mattered little if any of them experienced doubts. The rogue nations had selected their martyrs themselves, so there was a chance of failure in that link, but they had taken the necessary measures to ensure that the operative within the USA would carry out the mission, just like the pawns that initiated this conflict. And of course, then the US would retaliate. He was unperturbed if this crisis escalated to its culmination, he cared nothing for the millions that would lose their lives, there was always billions more to take their place. The continued power held by the Cult and the will of the Masters was all that mattered. Unlike MAJI, the security of the United States meant little to him, the Pindar was more concerned with the locations they had targeted, each one carefully chosen by himself to reinforce their agenda of a New World Order, as well as the smallest perceived impact to their partners. Locations whose impact would be unclear to anyone until it was too late. No conceivable event could prevent it now.

The President of the United States of America paced up and down the command bunker buried under six hundred metres of

Granite deep within the Cheyenne Mountain Complex. Based in Colorado Springs, the Cheyenne Mountain directorate was formerly home to NORAD until a number of years ago when its operations were moved to the nearby Peterson Air Force base to avoid duplication of functions between the two sites. Since then it had been on 'warm' standby ready to be brought back on line when the need arose. Bored into the heart of the mountain and housed in a steel building behind twenty-five ton blast doors, it was designed to withstand a thirty megaton blast as close as a mile away, and therefore during this uncertain time provided the ideal facility to house the president and his strategic command.

Two soldiers and an accompaniment of defence advisors marched into the command centre. Weaving between the rather ordinary lines of desks and flat display screens, the soldiers dressed in full military regalia stepped up to their commander and chief and saluted.

"Mr. President Sir, I have the launch command codes." notified the officer carrying a metallic briefcase that was handcuffed to his wrist. The nervous looking soldier took out the key and unlocked the briefcase. Placing it on the table in front of the president, he entered the security combination, opened it up and took a step back.

"Son you have further information for me?" asked the president to the second officer still standing there.

"Yes Sir, Mr. President" he replied with a slight hesitation, "General Allen is outside asking to speak with you."

The president knew General Allen was staunchly opposed to his election as the new leader of the US, and decided he could only be here to put his two cents in where it did not belong. That was the last thing he needed. "Soldier, tell the general I am a bit busy right now."

"Right away Sir." he responded with a nervous intake of filtered air realising he would have to turn away such a high ranking general.

Within a desert palace carved out of the sand stone of an ancient gorge, the Iranian President is intrigued to hear of a foreign visitor to his stronghold. A man called Dr. Kuzminski. At the same time across the Asian continent situated inside a jungle hideout deep in the undergrowth outside Pyongyang. The Supreme Leader of North Korea receives an equally unlikely guest brought in by one of his generals and going by the name of Mr. Pierron.

45 – Enter the Leviathan

Seber skimmed the peripheral of the Sun's corona towards the immense solar flare that reached out into space on the far side of Sol. An ejection of super-heated charged particles that covered an area easily capable of engulfing the Earth many times over. At a minimum safe distance from the wind of ions, they could visually make out huddled groupings of dots illuminated in its glare. Hundreds of objects, some blacker than space itself and others glittering like diamonds in the sky, but all maintaining a cautious distance from the hulking ringed destroyers. Krill looked out with dismay, these numbers were insignificant to what the Sin could bring to battle, and although they had come together in a common purpose, it appeared as if they were fighting for themselves. Even the Earth defence force and the Ashtar Co-operative had separated from each other to form their own ranks. This fragmented coalition of free races was Earth's last hope, the fledgling forces of the new alliance. *Soon they would realise how much they would need each other* Krill thought to himself outside the throng of the Co-operative link.

"Dr. Tesla, please establish a channel with the group leaders of the Earth defence force, Ashtar Co-operative, Hyekera and Raqzzon fleets.

"Channels secured Krill. The Hyekera supplying audio only."

"Very well."

Three holographic displays materialised into the air around Krill with representatives from each of the assembled civilisations. "Jaguar tooth, what number have we managed to get operational?" The man in the crystal-clear projection was obviously of Mayan decent. He was adorned in traditional Mayan garments and decorated in war paint, one of the Mars populace.

"Egregor Krill. We have about forty-five per cent of the current Earth defence forces operational. My people and yours have been working full day cycles, but this is the most we could muster in such a short time. The rest of the unfinished fleet at Cydonia should remain safely hidden beneath the newly installed Altairian holo-cloak."

"You and the Mayan people have done admirably." Krill turned to the short greyish figure with brown facial patching in the far display. "Ka'er Myas, has it been completed?"

"I supervised it myself" Ka'er Myas's large eyes blinked much slower than normal, showing about as much emotion as any of them had witnessed from any of their species. "The others will arrive at the rendezvous coordinates as soon as circumstances dictate."

"I will take command of the alliance fleet from now." As Krill finished his audible order, he momentarily shut his eyes as if he was sending a personal message to the Ashtar Ka'er over the Co-operative link.

"Very well." acknowledged Ka'er Myas also seeming to tune into the invisible tele-link.

"Hyekera and Raqzzon forces, we thank you for your contribution. I had hoped for more numbers, I still await the arrival of Altairian forces, but for now this is what we possess. Our plan of action is this. The Sin Supremacy scout fleet is near, I have no exact information on their quantity, but whatever comes we must be ready for them. We have one advantage; they do not know of our new alliance. As soon as they emerge into the solar system, we will use this surprise to our advantage and strike them with everything we have before they are able to organise their forces. I will position Seber in a sensor clear area out of the range of the solar flares interference and wait for contact. On my signal we will attack."

Seber veered in direction, twisting between the high temperature gases of coronal loops and high energy particle geysers, out towards an area where they could detect the Sin incursion into the solar system without electromagnetic hindrance and still maintain a line of communication to the alliance fleet.

Michael felt the immense power of the Sun upon his back. The ancient nano-fluid exterior filtered out most of the UV rays but enough penetrated through Seber's shell to make him begin to sweat. The whole thing felt surreal, behind him the Sun was lapping at the hull, and he was looking out into space while various alien envoys monitored a display screen of the solar system, waiting for the most feared enemy in the galaxy to arrive. He thought how blissful life must be for the people down on Earth that were unaware of the impending doom of the Sin. Then again what was happening on Earth right now, World War 3? He didn't know, maybe things weren't so great for them, but he knew he would rather be there holding his daughter with only the destructive stupidity of the human race to worry about. Unfortunately, Michael never had time to dwell on such matters as red dots flashed upon the display. His heart began beating hard when he saw where they had emerged.

"A large fleet of ships has just exited sub-space. They are within weapons range of Earth. Krill it's the Altairian!" stated Emile with some surprise.

All eyes except those of Krill shot towards Varantis. The Altairian Prime returned an icy glare but still maintained a facade of indifference toward the sudden appearance.

"I told you they would come!" chorded Varantis.

"They are assuming combat formation. Power surges in all vessels!" said Emile nervously.

"Just normal procedures after exiting from a long tunnel. The ships begin recharge of all systems. Like a creature taking a deep breath at the water's surface after an extended dive!" scalded Varantis.

"And their formation?" Krill questioned with an even tone.

Inside the enormous Altairian mothership heading the throng of the empire's warships, Xantis At Rae stared down towards Earth. "My Altairian, look upon your ancestral home, perhaps for the very last time. Now we must do what is required of us to ensure the survival of the Altairian civilisation and take care of these humans."

Michael monitored the display confused as to why some of the sensor spots had multiplied into a plenitude of additional blinking red lights.

"Krill, several of the larger vessels have released further batches of warships. They are moving towards Earth!" she glanced Varantis another look of mistrust.

"Egregor we must alert the alliance fleet right away!" Biriqzz made sure her opinion was heard.

"What are you suggesting rodent!" growled Varantis looking as if he was ready to unleash himself on everyone.

Emile's voice broke the alien stare down, "I have lost all communication to the alliance fleet, getting a massive surge of interference."

In the melee of confusion, no one noticed the giant Hyekera automaton mysteriously leave the command deck.

"Also detecting energy spikes from the Altairian warships! Do I turn around the Luna defence launchers?"

There was no answer, Emile shouted, "Egregor Krill, what do we do?"

46 - Doomsday Button

The defence secretary looked once more at the ticking clock on the wall of the newly relocated command centre. "Thirty-seven minutes to deadline Mr. President."

"Thank you Jim, but I don't need a countdown. If I want to see how close I am to the point where I might have to press this button and kill millions of people, then I will just look at the bloody thing myself." The president loosened his tie again and undid another shirt button trying to relieve some of the pressure pumping through his jugular.

"Yes Mr. President." The secretary replied also feeling the anxiety of the situation. He needed to keep himself occupied even if it was acting as a talking clock to the president. "Ok people do we have any updates? Radiation signatures! Suspicious civilian movement, unauthorised vessels, news from the other nations?" There was silence, just faces turning to their colleagues hopingly and shaking their heads in disappointed responses. "Do we not have anything at all?!"

"Nothing showing up on ours or anyone else's satellite imagery sir. Also no leads from our operatives in the field, and no breakthroughs reported by the UN." Finally spoke the command centre coordinator running his hand back and forth through his hair.

"Well, I for one don't believe those bastards will go through with it. We'd blow them all back to the stone age. I say it's a bluff!" spoke up a gruff voice.

"I hope to god your right General Milton, but you know how little life can mean to these terrorists." answered the president in detest.

"Perhaps they think we won't go through with it." commented a rotund man, the president's secretary of state.

"Then they would be terribly mistaken Mike. We as a nation can only deliver one response to a second nuclear strike against us. I'm sure as hell not going to give them a chance of a third. Jim, you have your authenticator."

The defence secretary took a deep breath, opened the metallic suitcase and removed the red package that had been delivered to the base each week since its relocation. "Yes sir." He ripped off the tamper proof plastic seals of the package and pulled out a glass key ring. "Here goes.", the secretary cracked open the single piece casing and slipped out the authenticator. "General Milton, CC coordinator Draper. You will need to witness this." The defence secretary adjusted his glasses and read what was printed in bold letters upon the thin film. "Authentication code Xray-Lima-Zero-Seven-Zero-Eight-Mike-One-Juliet-Two-Hotel-Papa-Seven-Nine-Lima-Lima-Zulu, codename Icarus." The witnesses confirmed and looked to the president. He had mimicked the process with his own authenticator that he wore around his neck. His witnesses, the secretary of state and another NORAD commanding general verified that the authentication code and the codename matched the president's own codes.

"Ok, Jim your key." asked the president as he took a second chain from around his neck, this one holding a large complex looking tubular key.

The defence secretary took his duplicate key from the sealed red package and joined the President of the USA at the metal suitcase. Inside the armoured container was housed a compacted electronic device consisting of a small display screen, two circular holes and a strip of inset red glass covering something. All eyes in the command centre fluttered between the two men and the clock. The seconds seemed to fall away too quickly, only insignificant minutes remained before the deadline.

47 – Stand Off

The flock of warships had surprised the alliance with their last-minute emergence into weapons range of Earth. Seber had lost contact with the alliance fleet and tensions were building as distrust filled the air. Now the Altairian were accelerating towards the planet with energy levels building up in the organic organs of their warships.

Emile initiated remote fire control of the Luna defence systems waiting for the command from Egregor Krill.

"Dr. Tesla….." began Krill.

"Wait! More ship signatures and a lot of them!" interrupted Emile.

Enormous twists in the fabric of space opened up above Earth. The luminescent swirls of light were blocked out as, one after the other, hulking Hyekera dreadnoughts crawled out into the void between Earth and the oncoming Altairian Warships.

"What are you up to machine!" barked Varantis, swinging around just as the solid frame of Phalacreus ascended from the lower deck behind the Raqzzon scientists.

Baraqz quickly sidestepped from between the Prime Ethereal and the fighting automaton. And not a second too soon as the uneasy truce faltered and both motioned for each other with threatening intent.

"Do not dare put my daughter's life in jeopardy!!" shouted

Michael jumping between them arms outstretched. The two adversaries were forcibly knocked back in a mysterious blow. An invisible shield seemed to halt them in their tracks as if they were attempting to walk head first into hurricane winds.

"The Hyekera knew the Altairian could not be trusted."

"You deceitful viruses, first you turn on your creators, now you turn on the alliance!"

"Enough." Krill finally spoke, with extraordinary calm considering the situation.

"Dr. Tesla. Please release targeting controls back to the Luna automated systems. Then force a communication channel into each one of those Altairian and Hyekera warships."

"Erhhm. Done." Emile seemed relieved the Egregor was taking command again.

"This is Egregor Krill. These coordinates are not the scheduled rendezvous point. Please explain yourselves, the Sin shall be upon us soon enough."

The two enemies had slowed to their relative attack postures waiting for the other to make a move. Each warship targeting another ready to fire upon the command. This was a standoff that could easily end in disaster. One wrong move and every piece of the delicate jigsaw would unravel. They would do the Sin's job for them, if that was not what they were here to do in the first place. A holographic image was projected within Seber. It was slightly degraded by the surge in interference, but they could all see it was the Emperor, Xantis At Rae. With the appearance of his father, Varantis stopped fighting the ghostly field preventing him from testing diamond against Hyekera metal.

"Egregor Krill. The Altairian Empire does not need to explain its actions. I warned you about these machines. As emperor I lead these warships in our promise to fight within a new alliance and defend the human race. Earth is our ancestral home, it is likely us, and it will not exist past this day. So, we pay homage to the symbol of our beginning as we pass over it in battle formation. As soon as those things power down their weapons, the Altairian Empire will take their place at the rendezvous coordinates."

A buzzing emanated from the audio system in response. Phalacreus switched his attention from Varantis to the others.

Michael let out a groan of exhaustion and went and took a seat, grabbing his head in pain. His eyes were bloodshot from numerous ruptured capillaries and the warm red fluid he had become accustomed to, dripped from his nose into his palms. The effort in keeping the two foes apart had taken a debilitating toll on his body. He tried to conceal his pain to avoid the deflection of focus from the matter at hand.

"The main bulk of Hyekera forces have been tracking the movements of the Altairian warships. The Hyekera could not commit fully with a remaining probability of the Altairian launching assaults upon Hyekera systems while our defences are significantly weakened."

Further bursts of buzzing echoed around Seber, and Phalacreus listened, waiting to relay the translation. Be it words or actions.

"The Altairian did not show at the chosen coordinates and contact was lost with the other Hyekera dreadnoughts. I alerted the reserve Hyekera to their sudden emergence above Earth. The Hyekera suspected the Altairian would not hold to their agreement, the Hyekera are here to destroy them for their treachery."

"Dr. Tesla, jump Seber between them."

Seber materialised in the middle of the face-off, to fire now would be an act of violence against not only each other but the Ashtar Co-operative as well.

"This distrust must stop here now. An unexpected surge in the solar flare's energy has momentarily extended the range of the communication and sensor blackout. But electromagnetic interference cannot disrupt the Co-operative link. The alliance fleet remains in its entirety and await your combined forces to join them. If you do not comply immediately then your death will be swift at the hands of the Sin." As Egregor Krill transmitted the stark warning, static crackled across the living skins of the Altairian warships. In an instant the entire Altairian fleet followed the emperor's Mothership through their own quantum tunnels towards the far side of the Sun.

Aboard Seber they watched as the Hyekera followed suit, the machines hulking destroyers disappearing in a swirl of colours.

"Well another crisis averted, but how long until the next one." commented Baraqz with a toothy smile in an attempt to lighten the hostile mood.

"Dr. Tesla, jump us to the rendezvous point"

"No.... It's too late!" muttered Michael.

"What?....." The consoles flashed and auditory alarms sounded. "Krill. They are here!" the fear in Emile's voice was all too evident.

"Baraqz you old fool, I wish you would learn to keep that cursed mouth of yours shut for once!" chided his life partner Biriqzz.

"Dr. Tesla shut down all systems, initiate your camouflage programme." ordered the Egregor.

The viscous fluid of nanobots comprising Seber's hull began to colour shift and darken. Small ripples and sharp protrusions distorted the surface and solidified across the once amber shell. A minute burst of gravitational repulsion from the sub-light engine sent the ancient ship into a pedestrian spin. To any observer, unless they were specifically searching for the Elohim vessel, Seber was undistinguishable from any randomly orbiting space rock.

"Krill, asteroid cloak engaged. All non-essential systems on standby, critical operations running at minimal capacity." reported Emile. "Here they come..."

48 – Time Sensitive

Phillip Al Zwarhi laid motionless eyes wide open, but to him it felt like he was still in a dream. The clock beside his bed said 4:20am and it was still pitch-black outside. Although his mind seemed detached from his body, it lifted itself out of bed and towards the draw of work clothes. Concentrating with all his being he tried to force his consciousness out of the realm between dream state and wake, but some invisible obstacle pushed his consciousness back, confining his soul to be a back-seat passenger in his own body. After picking out the clothes, his head turned towards the bed, through the blurry tunnel vision he could see his wife still asleep unaware of her husband's sleep walking. Phillip tried to shout, make a noise or movement to wake her. Nothing responded to his commands and all he could manage was a rapid sequence of blinks. Phillip watched as he walked away clutching his trousers and shirt, passed both his children's bedrooms without hesitation, and made his way down the landing stairs. Once in his living room he began to change into his work attire while screaming out with his mind. *What am I doing, I'm supposed to have the day off to be with my family*. His head was a chaos of confusion; he could see and feel himself doing these things even though it was not his intention. Why was he compelled to go to work. There would only be a skeleton crew keeping things ticking over. Most people had decided to stay at home with their families and loved ones. Today was March 11th, deadline day, at 2pm GMT he was supposed to be with his wife and daughters, providing each other comfort in what might be a dangerous period for the world. The terrorists had threatened to explode a nuclear device somewhere in the US, possibly here, but still the irresistible compulsion drove him to his garage, to his car. He started the car, opened the garage door and flicked on the headlights. His family station wagon sped along the eerily empty roads into the Arizona desert and away from his Phoenix home. Phillip's mind and body were in autopilot, following actions and motivations he could not comprehend. Speeding along the empty West Salome highway he pressed down harder on the accelerator as if some biological countdown was determining his bodily reactions.

In the distance, huge columns of steam rose into the cold desert air, dispersing as the heated water was cooled and blown away on the easterly winds. The six huge cooling towers standing in the middle of nowhere told Phillip he was approaching the gates of his work place. Palo Verde nuclear power plant lay 45 miles west of central Phoenix, within Arizona state, and was currently the largest nuclear generation facility in the United States of America, providing power to around four million people each year. He pulled up at the security checkpoint and watched on as he lifted up his identification pass to the automatic weapon holding security guard. Phillip sat there silent as the armed personnel thoroughly searched his vehicle. As they rummaged through the space wagons boot, one of the guards from the checkpoint walked towards him with a clip board. Again, Phillip shouted out with his mind's eye, echoing around his consciousness without a sound.

"Mr. Al Zwarhi, I don't have you on the work rota today." informed the clip board holding security guard.

There was a moment of silence, a glimmer of hope for Phillip. Maybe the guard would notice something was wrong, would see the real Phillip behind his eyes, banging his fists on the pupils like a man trapped behind a glass window. From there, take him to a hospital to be checked. He wondered if he had accidentally banged his head or had some type of brain disease or worse a tumour. Then he heard his voice vibrate, a pressure wave pushing him back into the darkness.

"I was supposed to have the day off, but you know with everything that is going on this morning, they needed to make sure my generator is running smoothly. I should be at home with my family, but we all have to make sacrifices at a time like this, which as you're standing here, I'm sure you understand. Anyway, they decided to offer me triple time to come in, which goes someway to make me feel a little better."

"Well Sir, let's hope today passes without incident. I will just go shoot myself for not asking for triple time!"

Phillip let out a loud chuckle and moved his car through the opening barrier towards the staff parking area. Once his car was parked, he began walking towards the domed structure housing the generator he provided maintenance for. Using his ID card to gain access through the heavy turnstiles, he walked into the main collection of buildings. After changing into his work overalls and sticking on his bright helmet and protective goggles, he proceeded silently towards the main turbine. No one stopped Phillip or spoke, they were too busy carrying out the multitude of morning checks, today doubly time consuming considering the shortage of staff. His sleep walking body momentarily stopped at the turbine work station. It glimpsed at the gauges that usually he would scrupulously monitor, and fixed his eyes upon the terminal clock. On the fuzzy peripheral vision Phillip could see everything appeared to be working within normal parameters, but the attention of his trapped sub-consciousness also drifted towards the time, 7.25am on the Mountain Standard Time display. The 2pm GMT deadline translated as 7am here. The deadline had passed and no warning alarm had sounded. His body seemed to react with a renewed speed but Phillip's thoughts went back to his family with a slight relief, maybe somehow the governments had resolved the crisis, or at least Phoenix was safely away from any nuclear attack. As he marched onwards from the monitoring station, Phillip realised that this couldn't be right, today he got to work extra quick. The clock was saying he had taken a full hour longer.

If two weeks ago Phillip hadn't been sent on an unexpected work excursion to New Mexico, then he would have been aware of the reason for the strange discrepancy in time. He was persuaded to attend a meeting to discuss the reliability of the General Electric turbine generators, with which he worked, to a consortium representing the proposed construction of Desert Rock energy facility in the four corners area of New Mexico. Completely unsure as to why he had been selected, he went reluctantly. However, he must have enjoyed it immensely as his memories of the trip were pretty hazy. Probably the effects of over doing a rare moment of freedom with a few too many beers. While away there was a slight panic as the computer programmers and engineers realised their systems were susceptible to failure due to a new US energy initiative. A new law passed by the American president that brought forward Daylight-Saving Time from the first Sunday in April to March the 11th, today. After much tinkering and annoyance, the systems were adjusted so that the facility computers would automatically adjust to compensate for the earlier scheduled DST, and move the MST one hour forward like all the clocks in America. While at work, this change was significant due to the requirement to synchronise with other facilities and states, but in his Arizona home it would have mattered little. Phillip had remained blissfully unaware of the modification to daylight saving time as Phoenix and the whole of the Arizona state did not adopt DST even though it was part of the MST time zone. Only one of two places within the North American continent that didn't observe it.

With urgency his unresponsive body headed straight for the turbine room, which turned the giant generator 2 that he had worked on for the last two years. Moving between the pipes of super-heated steam in the humming ten storey building, he made his way to a large lockup that stored the newly reconditioned and installed diesel backup generator. Once inside he wrenched open the back compartment with the crow bar from his tool belt. Shrewdly hidden behind a grease covered panel were the glint of machined metal and a plastic protected number pad clinging to its surface. A wave of fear and comprehension passed through Phillips consciousness. His mind reeled in its prison, *it cannot be, my wife, my children! They would be up now wondering where he had disappeared too. I must do something!* With all the mental effort he could muster, he reached out his consciousness from the dark recess that dragged back the threads of his soul. The tears of desperate fear filled

Phillip Al-Zwarhi's eyes. His hand extended out in front of him and pressed 4-3-6...3...............1; then there was a bright light.

49 - Evil Tests the Water

Ship upon ship poured from the hope draining exotic punctures in sub-space. The sky was blocked out as if an angry swarm of space bees were descending upon an intruder, ready to strike and strike again until the target was no more. The last warships of the Sin Supremacy scout armada emerged from their worm holes of swirling night, at least a thousand vessels of destruction from their countless slave civilisations, many of them unknown even to the oldest of the alliance. The lunar defence systems immediately launched a salvo of rapid ballistic missiles at the oncoming fleet, managing to take out a few of the weaker armoured warships, but inflicting insignificant damage on most. The front wave of warships unleashed their weapons against the moon installations; relativistic projectiles, plasma pulses and lasers ripped apart rows of ground based defence silos. Plumes of lunar dust surged into the thin air, swelling and growing unhindered by the weak gravity. Out of the blurry grey smokescreen the sliver heads of secondary interceptor drones thundered towards the enemy throng. Most of the long-range launchers were well protected in underground bunkers and had a stockpile of about two drones per enemy ship. A few more enemy warships succumbed to the barrier of interceptor munitions, either destroyed or disabled. The launching tubes automatically reloaded for the next barrage, firing a small hail storm of drones and missiles at the wave of doom, dispatching more of their assailants in a cloud of explosions. Then from the droves of oncoming ships a solitary vessel accelerated to the front. It was a small craft, resembling a polished onyx pearl and completely unique among the enemy plethora.

Inside Rahab cursed, "Time to put a stop to this annoyance, and show them the real power of the Sin Supremacy!"

Dark hazy ripples fizzed across the vessels black surface, coalescing into a single point that undulated in upon itself as it quickly grew in magnitude. An amplifying hum filled the surrounding area even though sound could not permeate the vacuum of space. All the slithering strings of gloom terminated at the undulating disturbance as the alien warship let out a bone chilling scream more disturbing than anything in nature could produce, and unleashed a focused beam of pure shadow at Earth's orbiting companion. The shadow ray hammered into the Moon, its surface erupted upon impact, blowing chunks of metal and rock high into the air as the beam scathed the lunar ground. No more retaliatory launches came from the defence silos. All that was left of them and the landscape in the vicinity, were piles of smouldering rubble and a deep wound scorched into the crust. Miles long, it would never heal, a permanent scar, a reminder of the awesome power of the Sin.

"What the hell is that?" Michael said agape by the destruction it wreaked. He took another gulp of the Mayan alcohol to try and numb his banging head.

"It is a Sin hunter ship." answered Krill.

"Only one Sin vessel, this is very good news!" commented Baraqz.

"On the contrary, it means this armada did not destroy the Pleiadians. There is another significantly greater mass of Sin Supremacy forces out there." replied Krill before reaching out with his mind. Voices grew louder and louder as his thoughts traversed the subspace through the interfering coronal ejections and into the web of the local Co-operative link. "The alliance fleet is ready to launch our assault." notified the Egregor.

"Krill!" breathed Michael with a sick feeling running through his body.

"I know. The Ashtar in Alpha have updated me from the far side of Earth. There is nothing we can do."

Michael turned his back on the approaching doomsday armada and gazed down at his home shrouded in darkness. On the far side of the world beyond his help, he feared for his daughter.

50 - First Strike

It was 6:36am Arizona MST time and 24 minutes until the official deadline. After a quick search of the house, Mrs. Al-Zwarhi had noticed her husband's work clothes and car were missing. She had tried numerous times to contact him but his mobile lay strangely forgotten on the kitchen top, and there had been no response to her message at the power plant. She sat with her two children on the sofa listening to the minute-by-minute updates on the news, still both furious and worried about her husbands out of character departure. As they watched the journalist's reports from the efforts abroad, the room was drowned in silence as the TV flicked off. Mrs. Al-Zwarhi attempted to switch the box back on but it was completely dead. Next she turned on the radio but again received no response, not even static; in fact no electrical appliance was working in the house. *Typical* she thought, *just when her electrical engineer husband had disappeared there is a power failure in the house.* This just made her even angrier with him, but then the ground began to shake. The children rushed to the window that looked out to the west. She pulled the curtains apart and joined them staring out over the skyline of the city outskirts towards the cactus filled desert. A huge mushroom cloud rolled upwards blocking out the low rising Sun. The ground shook more violently, the deafening roar of the wind filled their ears, they instantly knew what was coming. A tsunami of fire blew apart buildings closest to the nuclear power plant, concrete smashed and steel twisted under the intense blast wave as it headed towards central Phoenix almost unhindered by the flat farmland landscape. Those at a far enough distance not to be blown apart suffered various degrees of burns from the release of thermal radiation, and those unlucky enough to be facing the explosion were victim to flash blindness.

In the home of Al-Zarwhi in the closest town of Buckeye twenty miles from ground zero, Phillip's family hid behind their sofa gripping each other in fear. A searing wind battered the outlying Phoenix buildings with enough force to blow in windows and cause numerous injuries from flying debris to those who were not adequately protected. But fortunately for them, they were a sufficient distance from the blast area not to experience the full might of the atomic discharge of energy. However the real danger was yet to come, the radioactive fallout. The winds blew easterly over the city, no matter what type of nuclear device had been used, be it atomic fission or the thermo nuclear fusion bomb, the detonation came from the Palo Verde area and that had an abundance of radioactive material to throw into the air.

In the next town of Avondale lying 30 miles from the detonation origin just on the outskirts of central Phoenix. The nuclear accident warning alarms wailed around the city. Within minutes of the nuclear explosion, even as the mushroom cloud continued to rise, the sirens of emergency services began to echo in the background. Having Palo Verde nuclear power plant located so close and accustomed to the danger presented by the easterly winds, the Arizona state emergency operations centre had a detailed contingency plan for this type of situation. Radiation suited response teams rolled into the streets in convoys of military carriers and fire trucks. Loud speaker announcements bellowed out in the streets, 'We have confirmation of an explosion at the Palo Verde power plant. There is a strong possibility of radioactive contamination within this area. Therefore, we ask you to gather only what you can easily carry, a change of clothes, identification and water. Once you are ready, please make your way calmly to your congregation point. This will be the parking area of Goodyear Municipal airport. From there you will be transported to a safe area.'

Elsewhere across the city similar scenes were beginning to be re-enacted as a strip about 20 miles in diameter straight across central Phoenix was in the progress of being evacuated from the inevitable radioactive cloud that would eventually sweep across the region. Anything directly east of ground zero, even up to 90 miles away would receive a lethal dose of radiation. Luckily the closest city easterly, New Mexico, was more than the predicted 250 mile distance where the radioactivity would reach levels considered safe.

Phillip's wife brushed the dust off her two children as instructions relayed by megaphones vibrated through the strained walls. Scrambling to her feet, she grabbed essential supplies and ushered her son and daughter into the once quiet suburb. Thoughts of her husband brought pain to her heart, but she dared not grieve now, it was up too her to get their children to safety. The streets were chaos, shell shocked people stepped from their houses carrying their possessions. Debris lay everywhere as if a tornado had just swept through their sleepy neighbourhood. But this was no natural disaster. Even at their extreme distance they could all see the awesome power of the atom.

51 – Decision Point

A red warning light flashed on the geographical display. "Sir, Mr. President!" shouted a nervous operator. "We are detecting a nuclear explosion!"

The president flicked a glimpse towards the huge digital clock then to the graphical computer display of the United States. "What the hell! There is still over twenty minutes to the deadline. Where is it?"

"Ehh, our data says it is localised to the Palo Verde nuclear power plant, Arizona."

"Can we confirm it was a nuclear device and not an accident at the facility?"

"Yes sir!" notified another head-phoned member of the operations team. A communication officer. "Receiving alerts and updates from Phoenix. Definitely a nuclear device. They are beginning emergency evacuation procedures and requesting additional aid."

"That's why we had so much trouble locating that bloody bomb, what better place to hide a nuclear device than a nuclear facility." commented General Milton.

"Notify everyone that their nuclear facilities could be targeted. Get Phoenix whatever resources they need people." ordered the president.

One of the multiple displays switched to a live image that

flickered every few seconds as it updated. "Mr. President we have imagery of the attack site from one of our satellites." instructed the command centre coordinator as the image zoomed into the southern American state.

The president stared in anger and disbelief at the images he was receiving from high above the Palo Verde area. The whole area was a scorched wasteland, and where the power plant once stood was now replaced with a deep crater over a hundred metres in diameter. "Damn those bastards. Confirm our pre-determined targets."

"Sir, all IBM launchers wait on your command authorisation."

"Roy, insert your key!"

The defence secretary placed his tubular key into the right-hand hole while the president done the same in the left-hand side of the apparatus seated in the metallic suitcase. Simultaneously they twisted their keys clockwise in the locks. Another long code appeared on the small red inset display and the plastic covering flipped back to reveal a single red button.

"Sir, I hate to say it but the death toll is …. Well we got off very lightly with its location. Shouldn't we wait until the deadline before we retaliate with our nuclear arsenal?"

"Sharon, you tell that to the tens of thousands of our people downwind from that attack. The majority of Phoenix will be uninhabitable for years to come! And I'm as sure as hell not going to wait for those terrorist murderers to strike a better target!" retorted the president with a harsh unsympathetic tone.

"Then why don't we launch a like for like solitary retaliation before we kill millions of people?" implored the secretary of state.

"No! They all had their chance. Authorise the B-2 bombers to proceed to targets and the submarines to prep for launch. All forces to wait on my signal."

"Sir, all forces standing by. Waiting upon your launch code."

With a grim expression, the president twisted the button that had been revealed behind the plastic cover. The button unlocked, springing upwards and the launch code on the devices backlit display turned green. He placed his hand over the button and whispered to himself, "For America."

But no one heard his words over the commotion coming from outside the command centre.

52 - The Disturbing Depths

Screaming and moaning rattled around UMBRA security level 5. Known as the 'the zoo' it was a place of rumour and mystery within the gloomy depths of the top-secret Dulce facility. The level was a maze of undulating tunnels dug straight out of the rock, devoid of any human necessity for the aesthetics of unnatural construction. Along the arched ceilings ran filthy cables bringing electricity to the chilling corridors and dimly illuminating the bloody handprints and stains across the walls and floors.

Lab assistants dragged the newest experiment to its cage. In haste to leave their disturbing surroundings they dumped the unconscious test result onto the cold, dank metal floor and locked it in like a filthy stray animal. One of the lab workers gave a quick shine of her flashlight around this particular room.

"I don't know what they hope to achieve from this but it's not right." said the scientist with a look of revulsion at the unnatural sights under the torch light.

"What, you don't believe this is a necessity to create cures to the world's biggest killing diseases as they keep reminding us." replied the other without any conviction what so ever.

"All I see us trying to do, is play god, I mean look at this mess, what are we really doing down here. I mean what good can come from these things?" As she turned her torch back to the door she reeled in fright as the rays of light reflected off four snake-like eyes in the dark.

A harsh hiss came from a tall jade masked figure in the exit, "Your work here is more important than you could possibly comprehend. Let me make a suggestion, that you concentrate on the tasks provided to you or face the consequences. It is not wise to question our methods or motives."

"Yes of course!" stuttered the male lab technician almost unable to speak with nerves. "We were just going back to work."

The two sinister Masters stepped aside to allow the panicking scientists to scurry past them. After the scientists had disappeared into the murky corridors to continue their enigmatic work, a labour so vital to the Masters that they have pursued it for almost as long as they had been on Earth.

"Kukulcan, it is time for that female to disappear. She smells fertile, a perfect test subject for the Meridian phase, do you not think?" spoke the humanoid serpent in a harsh tone.

Wearing a mask of polished wood carved with a strong square jaw, fangs and sunflower type frills. Kukulcan looked like he had a head of a wooden lion. In an equally menacing tone, he tasted the air with a flicker of his serpent tongue and nodded in agreement. "She will find herself in one of these cages soon enough; and I will see to it that the human male is also transferred to the Meridian phase, and is the one performing the experimentation upon her!"

"A fitting touch."

"Tezcatlipoca, although these filthy humans breed like vermin, progress is exceedingly slow, our real goals are two-fold but if we hope to succeed in either then we need more subjects than we can acquire with our current methods."

"I received an update from Quetzalcoatl an hour ago; the Overlords believe that our plans upon the surface are moving at the desired pace. As they begin killing each other with their most powerful weapons, our grip grows stronger. Everything is in place; we have weaved our intricate threads of control throughout the human population. After today, what we have achieved in the last thousand years shall be duplicated in a few. Once the Cult complete their New World Order, our grip will be absolute, our own work can go at the pace we desire, and it will be too late for the humans to mount any resistance as they did long ago. Our patience will bring its rewards."

The Master's long clawed hand closed the sound proofed metal doors on room 151, one of hundreds of similarly disturbing chambers. As the doors screeched shut, they shrouded the cages in darkness and muffled the screams and groans that echoed out along the foul-smelling corridors of the mysterious level.

53 - Choices

The Sin Supremacy horde swarmed past the wounded moon on course towards what appeared to be a defenceless world. Home of the Raziel, the race of the prophecy. The advanced scout armada was sent ahead because of lessons long ago learned; the Sin remembered the futile efforts of the unconquered civilisations. They had dealt them a crippling blow back then, the Pleiadians had recovered but revenge had been executed upon them, and the Ashtar were next. None of them possessed the unimaginable resources of the Sin; no one could ever mount such a defence against them again. The mission of the scout armada was simple; while the Pleiadians and Ashtar are punished for their ancient acts of resistance, travel to Earth, destroying all in their path and begin the destruction of the human race. Prevent anything from escaping until further forces arrive and land their extermination squads. The armies of the Sin will then eradicate every last human on the planet before the infinity weapon makes sure that every trace of the Raziel is wiped out of existence. No seed of the prophecy will be allowed to be born again from this world.

"I am detecting an extremely low powered transmission emanating from the lead Sin ship. It is organic in nature." informed Phalacreus. "Amplifying and projecting audible spectrum." A high-pitched repeating wail resonated from the automaton.

"Weird, what is that." commented Emile

"Subtle but it awakens a familiar memory. That is a message of herald, or one meant for hidden ears." confirmed Krill. "To whom or where, I expect is a question that will be answered in short order."

"The attack will be signaled as soon as they pass us by." notified Krill as one by one various configurations of enemy warships thundered past them unaware that the nearby rock was in fact the most powerful ship in the alliance fleet.

Short range laser beams and projectiles vaporised any of the geo-synchronous orbiting satellites that stood in the way of the swarms of vessels. Among the clusters of high Earth orbit machinery, Seber luckily escaped any pot shots or collisions from the surrounding armada. It was nothing more than a rock in the way of a stampeding herd of wilder beast. As the rusting hull of some type of heavy weapons juggernaut floated within touching distance of the camouflaged Seber, Egregor Krill closed his oversized almond eyes and let his consciousness float away from its physical bonds. Almost instantly his mind met others conversing in the higher dimensional plane. Each Ashtar connected felt Egregor Krill's presence as it joined the local Co-operative link. All minds focused, the background noise of a hundred psyches, a thousand thoughts, all went silent, clear for the Egregor to project the attack command. The mental transmission rippled across the web of Ashtar minds. "Give the message to the fleet, jump to these coordinates…. Wait…"

"No! Keep them hidden. Let the Sin ships get closer." Michael suddenly blurted out.

"But they are almost within strike range of Earth!" said Emile puzzled as she continued to monitor the movements of the Sin Supremacy forces.

Varantis roared his disproval to Egregor Krill, "What are you waiting for!!! Don't be a fool. The Sin Supremacy fleet contains a single Sin ship, a scouting hunter vessel. Our new alliance can match the rest in combat. We must attack now!"

"I can do little to help you, but Elyon told me to follow my intuition. Everything in my being tells me this!", Michael spoke in a softness that was out of place coming from him.

"I calculate no scenario of advantage with this course of action." added Phalacreus.

"Agreed." Krill's deep black eyes stared at Michael expressionless like he was trying to penetrate his thoughts. "Yet, we will allow them to approach. But as soon as they reach weapons range, I am ordering the alliance fleet in."

Emile's fingers raced over her holographic console screen, "Cannot determine weapons range of the armada, too many different designs of ships and weapons of just those we can scan. Increasing the power of the scanners might help but it will give away our location. For all we know they could be in weapons range already."

"No, the Sin Supremacy would have opened fire at their first opportunity." said Krill.

"Then can I suggest sweetie we use the distance they first fired upon your moon installations as our baseline."

"Good idea Biriqzz." thanked Emile while Biriqzz's life partner gave her a nudge and a wink. "Baseline inputted. Egregor we don't have long."

Varantis growled, "You are risking all the work and sacrifices we have made. You talk of the importance of the Raziel yet you would allow so many to be slaughtered on the word of this human aberration!"

"You must have faith in him as Elyon and I do." answered Krill simply as the leading wave of warships began to power up their assortment of weapon arrays.

54 - The Enemy of my Enemy

General Allen accompanied by Commodore Gaughan moved determinedly passed the two young soldiers guarding the entrance to the command centre. Receiving word from COM-12 headquarters of the nuclear detonation in Arizona, he decided that this was no time for diplomacy and the chain of command.

From outside the door to the heart of the Cheyenne Mountain Complex there was echoes of nervous shouts, "You can't go in there!" and "Sir I have orders that the president must not be disturbed!" followed by some hardboiled responses, "Son, I am a three star general. I'll have you both demoted so fast you'll get the bends. How do you like cleaning toilets?" and "I don't take orders from very many people and you are not one of them!"

"No, but I am!" shouted the president as the two military men entered the command centre, his finger hovering millimetres over the launch control button. "What the hell are you both doing here? The United States of America has just been attacked once more with nuclear weapons!"

The general just gave his commander and chief a dismissive look, "Do not send the launch authorisation!"

"We are at war general if you haven't noticed. We cannot ignore this attack on our own soil. The people of the United States are relying on me to protect them. Why would I listen to you!" Everyone's eyes were peeled on the two men, only breaking their stare to catch a glimpse of the clock.

"Because I am privy to information you are not! The bigger picture."

"A bigger picture! Americans are dying as we speak; the terrorist nations ignore our warnings. Even sending forces into their countries acts as no deterrent. We have no choice but to retaliate with massive force. Am I painting a big enough picture for you!"

"There is another choice; and that's to listen to me."

"And why should we trust you General Allen? We know you were opposed to the presidents election, not to mention that you have just flown into a restricted facility inside a black project spy plane. Its development was super top secret. Can you tell me what you are doing with an SR-ninety-one? Mmhh!" the secretary commented with a condescending tone.

Commodore Gaughan gestured to the general that he would deal with the secretary, "That Mr. Secretary is an Aurora. Now is not the ideal time to discuss this matter but we are part of, for the moment we will say a non-governmental agency that had a hand in constructing the SR-ninety-one. This should demonstrate to you that we have knowledge and influence that you do not have."

The president gave the general a hard stare, trying to weigh up every aspect, his stance, facial expression, attempting to extract any hint of deception. General Allen maintained his upright posture and stoic look. "Right General you have two minutes to explain yourself."

"Mr. President!" interrupted the CC coordinator, "We have lost communications with a number of our satellites. It's like they just disappeared!"

"Make that one minute."

Meanwhile somewhere inside western Iran, Dr. Kuzminski entered a narrow desert valley escorted by men in off white wrapping garments as his Aurora aircraft was camouflaged beneath a sand covered tarpaulin. The member of COM-12 walked deeper into the valley, its walls getting increasingly slanted so that eventually above him, the overhanging walls almost touched.

Unless you knew exactly where to look, this place would be perfectly hidden both from the air and ground. Here in the wilderness no sound could be heard of the explosions and gun fire from the UN invasion. Only the echoing noise of a sandstorm picking up strength as its winds threw sand into the hot air. Dr. Kuzminski now stood before a relic of ancient Mesopotamia, a magnificent part of Iranian history rarely seen by the western world. Carved straight into the sandstone cliff face were two towering statues of human-headed winged bulls situated either side of elaborately gilded wooden doors. The figures bearing the head of a bearded man stood either side of the archway, the gates guardian genies called Shedu and Lamassu serving as protection against enemies. The heavy-set doors were opened and Dr. Kuzminski was ushered into the torch lit doorway. The entrance hall was decorated with the carved body of the winged bull and immediately behind them, opposing reliefs of a monumental winged genius, placed to also protect and bless those that passed by them. Being a member of COM-12 brought him many privileges and the opportunity to see many wonders but what opened up before him took his breath away. He stood inside the audience hall of a palace dwelling painstakingly fashioned from the surrounding sandstone. The floor consisted of turquoise ceramic tiles embellished with scenes of Mesopotamian life, such as harp playing women, animals and the faces of scholars. Strewn everywhere were artifacts any museum would be proud to display, busts of past rulers, aged paintings of distant lands, pottery and armour, but one seemed to stand out amidst them. A black obelisk standing tall upon a spacious octagonal carpet. The basalt stele was etched almost base to tip with minute ancient cuneiform text that Dr. Kuzminski guessed would provide an amazing insight into the golden age of this region of the world. Atop this emblem of Mesopotamian civilisation was engraved a scene, a man receiving a scroll from a large masked figure upon a throne. Perhaps even portraying the handover of the very information that adorned the impressive stele. Dr. Kuzminski turned his interest to the rest of the torch lit hall. The high walls were adorned with immense friezes of polychrome glazed brick. The decorative blues and greens depicted warriors, archers and winged lions marching towards an unknown long-ago battle. All around him thirty-six colossal columns soared up towards the arching ceiling, their capitals carved with an arrangement of double volutes with rosettes topped by two kneeling bulls back to back. Giant wooden beams rested in the gap between the necks of the animals strutting between the imposing columns, helping to support the immense wait of the yellow rock above.

"So you appreciate what we fight for!" said a mystery voice in a strong middle eastern accent."

Dr. Kuzminski looked around the grand hall to see a man come into the fire light wearing a simple brown suit and tie less pink shirt.

"What do you mean?" answered the COM-12 representative brushing the sand from his own suit.

"Iran is a country full of wondrous treasures from back in time to Mesopotamia and Babylonia, great civilisations of Parthia and Persians. The list goes on and on. We have a vast and proud history, one where we have always fought for what we believed in, even against overwhelming odds. Take the frieze covered walls for example. It is said by our scholars to depict a time very long ago when our freedom was once again threatened by an evil who planned to control and enslave us. Do you wish to know what happened Doctor?"

"Please tell me."

"A fantastic army rose up against this evil and through rivers of blood, drove them back down to hell!"

"Most fascinating, however, shall I cut to the chase?" suggested Dr. Kuzminski checking his watch.

"Yes lets. You would be dead right now if some people I consider friends had not requested this audience for you. Still, even then I would have been wary of allowing you here if those same people had not warned me of a planned attack against my family. God willing, I headed their warning and removed them to a safer location before a western bomb devastated my home and half the town around it. Many innocent lives were lost that day, so explain to me why you are here while your governments destroy my nation."

"To tell you to call off your attacks!"

The Iranian man with a black trimmed beard, let out a fake laugh of amusement, "You mean give up our only advantage! While you flew over in your strange plane, did you not see the brave warriors falling at the hands of your weapons? An unjust attack over fabricated facts contrived because we do not bow to their rules like servants!"

"First of all, these armies do not fight for us. They invade your country because they, like the world and yourselves, have been tricked into a conflict by parties pulling the strings in the shadows, those that would benefit from such a war", Dr. Kuzminski paused as he moved closer to the leader, put his hand in his pocket and in a quieter tone asked, "I hear you say unjust, yet did you not strike first with nuclear weapons. An act of terrorism that could only bring about one response, a response that you see now!"

"It was the American lap dogs, the UN, who did this to themselves! They are the evil ones, slaughtering their own people so that they may do the same to ours!" he responded with anger across his face.

Seeing that COM-12's fears could well be true, Dr. Kuzminski pushed further. "So, you are saying that your so called axis of evil were not responsible for the initial attacks?"

"No! But we know we were being framed to justify these invasions to the world. Now we must do what is necessary to fight back. Our nations are like cornered animals with no choice left to us but to bite back with what we have. Our teeth are those nuclear devices and our martyrs!"

Mr. Pierron's Aurora lay half parked, half crashed in a cove of dense trees and foliage. They had just managed to escape the attention of the both the American and Chinese air forces sent to intercept them, but as a result had to land a bit faster than they had wanted on what was not much more than a dirt track in a jungle clearing. With the Aurora's superior acceleration and speed produced by its pulse detonation engines, it easily left the J10 Vigorous Dragons of the People's Liberation Army Air Force far behind and out of sensor range. However, the American Air Force's F-22 Raptor stealth fighters were a little harder to evade with their state of art detection systems. They still remained out of detection range of the Raptors but the persistent pilots had formed a net around the area he needed to be and were now performing sweeps at their ceiling height way below the Aurora. They weren't going to get to their location with any conventional flying. Luckily Mr. Pierron was far from a conventional man, innovation was one of his specialties, one of the reasons he had been drafted into COM-12 in the first place. He ordered the Aurora pilot to cut all power, literally drop like a stone through the net and hope that the COM-12 engineers that built the craft were as good as they were supposed to be. He looked out the cockpit towards the edge of space and took a deep breath. Then just as he thought he saw a distant flock of birds cross the full moon, the afterburners cut out and the Auroras black curves plunged into the night. The dropping aircraft quickly reached the altitude of the searching Raptors and into their radar net. As the feet rapidly ticked away on the display, the Aurora crashed through the floor of their sensor range still undetected. Immediately the pilot ignited both the afterburners and the pulse detonation engines and cranked them up to maximum. Even with both propulsion systems leveling the descent they plummeted too rapidly and at an angle that was going to test the stealth composite and framework to its breaking point. Coming in hot the Aurora smashed into the saturated soil, every piece of bolted and welding material creaked under the strain of the impact, yet the under carriage held. The aircrafts extreme momentum ploughed up the mud, aiding in their deceleration. But the makeshift runway disappeared too quickly and the black jet tore into the tangle of trees, its wheels screeching to a halt a hairs breath from a rocky outcrop. As soon as they popped the hatch, gun barrels and heads sprang from their underground hide holes shouting orders in Korean. Mr. Pierron stepped from the cockpit, adjusted his tie and responded in their own dialect. Suddenly the atmosphere changed to a more welcoming manner as if they knew him. Now he had been led down into an extensive underground network into the command hub, an old relic from the Korean War, where he was met by a short, bottle wielding man.

"Mr. Pierron, welcome back to paradise! A glass of Johnnie Walker eighteen oh-five, I was saving it for a special occasion yet...", he nodded up towards the surface, "that time is looking unlikely."

"I would be a fool to turn down such an offer." he responded in perfect North Korean Pyongan dialect, "Considering only two hundred of those bottles were ever made." There was a crackling static from his expensively tailored jacket. He reached into his inner pocket and pulled out an object.

The tubby man's eyes lit up with curiosity almost dropping the glass of brown liquor, that he had just poured, onto the floor. He slipped off his oversized spectacles, "Is that…."

"It is indeed Dear Leader." The COM-12 representative held a golden pendant depicting a figure wearing the mask of a ram with curved horns and a tall double coned crown. From an elegant throne the figure held a snake headed scepter upon the shoulders of an Egyptian pharaoh, a female.

"The oracle of Amun! The Egyptian god is wearing the ram guise of fertility. I would say it would have been worn by Hatshepsut, Egypt's first female pharaoh. But she disappeared from history after twenty years of rule. Her remains were never found; how did you come across such a truly magnificent find?" the Korean supreme commander asked intrigued.

"The people I work for happened to have gained access to a previously unexcavated site under one of the Egyptian pyramids. A most puzzling discovery, yet full of treasures. You always had the eye for the finer things in life. As soon as I saw this, I knew you would appreciate it." Mr. Pierron switched back to English, "And also hoped you would realise how much you stand to lose. Now tell me, how did you get your hands on nuclear devices!"

"The Democratic People's Republic of Korea created them. We are a nuclear power that has the capability to punish all those that have targeted us." he responded in a poorly pronounced English accent.

"Dear Leader, we have known each other for a long time, no?", the Korean man nodded with a stern face as he sipped his whiskey, "I know no matter how great your nation may be, you do not yet have the ability to create a single viable device, let alone multiple nuclear bombs. Neither do the others, and those that are capable, are the ones facing the nuclear threat. I believe you are being manipulated, so again please, who has supplied you with these weapons?"

"I am the ruler of the Democratic People's Republic of Korea, and am nobody's puppet." he retorted fiercely.

Mr. Pierron placed the priceless pendant on a map covered table and removed a handkerchief from his other jacket pocket, dabbing his brow, "Then tell me why you accepted responsibility for the terrorist attacks."

"What choices were there? We were to be blamed anyway. The world had already heard about our nuclear tests, so why not let the world fear us. Show them that we will not be pushed around, that we have the means to fight back."

"I am interested to know, who told you that you were to be made the culprit. That you and the other nations must accept responsibility for mass murder? The same people who gave you those weapons I suspect!"

"Why do you insist that we bullied nations have nuclear devices if you do not believe I or any of our allies could create such a device or even obtain one?"

"Because the UN received irrefutable evidence. Satellite imagery and close quarter pictures of your forces taking delivery of one such device. Not just here but Iran as well." Mr. Pierron placed a copy he had obtained of the framing documents on the central table.

The North Korean dictator picked up the images and flicked through them with marked surprise. "Impossible, only a handful of my most trusted people knew of it. The location and details were highly classified."

"It was that evidence that persuaded the Security Council to take such forceful measures."

"What are you saying?" he asked as if the development of certain actions and reactions were falling into place.

"I am saying old friend, that you are centre stage on a grand play, where you and the audience are blind to all that is going on backstage to put on the performance. You are the proverbial Romeo and Juliet. If you do not listen, then you and the rogue nations will die and the rest of the world will wake and realise they have lost too."

"The Pindar!" shouted the supreme commander, throwing his

glass to the dirt floor. What do I do, it's already too late! The only way to stop them is to strike back."

Mr. Pierron pulled a walkie-talkie type device from his handkerchief pocket, "You know I am a man with many connections, maybe all is not lost!"

As he did, a muddied guard came running in, "Supreme commander, American jets have somehow located our complex. They are heading our way!

55 - Siege

Seber still drifted concealed under the rock mimicking nano-fluid. The last of the Sin Supremacy armada rumbled above; still unaware of the small hidden vessel beneath them and the alliance of free races waiting on the other side of the Sun. The menacing forms blocked out the tranquil green and blue of Earth as they loomed closer and closer to the planet. Yet the alliance fleet held back acting upon Michael's gut feeling, one that could be disastrous, and the consequences showed on the faces of those around him.

"Krill there are power build-ups in a number of enemy ships" alerted Emile anxiously.

"Michael?" queried krill.

"Just wait!"

"They are firing!" warned Emile.

"Hold it." reiterated Michael, his words spoken as if detached from his actual thoughts.

Strings of chemical projectiles accelerated out in front of the advancing armada. A wave of explosions lit up space like an elaborate firework display as lines of low Earth orbit satellites were torn apart.

"They will be within striking range within twenty seconds" yelled Emile. But Egregor Krill's eyes had already closed, letting his mind ascend into the invisible ether and flow out amongst the sea of the

Co-operative link. *Attack*. Even with the belief he held in what Michael represented, he could wait no longer. Too much was at stake.

Ripple after ripple, flash following flash, alliance ships appeared on the border of the upper atmosphere standing as protective shield against the oncoming hordes of the Sin Supremacy. The Ashtar tri-defence orbs lashed-out cutting lasers that cleaved through the oncoming ships with ease. Orange atmosphere vented from a pack of red lobster looking vessels that had been sliced by the intense Ashtar weapons, sending crustacean alien bodies and glassy equipment into the path of the closely formed masses. The huge quartet of concentric rings began to revolve around each of the hulking Hyekera destroyers as they exited their bright Einstein-Rosen bridges. As the gyroscopic like rings rotated in their random azimuths, they spewed out clusters of robotic sentries that zigged-zagged towards the abundant targets, individually zeroing in on any bio-signature within the enemy ships.

Taken by surprise the initial alliance salvo obliterated hundreds of the Sin Supremacy ships before they knew what had hit them. Still the armada poured forwards towards the cavalry returning fire with everything they had.

"Dr. Tesla, get us into the middle of that Armada. Everyone else operate a weapons station. Including you Michael." ordered Krill as his consciousness became fully focused once more in his physical body. "Baraqz, Biriqzz, are you familiar with the weapon systems of this vessel?"

"Would a Chaste hound of Doros Eight try to impregnate you during the blood moon cycle?" replied Baraqz.

"The dope means, Yes!" translated Biriqzz, "Emile was quite informative during our journey here."

Baraqz nodded, ignoring the jape and slipped on his antique goggles. Cracking his knuckles with serious intent, Baraqz took his station, yet Michael was still staring out through Seber's transparent hull, mesmerised with the distant battle.

"Oi, this is no time for day dreaming. How about you park your butt at one of those weapons stations." rebuked Emile still trying to fathom why he would wish to allow enemy warships to launch first strikes against Earth.

"Ehm.", Michael answered slowly coming out of his daze, "Yes ok."

The harmless tumbling asteroid maintaining its geo-synchronous orbit suddenly steadied itself and accelerated towards the space battle as patches of smooth amber migrated across the jagged rocky surface.

The elongated Earth defence carriers opened their forward triangular prows along with scores of side hatches. Quads of circular gravimetric generators glowed in the darkness as squadrons of TEAF fighters climbed from their launch bays and accelerated into battle formation. Using their superior maneuverability, the nimble TEAF fighter's formed attack wings and ploughed head on into the throng of the Sin Supremacy. These black triangular craft were designed for speed and close combat capabilities, weaving between ships they unleashed internal rail guns that punched through some hulls while barely scratching others. The TEAF fighter's disruption began to cause mini chaos among the ranks of the enemy armada allowing the other alliance vessels to continue their longer-range assaults before they could organise themselves.

Seber ate up the distance towards the back of the armada. The heavy juggernaut type warships had begun to spread out behind the main lines of battle. Escorted by columns of single seater spear shaped ships they began to fire searing balls of plasma towards the alliance lines of defence, incinerating TEAF fighters like they weren't even there. Further volleys pummeled the Hyekera destroyers, several impacts smashing apart sections of their dense metal rings. Still the protective electromagnetic fields generated by the spinning rings held fast. Even with three of the outer rings damaged, the destroyers were able to generate an EM shield, albeit weaker, as long as one ring continued its revolution. The stray balls of destruction that evaded the tiers of defence and blazed towards Earth were swiftly mopped up by the Ashtar rear-guard. Although some orbs experiencing direct strikes were destroyed, the plasma balls hitting the Ashtar warships caused only temporary damage as the depressions and wrinkles in its absorbing armour recoiled and sprang back into its original configuration.

"Everyone target enemy fighters around the nearest Sin Supremacy juggernaut." ordered Krill. "Dr. Tesla, the juggernaut please."

The two forward weapon protrusions, that had extended to the exterior of Seber's shell, released a pair of pure white beams that intersected in front of them and burst out in a single intense cone of white light towards the huge enemy ship. As the ray left the intersection point a sound like a chorus of vibrating crystals permeated space. The shaft of blinding light struck the stern of the juggernaut, ploughing into the rusting hull and out through its bow, exiting in a short-lived rainbow like a lighthouse beacon penetrating and diffracting through a rain cloud. A clean hole ran the length of the juggernaut, everything in the beams path disintegrated under the pure photonic energy. The nose of the dead vessel dipped, no longer able to propel itself under its own power and plunged through the melee of combating vessels.

"Signal the closest TEAF fighter attack wing."

"Egregor, channel open to Squawking Parrot's squadron." informed Emile.

"Squawking Parrot, this is Egregor Krill. Form defensive ranks around Seber; keep those enemy fighters at bay. We must destroy those juggernauts."

"TEAF wing Eagle assume attack formation Clarity." ordered Squawking Parrot to his Mayan brothers. "We are on our way Egregor."

Ten black triangles swooped through the onslaught of enemy ships arranging into shielding ranks around the ancient Elohim ship. As Seber assailed the bombarding juggernauts, all the accompanying TEAF fighters unleashed reams of strafing fire against their spear shaped escorts, filling their unknown enemies with rows of puncture wounds. Meanwhile the Ashtar contingent moved to meet the oncoming wave of Sin Supremacy invaders preceded by a wall of cover fire from the new alliance members. The rest of the scout armada now within weapons range of the alliance fleet unleashed their own hail of fire towards the oncoming Ashtar and alliance defensive lines, taking out numerous vessels that succumbed to the deluge of diverse weaponry. In the space above Earth the two mass forces ploughed into each other colliding in a plethora of explosions and flying firepower.

The Sin had never expected such a resistance if any at all. This arrogance had allowed the alliance in their surprise attack to destroy a great number of Supremacy ships, but still many, many more remained. Columns of Hyekera destroyers picked off enemy vessels as quickly as they came, the concentrated swarm of targets making easy prey for their sentries, although suffering significant damage in return. The powerful Ashtar warships spread amongst the Supremacy hoards, exchanging fire at the heart of the scout armada in an attempt to drive disorganisation into their ranks and isolating their frontline to the rest of the alliance. Even though the Ashtar were vastly outnumbered, they were more than a match for the majority of the enemy races amongst the scout armada. They knew the most dangerous enemies had not come yet. However, the Raqzzon arks were being overwhelmed. The enormous cigar shaped ships spewed out their super-hot beams of charged particles effectively melting alloys and hull composites on contact, but with their short numbers of cumbersome arks and their weapons recharge requirements, they could not hold back the tides of Sin Supremacy warships. Their charged clouds of ions created a misty barrier between the enemy and Earth, dissipating huge amounts of weapons energy and absorbing anything that could possibly penetrate the planet's atmosphere and strike the surface. However there was a huge hole in the alliance defensive lines where the Altairian had filled momentarily. The Raqzzon could not compensate for their sudden disappearance and throngs of Supremacy attack ships were about to punch through.

A congested sounding voice came over Seber's communication system, "Egregor Krill! This is lead Shepherd Zonnoq. We cannot avert the Sin Supremacy stampede." sounds of rumbling from weapons impacts interrupted the Raqzzon's words, "The Altairian have disappeared from their agreed positions, we are being overwhelmed by enemy numbers. I fear they will shortly break through towards Earth."

Emile scanned her tactical console images, "No quantum tunnel signatures, just a single partial echo. Krill, they were never there in the first place!"

Krill turned his expressionless stare towards Varantis, but the

Altairian Prime showed no acknowledgement and continued to attack the Sin Supremacy forces from his weapons console.

"Advise the TEAF fighter squadron to continue their assaults on the juggernauts. Ashtar warships will shortly join them. Dr. Tesla we need to assist the Raqzzon lines." notified Krill, but before Seber could jump to their aid, two Raqzzon arks split apart in an eruption of explosions. The small obsidian death sphere emerged from the melee. An attack squadron of TEAF fighters accompanying an Ashtar warship sped towards the solitary Sin hunter ship slamming lasers and rail gun fire into its sides. Neither seemed to have much effect. The Sin ship let out a chilling scream as its beam of shadow obliterated three of the triangular craft in one foul sweep. The remaining TEAF fighters swung around the potent enemy and unloaded all rail guns and Tesla lances at close quarters. The uranium tipped shells and high voltage arcs only managing to chip the dark glassy exterior. In a swift attack run, the companion Ashtar warship fired all tri-defence orbs, the sharp lasers sliced into the super hard material of the Sin craft but were only capable of inflicting deep etches into its obsidian hull. The Sin hunter ship retaliated once again with its shadow beam. The shaft of pure darkness pummeled the Ashtar warship, the terrible scream increasing in pitch as the mirror-like surface collapsed in stages under the intense dark energy. The warship attempted evasive maneuvers but the shadow beam followed its victim, the metallic material eventually succumbing to the awesome force of the weapon and tore apart around its occupants. An explosion incinerated the inside of the ship barely contained by the malleable hull. The empty crumpled shell of the Ashtar warship floated by like tin foil on the wind as the deceptively lethal Sin vessel finished off the remaining TEAF fighters. Now groups of Sin Supremacy ships were on a free run towards Earth.

"Where are the bloody Altairian." shouted Emile while juggernauts overhead continued their heavy artillery bombardment.

"There's your answer." commented Michael pointing out past his weapons console towards the back of the Sin Supremacy armada.

Like many tailed tadpoles hundreds of the biological warships tunneled into normal space, out of position and late. "Holographic projections." Varantis wore a crooked and satisfied scowl as his people finally appeared ready to do battle. Unbeknownst to the rest of the alliance, the Altairian had transported devices to their pre-designated coordinates capable of temporarily projecting multiple ship images and bio-chemical signatures. A diversion to give them time to accomplish whatever they had planned to do.

"Damn it, they are powering weapons. We and the TEAF fighter squadrons are right in their line of fire!"

Taking their cue from the emperor's Mothership, each of the living vessels bristled with static energy and in one huge synchronised discharge, branches of lightning struck out straight for the warring ships.

56 - The Truth out There

General Allen and Commodore Gaughan had placed two communication devices on the table. Voices crackled out from them, captivating the ears of everyone in the command centre.

"How are you getting this? These could easily be faked!" demanded the President of the United States.

"That's not important, but the content is." The general turned to the command centre coordinator, "Has any American planes just been dispatched to an area of jungle within North Korea?"

The coordinator paused waiting for the go ahead from the president. The general was about to snap at him when the president gave him a nod. "Answers people, quick!" he shouted to a group of operators as he took his place in front of one computer terminal. Seconds later he reported that, "Three Raptors were on route to jungle coordinates in North Korea after intercepting a transmission. They were already searching for an unknown aircraft fitting the description of an SR-91."

"Right, and what radio frequency was that communication on?" the general encouraged.

"Erhmm, one point six giga-hertz." answered the CC coordinator.

The president snatched up one of the communication devices and looked at its dialing knob. "One point six giga-hertz."

"Ok General you've made you point. So we don't know which one was responsible for the initial terrorist attacks, but what I have learnt from this, is that they indeed have other nuclear devices and intend to use them. I still must defend my country. And it appears we are losing our communication networks so I need to act now!"

General Allen sighed with frustration and looked to Commodore Gaughan who gave him the support he needed, "We have no choice."

"Mr. President, we need to tell you something that requires privacy. It relates to the failures of your satellite systems. If afterwards you still believe this is for the good of the US, then I will push that damn button myself!"

"Very well but I insist that the secretaries and CC coordinator remain." The president dismissed the others as Commodore Gaughan sat down with the CC coordinator at his computer terminal and asked him to do something.

As soon as the staff had exited the command centre the general switched his attention to the remaining parties. "The US and the world are threatened by a greater danger than you can possibly imagine. These rogue nations pale in significance! There is a force out there, intent on not just killing people of a few nations, but wiping out all human life. They are called the Sin."

"Never heard of them!" groaned the secretary of defence, "anyway what do you mean out there." He added gruffly.

"Commodore?"

"Have it!" the coordinator rerouted the computer monitor so that the image was displayed on the huge viewing screen. "This is the last image taken by one of your spy satellites before you lost contact with it and a number of others."

On the display was an obsidian globe passing within a backdrop of Earth and a purple beam from some other machine heading straight for the satellite.

"Sir we are now losing communication from the lower Earth orbit satellites." updated the coordinator.

"Get me a live link up to whatever we have left!" ordered the President.

"Live feed coming from a weather satellite positioned quite a distance from where we are experiencing problems. Infra-red only, Sir"

"It will do, put it on the display!"

When the real time images came on the screen, the others gasped. In the normally cold of space, thousands of red blips were coming together with many of them igniting into red hot flashes and disappearing. "What the hell is going on in our skies!" requested the president with his gaze firmly fixed on the massive command screen.

"You know that saying, the Earth is not the centre of the universe. That may be so, but the human race seems to have found itself there! What you are seeing is a massive alien force hell bent on destroying us, not just the United States, the United Nations or a bunch of so-called rogue nations, but the whole of humanity. The only thing stopping them is an intergalactic alliance that I and the commodore are part of, however this is not enough. The threat is real; you have already lost half your satellites. Do you now see that everyone's future depends on what we do here? We must all work together!"

"How? Why?...." the president's face was pale as a ghost.

"We don't have time, the deadline looms!"

"What do I do?" he asked now entirely submissive.

"Talk!" answered General Allen simply as he picked up one of the communication devices.

"And call off those fighters heading for our colleague!" added Commodore Gaughan hastily.

In the underground jungle complex another North Korean soldier sprinted into the supreme commander's bunker, struggling to catch his breath. "Dear Leader, the American planes.....they were right on top of our position....they definitely saw us as we were firing anti-aircraft rounds at them......but...but they just pulled away and left.

Mr. Pierron gave a wry smile and switched the radio transmitter to two-way communication. "General Allen, was that your doing?"

"It was the Presidents of the United States. I have him here with me." The general's deep voice crackled into the command bunker.

"What is going on?" demanded a confused Korean ruler.

"Your way out, old friend"

At the same time in the hidden desert palace an aid brings news to the Iranian President. His face looked grave as he spoke. "The invading infidels show no sign of stopping. And they will not stop now. I have just received word that a nuclear device has already detonated in America. The deadline is at hand; I must go and give the order to our martyrs. I bear no grudge to you Doctor; you may take your leave if you wish."

"Why did you not wait until the deadline before striking?"

"It was not my command, nor any of the others. Phoenix was not a target of ours. I don't know whose bidding that was. It must have been controlled by…." He stopped mid-sentence, "It does not matter, we have struck them hard yet they continue. We will die proud that we fought to the end!"

"Does that not tell you that your nations are not in control? Some other power is determined for this conflict to take its full course whether you wish it or not!" implored Dr. Kuzminski.

"No doubt another ploy by the Americans or the UN to justify what they are about to do!" replied the Iranian leader with spite in his voice, "Only I or the Leader of the Democratic People's Republic of Korea can give the martyrs their orders if the invasion forces do not withdraw.", he took a mobile out of his pocket, "My Korean brother may have been compromised so it is up to me to make the call."

"The deadline is still minutes away, please, I ask, wait one moment!", he pulled out his communication device from his long coat that immediately instigated the pointing of guns towards his head. "Shoot me if you need to but it is important that you listen!"

"Hold fire!" ordered the Iranian President as he looked to the phone and rubbed a thumb over the buttons.

Dr. Kuzminski held out the radio transmitter at arm's length for all to see and switched the device to two-way communication. "General Allen, this is Dr. Kuzminski, I hope you have been listening."

"Yes Doctor, I have the President of the United States and the Supreme Commander of North Korea on line too. They wish to speak with the Iranian President."

The voice of the Korean leader crackled over the radio to the Iranian President's surprise, "The Pindar has made fools of us! We need to discuss this before our nations are destroyed."

"I have heard what you said. I can tell you categorically as the American President that the United States of America or the United Nations did not strike our own people with nuclear weapons to justify taking actions against you. Neither were we responsible for this latest attack on our home soil! If your nations are not responsible, then this can only mean that someone of great power has played you as well as my own country. I don't know how we were so blind to such influences, maybe our current climate of hostility has made us oblivious to such obvious manipulation, but we must end this right now!"

"Then you know what must be done, we cannot back down unless you concede to our demands!" replied the Iranian President fighting the hatred for the American.

The high-pitched voice of the Korean ruler added further, "Call an instant stop to your attacks and begin a full retreat of all UN and US forces from our countries and I will recall the martyrs!"

"Roy, make it happen. Tell them we have reached an agreement with the rogue nations. Speak to whoever you need to and I don't care if you bypass any chain of command. I will take the heat. Just get it done now!"

"Get me the CF7 Commander on USS Blue Bridge, Lieutenant General Wolfhower in forward command, Azerbaijan, and the British Secretary of state for defence."

The seconds of the clock ticked away as the COM-12 members and the three leaders waited anxiously. One minute to deadline and a voice finally spoke over the radio. "I can confirm your air strikes and aerial bombardment has stopped. I have sent orders to all my army to cease fire as soon as your troops begin retreating."

"I wish I could say the same my North Korean brother, bombs still fall on our lands.", an urgent voice started shouting in the background, repeating the same Persian phrase.

"The tanks have stopped; the infidels are running!"

"We shall call off our martyrs." confirmed the Iranian President as he picked up the phone and gave the signal to abandon their sacrifices. "There will be no more nuclear attacks after the deadline from us!"

"But be sure, our ability to do so will not be retracted until the last of your soldiers leave our territory" warned the Korean supreme commander.

"I understand. However, once they are withdrawn, I insist that our peoples talk. Resolutions must be found."

"This we will make sure of!" concluded General Allen with determination deep in his voice.

57 - The Cavalry

Originating in clusters of electro plaques grown in the warship skin, the biologically generated lightning strikes crackled through space towards the rear of the ensuing battle.

The shards of forking electrons reflected in the deep black eyes of Egregor Krill, "Dr. Tesla …", "I'm on it!" Emile cut him short. From within its escort squadron of TEAF fighters, Seber flickered and vanished in a split-second entanglement jump.

Squawking Parrot's TEAF squadron and the many others engaged with the enemy fighters accompanying the juggernauts braced themselves for impact from the Altairian attack. The energetic lightning flashed all around the squadrons, missing the TEAF fighters and the area once occupied by Seber, though not by much. Like portable wielding torches the high voltage bolts conducted into the rusty metal of the juggernauts, melting the hull wherever the caressing fingers of lightning touched. After their initial simultaneous lightning storm, the smaller most agile bio-ships joined the close-range attacks to the rear-guard of the Sin Supremacy armada, while the more mature Drain warships continued their electrical strikes to the sandwiched enemy forces.

Although the alliance had one less problem in the Altairian, still, a host of Supremacy attack ships lead by the destructive Sin globe continued to push through the alliance defences towards Earth. As Seber raced to intercept the enemy penetrating the space vacated by the Altairian; Emile glimpsed at the battle with little relief. The Altairian were fighting for the alliance, but in their trickery, they had left her world vulnerable. She watched on as the flocks of newly hatched bio-ships dived into the fray, whipping their multiple tails and ejecting high pressured waste gases to perform maneuvers that would be impossible for most artificial craft to match.

"Dr. Tesla, as soon as we are in weapons range, fire on the Sin sphere, and get me a communication channel with Emperor Xantis At Rae." ordered Krill.

"Yes Egregor, I am quite busy at the moment.", the holographic projection of the old Altairian leader turned to one of his Ethereal, "That juggernaut still has weapon functionality, destroy it now!" The Mothership bore down on the destructive vessel. Electrical arcs exploded against the firing turrets sending out showers of sparks.

"Why did you not adhere to the defined alliance plan emperor? Without your presence in the defensive lines, the Sin Supremacy has managed to breakthrough our protective shield. To prevent this was the alliances primary objective."

"Was not our most important advantage surprise? With our delayed assault we now have the Sin Supremacy armada blockaded with no means of escape. Can you not see victory is at hand! Those ships represent an insignificant number and threat!" he said with disdain at Egregor Krill's questioning.

"Then you consider the Sin insignificant. Please let no Supremacy ship escape."

"Do not worry Egregor, we have not left our position unguarded. Varantis activate the Scarap web!" Xantis At Rae turned his back and the holographic image terminated.

"What is this Scarap web Varantis?" challenged Krill.

"Watch!" Staring ahead towards the far-off obsidian sphere, Varantis tweaked the organic object at the centre of his robe collar.

Just in front of the attacking Supremacy ships where the Altairian forces had vanished, the space vaguely rippled like the hot hazy air of a desert.

"Magnify the imaging scanners!" barked the Altairian Ethereal.

A crystal-clear display of the distant space appeared around them. At this magnification they could see thin tendrils crisscrossing the open territory like a spider's web. The multiple clear strands where intersected by what looked like hundreds of ochre coloured urchins. These newly materialised urchins were affixed with objects analogous in structure to the neck device Varantis had used to conceal his true identity. Crusty pustules leaked bubbling brown fluid as the urchins pulsated in the vacuum, they were clearly alive. As the first of the Sin Supremacy ships hit the almost invisible net, the sticky threads clung to their exteriors, breaking off and wrapping around them like strings of super glue. Then the throbbing urchins reeled in any slack, attaching themselves to the vessel hulls and exploding with a concussive inward blast. In a matter of seconds about sixty enemy ships found themselves entangled in the web of biological mines, the multiple explosions shredding and destroying them swiftly.

Varantis turned with arrogance to the expressionless Krill. "That is a Scarap web. We planted it at our pre-ordained coordinates. Each Scarap is embedded with one of our camouflage devices, and able to project a holographic representation of what we desire, be it empty space or an Altairian warship. The enemy will not know what hit them until it is too late!"

"A Sin sphere is not so easily dispatched; it may not be enough." answered Krill. Immediately as if on cue, a portion of the Scarap web ensnared the Sin scout ship and multiple blasts erupted across the obsidian glass. A brown mist expanded into space obscuring the damage dealt to the sphere. A handful of trailing enemy ships shaped like triple-winged anvils shot through the spray, dispersing the remains of the ochre urchins. Once again visible they could see the black globe was scarred with several rounded pock marks, but far from destroyed. With a blitzing spread of its shadow beam the Sin sphere annihilated the remaining Scarap web and passed the last line of resistance between Earth and its dark form of destruction. Behind their ruler, scores of the Supremacy attack craft closed in on Earth, the alliance forces had no chance of intercepting them before they could strike the populations on the planet.

"Krill, we can't get there in time. The enemy ships will be in weapons range within seconds." Cursing herself that she could not push Seber any faster. Even calculating an entanglement jump couldn't be completed in sufficient time.

"We need to do something! You saw what that thing done to the Moon." Michael appealed with a look of foreboding across his face.

Seber dashed past the struggling Raqzzon arks as the ripples of shadow built up upon the obsidian globe and weapon turrets sprang from the tops of the anvil shaped vessels.

Michael grabbed his temple and switched his intense gaze from the deadly sphere towards a nearby empty patch of space. "Emile..." his voice tailed off weakly.

"What the Frell!", Emile stared at the same area above Earth. "Detecting gravimetric distortions. A whole load of them!"

"The others." stated krill.

Just a short distance from the break-away enemy, over five thousand ripples deformed space. One blur after another focused into Ashtar warships. Thousands of ships like the reflection absorbing spinning tops battling in the midst of the Supremacy armada, and many more thousand in varying connotations of similar designs.

As soon as the cavalry arrived each one of them was aware of the situation through the Co-operative link and in response immediately opened fire upon the Sin hunter ship and its cohort. Their attentions momentarily removed from Earth, they took evasive actions. The tri-defence orbs of the newest warships fired relentlessly, joined by generations of earlier models, some with their defence orbs fused on the circumference of their bases, others clearly of older boxier designs without orbs altogether but discharging their laser weapons from various protrusions. The Sin sphere drove straight for its assailers unleashing bursts of destructive shadow as the black glassy material splintered and cracked under the battering of concentrated laser fire. A faction of glowing orange craft all with four long radiant turquoise stanchions chased down the eluding enemy vessels. From within the bright orange ovaloids, balls of fire obliterated the breakaway Supremacy attack ships, all except for one that had somehow avoided the intervention.

"There is still one Supremacy ship on a heading towards Earth. They have high yield dirty bombs, radioactive and biological. Krill its weapons are hot and targeting somewhere in North America." warned Dr. Tesla.

No! Michael's mind shouted. The US was a big place but he couldn't take the chance, no matter how insignificant the probability that the vessels attack might strike the area where his daughter was. With those desperate thoughts he reached out through space and with a crushing anger he concentrated his entire mind towards the enemy. It was like he was stretching out an imaginary hand frantically trying to grasp something out in the distance. He felt the fingertips of his projected thought brushing the deadly foe, but any tangible grip was just out of reach. With overexerted determination his concentration lunged out in a last-ditch effort, finally sensing his supernatural touch entangling solid matter in a forceful clench. On Seber's holographic display, the others could see the ships weapons turret begin to vibrate, and then metal plates begin to break off the exterior of the anvil structure. Michael let out a teeth-clenching roar as the ship shook in its trajectory and began to fold in upon itself as if a giant pair of invisible hands were crushing a tin can. Michael collapsed to the floor with blood running from his nose. Emile went to run to him but Egregor Krill stopped her with a few swift words.

"Dr. Tesla, take us back to the main battle and notify the entire alliance fleet that we cannot allow any Sin Supremacy ships to escape. Biriqzz please attend to Michael."

No longer a polished sphere, the broken and chipped chunk of obsidian that was the Sin hunter ship continued to push forward on its single-minded charge for Earth.

"How dare you challenge the might of the Sin!" bellowed Rahab from within his sullied death globe, the destructive shadow amplifying around him.

A myriad of lasers and fireballs slammed into the dark craft.

"You will never stop us!" he raged defiantly as intense light penetrated the harnessed gloom.

The Sin scout ship finally succumbed under the powerful assault from the plethora of Ashtar warships and mystery orange vessels. Shattering into cold shards of night and then incinerating to dust as a blast of shadow pulsed out from the wreckage.

The wave of murky black blew across the alliance fleet, bringing with it a ghostly echo full of spite and hatred, like a whisper on the breeze it was barely audible.

"Your end is coming!!"

The Ashtar had left Co-operative space unguarded to the Sin Supremacy so that they could contribute in the vital defence of Earth and the Raziel. And now the impressive show of force aided the Raqzzon and Hyekera in driving the enemy armada back into a contained mass while the Altairian and the squadrons of TEAF fighters prevented any retreating ships. Seber materialised back into space behind one large vessel akin to an almost transparent tentacle-less jellyfish. From a ridge along its varicoloured back it ejected glistening purple seeds at the Elohim ship, these dense pellets slammed into the amber shell in fireless explosions. Sections of the stony hull crumbled under the impacts but were rapidly repaired as amber nano-fluid flowed into the cracks and instantly solidified against the vacuum. Seber returned fire with surges of white light that pushed through its opaque rubber type skin and burst out in an array of intense rays. The wounded enemy ship began to drift lifelessly and its cloudy interior turned black and melted away into the cold of space. The silver spinning tops of Ashtar warships scattered the enemy around them tearing apart one after the other. TEAF fighters chased down stray Supremacy ships unloading their rail guns and launching chambers of Tesla lances, the metal spears puncturing diverse hulls and discharging their electrical payload. Meanwhile Altairian lightning immobilised and disintegrated fleeing ships, swiftly depleting the enemy armada and leaving nothing but a new nebula of battle debris.

Emile looked towards Krill as she dispatched two more enemy craft analogous to V2 rockets, "The armada are nearly defeated, the alliance fleet are mopping up the remnants of the enemy."

Michael groaned as he held his head on the command centre floor. Biriqzz had retrieved a tiny box from below and now held the contents under Michael's bleeding nose. A purple and black striped beetle which seemed to be releasing a stinking vapour from its distending duel anus.

"Ok, ok. Enough…. I'm conscious already."

Biriqzz, holding the insect's abdomen, gave it one last hard squeeze and placed it back in its miniature container.

"He is ok Egregor. I think his typical human male brain could not cope with such a level of concentration!"

Michael just gave her an un-amused glare as he wiped the blood and stink from his nostrils. He pulled himself to his feet and stared out towards the vast battlefield of ship rubble and floating alien corpses. He watched on as the last of the Sin Supremacy armada were chased down and destroyed.

"Did any get through to Earth?" asked Michael as Emile ran over and hugged him unexpectedly.

"No, our reinforcements were able to drive them back, and of course the demonstration of your potential prevented the attack ship striking the planet." confirmed Krill.

Almost welcoming the affection and assistance from Emile, he gave a weak sigh of relief. With the surge of exhaustion that had beset him, he was still a little groggy as he stood up. "Maybe the Sin will think twice about mounting another attack on Earth." he said with a tone that suggested optimism.

"On the contrary this was only a scout armada. They will never stop. The Sin will most definitely return; but next time they will come with such a force that would make what we have seen here today pale in insignificance." warned Krill. "This is only the beginning."

58 - Ceasefire

Just over a day had passed since the Earth had come seconds away from a nuclear third World War and the new alliance had fought back the Sin Supremacy. In orbit the Earth defence fleet had cleared the skies of battle debris and transported it too the Cydonia Mensae Mars base for the Mayan technicians to dissect. In the wreckages they hoped to gather more information on the Supremacy forces, using surviving data devices or examining the remains of alien species they would try and extrapolate the Sin movements, possible numbers and maybe a hint to when they would strike. The rest of the useful material would be recycled and used to create further TEAF carriers and fighters.

Down on the planet surface, other clean up jobs were being executed in the light of the conflicts, mainly political. All UN forces were slowly but surely withdrawing from North Korea and Iran. Not only there but the call to return home was given to the American, British and foreign troops stationed within Iraq and Afghanistan. With the full withdrawal, no more terrorist attacks had happened past the deadline, and for the first time many people woke up with a renewed hope that did not involve taking up arms. Instead they looked out upon their devastated nations and realised how much they had lost and how much they would have to rebuild, still freedom from western tyranny was what they had fought for and this is exactly what they had. Despite what hardships they were to face, they now had hope for their children. Every news channel and tabloid from every country ran the story of how last-minute evidence had proven that the rogue nations had not been behind the nuclear terrorist attacks, although foolishly admitting the responsibility in the light of faulty information provided by a mysterious third party. Many images and on-scene movie footage of the deserted Phoenix area were used to show the levels this new player in world terrorism was prepared to go to achieve what they intended. There were round the clock interviews and documentaries about the attack and evacuation accompanied by the scientific analysis of the time periods involved before human life could inhabit the hundreds of miles of irradiated lands. But the focus was on this third party, which was vigorously promoted as the real enemy, a formerly unknown terrorist organisation whose agenda was to cause worldwide instability and conflict for whatever advantages this presented them. But what was clear from past events was that it was a threat much greater than had been faced before. It was still very early days yet and there seemed to be a strong motivation to work together, to root out this new enemy and begin a new era of co-operation and peace.

The president took some solace in the fact that the United States had rode out this storm without further American deaths. Even though he believed that nothing would change in these rogue nations or other countries of concern, he had to do this. The original reasons for the American and UN interventions would still remain, deeply seeded in the psyche through decades of conflict, one day was not going to change this, no amount of talking had changed this and the years of military action certainly hadn't made anything better. Only time could heal the climate of hatred and fear that had been sewn, and if it didn't, then he might just have to turn a blind eye to it. Only he and a select few knew about the danger out there, the very real possibility of the extinction of the human race. Shortly after the last transmission to the North Korean and Iranian leaders, General Allen took the president and his three closest advisors to planetoid Alpha. After what they had discovered, they still seemed surprised when a black transport ship, based on a TEAF fighter, landed at the former RAF base Machrihanish to pick them up. However not as shocked as when the diminutive form of Egregor Krill introduced himself from within the primary ready room of the colonised space rock. The president and his aides were a treasure trove of questions from the moment they boarded the transfer vessel piloted by Emile. She was all too pleased to answer everything they had asked and bring them up to scratch with the basics of the situation, but she was relieved when they finally reached Krill's location. It was probably the only time that the president had been lost for words and stood there speechless while the Egregor told him in no uncertain terms that the Sin would return.

"When they do, it will be in numbers and strength that are incomprehensible, and which we stand little chance of defeating. The galaxy is a vast expanse, much of which we know little of, and much of which is dominated by the Sin. Let me explain to you that there are terrors and powerful civilisations out there that are unknown to the alliance. We have no way to predict what enemies we will be required to defend against, yet there is one thing I am positive of. The Sin will send their hordes down to Earth to exterminate the human race one by one, and your nation had better be ready to fight for their very existence." Egregor Krill stared inexpressive with his large deadpan eyes allowing him a moment to absorb the full gravity of what they would be facing.

Once the president eventually regained the use of his vocal chords, he spoke with an almost glazed look, "The people of the US and the world shouldn't know this truth. Such knowledge would cause a mass panic that would undermine any effort of mounting an effective defence against a full-scale invasion. Even just telling select governments or their military forces would be a huge risk. With so many variables and such a heavy burden, not to mention the mysterious organisation that had somehow infiltrated the world's hierarchy, the truth would find its way out and the consequences of this would be far worse. I will work with General Allen to do all that is necessary to prepare ourselves."

"I concur with that assessment. But when the time comes the world will need to be warned." acknowledged Egregor Krill.

"Only a few of us know the truth, we are all fully aware of what it would mean for this information to get out, and we have each sworn to secrecy. The satellite imagery and the live feed of the space battle have been disposed of. The loss of satellites has been attributed to a major meteor shower which happens to tie in nicely with the debris that managed to hit and burn up in the atmosphere, and the remains of an alien craft that crashed to Earth in a desolate Andean plain in southern Peru. The crumpled ball of metal created an impact crater near the Bolivian border about sixty-six feet across and sixteen feet deep. Luckily there were only a small number of locals in nearby Puno. Around two hundred people complained of sickness from inhaling toxic gas at the crash site, but we have already explained it away as pockets of gas being released from under the soil." announced the defence secretary.

"Ok then…" General Allen laid out a plan of action. "The fact is Mr. President that your military is never going to be able to protect everyone inside US borders, therefore your efforts must focus on rapid mobilisation rather than drafting more recruits. After recent events people will expect to see less need for recruitment into the military, we cannot risk further worldwide suspicion by openly expanding your armed forces. Therefore, concentrate on constructing more heavy artillery which needs to be operated by your existing forces, and most importantly stockpiles of close combat weaponry that can easily be distributed amongst the populace….. Yes, and before you say it, every man woman and child is going to have to pick up a weapon if they are to survive. My organisation will help with whatever we can. COM Twelve is already setting about initiating an enrolment drive for a new multinational task force to combat this new unseen terrorist faction. Yet their real reason for creation, although they will not know this, will be to combat alien forces on the ground and too use civilian resources to supplement their numbers." The president nodded in agreement and looked to his advisors, the secretary of state, defence secretary and General Milton for their input.

"Well General Allen, I am sure we can go about manufacturing mass stores of weapons in secret." answered General Milton, "Hell we've been doing black projects like this for years without anyone knowing outside certain agencies. We just have to be clever about how we approach it."

"That's all well and good but, how are we going to pay for this and what kind of timescale are we talking about here?" asked the secretary of state, well aware that this kind of undertaking would take considerable preparation.

"As to budget issues." General Allen answered, "I can tell you that NASA won't be needing its annual eighteen billion-dollar budget for the foreseeable future!"

"And with respect to timescale, I regret that we cannot give you any sufficient answer on this. To the Sin, the task of destroying the human race is their ultimate aim. As I am sure Dr. Tesla has explained; this single-minded crusade is the result of an ancient prophecy that humans will somehow bring about their downfall. They will eventually discover that their scout armada has been lost. Although, so far, they do not know how this has happened, this remains the only advantage the new alliance currently possesses. However, once the Sin know their armada has not completed its mission, it will gather every resource that they control throughout the galaxy, and only then will they return with such as force as to ensure the prophecy is not fulfilled. So, I suggest you labour at a rate as if tomorrow was your last day and then maintain this for however long we have given to us." responded Krill in his ever present melodic yet emotionless voice.

"Then we shall take our leave and begin work, but before we go, what can we do about the organisation that is headed by this Pindar? It is likely that the governments and people of the world will now be harder to manipulate, but their threat still remains." asked the president.

"Firstly, you need to place a halt on any further law changes, global agreements such as this United Nations Parliamentary Assembly. We believe that this unknown influence has been manipulating the global community for their own ends, this could be part of that. You will need to work with the leaders of the world as a singular entity, but right now this must be done within the boundaries of trust and the best interests of the world, not just the US. So go about your job as if they didn't exist, there is a focus to be maintained that will only be hindered by constant second guessing. This will be time consuming enough for you as it is. COM Twelve will be watching out for them. Dr. Tesla shall escort you back to the transport along with Commodore Gaughan who will act as our liaison and help you where he can." notified the general.

As the ready room door closed behind them, Egregor Krill spoke to the general who had remained. "Since your father rescued me from the wreckage in Roswell, I valued his advice as I do yours now. We need every resource we have working to prepare for the coming of the Sin. We cannot allow ourselves to be distracted from the real danger. What is your view on this influence in the shadows?" invited Krill.

"I have grave concerns about them. Now they are aware that the world knows about their existence, it will be much more difficult to root them out. Who knows how far they have infiltrated the governments of the world. They would already have to be firmly seated in the higher echelons of the US or UN to have orchestrated a deception of such magnitude. It is not unthinkable that the president or his aids are part of this group. This time we were lucky, without the destruction of the United States satellite network I don't think we would have convinced them to withhold their attacks. Although these people don't pose the threat the Sin does, we have seen what they are capable of and if we hadn't stopped them, the Sin Supremacy would have had half a job to do. COM Twelve will be stretched but I think they cannot be ignored. We need to direct significant efforts towards tracking them down and removing their threat."

"We detected a long-range transmission in the direction of Earth, 'Your Masters have returned, submit your servitude.', where that message was directed to, and to whom, is something we could not determine. Yet, this is not the first time we have seen such a message. As you will know, we detected a similar one during the Roswell incident. For all we knew, it was a message to humanity in general, a similar message they decree to all whom the Sin are about to conquer or judge. Without evidence, we must suspect the very real possibility that there could be an agent of the Sin on Earth. And that worries me the most about this unknown foe."

"Mmmh...... I think no matter the origin of this internal enemy, our focus and strategy will be the same."

"Agreed. Then do what you must. The alliance will have to hope that we severely weaken the enemy forces before the Sin Supremacy begins its planetary eradication on the ground. I am required to join the others and the representatives of the new alliance to determine what we must do next. Good luck General." wished Krill as he is slender frame left the ready room.

General Allen remained in the briefing room for a moment longer staring out the reinforced windows into space. His mind wandered towards the task at hand. *How would COM Twelve begin to bring down such a powerful and enigmatic organisation? Despite the countless facets involved in practically manipulating the world, they had managed to stay even out of sight of his own people. COM Twelve really didn't have much to go on except for this mysterious figure, the Pindar.*

59 - Another Path

The Pindar strode through a deserted city complex. He was in a strange murky street, although the Sun was blazing, none of the light was able to illuminate its stuffy air or penetrate onto the tarmac road. In front of the Pindar were rows of rusting metal fences running parallel along the four lane boulevard he was now crossing. These ten feet high barbed wire topped meshes rose at a shallow angle with the road, and disappeared in the shadowy distance. He approached the wire fences, behind the outermost rusty boundary the enclosed mesh divides expanded out from single file alleys into a large open area full of tall wooden storage crates. Set in the background beyond what seemed to be a checkpoint, there were numerous lettered archways in a rock face located straight ahead of him. The Pindar ignored the unusual street scene, stepped across the wire doorway in the fence and made his way through archway X. Inside were a selection of further dusty crates and an enormous curving desk laid there as the focal point of what was a mural decorated atrium. The blue photo fluorescent lights flickered and dust dropped from the high ceiling as rumbling noises and loud screeching echoed from above. The shimmering lighting making the painting covered walls a more eerie vista. Each mural was a surreal amalgamation of men, women, and children in scenes depicting peace, war, hate, death, order and rebirth. Highly symbolic artwork of what the Cult of the Serpent and the Masters would hope to achieve from here and across the world. The Pindar tapped his jacket pocket with the golden triangle and eye emblem to check on the contents concealed inside his suit, brushed the specks of dirt off his shoulders and headed towards the back of the atrium. Weaving between unused boxes he could feel an unmistakable buzz in the air that made the hairs stand on the back of his flaking neck and made him nauseated. Still it was nothing compared to the nerves he felt having to deliver news that would greatly displease the Masters. He reached the back of the atrium that opened up into the rest of compound. It was an impressive site, a drop of eight levels down, each floor a semi-circular array of empty detention cells gathering cobwebs. As his eyes inspected the immense prison construction his nose winced at the appearance of a vile smell.

"Pindar!" came a rasping voice, "You bring me news."

An elongated forked tongue flicked in the air, "And bad news at that I judge. I can taste the anxiety under the overpowering essence of caffeine infused sweat." added a second voice behind the mask of an old skull faced woman. From a side profile her pale gaunt mask was slightly elongated like that of all the Masters.

The Pindar jumped with the unexpected emergence of Quetzalcoatl and another figure draped in gaudy layers of rags and adorned with small skulls.

"Masters, I do bring news but I am disheartened to say it is most disappointing."

Quetzalcoatl let out an aggravated hiss, "Pindar we do not like to receive such news when we have so painstakingly weaved our threads of control. There was nothing that could have unraveled our plans. Speak now!" The large horned beak jointed to the golden straps of his feathered head dress hid the true anger upon his face.

"Everything was on schedule; the UN and US were in the process of invading our scapegoats. In turn those nations were ready to strike back with the nuclear weapons we had provided. It would have escalated to the outcome we had expected, but as the deadline time approached, the backup device we had planted to ensure a terrorist strike even if their martyrs failed, well it was activated early. We determined that the programming our operative received in Dulce did not take into account a recent change in day light saving time."

"Pitiful excuses! Still shouldn't such an early attack have instigated the required US response!" spoke the emancipated looking female Master in a high cracking voice.

"Eh, eh, yes indeed but it seems a group of people we were previously unaware of interfered."

"That you were unaware of!!" rasped Quetzalcoatl, "Our influence traverses all the most powerful organisations across the globe. Explain yourself and hope it is enough that I do not kill you right here, or even worse, allow Chihuacoatl to take you below."

"A man that has so obviously over indulged in toxic chemicals would be of little demand among the others." answered Chihuacoatl as she tasted the air once more.

The Pindar nervously reached into his jacket pocket and pulled out two prints. "Masters, our sources say that these images somehow led to our plans being foiled. They were brought to the attention of the US by that unforeseen group. They are supposed to be satellite imagery from yesterday around the time of the deadline." The plumed serpent snatched them away with his long thin fingers.

Both their snake eyes gazed at the pictures with silence. One held an image of a single obsidian globe and the other a mélange of red dots coalescing in great numbers above Earth.

Finally Quetzalcoatl spoke, towering over the Pindar. "These are nothing! …. What concerns me is how the Cult managed to allow this to happen. Now we cannot achieve the New World Order as we envisaged. We can now be certain that our persuasion in certain parts of the world has waned."

"Master, the world has pin-pointed our hidden influences as a new organisation hell bent on creating instability in the world, a new terrorist organisation." His voice was broken, fearing the retribution of the serpent like humanoids. The only force on Earth that could threaten his life and carry out such an action against him.

"They use our own tactics against us. Cut all our ties with those nations, they are of no use to us anymore. We have been forced to take an alternate route to our new world government. You shall concentrate closer on our own base of power and crush this quantity that dares to interfere with us. Put our alternative plan into immediate effect Pindar, you can see for yourself that this complex requires much work. Chihuacoatl will oversee the project here. Is that understood!"

"It is clear Master."

"And see to it that the HAARP is ready, its full capabilities will now be a necessity." added Chihuacoatl.

"Of course Masters. I will begin preparations for our new initiative right away. I have full confidence that Frau Wulf will have the Alaskan facility fully operational for when we need it." he dabbed the beads of sweat from his forehead and motioned away.

"And Pindar! Do not fail us again, though you are our blood, it will be the last thing you do!" warned Quetzalcoatl with genuine menace.

As the Pindar exited the processing hub the two Masters turned to each other. Quetzalcoatl waved the images too Chihuacoatl, "The Sin has finally returned yet the human race still survives! This changes everything; we must tell the one that lived."

"The Overlords are down below. They have come up to feast and the one that lived accompanies them." notified the skull wearing Master.

"Then we shall join them."

From an adjacent plain concrete structure, the two Masters stooped to fit their 7ft frames into an elevator. After dropping many more levels than the eight that could be seen from the atrium, they exited into a compound created from the natural cavern systems of the sandstone strata. The whole murky area was claustrophobic and exceedingly warm. Their slit pupils enlarged to absorb the scarce light from flaming pools of oil scattered throughout the chambers. Carved inside the rock was a multi-tier honey comb maze of countless enclaves, each one penned in with thick metal bars. They paced down one passageway. Chihuacoatl scratched a long-clawed finger along the cage bars sending their contents scrawling in terror. Quetzalcoatl peered into each, seeing group upon group of children cower to the back of their pens.

This was except for one cell where a diminutive form stood motionless, its young face looking out through the bars.

"Your child labour all appear to fear you except this one. Maybe he would make a good delicacy for the Overlords." questioned Quetzalcoatl.

Chihuacoatl answered while she stared maliciously at the child, "They have devoured enough children today but maybe they have room for a small dessert."

"He will not be touched! This one will be coming with me!" The voice was deep and extremely hoarse with a persuasive edge that commanded obedience.

The two Masters spun around as the child's head dropped and he took a couple of steps backwards. They immediately bowed before the one that lived. "We have come to bring you disturbing news."

From the dark shadows his eyes glowed a deep red. "Yes, I have felt your inner turmoil. Tell me of your concerns.", the flickering fires produced just enough light to outline his form and provide fleeting glimpses of the mysterious figure. At over 8ft he rose above Quetzalcoatl, the tallest of the Masters. Upon his head two pointed protrusions grew from each side. His skin was not quite as serpent like as the others, possessing a very patchy array of scales with reddish raw pigment and eyes slightly rounder unlike a snake.

"The Sin has returned here as they forewarned. Yet the humans remain alive! The evidence we have in our possession shows an external force has somehow managed to hold them back."

"Perhaps those Ashtar have once more mounted a defence of this planet." added Chihuacoatl.

"Not only the Ashtar I suspect. I can sense a growing disturbance that is in opposition to me. An energy that hasn't existed for a very long time." The one that lived's voice sounded as if it was remembering a past age.

"This will only be a temporary reprieve for us. We know the Sin will return with their full might and nothing can possibly stand in their way. The human race will be destroyed along with our ultimate goal. The Akhuforge phase is still a long way off and aspects of the Meridian phase remain just out of our grasp. I fear our time has run out!" hissed Quetzalcoatl.

"Let them come, the Sin have commanded our fear for long

enough. As of late I have felt a change all around us, I feel the walls decaying between here and where we have been forbidden. A weakening brought about by the Sin; they are disrupting the balance of things. We may not need the key of the Akhuforge, to accomplish our ultimate objective. We know why the Sin fears the human race and we have discovered the reason they should. Continue your work as you have always done. They broadcast a message once again, but I have made sure that it fell on deaf ears and that no reply was forthcoming. There can be no doubt that the Sin will return. They will eventually wipe out the human race from existence; however, we must make sure we do what we need with them first. The Sin's return might present us with an opportunity that they do not even realise." He gave a malevolent grin that momentarily exposed his razor like teeth.

"What do you mean?" opposed Quetzalcoatl, "The Sin will destroy us also, or at best enslave us. There is no scenario we can conceive where we can defy the Sin or bare fruition of the work we have done here."

"My strength ever increases. The Sin knows nothing of me and unbeknownst to them, their goals may be merging with that of my own."

"I do not understand" replied Quetzalcoatl.

"You do not need too, do as I say and let me contemplate the return of the Sin." The one that lived held up a finger with a thick black claw and pointed it towards the child's cage. The lock broke and the metal bars of the cell swung open. "Come with me now!" ordered the one that lived.

"Wouldn't you prefer one less tainted. This one was just another sewer rate in the slums of Brazil. We have a host of much fresher children." suggested Chihuacoatl attempting to appease.

"This child has a much greater purpose than to placate my appetite."

"But it doesn't even talk or interact, just stares, a retard with some kind of brain damage." said the serpent with the façade of an old women.

"Not damaged, just altered. You do not see the legacy of your work within this child. I however can sense not only his flaws but also his minds potential." The one that lived retreated into the darkness. "Follow me to your destiny!" he commanded in a tone unpleasant to the ears. The boy walked out of the cell of cowering children and without a word or second glance disappeared into the gloom.

60 - Observer

Somewhere between the orbits of Mars and Jupiter, in the midst of rock and ice, a construction akin to a polished shard of onyx lay in silence, observing. From within our solar system's asteroid belt a member of the Order of the Night turned-off her long-range surveillance imagery. Using the Sun as a gravitational lens to focus the dispersed photons, Malkiyyah had just witnessed the entirety of the huge battle. For weeks now she had drifted, concealed by space boulders in the main belt waiting for vital clues. Patience was a trait deeply instilled in her being, she had already waited for millions of years just to reach this point, and now things were suddenly changing. Malkiyyah pondered on what she had seen. *An unexpected turn of events. I did not foresee that those persistent Ashtar could muster and unite such a number of free civilisations to defend the Raziel. Not only that, they have somehow defeated the Sin Supremacy advanced armada, although an insignificant one at that.* The words of the prophecy were weighing heavy on her mind. *The path to what I desire has long been hidden from the Order. Billions of years have passed since our greatest prize was stolen from us, now I Malkiyyah of the Order of the Night will finally uncover its whereabouts......... and maybe the fate of my progenitor. One of the Elohim had brought him back to the system of the Raziel after the last great battle. Now it is another that has brought me back. In my soul I can feel I am close.* Malkiyyah zoomed into two images in front of her, one of an amber vessel; a sight she had not laid eyes upon for thousands of years, and the other, an ancient enemy on the fourth planet from the star accompanied by one of the Raziel. A hooded figure, but the glow inside was unmistakable; one of the Elohim was here. *I must remain and see where this takes me. The others have chosen to forget that there is another way. The Raziel is not the single portent to our fate. They remain blind to the whole prophecy. Still, my Sin brethren must know of this, the mistakes of the past cannot be repeated. A warning shall be sent.*

The black crystal began to spin on its axis, faster and faster it rotated as fluid shadow rolled around its glassy surface. Only the Order had this capability and rarely was it used. Once Malkiyyah's craft was no more than a blur of darkness, the signal of the night pulsed out in countless shards of shadow towards the distant corners of the galaxy.

As a consequence of sending the warning to her brethren, all energy had drained from the crystalline structure. Now she would have to wait, defenceless, in the long silent darkness until her vessel could absorb enough power from the zero-point energy that permeated the very fabric of space. Although born of the Sin, the Order of the Night lived separately from other Sin, they believed in a goal that the rest had long abandoned, existing for one reason only. Once recharged their hunt would begin.

61 - The Masters

The clunk of thick glass against concrete echoed throughout the extensive chamber of tunneled rock and supporting steel. Tezcatlipoca awkwardly walked beside Kukulcan inspecting their work. Apart from the sound of the snake replica fused to his knee, the place was a ghostly silence. They were in the bowels of the Dulce facility, level 7: incubation and cryogenic storage, where certain work on the Akhuforge and Meridian phases were carried out. Work which no human was ever allowed to see and must never know about. The whole level was just an immense basement blasted from the surrounding rock layers and reinforced with giant metal girders that formed the foundations of Dulce. Underfoot they poured tonnes of concrete to create a flat even surface and excavated an adjoining power plant that generated electricity for the facility by tapping deep into the geo-thermal energy stored beneath. Towards each corner of this open level were rows upon rows of bath like apparatus made from some type of purple plastic with several small transparent windows inserted. Each vibrating bath contained a soup of amber liquid and chunks of body parts still on the bone. From somewhere in their base a dull pink light shone upwards making them glow eerily. The two Masters moved through a grouping of these baths, stopping at one, Tezcatlipoca dipped his finger into its contents and tasted the ooze with a lingering lick of his fork tongue.

"The mixture is slightly off, it needs more human flesh, preferably fresh." he muttered.

"It is difficult to acquire fresh meat in the quantities we require for our accelerated work. Even in their third world populations. Gone are the times when the western world turned a blind eye to the plight of their poorest people. Anybody can hijack a global platform for their voice of adversity now." answered Kukulcan also sampling the digesting solution.

"Well Kukulcan, if things go as we planned, supply will no longer be a problem."

As they finished examining the fourth extensive array of baths, the churning amber fluid came to a rest. Each apparatus had a control panel that was suspended from a metal arm shaped like a lamp post. The stanchion of the arm rose up 7ft into the air from one end of the liquid bath. A red LED flicked on at the bottom end of the lengthy control block, and the copper alloy stirring arm began to once more vibrate. The agitating stanchion sent ripples through the soup breaking down the muscle, ligament and bone into its constituent nutrients. The amber fluid sloshed over the sides and down into moat like troughs cut into the concrete floor. These etched channels ran from each trough, merging into a larger channel, and down a gentle slope towards the centre of the underground chamber. The flowing fluid met in a central pool of amber now devoid of decaying human flesh. Growing out of the stinking pool was a thick column, an amalgamation of twisting organic tubes, electronic cabling and metal. The metallic pillar was similar to a colossal tree reaching all the way up to the ceiling of the chamber. Its branches a mixture of cables and tubes, each grasping an amniotic sack and forming a series of embracing veins in their exterior membranes. There were thousands of the yellowish-brown sacks grouped together in what resembled giant bunches of grapes, although containing something more sinister than fruit seeds. Each one seemed to be illuminated by a creepy pink light buried somewhere within the tangles of the column, the glowing light bringing clarity to the forms being incubated inside. Bodies, human bodies, male and female, ranging from mere fetuses to adolescents, all floating serenely attached to numerous wires and umbilical cords. The older humans, just reaching puberty, were clustered at the bottom, slowly decreasing in age and size as they moved up the length of the column until they diminished to the size of marbles. At the pinnacle of the Christmas tree formation, further data carrying cables and fluid pumping tubes sprawled out in bundles, spreading across the cavern ceiling like a mass of clinging vines running down the corner of the chamber and into a plethora of computer equipment and machinery upon a mezzanine platform.

All along the walls of natural rock on a raised peripheral level, stood lines of tubular vats radiating in a dull purple hue. Inside the lava lamp like structures artificial wombs held undefined forms, some looking humanoid and others of unknown shape, blurred behind bubbles that ascended between the womb membrane and the purple plastic exterior. Atop of the metal capped containers, fat red veins ran up onto the wall and crawled across the sandstone. At the opposite end to the mezzanine platform, the clinging veins descended the chamber walls and down into gigantic stainless-steel clad tanks. Inside the tanks large slow-moving copper lined blades mixed its red contents ready to be pumped into whatever was developing within the strange wombs.

From an entrance under the control platform, Quetzalcoatl paced into the gloom of level 7 and made for his compatriots currently examining the incubation tower.

"Ahh Quetzalcoatl, we were not expecting you yet, where are the Overlords?" welcomed Kukulcan.

"Trouble in Bhoga-Vita prematurely called for their return. They feasted and took their pick of slaves; the tour will have to wait." answered the plumed serpent.

"Quetzalcoatl, you do not need to wear you mask here. There are no humans around these depths, apart from the obvious. Down here we are Annunaki and have no need to mimic the human gods of old!" admonished Tezcatlipoca.

"I have not forgotten, there are other more important matters that occupy my thoughts than where our traditions begin and end." As he responded, Quetzalcoatl removed his elaborate feathered head dress and horned beaked mask, revealing his dark scaled serpent head. Although reptilian in guise, as humans are to apes, the Annunaki possessed many differences to the reptilians of

Earth or the humanoid Altairian. The main features perceptible behind their symbolic masks, the slit pupil eyes and forked tongue were that of a snake, while the Altairian equivalent more closely matched the characteristics of an iguana lizard. Their faces were covered in hues of deep red, dark brown and black snakelike scales, some possessing varying patterns to create unique colour combinations across their smooth heads. Pointed bat type ears extended up from the side of their heads and between them, two small slightly curving horns grew backwards from their forehead. The Annunaki nose and mouth were akin to a cross somewhere between a snake and a dog, protruding into a semi-muzzle but with a wide upwards slanting jaw line. This coupled with their mouthful of needle like teeth gave them all an evilly menacing and demonic appearance.

Apart from the Masters, there was a number of other Annunaki spread out among level 7. Many tended to the incubation column, others the vats and liquid baths and a select few upon the mezzanine level of electronic equipment. These however wore no decorative garments but bared their full scale covered body. And like a snake their chests were lighter than the rest of their body, with large plated scales covering humanoid features of a chest and stomach muscles. They were taller than the average human but still shorter in stature and build than the three Masters. Their limbs were long and thin, but muscularly defined and always in a posture mildly bent at the joints, never straight. Their feet were equally elongated as their hands and also ended in sharp yellowish claws that could quite easily cut through flesh. These labouring Annunaki also possessed a horned head, but theirs were more rounded bony stumps than the pointed protrusions of the so-called Masters. Also, another feature not evident under the decorative garments of the Masters, were a pair of bat like wings folded up behind their back. These appendages were diminutive enough to suggest that they had evolved to a point where they were no longer capable of flight, akin to what you find with such flightless birds as the ostrich.

As Quetzalcoatl fastened the enigmatic mask upon his belt of bird beaks, two Annunaki labourers strode past pushing some levitating piece of equipment. They stopped beneath the incubation column and removed a blood-stained knife from a utility compartment. With a couple of quick slashes, one of the labourers hacked through two twisted umbilical cords and cable combinations, squirting amber fluid in all directions. The large amniotic sack dropped onto the wheel barrel type device and continued to drip reeking fluid into pool below the Annunaki feet.

"Schhaal, state your agenda!" ordered Kukulcan to the slightly smaller workers.

"I and Fahsshhaa are taking the ripe crop to cryo-storage. Then we shall reseed the Meridian column before returning to our quarters on level five." answered the slimy labourer.

"Good, but before this is done. Take some of those to the zoo," Kukulcan pointed a long finger at a group of bubbling vats on the exterior of the chamber. "And attain more fresh meat for these nutrient baths."

"We have no fresh supplies."

"Then I shall send our humans to retrieve more. With attention above elsewhere, we can plunder unnoticed." replied Kukulcan. "I guess snatching what pickings we can, should not be a problem for long!" They both turned their interest back to the plumed serpent.

"So tell us then Quetzalcoatl, has the non-conformist pawns of the Middle East and Asia been quelled? Having played their role to bring fear and instability to the world, everything should be ready for the Cults' New World Order to progress swiftly." questioned Tezcatlipoca.

"Yes, and under our global government we can dictate all facets of the human population. The scale of our work here can grow indefinitely!" added Kukulcan.

In an expression of pure hatred Quetzalcoatl answered, "The humans have shown their stubbornness once more and hampered our best laid plans. An overlooked entity somehow intervened at the eleventh hour."

"How can this be! The Annunaki do not overlook details. Still, what conceivable variable could have unraveled what we have so meticulously put into place!" hissed Tezcatlipoca.

"Since we announced ourselves over twelve thousand years ago, the humans have always managed to find a way to thwart our plans for them." complained Kukulcan. "It was their tenacity and strength of free will that drove us from our thrones and into the shadows in the first place."

Long ago when mankind was still in the stone age and they feared or worshipped what they did not understand, the Annunaki showed themselves to the planets ancient civilisations, and did so as omnipotent beings. With their advanced technology and superior wisdom, they painted themselves as the creators of humankind, to be worshipped and served as such. Through the millennia they grew too comfortable and did not predict the resistance of the human race. Never before had such a primitive species shown such resolve in their being. Since their unexpected setbacks at the hands of Earths ancient civilisations, the Annunaki regrouped and once again began their grasp for power over mankind, this time from the darkness, a mysterious voice, patient and unnoticed. continuing to weave their claws of influence from the darkness.

Tezcatlipoca spat, "But we plotted to a degree that spanned generation after generation, the age long and cunning approach that had served us so well so many times before. For how could the human race fight to regain their freedom and free will if they didn't even know they had lost it! This time there was to be no conflict of the long ago past, piece by piece, string by string, the Annunaki were to gain control until there was a leash around the population of Earth, so tight, that they would have no choice but to obey. How could these humans foil us once more! Did we not anticipate every conceivable scenario? No matter the human response our desires were inevitable!"

"This is different! We did not plan for this because there is nothing we could do to prevent it." Quetzalcoatl pulled out the satellite images from within a compartment in his feathered garments. The faces of the two Masters immediately contorted in horror and panic.

"How can we hope to achieve any of our plans if the Sin have returned!" burst out Kukulcan with alarm. "We will meet our demise!"

"The Sin's initial attack was repelled by some galactic alliance, no doubt instigated by the Ashtar. We have a reprieve." replied Quetzalcoatl.

"For how long!!! You know as well as I that this means nothing!"

hissed Tezcatlipoca "We have only been successful to this point because our life energy has allowed us to plan not for the now, but the bigger picture. It is not possible to suddenly complete everything. The Meridian phase was our greatest hope if the Sin ever returned. Without it how can we ever achieve our ultimate goal of the Akhuforge. We all know the consequences of failing that."

"Should we consider recalling the pyramid ship? Take our research and enough subjects to continue our work elsewhere. We have the same decision we faced in nineteen forty-seven. Remaining then was the right decision as we have accomplished so much since that time. But now?" suggested Kukulcan.

"The cowardliness of running is a last resort." dismissed Quetzalcoatl.

"Quetzalcoatl you seem unworried! You do know the Sin will hunt down and kill every last human, including every single one in this facility! They will not be happy with our servitude of late. The Annunaki will be fortunate to survive their wrath." Kukulcan commented with fear in his voice.

"The one that lived told me that the Akhuforge may not be the only way. The return of the Sin has presented another opportunity. He has suggested we concentrate on our work here as normal. He will worry about the Sin's return."

"Another opportunity! He does not know the Sin as we do. The Sin will come with their full might and destroy the human race. Us, him, no one can stop them! What other way could there possibly be." stated a disbelieving Tezcatlipoca.

Quetzalcoatl replied with conviction, "You know full well what he is! The reason why we need the Akhuforge phase and what we seek in the Meridian phase. He has a sight far beyond what we know. Who are we to comprehend or question the one that lived."

For thousands of years they ruled the planet and its population as god's. But after their great downfall at the hands of the ancient human civilisations, and the secrets they had discovered through them, the price of Annunaki failure had brought catastrophic consequences that could only mean the existence of the human race and the Annunaki were forever entwined. So with little choice, the Annunaki hid upon Earth, becoming mere legends, mythology, then the unknown, always attempting to regain what they had lost.

Tezcatlipoca paced up and down in thought, his glazed appendage clanging against his shattered mirror robe. Another worker Annunaki entered the chamber dragging a levitating barrow of what appeared to be cattle parts and dumped them in one of the huge red tanks. When the splashing of crimson fluid broke his concentration, the one-legged Master spoke up. "So then Quetzalcoatl, has the alternate plan been initiated?"

"Yes it has begun. We have been patient and all aspects are in place. We have let our control and manipulation grow slowly at a speed the humans have dictated. Now we will force our hand, the laws they have created themselves will now ensure their downfall. Although our route will be different, we shall remain unknown and the result the same. First the US will fall into our absolute control, and as in the world of old, the rest will follow."

"Then we will have the resources we need to complete our work. That is only if the Sin does not return so swiftly." said Kukulcan with doubt in his whispery voice.

"Perhaps this new alliance and the Sin's mistakes of the past will delay their immediate return; their fear of what the human race might become will stop them from coming anything less than fully prepared. Still in the time we have given, it is imperative that we concentrate on doing what we need, what we must accomplish. In many respects the human race has been our bane, but now in others they may become our saviours."

62 - Conquer in our Name

Over twelve thousand years ago in the damp mist of Jaehager, above the flowing orange stained estuaries, row upon row of giant rusting juggernauts were spread-out in a ceremonial formation.

The thick metal hulls of the giant battleship-looking craft hovered over a plethora of black stone spheres. Arranged in configurations mimicking the constellations that now held symbolic importance, this was a grand demonstration to welcome a historic arrival, the Sin apocalypse Ship. Explosions of chemical rockets lit up the gloomy sky around them. From out of the colourful explosions appeared a hulk of shinning metal. It was the last of their tributes, fresh out of the bountiful war factories of the humid planet. The larger carrier like construction creaked loudly as it edged forward, approaching the long-anticipated obsidian fragment.

"Welcome our Masters. Our Saviours! It is with everlasting gratitude that we welcome you today." the message echoed out across the excavated landscape, but remained unanswered.

The unknown source continued, "We found ourselves falling into a state of chaos, societies segregated themselves, sought differing desires, these factions began great wars which decimated us. We were on the brink of global self-destruction, on a path with no foreseeable way back. But that was until your heralds saved us, they brought us the wisdom and weapons to eradicate the diseased ideologies that were held by those that wished to destroy us from within. We now prosper, one voice of order, spoken in unity. We have built monuments to you, and an army for you to guide, this before you, just the first of many our empire will dedicate to you."

The obsidian fragment still hung there silent in the mist; its judgement still not passed.

"We beg of you, tell us where we should point our weapons, that we may bring the same clarity of wisdom and order to those who don't know they need it. We will bring the saved into your Supremacy, through our histories lesson or by force, for liberating or destroying non-believers, we will do the galaxy a great service on your behalf."

*

A monolith of shinning obsidian stood at the centre of the cavernous symmetrical chamber. The sound of a trill breath reverberated around the four equidistant walls, and the black stone surface fuzzed and quivered. The monolith came alive with the insidious figure of, the Witch of Endor.

"Moloch has received your latest offering and judged the Jaehagen. We are pleased with them. They will serve the Sin well."

The surrounding group of figures bowed their heads in acknowledgement.

"You have proven yourselves to be unique to all Supremacy races. Your voice is small in number but its influence compelling in its greatness. You have a comprehension of your place within our Supremacy and that of the galaxy's future. This is because you think on a scale beyond others, across a timeline of potentials and a temporal reach as close to the Sin as it is possible by this Garden's after-thoughts. Strategy beyond the constraints of common fleeting life, through generations of change, insignificant in cosmological terms, yet long enough to serve the requirements of the Sin. Through such tactical outlook, you have perfected the command of conquest without war, slavery without shackles. To infiltrate worlds and societies, to manipulate their fears and desires into an eagerness to serve, give conformity to the Sin willingly, our god whisperers."

The so-called god whisperers bowed lower with arms raised upwards as receiving a blessing in these words. As a race they were extremely intelligent, able to fathom how millions of complicated strands and possibilities would stitch together within a tapestry of the distant future. Able to manipulate the tiniest pieces of a jigsaw with a clarity to foresee its all-encompassing picture. A mental level of consciousness on such massive timescales that most species could not comprehend.

They knew well the power of the Sin and their Supremacy, better than any other in this sector of the galaxy. Even before the elder races of the spiral arm had set eyes on the galaxy's ultimate adversary, they were firmly in their servitude, using their calculated and epoch spanning methods to bring new civilisations into the fold of the Supremacy. It was their unfamiliar ways of subduing a race, and have them willingly pledge their allegiance to the Sin without the need of threat or extreme force that made them such a valuable cog in the Sin Supremacy framework. And now for their immaculate servitude over a hundred thousand years, they had reached this point.

The Witch of Endor's presence was manifested on both sides of the monolith, and from any angle, it was if she was talking directly to the individual that gazed upon it. "You have laid countless civilisations at our feet, and appreciate the need for countless more. It is true that many of these, the Sin could have enslaved on a whim, conquered in an original state that held little value. But you, our god whisperers, you see the potential in the worthless, able to mould on mass with a development of order, the transformation of a civilisation of futility, into an effective tool or weapon of substance."

"Rise for your judgement!", the Witch of Endor commanded with an authority that drove fear amongst its audience. No matter the words of accolade that had come before it, if their use had been fulfilled, death would bring an end to this known level of existence. They had seen it too many times before. "You no longer require your leash, a leash is for a beast that needs direction, regular course-correction from their masters. But your long servitude has proven to the Sin, that your dedication to your masters is unwavering. You will bring favourable tributes to the Sin, and reap your rewards under the shadow of the Supremacy."

They all rose with apprehension to hear the Witch of Endors decree, "Go to the unexplored corners of this galaxy, find jewels for our Supremacy crown. We have seen that the best instruments of destruction are those that wish to be wielded. Using intellect to conquer is a slow path, but most effective. Successful enslavement, such willing enslavement, cannot be accomplished in the space of a populations' generation, it spans lifetimes, where your intricate plots and actions can be lost to legend and myth. The Sin appreciate the time your methods require, so it will be afforded to you. But be under no illusion, I have no doubt your intelligence will attest to this truth. If we beckon, and you do not answer, if tributes of subjugation and the vanquished do not materialise. There will be no leash again, but a noose around your necks."

A single member of the gathering responded in confident submission, "We will not fail you. It is an honour to serve the Sin in such a way. We know what is needed from us, and we will forge civilisations that will build monuments to your glory. And when the time comes, legions will welcome your mastery with open arms. Only those most ripe will be matured for your judgement."

The Witch of Endor surveyed her god whisperers intently, "There is one more task that we expect from you. Taste the solar winds of the unknown, for you know what we seek. The knowledge of our search for the Raziel is bestowed upon you. But never whisper of this, as you will see their destiny become entwined with yours."

"If such a seed exists in the unknown regions, then we shall bring it immediately to the attention of the Sin." the same figure acknowledged.

"Then, go forth and conquer in our name." The image of the Witch of Endor blew away like smoke under the dying breath released by the monolith.

On the far outskirts of known Supremacy space, the obsidian fragment broke its connection to the monolith of communion and initiated the wormhole to the unknown. A grand swirl of darkness opened up ahead of the Pyramid ship that stood poised before it.

A monstrous vessel consisting of a grey rough stepped base, the smooth white surfaces of the triangular body, with a capstone of black obsidian. Beginning a silent rotation, it sluggishly moved forward, passing the deadly apocalypse ship that was dwarfed in its presence. The event horizon of exotic night slowly swallowed the perfectly symmetrical vessel, inch-by-inch it left behind the regions of the Sin Supremacy, until its perception was finally lost to the Witch of Endor.

Exiting through the other side of the wormhole, the giant pyramid ship found itself in virgin space, unmolested by the reach of the Sin, trillions of souls who had yet to know the fear and destruction that was inevitable.

They immediately scanned the local star clusters. Such diversity of life, where it can take hold it invariably does. But on examination, no life in their vicinity exhibited the qualities they were looking for.

"Charge the Apogee. Target the centre of the next search area." commanded a crass voice over the flapping of reptilian wings. The obsidian summit of the pyramid distorted the space above it, a tornado of twisted space-time erupted and the white triangular sides begun to slowly spin as it elevated upwards to be consumed by the distortion.

Within the glistening white of the crystalline command chamber, the low-level buzz of the obsidian monolith had gone silent. Tezcatlipoca strode over, his mirrored robes clanging against his legs, and threw a red sheet over it, hissing loudly as he did so.

As the Sin communication device was unceremoniously covered, there were words of discontent between the Overlords. An, voice of the Overlords spoke out with the strongest grievance, "It disgusts us, that they believe it as an honour to be unleashed. We are the whisperers of no one, we are the Annunaki! We are conquerors, masters of ourselves and those that chose to worship us."

Other members of the Overlords spoke out, "It is Royal blood that runs through us.", "We are not mere servants fulfilling a destiny of servitude.", "Royalty is destined to rule."

The Overloads were very similar to the other Annunaki in the photo-fluorescent chamber, except they were practically albino in their colourisation, barring some whom exhibited a staining of maroon red.

"Why is such displeasure displayed?" questioned Quetzalcoatl.

The Annunaki royalty looked to their collection of great minds.

"Quetzalcoatl, Enlil, Tezcatlipoca, Loong, Ninhursag, Marduk, Lelwani, Apep, Nummo, Nagaraja and Boreas. You are the chief conspirers of the Annunaki. Tell us what we should be thinking, tell us what courses of action have you contemplated?"

"It is not just the Sin that have reaped the benefits of the worlds we have enslaved." started the dark-brown Nagaraja, more serpent looking than the rest with a flattened pronounced neck that resembled a narrow cobra hood. "Every civilisation and empire we have conquered has brought with it a glut of useful knowledge. And how much have we learnt of the Sin in that time?"

A muscular Annunaki, distinguishable by his rare green patches of scales, offered their further thoughts, "It has been an eternity of planning, but our guidance has taken us to this point. This freedom is an honour we have bestowed upon ourselves. Now we find ourselves with countless strands of unknown possibilities. Now let us see what opportunities these bring us."

"Enlil and Nagaraja have it right. Maybe one of these strands offers us the path to becoming our own masters." declared Quetzalcoatl, "We have time afforded to us."

The Annunaki were arrogant in nature and detested servitude to anyone, yet when the Sin came to their world Alpha Draco, their conquered systems of Sirius and Kochab, and finally their Orionis strongholds of Altinak, Mintaka and Alnilam, the Annunaki knew there was little choice but to welcome them with open arms. They possessed forewarning and awareness of the Sin, so it was immediately clear to the Annunaki that non-committal to the Supremacy was a response of futility, the tales they had heard had testified to the fate of those that refused. With servitude they had earned time. The Annunaki were intelligent and possessed a life-force that blessed them with a life-span over a hundred thousand years, they would bide their time and eventually seek a renewed freedom in the only way they knew how. Meticulous planning, ingenious cunning and the application of skillful influence.

*

The Pyramid ship exited from its twenty second wormhole since leaving the Witch of Endor and Supremacy space. The Annunaki had travelled through unknown space in their veiled and secretive manner, creating vast distances between them and the Sin. Now they were in a sector of space on the outside of one of the spiral arms of the galaxy.

As they had done in their previous jumps, they scanned the local system for advanced life and the signatures of technology. Again, as all those jumps before it, the results did not match the parameters required, yet something held their interest. In front of them stood a blue and green gem of a planet, with hemispheres of retreating glaciers, like white eyelids opening to the touch of a new warmth after a long hibernation. It's very appearance from orbit spoke habitability. Curiosity drove them to begin their detailed analysis of the planet, it's ecosystems and biological evolution of life. Scanning the layers laid down over billions of years, tracing its history from the fiery volcanic start, to its bombardment by water carrying comets, and right through its fossil records of mass extinctions to its current explosion of life.

It's formation and planetary evolution were standard for a rocky world this far from a G2V type star. But the data before them was an intriguing puzzle, the ignition of life had started significantly earlier on this planet than should be possible, at least on any world they had knowledge of. And the sheer scale of complex diversity from a single tree of genesis was equally surprising. It was as if this world had discovered upon the magical formula for life.

An intelligent mammalian species had seemingly rose above them all in its habitation range and dominance. A hunter-gatherer species, it was primitive on its technological and social path. But it was capable of complex social interactions and society building, the creation and use of tools, creativity in art, domestication of other living creatures with a move to pastoralism and agriculture. Intelligent life had appeared incredibly early in this planet's lifecycle, much earlier than the scientifically possible galactic benchmark. Not only that, this dominant mammalian species from its first appearance, had evolved to its current point at a significantly accelerated rate. Not with its physical biology, but through the complex development of their mental capabilities. This place, existing in a mundane and unremarkable location in the galaxy, was a beautiful oddity that clearly held new secrets waiting to be unraveled.

The chief conspirers of the Annunaki, were scrutinising the fascinating data when the Overlords returned to the Kings chamber within the centre of the Pyramid ship's main body.

"The view from the grand gallery has not changed. What is our status?" questioned An, attended on both sides by lesser Annunaki labourers carrying trays of raw bloody meat.

There was a long pause, before Apep responded to the Overlords. Apep differed from the other chief conspirers in that he shared the tail possessed by the Overlords, albeit thinner and considerably longer, as if dragging a snake behind him. "We still analyse the planet beneath us."

"Why waste our time here? Apart from an endless food supply, what use would these creatures have to us or the Sin?" countered An, his mouth dripping with fresh blood.

"These dominant creatures, there is some abnormality about them that irritates me. I must know what it is." countered Tezcatlipoca.

"I must agree." added Quetzalcoatl, "This world, we can perceive so many possibilities, given the time. Imagine what we could achieve, being able to dictate the path of a civilisation who have evolved so quickly, whom reproduce so fervently, but live and die in such fleeting time periods. What would take millions of years could be achieved in a fraction of the time. Perhaps within a timescale afforded by the Sin, the Annunaki could build a great empire. This place is worthy of our further attention. A great prize for the Sin or possibly the perfect opportunity for the Annunaki."

"A great prize of an empire you say. A million years would still be a flicker in the creation of the Sin Supremacy." challenged another Overlord.

"You must not suffer such narrow-mindedness." rebuked Tezcatlipoca as he continued to pour over the data, "I smell the scent of nature's tampering. Its unpredictability could have presented us a head-start of billions of years."

"Leave the conspiring amongst us, revel in the comforts you will be given while we determine the most favourable path for the Annunaki." Quetzalcoatl impressed upon the listening Overlords, "It is a decision that cannot be made now. We must explore all the paths of possibility to its ends. With choices of such consequences, our actions must remain undetectable. Once we have established a foothold, no chances should be taken, we should send this vessel into a dormant state."

"Then we should utilise the natural shroud of the large gas giant." suggested Enlil.

The Overlords hissed their approval, and took their feasting to the lower temples.

The great Pyramid ship descended into the atmosphere of the enigmatic planet, glowing like a falling star. Scouring the lands for the greatest population densities, the sign of fledgling societies, the Annunaki released their saucer shaped transport vehicles. Launching from the four sides of the pyramid, they originated in the voids of the internal structure and out through tunnels rising at forty-five degree angles. As each stabilised itself in the planets strong magnetic field, the flying saucers headed to their carefully selected sites on each continent. Appearing under the searing Sun, pale moonlight or through the clouds of the heavens, to all that laid eyes upon them, this fearful herald in the sky represented a higher power that they could not comprehend.

Once the points of infiltration had been approached, and the first gods had descended to their new worshippers. The Pyramid ship rose through the ceiling of the world and disappeared into the shroud of space on a vector towards the nearby gas giant. Obsidian tip first, it plunged into the violent and thick gas atmosphere of the largest planet in this solar system. As the black apex plummeted into the dense hydrogen and helium air, the mixture of gases began to swirl, increasing in strength and diameter as the pyramid sunk deeper and deeper. As it finally reached its hidden resting place, the swirling region of high-pressure had become a monstrous rotating storm a hundred thousand miles in diameter. All trace of its existence and location now concealed apart from the fierce lesion left by the Annunaki thorn that had pierced it. A great red spot on the surface of Jupiter. The mark of a new era in human civilisation.

63 - Sacrifice

Over the alliance frequency a communication came from the Ashtar Co-operative forces. "Egregor, this is Ka'er Myas. I request to take the majority of the galactic fifth fleet back to Co-operative space. I will leave a contingent behind with the older and worst damaged vessels to be rectified at Alpha and Gamma.

"Agreed Ka'er. Let us hope that in saving the human race we have not brought an end to our own civilisation. I will check the link for your update." Krill paused for a moment as if he had more to say. Then without another word spoken closed the transmission.

Michael stepped up beside him, "Your people left your own space unprotected to save ours. Why would you risk the extinction of your own race?"

"You still struggle to fathom the larger picture. The Sin is too powerful. The Ashtar Co-operative inhabits a tiny region of the galaxy. The dominion of the Sin encompasses much of it. We may not have fallen today, but eventually the Ashtar would perish at their hands. We chose this fate long ago. All our hope lies in you and the human race. You are the Raziel, the seed of their demise. If we are wrong, then we, you, your daughter…everyone is doomed."

"And if you are right, I will do everything in my power to prevent that." Michael replied with conviction, rubbing his fingers over the silver bracelet in his hand.

*

Over seven thousand quantum disturbances rippled on the outskirts of Ashtar Co-operative space. With all the speed possible Ka'er Myas led her fifth fleet back to their home territory. With weapons still warm from the battle above Earth, the Ashtar warships decelerated into the outer systems.

Concern immediately flowed through the fleet's local Co-operative link. Their fears had become a reality; the Sin Supremacy had come to wreak revenge on them.

"Command group, scan all systems within range and report." communicated Ka'er Myas through the local fleet Co-operative link, trying to separate her own apprehension from the collective mind.

The first analysis from the outer systems started to download into the terminal of Ka'er Myas. Outpost after outpost, world after world, every system came back with the same status. No life detected. Everything was annihilated, anywhere they had ever inhabited lay blackened husks, without a shred of organic life or even the remains of a single structure. All were now dead worlds of ash without any signature of Ashtar civilisation surviving.

Yet all was not immediate despair to Ka'er Myas. Knowing that the death of the Pleiadians meant they would have to sacrifice the defence of their own civilisation to aid the human race, the Ashtar had evacuated many of the outlying systems and relocated their populations towards the core of their space, consolidating most of Ashtar populace on their most important worlds.

"Take us to our core worlds. This is where the Ashtar hope lies."

Seeing the embers of Sin malice still glowing bright on their once magnificent colonies, the Ashtar war group left with urgency straight towards their inner systems.

As soon as they reappeared above Zeta Mimeo, the tumult of uncharacteristically chaotic thoughts hit them through the link. They were too late. Zeta Mimeo was a key world in the Ashtar Co-operative, an industrial planet named so due to the geological similarities it shared with Zeta[1] Reticuli. The Co-operative link was swamped with dismay, unprepared for the psychic blow, it momentarily disorientated the fleet. They were too late again, overwhelmed with the terrible scenario, the only thing steadying the thoughts within the fleet was the saving grace that there were so many defeated minds. Meaning that all was not lost.

"Maintain focus, find strength in the local fleet Co-operative link. The wider link is providing us insight into what has happened to our people, but right now it is far too chaotic. Command group, please initiate scans of our core worlds and provide reports. Yet keep the knowledge of our findings from the wider Co-operative link until we have the full picture." commanded Ka'er Myas, "All others, start piecing together and integrating the information from the memories in the wider Co-operative link. Bring solace where you can with the knowledge of our arrival and the success at the Sol system."

Debris clogged the orbit of the industrial planet. The atmosphere was lit with red hot wreckage burning up as it streaked across the skies. These meteorite showers would persist as a sign of how close they had come to destruction for months to come.

Each thought, image and memory in the shared mindscape worked to weave rare discord within the usual clarity and order. As each fragment of recent experience was processed and assembled, a sequential story of the key past scenes started to piece together like a movie filmed from a million different viewpoints. Reports of the harrowing events flooded into the mind of Ka'er Myas, not only from Zeta Mimeo but from each planet within the range of the Co-operative link. With each voice, the pieces of the jigsaw began to fall into place until the link had given her a full picture of what had happened. Ka'er Myas began to replay the critical moments from the beginning.

The first images came from those that were inhabitants of the furthest peripheral colonies. They filled her minds-eye as if Ka'er Myas was experiencing them first hand. Society leaders, scientists and families crammed together in an underground bunker, connected to their distant settlements through a series of communication and monitoring relays. Viewing these multiple feeds to see what fate awaited the homes they were forced to abandon.

"Initiate the imagery from our nearest deep-space observatories."

requested one of the society leaders as visual displays and sensor outputs appeared on the malleable metal walls of the bunker.

Before the deep-space observatories, countless swirls of darkness twisted and buckled space across the edge of Ashtar territory. The Sin Supremacy had arrived at the peripheral colonies in force, ships pouring out in the hundreds of thousands.

By the time the swirling omens of evil had unleashed all its contents, the scientists' analysis was almost complete. The data poured across the displays; they were ready to upload their reports for the knowledge of the wider Co-operative link in hope that it may provide some insight on how to better defend against them.

The synchronised message broadcast, "All data amalgamation from the visual observatories, planetary scanners and monitoring outposts complete. Much of the vessel designs and biological signatures of this Sin Supremacy armada are of unknown origin or have never been seen before by the Ashtar. All data is now packaged and being transmitted."

The Ashtar were an old species and the Elohim had shared much knowledge with them, yet this armada alone must have held more advanced civilisations than they even knew existed in their long extensive history. What it immediately told all that observed the data, was that they were entirely unprepared for what was coming.

The inhabitants of the Ashtar bunker continued to watch over the enemy. There was no usual heralding of the Sin or the gift of surrender, no hesitation, no time for escape, for as soon as the armada arrived, destruction rained down on their worlds. Crusts fractured, as tectonic plates were ruptured with deep explosive weapons. Bodies of water spontaneously evaporated and the skies were scorched with fire. A sequence of events repeated across every system that the Ashtar had ever touched.

The sources of imagery and sensor data flashed-off one-by-one, the final images downloaded from those connected to the space outposts and orbital monitoring systems before they lost all sight, were of the armada of Supremacy ships swarming past on their methodical and vengeful hunt to wipe out any sign of the Ashtar civilisation. The Ashtar watched on helpless from their bunker, they had abandoned those worlds and settlements in preparation for their survival and now their minds focused on the skies above them in trepidation.

Then the forming story switched to the core worlds. Most of the memories swamping the Co-operative link coming from Zeta Mimeo. But unlike those coming from the outer settlement inhabitants, this was an Ashtar stronghold and a lot of the thoughts were more focused and resolute, supplemented by many battle-hardened minds. Remaining so, even when the first images of the Sin Supremacy armada arrived. A terrifying site of a huge dark crystalline vessel looming over the planet. One of the Sin apocalypse ships, like a fused collection of onyx fragments cut from the deepest black gemstones, its geometrical structure was flawless. These fear inspiring vessels were the embodiment of the Sin, more often than not they were all some slave civilisations knew of the Sin or had laid eyes upon, but this was more than enough. The apocalypse ships contained awesome power, that some say came straight from channeling pure evil, but whatever their origin, for billions of years they had been the enforcers that controlled the Sin Supremacy. Though all-powerful, the Sin would rather see thousands of their Supremacy minions sacrificed before risking a scratch to their great symbolic vessels or themselves. This malevolent mind-set was demonstrated above Zeta Mimeo as the Sin apocalypse ship slowed to a halt above the Ashtar industrial world.

One Ashtar voice elicited an intense emotional imprint on the Co-operative link, one whose echoes still continued strongly, "The decision of no return is upon us. Send out the activation pulse."

The movement of an Ashtar hand played-out before Ka'er Myas, the long spindly finger reached out to a terminal and pressed a variety of symbols. The display reacted with a plethora of flashing warnings.

Then hundreds of processed memories became fused together in a kaleidoscope of imagery, filled by vessels of war as the Sin called forth its subservient to attack. These memory feeds constantly switched to various sources that provided the best viewpoints as the waves of Supremacy ships descended towards the planet. Then like a fireworks display, angry outbursts of fire and metal lit up each image, one after the other, as each warship exploded before it was able to get close. No matter what coordinates, sides or vectors they chose to attack from, the same pattern resulted, yet the evil Sin ruler threw more and more sacrificial lambs towards the world below.

In a logical act of last resort, the Ashtar Co-operative had mined the space around their most important planetary bodies in an eleventh-hour attempt to protect the populace and their worlds. A course of action that was working, but at a massive price. No conventional defence would have held back a Sin Supremacy armada; the Ashtar knew this and had to make the difficult decision to resort to what was known as a chaos minefield. An extremely rare and difficult weapon to create. Once activated by a low-powered pulse, the atomic sized mines would bury into sub-space and create a network of unstable micro-wormholes whose mouths would continue to rapidly shift between random points throughout the dense network. Any ship or projectile that wandered into the unpredictable melee would instantly be pummeled by hundreds of microscopic singularities, and quickly torn apart by the dimensional warping. Extremely effective, yet unlike any other mines, they could not be destroyed by conventional weaponry, circumvented, withstood by any known material or even switched-off. Even electromagnetic radiation and particles were partially affected in both directions, which meant star-light itself underwent a percentage of scattering through the micro wormholes before some of it was directed to the planet.

As planet-based imagery of explosions coloured the dim sky of day, and lit up the night across Zeta Mimeo, many telepathic fragments formed memory impurities in the Co-operative link. They were not those of Ashtar origin, but surprisingly random thoughts and feelings of their attackers. An infiltrating noise originating from those species that had also developed telepathic communication, fledgling capabilities or degrees of empathy.

Ka'er Myas reviewed several of the intriguing fragments.

The first from a group of unknown assailants looking out through the command deck of their warship, viewing their target world between others of their species. Their vessels were towering like a glass skyscraper built from multiple floors that grew in diameter upwards, but each cluster of decks strangely misaligned and joined by columns covered in hairy glass filaments. The most advanced of these unfamiliar warships hit the invisible event horizon of the chaos minefield, immediately distant puffs of powder blew across its surface, like sugar being thrown into the air. Accelerating in fury as the warship stubbornly pressed on, quickly annihilated piece-by-piece, not in a crash of force analogous to hitting a wall, but evaporating as if driven through a fine sieve where the exiting product was nothing but a glistening cloud of dust. The feelings exuded by the telepathic owner were clear, satisfaction that its comrades had perished in battle, and euphoric excitement that it may be next to die in service of the Sin.

Quickly that moment blurred into another fragment.

Ka'er Myas was in a tightly confined pod surrounded in fluid. The smell was rancid to her, but it elicited a degree of olfactory pleasure to its occupant. The visual aspect of the fragment was strangely warped there was a clear understanding of the situation. From orbit the occupant had fired a series of spore-type projectiles towards the planet. It followed them as they accelerated into the chaos minefield, then in bewilderment, witnessed them disappear and a portion of them re-appear but redirected straight back at the pod. In a moment of situational acceptance, there was relief that the ordeal would be over, no more life had to be taken, then all thoughts and feelings focused to a distant memory that held a strong emotional connection. A deep sadness of a promise to return broken, a life that lost its real meaning a long time ago. Then peace as the mind faded under the explosive decompression.

Wailing sirens and flashing lights emerged as the freezing fluid dissipated to hot steam. Ka'er Myas could sense that the origin of this fragment was from a species with a fledgling form of thought sharing telepathy, one that was developing, and a trait in which they probably had not even realised they possessed.

She reached out to the related fragments that had managed to be absorbed by the Co-operative link. A collection of broken imagery and echoing voices that were reminiscent to a dream state. An unknown figure turned towards the originator of this clouded memory, "Is this what you hoped for us Soloc! The guilt of what we have done, the fear of what we are involved in, is not a better replacement for that feeling of boredom or meaningless we had on Nusima Minus."

"At least we fulfill a purpose Ethnik." neighed Soloc in an aggravated reply.

"Yes, look around you. It is cannon fodder!"

The little forward momentum they had, suddenly ground to a halt with the sound of twisting metal.

"Help, help!" brayed Ethnik into his communication console, "We are stuck in some invisible obstruction, systems are failing fast."

"We need to break free and show our worth.", Soloc's forepads hit the weapons controls, still trying to fire their cannons at the strange world they had been sent to attack.

Ethnik kicked the navigation pads with his hoofs, trying to get some response from their vessel as sparks ignited around him.

What seemed to be an overloading power unit exploded out of sight. Flames burnt across the left side of the vision. The next sight was significantly blurred to one side, but the figure named Ethnik could be seen slumped in the propulsion stable, elongated neck hanging to the side.

Soloc then had him in his arms, "I am so sorry. I did not mean this for you. We were to gallop across the fields of stars, together a stampeding force in the Sin Supremacy." He closed the lids over the ocular stalks as Ethnik's snout gave a final weak snort.

"May you forever graze amongst the fruiting Ickaba trees." hooted Soloc, before realising the explosion had knocked them free, drifting out-of-range of whatever invisible snare had gripped them.

"I will avenge you in the name of the Sin. Our lives will mean something!"

Ka'er Myas took a moment to reflect on the insightful Co-operative impurities. There was such a full spectrum of emotions, motives and circumstances. Clearly they were not all inherently evil by the definition held by the Ashtar and its allies. Yet the experienced fragments did reinforce one undeniable fact, the unbreakable hold the Sin had over them. So many civilisations and species irrelevant of their culture, history or beliefs shared the same acceptance. A choice to turn their back on morality, to accept the destruction of the helpless, the extermination of the innocent, to ultimately elect to take away the gift of life as a focus of their existence.

The chaos minefield had meant that the Sin could not get close to Zeta Mimeo and their planetary bombardment capability was severely diminished. It also meant that the Ashtar inhabitants could not leave, and their own planetary defensive systems unable to be used to attack back, only utilised to combat any weaponry that escaped through the chaos minefield towards the planet's surface. This was a frustration affecting the Sin Supremacy not just above Zeta Mimeo, but one repeated across every Ashtar world that held significant populations towards the core of their space.

However, it was not the chaos minefield that stopped the Sin's attempted purge. Zeta Mimeo was a key world to the Ashtar; producing the bulk of its new design warships, it therefore possessed greater defences. Not all worlds had the protective measures it had, and many of those that did, could not create a chaos minefield nearly as dense as Zeta Mimeo's. If they continued to send ships recklessly against these chaos minefields, eventually many would have gotten through.

A situation that was described to Ka'er Myas through the coalesced thoughts of one colony world called Ma'cion.

Supremacy vessels had eventually broken through their deployed chaos minefield due to sheer numbers. The Ashtar had manned their mobilised defence systems and retrofitted structures acting as armed fortresses. Atmospheric defence orbs where released from their containment units which quickly ascended to meet the scattering of black dots growing in size, and laser turrets sent up a web of strafing fire against the projectiles accelerating ahead of the wave of warships. The Sin apocalypse ship sent swarm after swarm to run the gauntlet of the orbital minefield, the unrelenting weight of numbers allowing hundreds to evade the fluctuating minefield. The following scenes were hard to assimilate as enemy vessels impacted into Ashtar city structures, devastating the landscape. Connections to the Co-operative link aggressively severed as weapons tore apart the defensive batteries and their Ashtar controllers. Whole families and generations buried alive, psychically calling out for help as deep-strata bombs ruptured the underground geology, and blasts of night from the apocalypse ship melted through the crust. The colonists and their refuge seeking guests fought back desperately, progressively losing the battle of relentless attrition. Then out of the blue when things appeared to be turning for the worst, the bulk of the Sin Supremacy armada ceased their attack, abandoning their forces within the chaos mine fields and departed the system without another shot fired. Disappearing back to unknown space with no explanation, leaving huge regions of wreckage from many thousands of Supremacy ships scattered throughout the Ashtar systems. A strange scenario that was simultaneously duplicated across Ashtar Co-operative space. Even on those worlds that did not possess a chaos minefield to shield them.

The only reason Ka'er Myas could determine for the entire sudden retreat of the Sin Supremacy was that they had discovered something so important that it made the destruction of the Ashtar irrelevant, and that could only have been one thing. The fate of their scout armada at the hands of the new alliance. Somehow, they had been warned that the free races had rallied around the Raziel once more.

The local fleet link connected back with the wider Co-operative link, bringing a layer of order and clarity to the tumult of thoughts as they uploaded a comprehensive update and re-integrated the fleets strength-of-mind. The Co-operative link was the only contact the Ashtar worlds had with those that had joined the new alliance in battle. The nature of the chaos minefields had meant that they had fundamentally chosen to imprison themselves, with standard technological communication rendered almost inoperable and space travel exceedingly dangerous, they had been cut-off from the rest of galactic society. A choice that was a last resort, an option accepted with its consequences fully understood. But it was a hard decision that would give the greatest possibility to keep their civilisation alive until such time as methods to disable the chaos minefield were designed, or it naturally dissipated. The chaotic wormholes had a half-life decay rate of almost a thousand years, meaning that it would eventually be relatively safe to pass through in a few thousand years. That figure being dependent on the quantity of energy absorbed from what it destroyed in its field, the more chaotic energy the quicker the decay rate. But no matter what came first it would only buy them time, if the new alliance could not defeat the Sin and save the Raziel, then there would be no hope, the Sin would eventually return and finish the annihilation of the Ashtar race that they had started so completely, while victory still meant solitude to billions of Ashtar that had embraced a space-faring culture.

The sacrifice of the Ashtar had achieved its goal, the Co-operative link was awash with millions of messages being exchanged between those who now had to endure a difficult isolation. Thoughts that this choice was the right one and the only logical action available, those of proudness and encouragement to the fleet, that they can lead the new alliance to triumph, and thoughts to a time when they can all be reunited. Although most of these messages were conceived in positivity, none could hide the underlying sadness permeating underneath. The Ashtar fifth fleet did what they could to reinforce the construct of positivity. Yet those that had lived through the ancient history of the last great battle could only feel despair. Their single advantage of surprise and secret formation of the new alliance was lost, meaning one singular outcome. The Sin would gather the entirety of their Supremacy, including their most powerful minions that still remained unseen, and in a galactic sized armada return to Earth and wipe out the Raziel and anything that dared to stand in their way. Had they only achieved the prolongment of their extinction?

64 - Calm before the Storm

Most of the new alliance fleet had parted ways. As soon as the last of the Sin Supremacy armada had been destroyed, the Altairian and the Hyekera forces signaled their departure and hastened back to their own space, unwilling to leave their territory open to advantageous attack from the other. Even such as momentous collaboration could not suppress the deep mistrust instilled within the Altairian hearts and Hyekera cores.

Although the assembled forces had left the battle ground of the solar system to attend to their own civilisations, many hundreds of ships belonging to the Ashtar and Aurora defence fleet still patrolled the space around Earth and Mars. Queues of the most heavily damaged vessels waited to be brought into the hollow rock of Planetoid Gamma for emergency repair work. Meanwhile the orbit of the red planet was littered with limping warships, holding position until they were cleared to land in the vast work hangers of the Cydonia Mensae shipyards. Among the battle-scarred warships, Seber glistened in a hanger deck of Athena, appearing like new, all its wounds healed by the efficient nano-fluid flowing beneath its outer hull.

Elyon was in the observation alcove of Athena looking down at Earth. At night it was so apparent to him how this world had changed over the millennia. He remembered gazing upon this new world for the first time from the deck of an Elohim transport, barely able to make out the light of civilisation. Now everywhere it shone brightly, illuminating the remarkable progress of the human race. But all the growth of humanity meant nothing now; *what knowledge or intrinsic thought must glisten when you gaze back at me to the stars, that all your radiance could be snuffed out like candles under the breath of the Sin?* Elyon sealed the viewing window and headed down the slim corridor towards the star room. The natural luminosity instilled with Elyon flickered like a failing light bulb; he steeled his emotions, channeling his concentration to the task ahead. The glow stabilised throughout the shining one, Elyon pulled his hood over his glassy head and pushed open the wooden doors gilded with azure and emerald.

Inside the star room many had gathered for what would be considered the first war cabinet of the new alliance. With its astronomical tools and displays, the star room was tactically ideal for such a purpose, and the Ashtar had already refitted it with a round table and chairs of asteroid rock. Egregor Krill and numerous Ka'er stood opposite the door waiting for the Elohim's entrance. Also joining the Ashtar inside the room were the representatives of the new alliance. The Altairian Empire; the first sentient beings of Earth, a saurian race with a history that had moulded their strength. The Hyekera; a fledgling machine life, although created by others and the youngest civilisation in the free galaxy, it had not hindered their rise to power. The Raqzzon; herders of the galaxy, a small and fury appearance which did not symbolise their fierceness to protect others and fight for what they believe in. The human race; technologically primitive yet with endless potential, the Raziel of the prophecy and the doom bringers of the Sin.

Michael stood there rubbing his exposed shoulder, trying unsuccessfully to locate the raw tender lump. Biriqzz looked on confused. In her vast experience, no one should have healed that quickly from a boring larvae extraction. There was effectively no sign of the entry wound, bruising or swelling. "Well, you see, I told you there was no need for all that whining and fuss."

Michael didn't respond, distracted by the entrance of Elyon.

Elyon held aloft his arms to these five races, these were to be the ones that formed the foundation of the stand against the Sin Supremacy, "My emotions cannot translate to words, what proudness dominates my soul, for what you have achieved this day. For that you have my undying gratitude. Yet, monumental as this triumph is, it is but the first step on a more arduous journey of survival. We have stared directly at the mask of death, but revealed behind it, is the face of something far more terrifying, a horror of truth that paralyses hope, where to endure is a vision that cannot be conceived. Though, lessons of history and the lives lain down before us, teach of a prevailing theme. Hope always finds a way, as long as there are those like you who stand before me, giants of courage and strength to carry its torch, protecting its light for all those cowering in the shadows to feel its warmth. I have beckoned you to Athena because in despite of victory, we catch our breath in the calm before the storm. Time does not acknowledge our need to grieve or rest, representatives of the free races of the galaxy, we must plan our next moves with great care and collaboration. Emile, would you be so kind as to enlighten us with the current situation upon Earth?"

"Excuse me, what was.. oh, yes of course." Emile fumbled with some notes in front of her, and gave them a quick glimpse. "Ehmm, right.", she stood up adjusting her ever present lab coat looking somewhat flustered. "Ok, I have spoken with John, sorry, that's General Allen of COM Twelve, our Earth based organisation for those of you who don't know. And we have managed to avoid a planet wide war because of their efforts, and some inadvertent events caused by our delayed intervention. Which is great!" Emile gave a quick thumbs up too Michael who looked like he was holding back a smirk under his serious demeanour, but returned a nod of recognition. "They are continuing to work so that a similar situation will not arise again and undermine our efforts here. The human race to the most part is still unaware of the existence of the Sin, the new alliance, or any extra-terrestrial life for that matter. We had a little incident regarding one of the Sin Supremacy warships falling to Earth, and its remains hitting an area of Peru. There was some news coverage and a number of locals from nearby villages became ill from toxic gases released by the surviving engine wreckage. Luckily the crash site was pretty much a deserted region, and we were able to pass it off as a falling meteor that burnt up in the atmosphere. The remains of which released a layer of noxious gas from under the surface when hitting the muddy landscape. In turn this was inhaled by the people who first came to inspect the site. So no harm done there.... Mmmhh, I think that's everything."

"The containment of this situation brings glad tidings." Elyon gestured to Emile that it was ok to sit back down. "Egregor Krill, I leave the floor open to you."

"Thank you Elyon. Long ago the Ashtar realised that the human race must persevere at all costs, even if it meant the end of our race at the hands of the Sin. As soon as we discovered the demise of the Pleiadians, the Ashtar as one of the elder civilisations and the last of the old alliance, had no choice but to commit our entire defensive capabilities to the battle above Earth, and leave our people at the mercy of the Sin. Over the Co-operative link I have received the report from our forces in Ashtar space, and I am afraid the news is dire. The Sin Supremacy came with numbers a hundred times that of what we were able to hold back here. The only reason the Ashtar still exists is not because we abandoned our worlds and barricaded our race behind chaos mine fields, but because the Sin discovered something of a magnitude that made them rethink their plans. This could only be the formation of the new alliance." The consequences of this information could be seen in every set of eyes in the room. "We know they will return with their full might, be it tomorrow or a solar year. This time it will be different to the last great battle. Even though we all work night and day to create more warships, our numbers will remain significantly lower than before, and the Sin Supremacy's greater than ever."

"Yes! What we have mustered today is but a drop in the ocean compared to what the Sin command." Elyon's radiant eyes met Michael's, who looked back with uneasiness, "But even the smallest pebble can cause a ripple of change."

Elyon took the time to scrutinise the people around the stone table, taking in each one in turn. For him, Egregor Krill and the Ashtar Co-operative were the glue that held together the new alliance, the oldest allies of his people, the Elohim. They showed little emotion, but inside they possessed an unwavering selflessness. He knew they would fight to the last against the Sin. Then either side there was the warring races, the unpredictable younger species that did not fully appreciate what the Sin represented outside the agenda of their own civilisations. Varantis, Prime Ethereal of the Altairian, and son of the emperor, was flanked by a contingent of royal guards and advisors, all staring furiously across the table at the giant Iyekera machine, Phalacreus, whose cycloptic optical device un-movingly reflected back the faces of his civilisations nemesis.

To his right sat life forms that embody to him what was good in the galaxy, what the new alliance stood against the Sin to protect. Emile the brilliant human physicist, fascinated with understanding the unknown and possessing a vigour for discovery. The Mayan descendants of Cydonia Mensae, the very representation of determination and persistence. Biriqzz and Baraqz, embracing the wondrous diversity of the galaxy and nurturing its growth, the Raqzzon society was small in stature yet giants in heart.

And then finally, to his left, Michael, the key that may tip the balance either way; to the total annihilation of all who stand against the Sin, or the slenderest of hope. And like human nature, which way the scales would sway was unpredictable, the Raziel were capable of such love, and yet at the same time such evil, extinguish a life without the slightest remorse or sacrifice their own for another. He looked at Michael's hands that clutched representations of the two very different paths he may travel down. In one, his love, the bracelet of his child. In the other, pain, anger and hate, a dangerous concoction flowing in his little veneered flask.

However, the Raziel were his task, one that would come to an end soon, in either failure or success, the deeds and mistakes of his past had put him on this course and left him with no choice. Elyon's voice resonated throughout the star room, "Go now, prepare your people for the trials and sacrifices to come. As something that opposes natures instinct, my ask of you is one that is difficult to swallow. Your survival, your future, does not rest on the protection of your own people or borders. It is here that fate will be decided for us all. When judgement called upon us, together in unison we responded with our defiance against evil. Our strength bound by our common goal is a formidable wall that cannot be easily scaled or broken. But its foundations and resilience are only as strong as its weakest bond. So, we must forge onwards with building our new alliance, direct focus away from petty differences and the distraction of folly, to once again stand here united beneath the new dawn of the Raziel. May good fortunes follow you all!"

Their faces before him showed resolve, his own words had suggested a ray of hope, but beneath Elyon's glowing façade, he harboured none for the human race.

Everyone had gone their own ways to prepare the best they could. Michael was alone in the observation alcove, looking down on the beautiful vista of Earth. To him it looked so peaceful from here. It was the night's shadow and not the Sin's that was now on the move as it shrouded the American continent. Were they even aware how close they had come to destruction? His mind wandered, trying to imagine what his daughter was doing right now, was she happy, was she safe? Was she staring up at him counting the stars and thinking of him? What he did know though, was however small his participation was, he was going to do everything in his power to help protect her. He sipped from his hip flask while he looked upon the picture he held of his daughter. It was becoming increasingly hard to maintain focus as his eyelids grew heavier and heavier, mentally and emotionally drained, sleep crept-up and took him, quickly dragging him into the realm of slumber.

Michael stirred, there was a cold darkness blowing across him, then bright rays of light flooded his eyes, blurring his sight. An unknown figure moved on the edge of his peripheral vision as he struggled to make sense of his surroundings. He was laid out flat on a horizontal surface with a weight pushing down upon his chest. Michael tried to move his left arm but it was constricted, held in place by an invisible force. Then with an effort, his right arm lifted, managing to rub his eyes. Fabric fluttered under the breeze, allowing the morning Sun to pour through the open window, illuminating his dream. He had fallen asleep on the bed again, fully-clothed with a large story book resting on his ribcage. He felt the touch of a warm breath on the side of his neck. He turned his head, Bella lay there beside him, hugging his arm and snuggled into his neck for security.

Back in the reality of the observation alcove, there was a sigh of contentment and a smile formed across Michael's face.

Epilogue

.... Bestowed upon each was life's greatest gift; a soul and the free will of choice, although born from the dust of stars, their destiny would not be controlled by the physical laws of the universe, unlike the matter that permeated the cosmos, they had no pre-determination, for them it would be a future of infinite possibility.

Yet divine knowledge was offered to guide and give meaning to their existence, to cherish the wonder of creation and life, a moral compass to light their way when they stray into darkness, to keep them on the fragile path towards the journey's end, that time when they will be released from the constraints of their worldly vessels.

The firstborns absorbed and contemplated the teachings of wisdom, some minds were more open than others, but all heeded the last words imparted on them, a warning to the firstborns that although they have free reign of the Garden which has been created for them, they must never take from the tree of knowledge, its essence a forbidden fruit. With this final testament, the shimmering beams that reached out from within each branch, began to retreat and fade as the threads of space and time weaved itself back together, and in one last mighty clap of thunder the rift flashed out of existence.

To be continued in
Volume Two of the Causality Saga:
Ascendency of the Sin